ABOUT SVEN HASSEL

Born in 1917 in Fredensborg, Denmark, Sven Hassel joined the merchant navy at the age of fourteen. He did his compulsory year's military service in the Danish forces in 1936 and then, facing unemployment, joined the German army. He served throughout World War II on all fronts except North Africa. His fourteen World War II books, which draw on his own encounters and experiences as a soldier, have sold over 53 million copies worldwide and have been published in more than 50 countries. He peacefully passed away in Barcelona in 2012, where he had resided since 1964.

BY SVEN HASSEL

SVEN HASSEL

O.G.P.U. PRISON

Translated from the Danish by Tim Bowie

WEIDENFELD & NICOLSON

A W&N PAPERBACK

First published in Great Britain in 1982
by Corgi
This paperback edition published in 2014
by Weidenfeld & Nicolson
an imprint of the Orion Publishing Group Ltd,
Carmelite House, 50 Victoria Embankment,
London EC4Y 0DZ

An Hachette UK company

3 5 7 9 10 8 6 4 2

British Library Cataloguing-in-Publication Data.
A catalogue record for this book
is available from the British Library.

ISBN 978-1-780-22818-1

Printed and bound in Great Britain by Clays Ltd, St Ives plc

MIX
Paper from
responsible sources
FSC® C104740

www.orionbooks.co.uk

Contents

Contents

Dedicated to my friend the Spanish poet, Joaquin Buxo
Montesinos

The one thing our Fuhrer is afraid of is peace, but he needn't worry his head about that. Our enemies wouldn't dream of making peace with him.

Porta in conversation with Tiny,
at a crossing of the Dniepr in July 1942

Happy was our laughter there where death became absurd and life still more so.

Wilfred Owen

'*Aprés moi le déluge,*' the Staff Padre explains, goggling up at the Oberst, who is gazing stonily down at him from the saddle of his horse. '*Me mum left me when I was just a little lad,*' he sobs, self-pityingly.

'*You're drunk,*' says the Oberst, and taps his riding boots with his whip.

'*Wrong, quite wrong, Oberst ol' pal,*' hiccups the padre, emitting a long cackle of laughter, which echoes in the morning quiet of the streets. '*Take a closer look, ol' Oberst pal, an' you will observe I am quite, quite sober. Even your horse don't notice it when I breathe straight in his face.*'

With the aid of a lamp-post he achieves the difficult task of getting to his feet and saluting. '*Oberst ol' sir, I will not attempt to deceive you,*' he says with solemn honesty. '*I am drunk. Terribly, terribly drunk!*' He gives himself a penance of ten "*Our Father's*" and fifteen "*Hail Mary's*", but then loses the thread and says '*God, sir! Permission to speak, sir? I am staff padre at Third Army Corps, sir!*' He embraces the neck of the horse and begs to be arrested, put in irons and carried off to jail. '*But please,*' he begs, with a sly cackle, '*please put me in Alt Moabitt jail. They're having beans for dinner today! Come with me Herr Oberst, ol' sir, an' you'll see. They're the best beans you ever, ever tasted in all your life!*'

1
Obstacle Race to the Glasshouse

Gregor Martin swears for a long time without repeating himself.

'*Escort* duty,' he snorts. 'Why in the name of the half a hundred heathen hells does it always have to be *us*? Why can't they just put 'em on the tram, or something? All that shit with leg-irons an' handcuffs an' loadin' with live! As if any one of 'em was crackers enough to bugger about *escaping*!'

'You don't understand a thing,' smiles Porta, happily. 'It is laid down in HDV[1] that prisoners are to be taken to jail in irons and under armed escort. The Army takes this kind of thing *seriously*. Send 'em on the *tram*! You must be round the bend!'

'Shut it, now,' growls Gregor, sourly. 'And if you start one of those stories of yours, and its about some prisoner, I'll bloody shoot you, I will!'

'My stories are not to be sneezed at,' whinnies Porta. 'You can learn a lot from 'em. We were once escorting prisoners from Altona to Fuhlsbüttel, an' when we reached Gänsemarkt, we all agreed to take a tram. But the escort commander, Oberfeldwebel Schramm, had some kind of eye trouble and had to wear tinted glasses. We *told* him it was a number 9 tram we were getting on and it ought to be a number 6, but he told us to shut it, like you just did. Wouldn't admit to himself his glasses played him tricks more often than not!

'*Up* you, Schramm, we thought, and nipped up on the number 9, which had its terminus at Landungsbrücke.'

[1]HDV: Heeresdienstvorschrift (German): Army Regulations

'All right, that's enough,' shouts Gregor, gruffly. 'We all know how its goin' to end.'

'Not a bit of it,' smiles Porta, condescendingly. 'We wound up, three days later, with *Marabou*[2] at Fuhlsbüttel, but before that Oberfeldwebel Schramm had gone bananas and we'd had to take him to Giessen[3]. When this lot was all over the escort became prisoners and the C.O. had to detail a new escort. *This* one was placed under the command of Feldwebel Schluckemeyer who had some kind of *ear* trouble. . . .'

'If you're goin' to tell us he went batchy too,' shouts Gregor, 'I'll do somebody or other a bloody mischief!'

'Oh *no-o*!' said Porta, looking insulted, 'I always stick to the facts. Feldwebel Schluckemeyer never went mad. He *did* shoot himself, just before we got to Fuhlsbüttel, and that caused us a bit of trouble, because, you see, we couldn't just march into the glasshouse and report without any escort commander. . . .'

Gregor snatches his P-38 from its leather holster.

'One word more an' I'll fill you full of holes!'

'Have it your way,' sighs Porta, shrugging his shoulders carelessly. 'But you'll regret not having drawn on my wealth of experience. *I* am *the* expert on escorts, from both sides of the loaded rifle.'

'*Shit*!' says Gregor, irritatedly, slamming his pistol back into its holster.

Porta, who knows Berlin like the inside of his own pocket, takes the lead, but as we cross Neuer Markt and swing into Bischoffstrasse, one of the prisoners, infantry Gefreiter Kain, points out we are marching the wrong way.

'What the devil do *you* know about it?' Porta bubbles, furiously, 'I might be taking a short-cut, mightn't I?'

'Balls!' says Kain, stubbornly, 'I was born in this town and know it inside out. Go down here and you run straight onto Alexander Platz.'

'Don't you tell *me* what's what, you jailhouse shit! I know what I'm doin',' says Porta.

---

[2]Marabou: Notorious Commandant at Fuhlsbüttel: See 'Wheels of Terror.'
[3]Giessen: Insane asylum.

12

'Prisoners speak when they're spoken to,' howls Tiny from the back of the squad.

'If we're goin' to the glasshouse,' interjects an artillery Wachtmeister, 'then we're *right* off course.'

'Chatter, chatter, chatter,' Porta chides, in a superior tone. 'You sound like a flock o' flippin' parrots in a knockin'-shop. Get the Christmas spirit going, Gregor, and free the slaves from their chains. I'm setting 'em up at "The Crooked Dog" on the other side of "Alex".

'There's always something doing at "The Crooked Dog",' explains Porta, with a cheerful, guttersnipe grin as we rattle to a halt outside 'The Dog'.

'Last Wednesday some feller rushed out after another feller, an' shot him in the arse for trying to nip off without paying. Last night a meeting between the railwaymen and the boys off the trams wound up with one of 'em getting a chronic case of hurdy-gurdy fever, and *every* night somebody or other leaves headfirst via the window.'

'You politicals?' asks Tiny, interestedly, as he unlocks a Pioneer Gefreiter's handcuffs.

'You *could* say that,' the Pioneer answers, phlegmatically. 'Accordin' to the evidence I ought've been a Cabinet Minister at least.'

'Red Front an' all that shit?' asks Tiny, with a sly grin.

'Worse'n that,' declares the Pioneer, darkly. 'I got chucked out o' "The Frog". The watchdogs swarmed around like a lot o' ducks gettin' onto a lump o' bread, an' *I* have to tell 'em about Adolf bein' just a liar from Brunau what the Austrians had sent us out of wicked malice.'

'You got just one chance,' explains Tiny, omnisciently. 'When they drag you up in front of the court, up with your bleedin' arm, click your 'eels an' shout, " 'Eil 'Itler!" This you do every time you answer a bleedin' question. *Then* what they do is they send you to the ol' trick-cyclist. Up with your arm again an' give 'im the same treatment. Then 'e'll ask you to do somethin' barmy, like puttin' bits o' wood in 'oles, or puttin' words together, or somethin'. What do you do? You shout out: "*Führer, befiehl, wir folgen!*" An' this you keep on with

13

even when they throw you into solitary. After a bit they'll find out as 'ow you're unsuitable for punishment, an' put you in the nut 'ouse for life. *Then* you're saved! You just sit there nice an' peaceful like, an' wait till Germany's got the shit knocked out of 'er. When *that* 'appens they'll kick your arse out o' the loony-bin an' fill it up with Adolf an' *'is* mates. In the new Germany you ought to 'ave a good chance of makin' mayor at least.'

'Bit dodgy this, isn't it?' protests the artillery Wachtmeister pessimistically, as they find seats in the smoke-filled, beer-stinking saloon.

The host, a tiny man wearing a big, black bowler hat, embraces Porta with a happy grin. The first round is on the house.

'Any of you lot due for the chopper?' asks Porta, after the second round has gone down. 'If so, don't be nervous. It's all over before you've time to think about it. I know the feller who does it, and *he* knows what he's up to. Only made a mess of it twice, an' one of *them* was a bint. Put him off by cryin' an' sayin' it was all a mistake. It *was* too!'

'I don't believe they're cruel as all that,' an infantry Feldwebel puts his oar in. 'We Germans are a humane people.'

'Tell that to the boys in Germersheim[4],' says Porta, jeeringly.

'You may not believe it,' says the Feldwebel, 'but I am really innocent.'

'Of *course* you are,' Porta nods agreement. 'We're *all* innocent. Unfortunately it's often more dangerous to be innocent than guilty.' He bends forward over the table and speaks in a confidential tone. 'I once knew a Herr Ludwig Gänsenheim from Soltau. He was a *careful* man. So careful he even walked along the street with his eyes shut so's not to see anything he oughtn't. When the talk turned treasonable he'd put his fingers in his ears. His toes too, if there'd been room. Well, one day he got mixed up in a KDF[5] march with everybody screaming "*Heil*

[4]Germersheim: Military prison near Karlsruhe.
[5]KDF (Kraft durch Freude): NAZI organisation, 'Strength through Joy', which arranged entertainments and travel parties.

Deutschland, Heil der Führer!' By the time they'd got to Leipziger Strasse and rounded the tramwaymen's building, our neutral friend, Herr Ludwig Gänsenheim, had got himself brainwashed into being a faithful follower of the Führer without even wanting to. When the happy crowd thundered over the Spree Bridge he went all to pieces and screamed: "Death and gas to all Jews and Communists!" He was so far gone he didn't even notice himself go down an' the mob tramp all over him. On *they* rushed to the Chancellory to get a flash of Adolf, an' while they were doin' it a Schupo squad was sweepin' up what was left of Herr Ludwig *an'* ten other poor innocents like him. Off to the morgue with 'em, and maybe somebody eventually identified 'em.'

'War's terrible,' the infantry Feldwebel breaks in, the corners of his lips drawn down so far they almost meet under his chin.

'All sorts of people get killed one way or another, innocent an' guilty alike.'

'Yes, yes,' Porta continues, enthusiastically. 'In wartime no worry! Some get their chops shot off at the front, others lose their bonce in Plötzensee. Sooner or later we all get it, so's our descendants can see we *did* do *somethin'* during the war, an' didn't just run round in circles like a flock of hens with a fox nippin' at their arses! World Wars *have* to wind up in blood and shit, to get a good word in the history books. You don't think Adolf'd accept a war nobody even noticed. It's the really *wicked* dictators and generals who get remembered!'

The rain has turned to slush when the prisoners and their escorts turn out of 'The Dog'. Outside the Hitler Youth hostel on Prenzlauer Strasse they are hauling down the flag. We turn the corner and march down Dircksen Strasse.

'*Shit*,' growls Gregor, wiping slushy snow from his face. 'I'm about tired o' this bloody war. Always goin' round waitin' for a bomb to drop on your nut.'

From a door a few steps up from the level of the street a man comes flying, rolls like a living wheel straight across the street, and crashes into the wall of the house opposite. His coat and hat come flying after him, and, after a pause, an umbrella.

Porta laughs, expectantly. 'Gents we're there! *This* is "The

15

Crippled Frog", and things seem to be livening up. Be nice an' quiet now,' he continues, in a fatherly tone, 'because this is a decent place, with a piano *and* a set o' drums, an' this is where the war-widows come to get consoled for their great loss.'

'I been 'ere before,' declares Tiny, his eyes shining. 'The cunt there is in this place you wouldn't believe. Not much room though. Can't go for a piss yourself. You 'ave to send your shadder!'

'What'll we do if the watchdogs turn up?' asks Gregor, nervously, depositing his Mpi on a shelf under the bar.

'No problem,' Porta laughs, unworriedly. 'Both the watchdogs and the Schupo always ring before they raid this place.'

The host, who has two wooden legs, embraces Porta heartily and asks where he is going. 'Taking four poor bastards to be strung up,' says Porta.

'Oh, *shit!*' says the host. 'First round on the house. Beer and schnapps.' After the first four rounds of beer and schnapps Porta begins to tell treasonable anecdotes.

'When the Tommy's get hold of *him*, they'll *really* stretch his Austrian neck for him,' he says in a secretive tone, to a tramdriver who is leaving at dawn with a troop transport.

' 'E'll be for makin' a speech before they pulls the bleedin' floor out from under 'im.' Tiny laughs uncontrollably and bangs his fist down on the table, making the glasses dance.

A Schupo in semi-civvies laughs so heartily he swallows his cigar.

The host hits him on the back with his third wooden leg, which is always kept in reserve behind the bar.

He chokes up the cigar which, to our amazement, is still alight.

Two women, dressed in black, white and red, and sitting under the picture of Hitler, begin to sing:

I once shot a copper
Now 'is wife's a'gettin' it proper. . . .

A party of wounded are sitting at the long table running their hands up the girls legs.

Sophia she was stinkin' drunk. . . .

16

sings Porta in a beery baritone. A medical officer, half-asleep by the stove, opens one eye in conspiratorial fashion and stares around the room.

'Malingerers! Malingerers, the bloody lot of you. What do you care about the Fatherland?' he thunders, ecstatically. 'I'll fix you, I will! Kv[6] the lot of you and off to the front!' With a deep sigh he slumps across the table and falls asleep again.

'Drunk! Drunk as a cunt!' says the host, shaking his head in disapproval. 'Farts about on some commission declarin' everything an' everybody Kv. Give 'im a medal for it, they did. Last week 'e declared a bleeder with only one leg Kv. Got right up to the front line with 'is false leg under 'is arm before they stamped 'im GVH[7] and sent 'im back to depot. Now 'e's at the Hauptfeldwebel School 'opin' some time to get back at that bleedin' M.O.!'

'Ten minutes for a five-spot, and twenty-five for all night,' the red white and black women are offering.

'But only if you're wearin' a rubber, mate,' titters the smallest of them, pointing suggestively up under her dress.

'Later, later,' Porta waves them away. 'Give us the one about the orphaned children first.'

'No, the one about death as turns up after midnight,' hiccups Tiny, laughing foolishly. 'We're on our way to the clink with four candidates for the chopper,' he confides to the two patriotic ladies.

'And they look such nice chaps, too,' giggles the tall thin one.

'They are that,' grins Tiny. 'They'll make four lovely corpses.'

'What've they done, then?' comes inquisitively from over by the long table.

'Nothing much,' smiles Porta. 'The footslogger there cut the throats of his two newborn twins. The gunner beat his wife to death with some part or another of a gun, and the fat chap, who's a butcher in civvy street, made sausage meat out o' two whores.'

---

[6]Kv (Kriegsverwendungsfähig): Fit for service.
[7]GVH (Garnisonsverwendungsfähig): Fit for home service.

'That's enough of that,' shouts the Wachtmeister, indignantly. 'None of us is a murderer. We're politicals, we are!'

Suddenly everybody wants to buy a round.

'The Fatherland has had it,' intones Porta, over the heads of the crowd, which exudes a mixed atmosphere of beer and street-walker love.

'After us the bleedin' flood,' announces Tiny, excitedly, and drinks a sleeping guest's beer. 'Our wicked enemies are takin' the piss out of us,' hiccups Gregor, staggering threateningly.

At the long table the convalescents and their lady-friends begin to sing:

Germany you ancient house,
Your blood-stained banner hangs in tatters. . . .

'As a servant of the state I cannot continue to listen to this sort of thing,' protests a long, thin man in a black leather coat. He resembles an eagle with a bad cold.

'Sit over in the corner then and stick your fingers in your ears,' Porta advises him. 'What you don't hear won't hurt you.'

'Let's get on to the bloody glasshouse,' begs the artillery Wachtmeister, unhappily. 'This whole thing is madness! As a military prisoner I must strongly protest.'

'Your lice must be ticklin' up your liver,' growls Tiny. 'What the 'ell's it to do with you, anyroad? You're not a servin' soldier just now. 'Ave a bit o' fun. It's the last chance you'll bleedin' 'ave before you get court-martialled. After *that* you won't be laughin' all that much. *Then* you may realise World Wars just ain't *funny!*'

The infantry Gefreiter is drunk and dancing a weaving tango with the patriotic little whore. She has a good grip on him to prevent him falling.

'I know a bloke who's gonna get his nut chopped off,' he confides to her, with a skull-like chuckle.

'The good go first, *always*,' she consoles him, and follows her words up with a hearty belch.

'Yesterday a rotten bastard give me a set o' phony ration cards for an all-nighter,' says a girl, sadly.

18

'You couldn't've satisfied 'im, then, could you?' says a one-armed Feldwebel.

'Aren't you scared they'll escape?' asks a civilian. He smells like police.

'They don't dare,' grins Porta. 'They'd get shot for desertin' as well as what they're gonna get shot for now, an' *that's* enough to give the toughest nut in the world the pip.'

'You must know, as an NCO, that it is strictly forbidden to take prisoners into public houses?' The plain clothes policeman turns to Gregor. 'I refer you to page 176 in regulations for military escorts. The prisoner is to be taken straight to the place of imprisonment and placed in solitary confinement. He is in no circumstances to be allowed to come into contact with other persons. If communication with him becomes necessary, such communication will be confined to as few words as possible.'

'Dead on, matey,' Tiny burbles, foolishly. 'Prisoners will be treated like tiny little babies, they will. They are not to be contaminated by contact with drunks, nor 'ores neither! Any on 'em as *does* talk to 'em'll be clapped in bleedin' irons an' took straight in front of the judge.'

'Fifty for a shot?' a ratty little man whispers. 'Dead good, it is,' he whispers, and nudges Porta conspiratorially. 'Ether an' benz. Three days time and all China's got the black plague. If you're the last German soldier alive none of 'em'll care tuppence.'

'Too soon, my son, too soon,' says Porta, without interest. 'I'm one of the happy few who're still enjoying a good, good war.'

Shortly after the weird little man disappears into the toilet with his hypodermic syringe and four war-weary infantrymen. When they come back they exude a new optimism.

The noise level in the bar increases. Two of the prisoners have dropped off to sleep in the dog's basket by the stove. The dog is not happy about this. It growls, shows its teeth and nips at their legs. But to no avail. Resolutely it lifts a hind leg and pisses all over their faces.

'A couple o' pints o' water a day is *good* for you,' mumbles the sleeping infantry Gefreiter.

19

'Chew your food twenty-seven times before swallowin',' snivels the Pioneer, working his jaws like a masticating cow in a warm stable.

'Take me home to jail,' demands the Wachtmeister, severely. 'I've the *right* to be taken straight to jail. I'm a bloody prisoner an' I've got more rights'n any other bloody soldier in the army. You lot don't only have to see to me not runnin' off, but also that I don't come to no harm. It's a very serious matter, it *is*!' He points accusingly at the two prisoners in the dog's basket. 'The judges aren't gonna like *that*, y'know! Prisoners drunk as lords.'

'I'm *hungry*,' announces Porta, with an echoing belch. 'What about a round o' "shit on a shovel" to stay the pangs? Eight "shit on a shovels" ' he shouts through the kitchen hatch.

Very soon eight steaming plates of hash appear from the kitchen.

The miserable grey morning light of November begins to appear and Gregor feels it's about time they rejoined the service and began to try to find their way to the jail.

'Maybe it's gone away!' slobbers the Pioneer in the dog basket.

'Think so?' asks the infantry Gefreiter, an expression of hope spreading across his face. He looks like a starving man who has found a well-filled wallet.

'They ain't gonna like it if we arrive in the middle o' breakfast,' mutters Tiny, darkly.

'Right you *are*,' admits Porta, thoughtfully. 'Particularly the way the boys in the dog basket stink of beer an' schnapps.'

'What do we *do* then?' sighs Gregor indecisively, suddenly feeling rather lonely.

'We bomb England to bits,' declares a drunken airman, banging his fist on the table. 'There'll be nothin' left but a bloody big hole in the sea!'

'God love us,' shouts Gregor, with a hashy belch. 'We never should have *had* a soddin' air force.'

'Just what I say,' shouts the infantry Gefreiter in the dog basket. 'Brave foot-sloggers an' artillery as can aim straight. A shower o' shells on top on 'em an' over the top *we* go!'

20

'Yeah, we've lost a *lot* of wars *that* way,' sighs Porta, tiredly. 'The foot-sloggers foot-slogged themselves straight to hell. When they got to the day of victory there was nothin' left of 'em but the rings of their arses. All the shiny Krupp guns were so worn out they shot backwards an' plastered the gunners all over the landscape.'

'If you don't come *now*,' shouts Gregor, angrily, blowing himself up like a poisoned pup, 'I'm off. Damned if I'm not.'

'Woof, woof!' barks Tiny. 'Barmy as a Prussian without anybody to give orders to, *you* are. Listen now, Gregor. *You* are an *escort*! If you're on your bleedin' own 'ow *can* you *be* an escort. They'll courtmartial you, they will. Count on it. The commander of a escort without no escort nor no prisoners neither. A very, very serious matter, *indeed*!'

'Oh, they'd kick his arse all the way up to the back of his neck, they would. He'd have to stand on his head to go for a shit,' confirms Porta, scratching his ear. 'One glance at Army Regs an' anybody can see it's no fun being put on escort duty.'

'What the Bible is to the Pope an' the Koran is to the Muslims that's what Army bleedin' Regs is to the German Army,' shouts Tiny, solemnly. 'If Moses's son Job 'ad 'ad Army Regs to 'ave a gander at 'e wouldn't never've been barmy enough to cross the bleedin' Rhine an' go walkin' in the German soddin' jungle'n gettin' the lot on 'em suffocated in 'eathen *sauerkraut*.' Tiny is firing off his usual strange mixture of history and the Bible.

'Tell me, gentlemen. Tell me please. Where am I?' asks the medical officer suddenly. He gets to his feet with considerable difficulty, his legs wobbling under him.

'Doctor, sir! You are amongst *friends*!' Porta assures him, smashing his heels together. 'You, sir, are in "the Frog", sir.'

'Comrade, shoot me,' the M.O. demands, with a very German look on his face. 'I am a boozy rat. Shoot me!' he repeats, tearing open his tunic and baring his breast.

'If you wish, sir,' replies Porta, obediently, placing the butt of his rifle with difficulty to his shoulder. He wavers dangerously, the muzzle of his rifle pointing all over the place. 'Stand still then, doctor, so's I can shoot you as ordered,' he shouts through the din.

21

'Fire!' orders Tiny, in a stentorian voice.

A deafening roar splits the air, and plaster powders down from the ceiling. The bullet ricochets round the room and ends in a beer cask, from which the contents begin to spout.

'I'm killed, I'm bleeding,' whimpers the M.O. miserably, as the beer drenches him. Wailing, he crawls under the table, and hitting his head on a supporting crosspiece discovers he is not dead yet. He staggers to his feet with difficulty, stands in front of the mirror, and points at himself. 'Aha, *there* you are,' he says, cunningly. 'Thought you could fool *me*, did you? I see *straight* through you, you doctor you. No malingerers with me. Fit for duty and back to the front! *Kick* me!' he orders, in a severe voice.

'Order carried out, *sir*!' shouts Tiny, sending the medical officer flying across the room with a well-directed kick.

'It's the *Russians*!' screams a tiny woman, who seems to be exceptionally patriotic, jumping up on the sleeping Schupo's back. She bites him savagely in the neck and pulls his ears back with both hands.

The traindriver, who has been lying across a table, snoring like a runaway circular saw, wakes up suddenly at the sound of the Schupo's screams.

'*Zurücktreten. Zug fahrt ab!*' he roars, sitting himself crossways on a chair with a traindriver look on his face. Whistling, and making steam-engine noises he hops around the room on the chair.

'They'll put that bastard inside for *sure*!' prophesies the Wachtmeister watching the whistling, steaming traindriver with a sombre mien.

'We'll *all* end up there sooner or later,' says Gregor, darkly.

'*Verweile Augenblick, du bist so schön,*' Porta quotes from Goethe, solemnly.

The traindriver knocks the M.O. over. He crawls along the wall and gets up in front of Tiny. 'I've found you, my son! I've *found* you!' he slobbers, idiotically. 'How's dad, son? Fit for duty is he?'

'Not really,' answers Tiny. 'They cut 'is bleedin' 'ead off in Fuhlsbüttel on New Years mornin', 1938!'

'The ways of God are mysterious,' sobs the medical officer, crossing himself. 'Head or no bloody head, who cares? He's fit for duty, *I* say. What use's a German soldier got for a head anyway? First day he gets in barracks they tell him to stop thinkin'. Leave all that to the horses. That's why God's given 'em such big heads. What am I *doin'* in "The Frog" anyway?'

'Replying as ordered, doctor sir!' hiccoughs Porta. 'You are getting yourself blind pissed, you are, doctor sir, and you are telling all the guests present that they are quite, quite fit for duty!'

'Impossible,' protests the doctor, his mind clearing for a moment. 'I am not on duty an' when I'm not on duty nobody can be declared fit for duty. You must report me. I am asking for a court-martial. Now I will fall down,' he shouts in a piercing voice, and falls limply across the host's table. 'It's *you* I've been looking for. Tomorrow we'll open up your lungs. People who ain't fit for duty don't need lungs anyway. *You* have been *ruined* by your milieu!'

'*Up* you, you drunken bastard!' screams the host, pushing him off the table.

'Jesus an' Mary!' cries Porta. 'The nerve of that shitty-arsed sod! What'll we do with it?'

'Cut it's bleedin' throat for it,' suggests mine host, oozing with the milk of human kindness.

'That's *enough*l' shouts Gregor, suddenly, tightening his belt. '*Up* you drunken shower. Up on your feet! Attempt to escape, and we will use our weapons.' He cocks his P-38 noisily. Suddenly the energy oozes out of him, and he orders another beer.

'Don't leave me, boys,' begs the M.O., looking up the taller of the patriotic ladies' skirts. 'Arrest me! Lead me to the scaffold! This head's too heavy for me!'

'Sounds promisin',' sighs the host, sadly. 'Do us all a favour an' take 'im with you!'

'Why not!' Gregor gives in. 'Put him in irons with the four other villains!'

'What, what, what!' protests Porta. 'You can't just do *that*. We are eight escorts and four prisoners, just like it says in Army

23

Regs. If we're goin' to take that bastard with us, *you'll* have to find two more escorts. Otherwise you go before a court for breach of regulations. Where'd we *be*, if just *anybody* was allowed to pick up extra prisoners on the road? 'Fore we knew where we were we'ld be looking like some kind of a pilgrimage, or a crusade or somethin'.'

'I'll go along as an extra guard,' says a Jaeger, who looks rather like a soaking-wet goat. 'My leave was over two days ago an' I could do with a good excuse for goin' over time.'

'Got a gun?' asks Gregor, prosaically.

' 'Ere you are, then!' brays the Jaeger, happily, taking a rifle from behind the counter. '*And* live ammo', too. I'm on me way to the Caucasus front.'

'Take you a while,' Porta nods. 'We need one more.'

'He's *here*!' rumbles a voice from the door, and an ebony figure in *panzer* uniform looms up.

'Has Africa surrendered, then?' asks Porta, in amazement. 'Where the devil've you turned up from?'

White teeth flash in the black face.

'I'm German. Stabsgefreiter Albert Mumbuto, *11. Panzerersatz Abteilung*. My father was staff-bugler in *2. Leibhusaren Regiment*. He has shaken hands with the Crown Prince and seen the Kaiser. *I* am now transferred to *27. Panzer Regiment*. z.b.V.'

'That's *us*,' grins Porta, happily. 'Heartily welcome, black man! *Now* we know what to do. Arrest the doctor!'

'Come 'ere you crooked son of a bitch,' shouts Tiny, clicking the handcuffs on the doctor's wrists in true American style. 'You're under arrest, buddy, so stop callin' *me* buddy, as of now!'

'Holy, holy, holy!' the M.O. intones, clapping his hand-cuffed hands together, and lifting them in priestly fashion towards the heavens. He breaks into a happy laugh. 'Let's go, boys. Now we're *all* fit for duty. I'm a swine. A giant swine,' he admits with drunken truthfulness.

The escort swings into Gips Strasse, and he shouts, to a sleepy couple.

'Hey you there! Hey! You want to get to know Dr. Alfred

24

Hütten? Not to be confused with his cousin Dr. *Oskar* Hütten, the veterinary, who's a drunk *and* some sort of a *heathen*! He does *not* believe in the Führer, *nor* in the Holy Trinity!'

'Watch it, crab-catcher,' snarls Gregor, irritably. 'Or you'll get your bloody nose flattened.'

'How right, how right, Herr Oberjaeger,' the M.O. smiles weakly, and spirals his body around a lamp-post.

'Let's dump him in the park,' I suggest, when we finally unwind him from the lamp-post. He has cocked his leg up against it as if he were some kind of canine.

A Feldwebel from the Luftwaffe watches us interestedly.

The medical officer salutes him.

'There you are at last,' he shouts, happily. 'Is England demolished? Is the German Sea washing over it? The Luftwaffe are a fine set of boys,' he states, a little later, imitating an aeroplane with outstretched arms. 'The Reichsmarschall bears Germany's highest order. Made specially for *him*!'

'Fat German throats have to have fat German orders,' Porta philosophises.

'*Halt*! Where are you taking these men?' comes a deep voice from the darkness. A corpulent Staff Padre with his cap turned backwards rolls out of a little door behind the *Erlöser Kirche*. 'Answer, man! Answer me!'

'Prisoners and escort, halt!' commands Gregor, with an unhappy look on his face, as if he is already regretting this meeting with the spiritual arm of the service. 'Herr Staff Padre, *sir*! Escort with five prisoners from Panzer Barracks proceeding to Garrison Prison.'

'Well, well, well, *well*!' says the Staff Padre, pleasure in his voice. 'So you're on your way to jail, are you? I think I'll accompany you. They've got a good cook in that officers mess, and if I'm not wrong today is brown bean day. Anybody here like beans? Take one pace forward and I'll *shoot* you!' He shakes his head so violently that his cap flies off and goes rolling across the street.

'Drunk!' says Porta, knowingly.

The padre falls down twice trying to pick up his cap. When he finally catches it he puts it on crossways.

'That's to confuse the enemy,' he confides, with a sly grin. 'Follow me!' he orders. 'By order of the Führer we will take over "The Rosy Maid", and there I will set 'em up. Don't I *know* you?' he asks Porta.

'Herr Staff Padre, sir, yes sir! I was formerly chaplain's assistant at 7. Infantry Division in Munich[8]. Transferred, sir! Transferred because my faith was not strong enough, sir!'

'D'd'don't he believe in *God*, then?' babbles the padre, holding on tightly to a lamp-post.

'Only when I'm scared,' Porta admits. 'Like when the enemies of Germany throw shells at me. Padre, sir, in ordinary circumstances I don't know the difference 'tween a Holy Roman pigeon an' a Finnish wild-cat with wings, I don't really, sir!'

'M-m-me neither,' dribbles the padre, kissing the lamp-post fervently. 'We forget God when things go well. Are you, by the way, a C-c-catholic or a P-p-protestant?'

'Well padre, sir, I'm a bit of both, you might say. Whatever is suitable at the time,' admits Porta, diplomatically.

'I like it! I *like* it!' laughs the Staff Padre, slapping Porta's shoulder, in friendly fashion. 'I've just been with the Bishop. The Vatican is asking after me. Something big's goin' to happen. I might be able to use you, Obergefreiter. I'll have you transferred to m-m-military sp-sp-spiritual service. It would be a pity to see a man like you wasted on the bloody altar of the Fatherland!'

'I *do* agree,' whispers Porta, making a rapid sign of the cross.

'Come on then,' says the padre, striking out at an invisible enemy. 'Right wheel, left turn, forward march! *You* know the way. "The Maid" in Berg Strasse.'

'Spiritual advisers who talk about friendship are not to be trusted,' says Albert, darkly. Moving away from the padre.

As we march along beside the tall hedges of the Stadt Park, a resounding 'Halt!' breaks the morning silence of the street.

The cloaked and capped upper half of an Oberst appears above the hedge. Gregor almost drops his Mpi in terror. The night silence is broken by strange sounds. The noise is like that

[8] See 'Blitzfreeze'

of a shipload of passengers struck simultaneously with sea-sickness. It comes from the Staff Padre who is getting rid of everything he has consumed at 5. Panzer Regiment Mess. It is not a little.

The hedge parts and a brown horse with an Oberst on its back comes through like a T-34. The horse sniffs at Porta and closes one eye as if to say: 'Watch this, now!'

'What kind of a pig-stye *is* this?' screams the Oberst, furiously, slashing his riding boots with his whip.

Gregor falls over his own feet, salutes, and cracks his heels together.

'Herr Oberst, sir! Beg to report, sir! Five prisoners and escort en route for jail, sir! All properly handcuffed, sir! Accordin' to regulations, sir!'

'We meet again, Herr Oberst,' shouts the Staff Padre, happily, pushing Gregor to one side, as if he were a piece of refuse. 'And how is your lady wife, sir? Does she still love me, sir? I hope soon to see her in the confessional, sir!' His noisy laughter rings along the street.

'You're *drunk*, man!' snarls the Oberst, nasally.

'R-r-rubbish, man. You insult my spiritual honour,' he strikes out at the Oberst, as if his riding-whip were a sabre. 'Y-y-you just watch yourself! I'll cut you up into *sauerkraut*, I will. Don't you think I'm frightened of an *ersatz* Oberst like you just because he's sittin' on a horse! You're ugly bastards, you *are*. *Both* of you!'

'Put that man in irons,' orders the Oberst, his voice cutting through the night.

Tiny throws himself at the padre like a hungry polar bear, and throws him to the ground. Filthy snow splashes up onto the Oberst's well-polished boots.

The horse whinnies and rears up in protest. The Oberst slides backwards, but saves himself by catching it round the neck. It rears again and this time he loses his seat and falls with a smack into the slush alongside Tiny and the padre.

'Welcome to our house,' sniggers the padre, saluting, flat on his back.

Shaking with nerves, Gregor assists the Oberst to his feet.

Nobody notices Porta give the horse a slap on its rump which sends it off at a gallop through the hedge and across the park.

'Beg to report, sir! Horse deserted, sir!' shouts Porta, clicking his heels twice over.

'Catch it!' orders the Oberst, brusquely.

Escort and prisoners dash off into the darkness after the galloping horse, which circles and comes back to the Oberst. He is in the process of having a fit. Putting on his hat, he has discovered it to be full of slush.

Tiny stands at attention in front of him with his hand at his cap, attempting to report. He gets out, 'Herr Oberst!' He is cut off by a roar of rage.

It is only when the Oberst has swung himself back into his saddle that some measure of relaxation falls over him. He bends forward over the neck of his horse and stares fiercely at the padre, who is still sitting in the slush talking to himself.

'Put him in irons!' rages the Oberst. 'He has attacked a Prussian officer! Put him in *irons*!' he repeats, revengefully.

'Herr Oberst, *sir*! Beg to report, *sir*! We ain't got no more irons, *sir*!' trumpets Tiny.

'Tie him up, then!' thunders the Oberst. 'Take that stupid look off your face, man! *You*, Obergefreiter! *You*!' he shouts at Tiny.

'Beg to report, sir! Born with it, sir! Marked down barmy, sir, by the Army psychopaths, sir, I was! In 1938, sir, by order of *Herr General der Kavallerie* Knochenhauer, sir, as I was batman for, sir! Beg to report, sir, 'e was Commander 10. Army Corps, Hamburg, sir!'

'I know General Knochenhauer very well,' shouts the Oberst, patting his horse on the neck as if it were the general himself. 'You must have been a wicked man, soldier, if you couldn't get along with General Knochenhauer!'

'Beg to say, sir! Beg to say as the general an' me 'ad contact problems, sir!' smiles Tiny, contritely.

'What kind of man *are* you, anyway?' snarls the Oberst, bending forward over the neck of his horse to get a closer look at Tiny.

'German, sir! A *German* man, sir! That's what I am, sir!'

roars Tiny. Banging the butt of his rifle down on the flagstones and sending up a shower of sparks.

'You'll hear more from me,' the Oberst promises him, with obvious distaste. He pulls his horse round and rides off into the park.

'What in the name o' hell do we do now?' asks Gregor, looking worriedly after the Oberst disappearing into the rain.

'You've got a problem, friend,' admits Porta, sombrely. 'An Oberst from G-Staff has ordered you to arrest the good padre and to take him in with the rest of your prisoners. You should have protested that order. You're skating on very thin ice. You can't take him with you because you're short two escorts. Do it, an' you'll be contravenin' Army Regs. You'll lose your tapes *and* you'll be lucky not to get two years in Germersheim. You can't *not* arrest the padre. An Oberst has given you a direct order to do so. Not do it an' you're refusing to obey an order. *That* can cost you your napper, my son!'

'What the *hell* am I to do?' whines Gregor unhappily. He curses the day he was made an NCO, and *could* be made escort commander. 'Get me out of this,' he pleads.

'Well, just this once then,' smiles Porta largely. 'Though I'm not much for mixin' in with NCO's decisions.'

'Cut that crap!' Gregor breaks in, hope gleaming in his eyes. 'Tell me what to *do*.'

'*Before* the Oberst an' his horse turned up, the Staff Padre gave you an order. He ordered you to take "The Rosy Maid" in Berg Strasse. The padre is a staff officer equivalent in rank to a major and to disobey his order could cost you a lot. *And* he has not recalled that order.'

'For Christ's sake what do I *do*, then?' Gregor almost weeps, feeling the ice get thinner and thinner under him. 'A prisoner can't give his escort commander orders. Specially not orders to go into a boozer!'

'Your birth must have been a difficult one,' considers Porta, in wonder. 'Can't you understand? You have not yet met the Oberst and his horse!'

'Got it, got it!' Gregor's eyes light up, as he sees a safe shore ahead. 'We march straight to "The Rosy Maid", and let

29

that padre sod fill us up with giggle water. When we leave "The Maid" we carry out the *Oberst's* order, an' arrest the bloody parson. While we're in "The Maid" we detail off a couple more escorts.'

'You keep saying "we",' puts in Porta, wonderingly. '*You* are the boy who carries out the orders, and *you* are the boy who carries the can. *You*, not "we"! *You're* the boss!'

'Thank God I never became an NCO,' sighs Albert, showing two rows of pearly-white teeth. 'It's dangerous, it is!'

'You're fit for duty,' shouts the medical officer, from the darkness, rattling his handcuffs menacingly.

'Shut it, shit'ead,' Tiny scolds, hitting him on the back of the neck with his rifle butt.

'Prisoners and escort, quick march!' commands Gregor, in a voice which clearly reveals he has given up caring.

The Staff Padre leads the column with his riding whip on his shoulder as if it were a sabre. Now and then he changes from a march to take a couple of dance steps. He sweeps his cap off in a courtly gesture each time he passes a civilian.

'Drinkin' spirits is vulgar,' declares the M.O. with a satanic grin. 'Don't think you're going to dodge the front line,' he turns to the artillery Wachtmeister. 'Even if your hobnailed liver gets big enough to choke you, I'll mark you fit!' He pokes the negro in the back. 'You want to get to know Dr. Alfred Hütten better? Now's your opportunity. I could send you off for a dry-clean job that'd turn you into a snow-white German. The SS Reichsführer has ordered everybody to become Arians. The ones with the hooked noses'll have to get 'em straightened. How'd you get yourself that colour, anyway, Herr Schwartz?'

'Can it, quack,' snarls Albert, throwing a punch which the M.O. ducks.

'Black or white you're fit for duty, and back you go to the front, my lad!'

'Live together in the spirit of the Lord, and you will go to Heaven,' intones the padre, swinging his whip around his head.

'Priests are like girls legs,' grins Porta. 'They promise you a better time when you get higher up!'

'Slay me,' the padre demands, with a saintly look on his face.

'Place my head on a pole outside the Garrison Church. I've always wanted to become a martyr.' He falls to his knees at a tramstop and passes his hands lovingly over the cast-iron base of the sign. 'We meet again, my beloved Copernicus!' His stentorian voice echoes round the square.

'This feller's got his arse where his brains ought to be,' groans Gregor, resignedly. 'Wicked Emil'll make a whole platoon of martyrs out of him when he gets him in the cage!'

Suddenly the M.O. throws his arms round Tiny and begins to lick his face, like an excited dog.

'I thought you were dead, comrade. Your disguise is fantastic but I've seen through it. You're the boy who used to fuck the stiffs in the mortuary at Klagenfurt. Take off your hat when you address an academician,' he burbles, knocking off Tiny's steel helmet.

'Keep your rotten paws off my tin'at!' roars Tiny, angrily, picking up his helmet.

> *My hat has got three creases,*
> *Three creases has my hat. . . .'*

chants the Medical Officer, happily, attempting to dance some steps of the charleston. His legs tangle and down he goes.

'*Jacta sunt alea*[9]' announces the padre in a loud voice as he leads the escort column into 'The Rosy Maid'.

'Oh no-o!' groans the host, dropping two filled tankards. 'That goddam parson again!'

With a sound like a pack of hungry wolves going into action the padre attacks a large dish of smoked pork with *sauerkraut* and dumplings. He uses neither knife nor fork but shovels away at the food with both hands.

The landlord claps his hands to his head.

'God help us he'll eat the lot. An' that was for six people! What'm I goin' to give the rifle club?'

'Let 'em eat the parson,' suggests Porta, practically. '*We* can do without him!'

' 'E's a terrible man,' moans the host. 'The seven plagues of

[9]The dice are thrown.

31

Egypt all rolled into one. There ain't an officers mess in the entire Brandenburg military zone as don't live in fear of a visit from 'im. They do say as he was at a dinner with the Reichsmarschall an' before the guests were finished with their hors d'oeuvres 'e'd eat everythin' laid out on the table includin' the bloody flower decorations. Another time 'e ruined Herr Göring's electric train by loadin' it up with diced pork. There was three cooks standin' at the other end of the track choppin' up suckin' pigs as'd been roasted on a spit into little bits an' loadin' up. When the train passed 'im 'e'd empty the wagons. By the time 'e'd finished the train was that greased up it took the Reichsmarschall an' all 'is train specialists three weeks to get it runnin' proper again. They do say as 'e was the indirect cause the Luftwaffe didn't win the Battle o' Britain.'

'Lovely food,' says the padre, clapping the landlord on the shoulder in comradely fashion.

'Glad you liked it, then,' answers mine host, sourly.

'It was good enough, landlord. A few more dumplings perhaps, but I'm not complaining. The pork was good. Homesmoked I'll bet. You're a crafty fellow, landlord. I know all about it. Illegal pigs in the backyard, eh? When're you slaughtering again? I'll drop by. Now let's have tea with rum. When we've had that I'll buy a round of beer and a nutty schnapps. Put it on the bill as usual, landlord.'

'This drunken skypilot'll *bust* me,' moans the landlord, miserably.

'Whyn't you throw him out, landlord?' asks Porta. 'A quick boot in his holy arse and out the door.'

'Can't,' sighs the publican, heavily. 'You 'eard 'im. Knows all about the pigs out the back. If only some rotten Englishman'd drop a soddin' bomb on 'im. The worst of the lot is the way 'e keeps on sayin' that tomorrow 'e'll be startin' a new life an'll pay all 'is debts.'

'Yes, yes, we all have our troubles,' says Porta. 'I once knew a stationmaster, a Herr Leo Birnbaum, who ran the main station at Bamberg. A nice, understanding sort o' chap, but with a weakness for the bottle. On even dates he drank Hollands gin with beer and on uneven dates he drank beer with Bommer-

32

lunder schnapps. Every New Year's Eve he'd make a resolution that from the first of January he'd be a good, sober citizen. When he woke up after the party it was always the third or fourth of January and so it was too late and he had to wait till next first of January. Where the German Railways were concerned he seemed to think they'd been invented for him to have fun with.

' "Plauen, all change!" he'd shout sometimes when trains'd come rolling into his station.

'When the passengers started fighting to get off, he'd shout at them asking what they were up to and couldn't they read? Didn't the signs say, Bamberg? He could get away with murder, because his father-in-law had been the Führer's barber before 1933 and was now the local Gauleiter.

'But it came to an end at last, and even the barber-Gauleiter couldn't save him. It was shortly after he'd first started to eat salt herring. Somebody'd told him it was good for a hangover. It was the forenoon of the 22nd of February. A little before eleven o'clock, I think it was, when everything started to go wrong. Stationmaster Birnbaum was standing on platform 5, chewing on a salt herring, with a green flag in his left hand and a red flag in his right, when to his great surprise he saw goods-train 109 coming in to platform 3, instead of platform 5. He waved both his red and his green flag, wildly.

' "109, 109! What are you *doing* on that platform?"

'Goods train 109 didn't seem to hear him. Over the tracks he went, still waving his two flags. On platform 3 he trod on a greasy old hat which someone had lost and slid straight between two full petrol wagons addressed to 35 Panzer Regiment, Bamberg. The brakeman in the last wagon tried to grab him. That was a mistake! Herr Birnbaum fastened on to the brakeman's arm and pulled him down with him under the tank-cars. The off-side wheels cut the head off Stationmaster Birnbaum, very neatly, while the near-side wheels cut the head, just as neatly, off brakeman Schultze. This was particularly sad for the latter who was still on trial for the job and never became a permanent employee.

'There was a nasty epilogue. Accidents seldom come singly.

German National Railways cleaning assistant (female) second grade, Mrs. Amanda Grimm, was standing on platform 2, resting her German chin on her German Railways broomstick, and wondering where the two officials had disappeared to. When the goods-train had passed she glanced tiredly at the track and saw the head of Stationmaster Birnbaum lying there winking at her. She emitted a German scream of terror.

' "The Stationmaster's lost 'is 'ead," she howled and ran into the telegraphist's office. He, believing she was drunk, slapped her face. She reported him for this, later. She was, after all, a kind of civil servant, *and* she was on duty at the time, which could be proved by the fact that she still had her broom in her hand. This was not the end of the matter. The Kripos[10] received the report and some fool of a clerk filed it under "homicide" because another fool of a clerk had marked the file in red pencil: Case no. 2988-41 — "Decapitation of Stationmaster." Finally the case got on to the desk of a reasonable detective, who was just passing the time until he reached pension age, and wasn't interested in promotion an' all that shit. This did not, however, end the matter. The same night the RAF bombed Bamberg. They weren't *aiming* at Bamberg, of course, but at Munich. This was discovered later when one of them had to make an emergency landing. The Kripo man who had the case in hand got hit during this raid, while relaxing gently in "The Crooked Goose".

'*Now* the case was passed over to another Kripo. A young fellow with a really *German* civil servant frame of mind. He started every interrogation with a burst of knowledgeable laughter, and made it clear to witnesses that repeated lies would only make things worse for themselves when they finally told the truth. When he saw the words "Decapitation of Stationmaster" he actually licked his lips. Here it was at last. The big, big case which could get him promotion to an inspector's chair in the RSHA[11]. He pulled down the brim of his hat, put on his leather overcoat and went into action.

[10]Kripos: Criminal Police.
[11]RSHA: Reichssicherheits-Hauptamt: Government Security Service.

34

' "Confess," he snarled at Mrs Amanda Grimm, the cleaner. "Lie, and you'll be sorry!"

'She was interrogated so many times that in the end she went quite crazy, and thought she herself had pushed the Stationmaster under Goods-train 109. She signed a confession in the necessary eight places. But she wouldn't confess to killing the brakeman.

' "I don't even *know* him," she defended herself.

' "You don't have to *know* people to kill them," the young Kripo explained to her, in friendly fashion. "Soldiers do it every day!"

'He should never have said that. Just then three snap-brimmed gentlemen arrived to question the station telegraphist about another case. The cleaner complained to them that the Kripo had accused German soldiers of being murderers. All three of them fell on the young detective and almost ripped him to bits. This started a new series of misfortunes. The telegraphist sat, with his hand on the key, preparing to stop the Eger express and allow the train from Munich to go through.

'The snap-brims activities made him nervous. He made a slip. The Eger express continued at top speed. The Munich train moved onto the wrong track. The telegraphist started to scream. The snap-brims were so busy knocking their colleague, who had insulted the Greater German soldier's honour, into a cocked hat, they didn't even hear him scream. They were used to hearing screams. They didn't even notice the telegraphist eating the telegraph tape to remove the evidence.

' "It's goin' to happen *now!*" he prophesied, looking interestedly out of the window.

'The express train, which was pulled by two engines, one moving backwards — it was no. 044376-2 — came thundering in the distance. With a roar of steam it flashed through the station. Two bundles of "*Völkischer Beobachter*" were thrown from the mail car. They carried the latest news about "straightenings of the front" and "strategic withdrawals".

'The telegraphist closed his eyes, opened his mouth, and awaited the meeting of the two onrushing trains. They met at

35

block 22. The Eger express seemed to eat its way through the fast train from Munich with a din the like of which has seldom been heard before. In typical German style everything became very complicated.

'The snap-brims completely forgot what they'd come for. They'd disappeared before the sounds of the smash-up had stopped echoing. It didn't help them. They were found and accused as parties to the rail accident. They were lucky not to be accused of sabotage. They'd've been hanged twice. As it was they got off with having their necks stretched only once. The telegraphist didn't want to become better acquainted with German justice. He blew himself and the station up with the explosives kept in reserve to blow things up with before the enemy could take them over.

'The railway cleaner 2nd. class also managed to avoid the long arm of the law. She had hidden herself in a cupboard in which the telegraphist kept his black market goods. When he blew up the station she went with it.

'You're lookin' a bit queer, landlord? You're not feeling ill, are you?' asks Porta, solicitously. 'Perhaps you haven't been able to follow me properly? What I've been trying to explain to you is that too much alcohol is *bad* for you. I used to know a chap who had a service station. Oskar Schleben his name was and he was a foundling. They found him on a doorstep in Schleben Strasse and named him after the street. He got himself a lovely little boy, with the help of a Chinese young lady, and every evening he'd give his little boy a glass of Bommerlunder to get him off to sleep. When this kid had got to the age of two without ever in his life havin' been really sober he ran away from home. Well, round he went for a while an' when he got tired he sat down on the pavement outside the Tiergarten[12]. By the sausage seller's wagon, it was! Nobody could understand *how* in the world the child'd managed to *get* that far. Some *thought* it might be because he'd got Chinese blood in him. Anyway, after a couple of hours time'd gone by people started noticing him and, of course, a Schupo turned up.'

[12]Tiergarten: Zoo.

36

' "Whatever are you doing here, my little man?" he asked with false copper friendliness.

"Poo-poo," answered the boy, and kept on saying it. It was all he *could* say, anyway.

"The copper got worked up."

"Talk German, or you'll go inside!"

"Poo-poo," said the boy, and so, of course, they arrested him.

'They took him to "Alex"[13] where they put him through the process and he ended up in a cell. He might even have been forgotten there because they hadn't been able to fill in an admittance form for him. They wouldn't put his name down as "Poo-poo" on an important German police document, you see. But when he didn't get his usual daily Bommerlunder he started up wailing. Stabswachtmeister Schlade who was a really *square* kind of German, opened the cell door and stared hard at the boy.

' " 'Aven't you read the prison rules? Singing and loud talk is forbidden! *Strictly* forbidden!"

'The kid couldn't've cared less. He wanted his Bommerlunder. They sent for the police psychiatrist and things really got moving. . . .

'What's up, landlord? You look as if you're going to choke?' says Porta, compassionately, serving himself a glass of beer.

'Not, not, not another bloody word! Not about police. Not about n-n-nothin',' stammers the landlord, pressing both hands to his ears. 'I can't *stand* any more . . . I'm going round the bend!'

'Round the bend or no round the bend you're fit for duty. Count on that, you wooden bastard,' announces the Medical Officer in a loud voice. Soon after he asks the Staff Padre if *he'd* like to get to know him.

'You are *drunk*, sir,' says the Padre.

'Wrong! It's *you* who's drunk, Padre. But *that* won't help you. You're fit for duty, you are. Off to the front an' get shot! Can a dog get into heaven?' he asks, after a brief silence. He has a strange look in his eyes.

---

[13]Alex: The main police station on Alexander Platz.

'Application should be made to the Bishop at Münster. It will be treated conscientiously,' answers the Padre. 'I will give it my recommendation. Don't forget the proper stamps are affixed!'

'Damnation, I can't *take* any more of this shit!' shouts Gregor. He becomes wildly zealous. 'Prisoners an' escort! Form up, you shower o' fucked-up sods! Prisoners in the middle! If one of you opens his mouth I'll knock his goddam head down into his arsehole! The party's over! We're back in the Army!'

Several of us stumble on the stairs as we leave 'The Rosy Maid', singing happily. The padre climbs a lamp-post and hangs there barking. He says he is a werewolf.

'See me fly,' he shouts, triumphantly, and ends with a splash in the slush.

Gregor orders us to line up to be counted, but we keep changing places and he can't get the numbers to tally.

'Everythin's goin' round and round,' he moans, unhappily. 'We're increasin' fast as blasted rabbits.'

'Let *me* count,' says Porta officiously. But *he* can't get the figures to agree either. He goes back inside and comes out with a piece of billiard chalk. Each man is to make a chalk-mark in front of his left boot and then fall out and go back into 'The Maid' so as not to confuse the count. The Padre messes up the whole thing by making a mark in front of both his feet.

Gregor feels he is going mad, and begins to knock his head against the wall.

Then Porta comes up with a new idea. Each man to be given a full tankard of beer, to drink it and place the empty tankard back on the bar. Tiny spoils that one by taking a couple of glasses extra while the others are draining theirs.

Gregor gives up all idea of making a tally.

It is well into the morning by the time we march across the Spree Bridge at Kronprinzen Ufer, and hear a military orchestra in the distance.

'A song!' the Staff Padre orders, and begins in a loud voice himself:

Willst du noch einmal sehen[14]
sollst du nach dem Bahnhof gehen.
In dem grossen Wartesaal,
sehen wir uns zum letzten Mal. . . .

'Straighten your equipment, pull your helmets straight!' orders Gregor nervously. 'Try for Christ's sake to look *something* like German soldiers! Get your carbine up, Tiny. You're carryin' it like a pissed poacher.'

'Whassup?' gargles Albert, with a crazy grin splitting his black face. 'Adolf coming?'

'Worse'n that,' groans Gregor. 'It's the new guard comin' on. They're marchin' straight at us, an're playin' the *Badenweiler*, the Führer's personal march.'

'*C'est le bordel!*' says the Legionnaire, indifferently.

'They must be celebrating something or other,' says Porta. 'A victorious retreat most likely!'

'What about droppin' into "The Lame Gendarme", till it's over?' suggests Tiny, practically. 'It's just by 'ere. Double quick time down the bleedin' alley over there an' we're inside "The Genny" quick as knife!'

'Too late,' decides Porta. 'The world's about to collapse.'

An infantry orchestra with a stick-swinging drum-major at its head comes swanking round the corner. It fills the whole width of the street.

'Pour on the coal, my son,' Porta advises. 'You are commanding a military escort with prisoners in irons. According to Army Regulations you have right of way over the tin-whistle'n bang-bang boys. That orchestra's got to give way! You only halt for heavy motorised units.'

'Yes, yes, but that orchestra's playing the Führer's own *Badenweiler!*' puts in Heide. 'Even heavy motorised units

[14]Freely translated:
If you want to see me again,
You must meet me at the train, then.
At a waiting room rendezvous
We will breath our last adieu. . . .

39

have to stop for that. Says so clearly in Army Regs, in the section on military orchestras!'

'Holy Mother of God, what do I *do*!' shouts Gregor, unhappily.

'Gain time,' advises Porta. 'Let prisoners and escort march backwards over the Spree Bridge, that's what I'd do. *Then* you can't be charged with having gone off the route. *And* the oompah-oompah boys can't say you've got in their way either!'

'*Tu as raison,*' says the Legionnaire.

'We can't go marching back'ards for *ever*,' screams Gregor, staring at Porta wildly.

'No, of course not,' Porta explains, patiently. 'Soon as they've finished Adolf's march off they're no more'n any other lot of Piccolo Petes an' you an' your armed escort come first. Then it's forward march'n follow your prick, and if that tarted-up drum-major don't get out of the way p.d.q., up his jacksey goes his old stick. *That* ought to teach him to respect the rights of the Greater German Army's escorts under arms!'

Suddenly a whirlwind seems to strike the middle of the orchestra. Two terrified cats come flying out of an entry with three bulldogs at their heels. One of the cats takes a flying leap onto the back of a tuba-player, who falls over his own feet and drops his instrument. Two staff horns trip over the tuba, while the other cat rushes between the legs of the other musicians with all three dogs after it. In and out they go amongst the bandsmen, creating a scene of indescribable panic.

In some unexplainable fashion the medical officer has got hold of a baton, and begins to conduct the drummers and flautists of the orchestra who are still on their feet. They follow him automatically and the opening bars of the forbidden '*Salus Caesari nostro Guillermo*' burst forth.

The drum-major comes to himself and, shocked, stops the forbidden march.

The medical officer goes for him bald-headed with the conductor's baton, and he defends himself with his silver-knobbed stick.

'Gregor! As escort commander you must put a stop to that,'

says Porta. 'The prisoners are in your care. I'm afraid you'll have to arrest that drum-major for striking a prisoner in your charge.'

'I can't, I can't, I've had it!' weeps Gregor, in despair. 'I wish I'd never been born.'

'That having already happened,' states Porta, blackly. 'Let's get out of here before they get time to think.'

'Prisoners and escort, forward *march*!' shouts Gregor, with the desperate tone of a condemned man.

'Down with 'em all!' shouts the Staff Padre, rushing to the head of the party.

In panic the soldiers of the new guard give way.

We press forward like a tidal wave on some day of wrath.

A good way down Lehrter Strasse, just by the football ground, Tiny suddenly gives a terrible scream and folds up as if fearful pains were shooting through his body. He throws himself down on the snowy asphalt and howls like a madman.

'What in the name of Heaven is wrong?' asks Gregor, his eyes bugging wildly and fear written on his face.

'*I* know *that* one,' snarls the M.O. viciously. 'No malingering here, man! You're fit for duty!'

'Me 'andcuffs, me 'andcuffs,' screams Tiny, rolling himself even tighter into a ball.

'Your handcuffs?' asks Porta, blankly.

'Me 'andcuffs, me 'andcuffs. They're nippin' me bleedin' bollocks off!' Tiny groans, heart-breakingly, writhing about on the wet ground.

When we get his trousers off the mystery is explained. He has been carrying the handcuffs in the way he has seen the American police do in films. Without his noticing it they have slipped inside his trousers and suddenly clipped themselves onto his private parts. His writhings have tightened their grip even more.

It takes Porta some time to find the key and release him so that the escort can continue.

'*Dominus vobiscum*!' the Staff Padre greets a shivering queue at a tramstop. He meows like a cat, and asks the M.O. to castrate him so that he will not fall into error when he meets

41

sinful women. He jumps on to a bench, and shouts out over the football fields:

'All dead report immediately to the Divisional Padre for last rites and sprinkling with holy water! Relatives must foot the bill!'

'I'll shoot that bastard, I will,' promises Gregor, tightly, pulling the padre down from the bench.

'We *made* it!' says Porta, pressing his finger on the bell-push outside the gate of the Garrison Prison.

'What the hell are you *at*, man? Trying to ring down the whole bloody prison, are you?' scolds the Wacht-Feldwebel, angrily.

'Herr Feldwebel, sir! Beg to state, sir, we're in a bit of a hurry, sir!' says Porta, cracking his heels together. 'We are considerably delayed, sir. We have been ordered to take up new prisoners all the way through Berlin. The last of these we were given by the *Standortkommandant* himself, sir!'

'You lot stink worse'n a whole bloody brewery,' growls the Wacht-Feldwebel.

'Orders, sir, orders! We have been *ordered* to drink alcoholic beverages,' states Porta. 'Wherever we went, we were given orders to occupy beer-halls, bars, inns, whatever. We *know* our Army Regs an' we know better than to risk a charge of refusing to obey an order. If we're to get out of this World War alive we've got to obey *orders*. No matter how stupid they are.'

'You can't pull the wool over *my* eyes,' the M.O. says, throwing a stern look at the Wacht-Feldwebel. 'You lot've been sitting here malingering for too long. You're fit for duty, all of you. Off to the front with you, so's you can get shot!'

'You keep a smart place here,' praises Porta, watching a party of prisoners, in fatigue dress, down on their knees polishing the floors.

'Thing an old soldier likes to see,' smiles Tiny, in satisfaction. 'Not often you see a thresh'old with such a lovely 'igh polish on it. These slaves o' yourn. They use ordin'ry polish, or is it somethin' special from Army Prison Supplies Depots?'

'When I've knocked three times and whip this door open,' whispers the Wacht-Feldwebel, 'you don't *march* in you *fly* in,

42

and don't forget to keep your toes back of that white line on the floor! Don't, and our Hauptfeldwebel'll turn you all into snails and have you eatin' your own haemorrhoids!'

'*We* know, Herr Feldwebel, sir,' promises Porta, self-confidently. 'We've been there before. Open up the gates of Hell, then!'

The door flies open and the escort rattles in and positions itself straight as a string behind the white line.

Gregor reports at a speed which runs the whole thing into one long word.

The face of the Hauptfeldwebel behind the desk radiates bestial wickedness enough to frighten even a war-hero.

His eyes gleam treacherously from between rolls of fat, as he looks us over consideringly one by one. He passes a hairy, ape-like hand over his totally hairless scalp. His gaze stops at Tiny as if he cannot believe what he sees.

'How in God's name'd you get shared out with a face as horrible as *that*?' he asks, in an animal-like growl.

'Beg to report, 'Err 'Auptfeldwebel, *sir*,' roars Tiny, his eyes fastened on the picture of Hitler, 'member o' Frankenstein family, *sir*!'

'Are *you* trying to crack jokes with *me*?' asks the Hauptfeldwebel, menacingly, getting half up from his chair. Without waiting for an answer he shouts:

'Prisoners left turn! Double march!'

The Staff Padre falls over his own feet, of course. Lying on the floor on one elbow, with his chin resting in his hand like a large cherub, be begins to sing a psalm:

> '*Hungry, tired and weak he comes*
> *Beset by thoughts of doubt.*
> *Be not angry. . . .*'

'That man's dead-drunk,' states the Hauptfeldwebel, getting all the way up out of his chair. 'What's the meaning of this?'

'Beg to report, sir,' shouts Porta, clicking his heels three times. 'That's how it *was* sir! That's why the padre is *here*, sir! We'd never seen him before, sir, until out he comes from the dark and orders us into "The Rosy Maid" where he runs up

43

a debt for comestibles consumed, sir. Then the *Standort-kommandant* arrives on a brown horse and orders us to take the padre with us under arrest, sir. Beg to report, sir, something like this has happened before, sir, with an escort and prisoners on the way to the Garrison Prison at Munich, sir. These unhappy men, sir, were marching down the Leopold Strasse when up came a *black* horse with General der Infanterie Ritter von Leeb. On the other side of the street, sir, there sat Oberveterinär Dr. Schobert, singin' dirty songs, sir. The Commanding General, sir, ordered that escort to take the singing vet with it. And so they did, sir, 'cause an order's an order just like a schnapps is a schnapps, sir. But then when they got to Luipold Strasse there came another horse, a red one, sir, with the Chief of Staff of 7. Army Corps, Oberst von Wittsleben, on it, sir. *This* horse was really an Austrian horse, sir, which'd done service with No. 2 Honved Hussar Regiment, but when Austria returned to the Greater German Reich, sir, then that regiment came back into the German Army. The Chief of Staff had picked up two Gefreiters from 40. Infantry Regiment, sir, who'd been holding treasonable conversation, sir. They were also handed over to this poor escort. . . .'

The Hauptfeldwebel grinds his teeth together so hard that it is a wonder his jaws don't go out of joint. His eyes begin to roll wildly in his head.

'Beg to report further, sir,' continues Porta, without stopping to draw breath, 'this escort wasn't out of the mire yet, sir. They were marching smartly over Maria Theresien-Platz when two soldiers came running so fast you'd think there was a blow-lamp playing on their arses, sir. Over from "The Golden Beaker" there came a loud bang, sir, and there was a Leutnant, sir, hopping around in the swing-door as if he'd just been given a swift kick in the arse, sir. Well, it'd all started with a Stabszahlmaster Zorn, sir. . . .'

The Hauptfeldwebel takes three or four deep breaths. Then he begins to roar. The words leave his lips so quickly that it is impossible to understand what he is saying. When he finally regains control of himself he falls back into the chair, which groans protestingly.

'You! You shut up!' he spits at Porta. 'You are driving me crazy. You chatter like a cage-full of lovebirds. I can't even hear myself think. What in the name of all the hells has your escort from 7. Army Corps to do with me? We're in Berlin. I don't want to *know* what happened in Munich. *I* don't give a shit for Munich, nor for the entire 7. Army Corps, and I *order you* too not to give a shit for Munich!'

'Sorry sir! No shit available just at the moment, sir,' Porta smiles in friendly fashion.

'Were you sent here by Satan himself?' screams the Hauptfeldwebel, foaming at the mouth. 'Maybe *you* were a prisoner that time, in Munich, Mr. Obergefreiter?'

'No sir, no indeed sir! I had nothing to do with that escort. Not as a guard. Not as a prisoner. I heard about it for the first time when a Feldwebel came to make confession to Wehrkreis-Pfarrer Weinfuss. It was the time when I was assistant to the padre there. That was at 7. Division in Munich, sir. There, by the way. . . .'

The Hauptfeldwebel hammers both fists down on the desk so hard that papers, pens and other impedimenta fly round our ears.

'One word more and I strangle you!' he threatens in a hoarse voice. 'Why are you telling me all this?' he asks, unhappily, after a short pause.

'Well sir, since you ask, sir, it's so as the Hauptfeldwebel can understand how it was we brought the Staff Padre along with us. . . .'

'Prisoners' papers,' the Hauptfeldwebel cuts in, sending Porta a killing look.

Pale and silent, Gregor hands over the few papers.

The four 'regular' prisoners disappear into the depths of the Garrison Prison.

For a while silence presses down on the office. We watch the Hauptfeldwebel, the notorious 'Wicked Emil', and he watches us back. Leather equipment creaks. Rifle butts scrape against the floor. A fly settles on the blotter and sits there cleaning off its wings. Everybody stares at the fly.

45

Porta opens his mouth as if about to say something, but gives up and closes it again.

Albert's black, round football of a head splits in a pearly smile.

'What the hell are you grinning at?' rumbles 'Wicked Emil'. 'Think you're back in Africa getting ready to eat some poor missionary, do you? Shut your head, man! In Germany we only laugh when we're ordered to. Got that? Tell me. How the hell did you get into a Greater German uniform? Far as I know the Führer's said all blacks are *untermensch* just like the Yids?'

Albert throws a pleading glance at Porta, who comes to his aid immediately.

'Permission to speak, sir. Albert, sir, he's not a real nigger, sir. He's a Reichsnigger, *he* is. His father was a Wachtmeister of hussars. I can explain it all to you. It's a long story. . . .'

'Stop! No explanations,' shouts 'Wicked Emil', with a look of terror in his eyes. 'Papers for the rest of the prisoners. Get *on* with it, man. Get *on* with it. Don't think you can come in here and jettison just anybody. No, not even a murderer who's slit his own general's throat will I take without proper paperwork.'

'Beg to report, sir,' Porta assures him, 'the paperwork's on the way. They'll be coming by post, sir, any day now, sir. Beg to report, sir, when we met the brown horse with the Stadtortskommandant, sir, Oberst. . . .'

'I don't want to hear about it, not about horses, not about Obersts! Have you understood me Obergefreiter! Stop begging! Stop reporting! You're driving me *mad*! Papers, papers!'

'Beg to report, sir that's just what I was *going* to report. . . .'

'No, no, NO!' sobs 'Wicked Emil' falling forward despairingly across the desk.

'Something to drink, sir,' Porta smiles, in friendly fashion, handing a glass of water to the Hauptfeldwebel.

'Wicked Emil' snatches it like a drowning man grasping at a piece of driftwood, and slobbers the water down with a noise like a choked-up sewer being cleared. He tears open his desk-drawer, pulls out an army pistol, and places it on the desk in front of him. 'Know what this is, Obergefreiter?'

Porta bends forward and examines the pistol with interest.

'Beg to say, sir, its a Walther, sir, Model 38, sir. I have one here just like it, sir.' He pulls a well-oiled pistol from its holster and points it towards 'Wicked Emil'. The Hauptfeldwebel's eyes begin to twitch at the corners.

'Don't point that thing at me,' he stammers holding his hands defensively in front of him. 'It might go off!'

'Beg to report, sir, that that has happened, sir. Happened to a cavalry Wachtmeister in the prison at Paderborn. The men used to call him "The Dwarf" because that's what he looked like, sir. Well, sir, *he* got shot by a cavalry Obergefreiter from Kavallerie-Schützenregiment no. 4, sir. The Obergefreiter was just showing the Wachtmeister his '08, as we might be doing now, sir. Not even three officers from the JAG Branch could ever find out *how* the gun happened to go off but somehow or other it *did*, and there was the cavalry Wachtmeister dead as mutton, sir. At short distances, sir, the old '08 makes a big hole in a man, and, sir, a P-38 makes a pretty big one too, if you take my meaning. I could prove that to you sir, if. . . .'

'Put that gun away,' screams 'Wicked Emil', desperately. 'I want this case closed, and no more horses or obersts or pistols mixed up in it. Why is this padre and why is this medical officer here? *You* shut up, Obergefreiter,' he fumes, pointing a fat finger at Porta. 'I never want to hear your voice again. Not even if you an' me're the only two left alive after this war! I'd rather talk to myself. Answer me, you! Unteroffizier,' he roars at Gregor.

But Gregor is on the verge of a nervous breakdown, and can only emit strange sounds.

'Wicked Emil' begins to tremble. His whole body shakes. He clasps his forehead with both hands, despairingly.

'Jesus, Joseph, Mary and all the Holy Family! What've I got myself into? Have I gone mad, or is it all my imagination.'

'Beg to report, sir,' rumbles Tiny, in his deep bass. 'Beg to report as 'ow the Standortkommandant for Berlin/Moabitt 'as ordered the arrest of the Staff Padre, sir, an' ordered us to take 'im with us seein' as we was already goin' to the glass'ouse. The Standortkommandant says as 'ow 'e would ring to the Prison Commander, an' 'ave a talk with 'im about the padre, sir.'

47

'But what am I to arrest him *for*?' moans 'Wicked Emil'. 'I *must* know what to book him for. I can't just write a receipt for "one (1) Staff Padre received herewith". This is a Prussian jail, not a left luggage office!'

'With your permission, sir, the Staff Padre, sir, 'as insulted the German God,' lies Tiny, consciencelessly. He watches, with considerable interest, as 'Wicked Emil' scratches feverishly on the prison arrivals form.

'Very well,' growls 'Wicked Emil' with satisfaction, as his pen continues to scratch away.

'No more, I hope?'

'Only a bit of defamation of the Führer,' says Tiny, giving out a long-drawn sigh.

'Couldn't you've *said* that straight away, you stupid turtle,' thunders 'Wicked Emil', furiously. 'Now I'll have to alter the form, and alterations have to be witnessed by three reliable persons. That's not easy to manage in Germany today. *Everybody* knows insulting the Führer comes before insulting God!'

He begins to erase desperately. He knocks over the eraser fluid, goes into an acute fit of rage, and begins to chew on the block of admission forms. He calls the guard and orders the Staff Padre taken to cell 210 in the officers' wing.

'*Dominus vobiscum*' we hear the padre's blessings receding into the distance.

'What about him, there?' asks 'Wicked Emil', pointing to the M.O.

'Beg to report, sir,' drones Tiny's voice. 'The doctor's 'ere by 'is own orders.'

'Holy Greater German God,' chatters 'Wicked Emil'. 'Where'd it all end if any German could just go and arrest himself? We'd have to build at least a thousand new jails!'

'Easy there! I'll take care of you,' shouts the M.O., swaying perilously. 'No malingerers where I am! You Hauptfeldwebel, you! You're fit for duty.'

'Beg to explain, sir,' Porta breaks in suddenly. 'Obergefreiter Creutzfeldt has got spots on the brain, sir. He once got kicked by a horse, you see. He's forgotten we met Major von Ott, acting commander of Wachtbataillon Berlin. He ordered us to take the

48

doctor with us, sir, because he interfered with the guard party and, against regulations, took a bandleader's baton from him and got the band playing forbidden music.'

'I heard something about that,' sighs 'Wicked Emil', shaking his head from side to side. 'It'll cost him dear!'

'Beg to state, sir,' continues Porta, unworriedly, 'there was this Field Apothecary with 8. Army Corps in Vienna. *He* wanted to conduct the Hoch und Deutschmeister Regimental Music Corps. Well, sir, it cost that apothecary dear too. He can't even. . . .'

'Shut your mouth, now. You, you Obergefreiter, you! To hell with your apothecary and to hell with Vienna too!' roars 'Wicked Emil' crashing his pistol down on the desk top. 'If I don't get those papers today, I'll hold you responsible. What'll I *do* with prisoners with no admission forms? I'll have to keep 'em here for *ever*. Till long after we've started on the *Third* World War. If they've not been admitted how can we ever discharge 'em? Nobody'll ever call 'em up for interrogation. No interrogation no confession, and no courtmartial can be held! Poor old Emil'll have these unlawfully arrested bastards on his hands for *ever*! You can see for yourself I'll be up shit creek. Some Kriegsgerichtsrat or other'll have me up for unlawful imprisonment of army personnel. And in *this* case a kind of an officer.' He gives a long despairing sigh and collapses into his own fat.

Porta sighs with him.

'Beg to say, sir, it's hard and merciless times we're living in. Why, sir, a world war *always* brings hard times with it.'

'How right you are,' 'Wicked Emil' gives up, in resignation, and orders the guard to take the M.O. to cell 209.

'Is 'e allowed to 'ave readin' matter?' asks the guard, a Gefreiter of Jaegers with an expression of quite unbelievable stupidity.

'No, devil take me, he read more'n enough when he was reading for his medical degree. I hate these stuck-up half-educated students who have to have somebody to hold their pricks for 'em when they go for a piss in the dark.'

'Beg your pardon, sir,' Porta begins, brightly, 'there was this professor of medicine who. . . .'

49

'Put a sock in it,' roars 'Wicked Emil', 'or I'll put *you* inside too. Don't you ever let yourself get put in *my* jail. The Devil's a Sunday School teacher 'longside o' me!'

'Beg to report, sir,' begins Porta again.

'Get *out*!' thunders 'Wicked Emil', and gives the desk a kick. 'God help you, Obergefreiter, if ever we meet again.'

'That Hauptfeldwebel of yours is out of his mind,' Porta confides to the Gefreiter clerk, as they clatter down the long corridor. 'First he says he'd like to have me inside here! *Then* he threatens me with all kinds of desperate things if he ever *sees* me again.'

'You wouldn't like to *really* get to know "Wicked Emil",' interjects a guard, with a dark look. 'If *he* kicks you in the arse you're shittin' from between your teeth for the rest of your life!'

'We're reckoned to be *the* toughest army jail. Not only in Greater Germany, but in the whole world,' boasts the clerk, proudly. 'There ain't another jail worse'n ours *anywhere*!'

'It's not half bad,' considers Porta, 'but compared with the old days it's a piece of cake.'

'You wouldn't talk like that if you were inside this place,' snorts the Gefreiter clerk, with a sneer. 'They don't only shout an' scream at you an' knock your teeth down your throat here. You'd be surprised, perhaps, at getting burned with cigarette ends or havin' your nails pulled out, or your balls bashed loose with a hammer?'

'You get to Heuberg,' interjects the guard, with a satanic laugh, 'and you end up in the stables. There they spreadeagle you like a plaice fillet, baste you with flour and salt and let some rough-tongued goats loose to lick you clean. You'd die laughing!'

'Bah! Small stuff,' shouts Porta, contemptuously. 'Wouldn't even make a Jap grit his teeth. You lot should've lived in the Middle Ages, when the Church used to look after the wretches and the heretics. They used to start off proving their innocence by walking on burning pitch and drinkin' melted iron. When that was over they'd pinch you here and there with red-hot pincers. After which they'd rip your tongue out and put out your eyes. They had that one where they'd harness four horses to the villain's legs an' arms, and when *they* were off people could see clearly they *must* be guilty. I have heard that when women were being persuaded they were really witches and had a pact with the Devil they'd scream so terribly you'd think knives and glowing pokers were being used on their backs. But then when they *had* confessed it wasn't all over. Oh no! *Then* they used to cut 'em in pieces and nail the bits to posts alongside the church or the Town Hall, as a dreadful example to the other wretches. People who'd been through *that* lot'd think the Gestapo was a band of suckin' infants by comparison. Getting yourself *dead* was a major problem then. Today they cut off your head or break your neck on the end of a rope and it's all over in no time. In the old days they'd take off a toe, and then a hand, and then maybe a leg, or perhaps an arm, before getting to your head.'

The heavy prison gates crash to behind us.

With slung carbines we slouch down the wet street.

'Must be rough being that "Wicked Emil",' says Albert, with a deep sigh. 'Not a hair on his head. He must feel very lonely. Nobody loves a bald man. Tell me, for example. Who loves Mussolini?'

'Shouldn't think anybody! Bald men are nearly always wicked men,' says Porta.

An hour afterwards we are back with the company, and the escort has been dismissed. Off goes the alarm warning. The whole barracks resounds to the noise of busy men packing ready to move. The regiment is to go to the front. New weapons and equipment are being issued. We march off by companies to the goods station.

> *The gates of mercy shall be all shut up,*
> *And the flesh'd soldier, rough and hard of heart,*
> *In liberty of bloody hand shall range*
> *With conscience wide as hell. . . .*

> *William Shakespeare*[15]

He straddles an armchair and uses his machine-pistol like a scythe. He sweeps it round the big room. Plaster and the dirt of years explode from the walls.

The Pioneer Feldwebel remains standing for a fraction of a second, made visible by the muzzle flash of the Mpi. Then his body rockets backwards across a long table, on which freshly killed hens are lying. The rain of bullets pours into him, making his body twitch violently. He falls to the floor, taking the hens with him.

The Russian grins and clips in a new magazine. There is no doubt that he is enjoying himself. As most people do when they can kill without penalty.

'Murder is fun,' said the SD men of Sonderkommando. It seemed that a great many other people were of the same opinion. There is a devil in all of us, and war brings it to the surface amazingly quickly.

The Russian spins round and almost falls off the armchair. The Mpi spits towards the door, through which a Pioneer Leutnant and two NCO's come rushing.

The Leutnant seems to hang in mid-air. His legs flap like a scarecrow in the wind as bullets smash into his knee. The two other soldiers are thrown back against the wall. For a moment the scene looks like an explosion in a paint factory.

Albert and Gregor fire simultaneously. After the noise of the Kalashnikov the P.38's sound like air pistols, but the results are different. The Russian swings round, hit in the shoulder. Then in the stomach. He lets out a roar and begins to collapse. The next burst rips his head half off his shoulders. He goes down with a splashy thud, his feet still resting on the armchair. More blood!

'Mad bastard,' says Albert, wiping sweat from his shiny black face. 'Hell! He could've got the lot of us!'

---

[15]*Henry V, Act III, Scene III: Before the gates of Harfleur.*

'Shithead!' says Porta. 'Now he's finished knocking people off, anyway. Let's go through the house just in case.'

Tiny shoots a cat by mistake. It sat w ashing itself on a w indowsill.

'Rotten swine!' rages Porta, and doesn't speak a word to Tiny for the rest of the day.

2
Infantry Attack

The Old Man greets the new intake and explains to them patiently, all the things they didn't teach them in training school.

'Listen now,' he says in his hoarse voice, and directs a dark brown jet of tobacco-juice into the snow. He puckers his lips and gives out a long, piercing whistle. 'Hear *that*, and down you go! Flat on your faces! They're the little devils to watch out for. They *spread*! Down in a hurry, if you don't want to see your guts dangling round your boot-tops. *This* noise!' he produces a drawn-out, grating sound, reminiscent of a goods-train braking, '*behind* cover, quick as a bat out of hell. Holes in the ground're no good. Those boys hit and *bounce*. So if you're in a hole the shit showers down on you from above!' He imitates the sound of every type of shell and bomb. Repeats them over and over again until he feels sure the new boys have got hold of them. 'One thing you've *got* to learn, my sons,' he goes on. 'Run! Run like hell! Run faster'n a rabbit with a buzz-saw sawin' away at his arse! you *can* run from shells, *if* you're fast enough, and never forget when you're in HKL[1], make yourself small and keep your head down! That's if you want to see home and beauty again! Snipers, kiddies,' he points round the ring of young men with the stem of his ancient silver-lidded pipe, and sends another long stream of spittle out into the snow. 'I know they've told you that our neighbours over the way are only half-trained. Forget it! Quick as you can! Siberian snipers are the best in the world! They can cut the head off a rat at two hundred yards!'

[1]HKL: Hauptkampflinie: The front line.

54

It is just after dawn. The Company arrives at the front line, and two minutes later the first man falls with a bullet through his head. A seventeen-year old tank gunner who has forgotten what the Old Man has been trying to teach him. The others stand staring whitely at their dead comrade. The explosive bullet has taken off his entire face.

'Crackerjacks,' grins Porta, sarcastically. 'That ought to prove to you Ivan's not usin' blanks! Take a German head off in no time at all, don't they? Don't be nosey, and you'll live longer!'

'You there,' orders Tiny in a voice like a blow-torch. 'You there, with the long neck. Yes *you*! Get that dumb look off your face.'

A long, thin seventeen-year old, in a uniform which is much too big for him, cracks his heels together and salutes.

'Cut the gymnastics,' Tiny says, blowing a cloud of smoke from his fat cigar. 'Take these ammunition boxes, an' fasten yourself on to my arse. If Ivan blows you off the face of the earth with a flamethrower, you *still* stay close to me. *Panjemajo?*[2]'

'I can't carry all six of them, Herr Obergefreiter. I've only got two hands,' the youngster apologises unhappily, holding out his hands in front of him.

'Tie a couple of 'em to your balls, then, son!' suggests Tiny, with a horsey whinney. 'You're *carryin*' 'em, anyway you like it. *Panjemajo?*'

Further down the line, Heide puffs himself up. He has been given command of a squad, and his barrack square syndrome is in full flow. His shouts can be heard far and wide as he chases his squad around.

'Julius is, and always will be, a military pig. *Il est con!*' says the Legionnaire, acridly.

'He was born in a uniform and a tin-hat, didn't you know?' says Porta. 'When he left his mum's womb, on the 20th of April, which is, of course, also the Führer's birthday, he came out with bayonet at the ready, and straightaway jabbed it in the midwife's gut, shouting a wild hurra! Then he cracked the doctor's head open with the butt-end, saluted, and took an ice-cold shower to

[2]Panjemajo? (Russian): Understood?

55

prepare himself for a career as NCO in the Prussian Army!'

Grinning, we watch Heide, who is in the process of working up the artificial NCO fury which he seems to feel is necessary when stupid civilians are to be turned into military robots. Julius Heide is a fine-looking soldier, straight-backed, well-trained, fair-haired and with ice-cold, dangerous, blue eyes.

'What a shower,' shouts Porta, from a hole in the snow. 'Not many of us old 'un's left, now. New faces everywhere you look. Soddin' arseholes! Come over here, Tiny, and keep me company. I never could stand strangers!'

'Me neither,' rumbles Tiny's deep bass. 'If I 'ave to go, I'd much rather it's in company with pals. I've always been against mixin' me blood, shit an' bones with a load of strange bastards.'

Looking down over the slopes we can just see the dreary village so many German and Russian soldiers are going to die to gain possession of within the next few days. Through the drifting snow it reminds one of a Christmas card rather than a place where danger lurks. But we know the Russians are down there and that they have strengthened its defences efficiently and well. It is the first station on the *via dolorosa* leading to the heights, and to the huge OGPU[3] prison which lies menacingly on the top of the farthest hill, appearing and disappearing through veils of drifting snow.

The road leads over heights and hilltops down through the valley where death beckons. Our battle units will have to burn their way through several villages and fortifications to get to the great prison. This morning we don't know it, but we and the Russian soldiers will soon be cursing it just as much as thousands of unhappy prisoners have cursed and hated it. When the snow clears, now and then, it looks like an angry threat, dominating us with its massive walls and rows of barred window openings.

'Wonder how many they've got locked up in *that* place?' says Porta, thoughtfully, examining it through his field-glasses. 'A knot with three walls round it and a soddin' lot of barbed wire on top! Never seen one of those before!'

[3]OGPU: Russian Secret Police organization which preceded the KGB.

'It's a big bleeder ain't it?' says Tiny, impressed, looking through the periscope eyepiece. 'Wonder if they'll let the slaves out, when we start smashin' it up? Or if they'll just give the bleedin' key an extra turn, like our lot do when there's a raid on?'

'They'll not let 'em out,' says Porta, with decision. 'They'll let 'em fry in their own fat when we start putting down incendiaries.'

'Wonder if there are women in there?' Albert says, licking his lips.

'Of course there are. It's both a men's and women's prison,' explains Julius Heide, who is always irritatingly well-informed about everything.

'What kind of poor social losers get put in there, anyway?' asks Barcelona, well aware that the expression will touch Heide on the raw.

'What do you mean, social losers?' fizzes Heide. 'Criminals, that's what they are! Political and criminal swine, who should be put up against a wall!'

'Don't forget now,' grins Porta, happily, 'this is a Communist *untermensch* prison. *Their* politicals are a kind of ally of ours. Liberators, you might say.'

'Traitors are traitors,' says Heide, categorically. 'A Russian who sympathises with us, is *still* a traitor to his country, a political criminal, and deserves to lose his head for it!'

'House!' Porta roars with laughter, and claps both his hands to his head.

'What about Vlassov's lot, then?' asks Gregor, smiling crookedly 'We've given *them* uniforms and weapons so's they can help *us* give their own lot a bashin'?'

'You're too stupid to understand any of it!' Heide gives up, angrily and almost lets his head show over the lip of the snow-bank. He suddenly remembers the snipers and comes down again like a flash. 'One of our classic authors has put it very clearly: *Der Feind liebt den Verrat, aber Verachtet den Verräter!*[4]

---

[4] The enemy loves treachery, but despises the traitor!

57

'What a load o' shit,' Tiny makes a contemptuous noise. 'Everybody wants anybody long as they're in the right uniform! Germany's got Swedes *an*' English *an*' Russkis servin'.'

'Negroes too,' puts in Porta, pointing with a laugh at Albert, who is sitting, chewing away at a piece of frozen bread.

'Shut it, man!' growls Albert, insultedly, 'I'm a pure-bred German, I am!'

'Maybe you are,' shouts Heide, jeeringly, 'but Germanic you'll *never* be!'

'That makes me happy, too, now that SS-Heini's said the Hindus are kind of Aryan!' snorts Albert, showing all his pearly teeth like an angry dog.

'Why's niggers white inside their 'ands an' under their feet?' asks Tiny, in an interested tone, looking at Albert's pink palms.

'*Anybody* knows that,' hoots Porta, moving farther away from Albert. 'Him and his tribe have to get down on all fours when they're being spray-painted.'

'Ha-ha-ha-a-a-!' hisses Albert. 'You're *funny*, man, *funny*!'

A sinister, hollow sound grows in the air. It is as if something is coming towards us, banging from side to side in a long tube as it gets closer. Snow sprays upwards in cascades as trench mortar projectiles fall in front of us. They explode with an echoing thump.

'It ain't right!' protests Porta, from down in his hole in the snow. '*We're* the ones who ought to be shooting the mortars, not that baggy arsed Ivan lot, the rotten sods. Always breaking the rules, *they* are!'

A scream pierces the night. It comes from the far side of the frozen stream. Loud and shrill. A man's useless protest against the shrapnel which has cut deeply into his body. If the scream is anything to go by.

Here comes the slobbering sound again, followed by a hollow-sounding explosion. We make ourselves small. Press down into the snow. This is the object of the drill. Not to let yourself get killed by a slobbering mortar. For no reason. Everybody is more or less scared to death. It's worst for the youngsters who've never been at the front before.

'Hell, but it's cold,' groans Gregor, blowing his own warm

58

breath up over his face. 'Must be hundred below!' Nough to freeze a polar bear's balls off'n stop him fuckin' ol' Mrs Bear for a month o' Sundays!'

'It's exactly 43 degrees,' declares Julius Heide, importantly. 'A German soldier ought to be able to stand *that*. The old Teutons had it worse.'

'Were you *there*, too?' pipes Gregor, stamping his feet in the snow.

'Course he was! Julius was an' his Führer was too. The Germans watered their horses in the Volga and Julius knocked the icicles off the Führers arse, after he'd been for a shit!' Porta laughs so noisily that the Russians open up with sustained machine-gun salvoes, thinking it's them he's laughing at.

Tiny unhooks the waterbottle from his rations pouch and follows the tracer tracks with his eyes. He takes a long swallow and hands the bottle to Porta.

'*Stolichnaya*,' cries Porta, delightedly, and puts the bottle back to his mouth, feeling the pure vodka run in a silken stream round his body and right down into his icy toes.

'Where'd you get it?' asks Gregor, passing the bottle on to Barcelona.

'GEKADOS[5],' answers Tiny, with a secretive grin. 'I 'appened to walk past a Luftwaffe depot, where they was 'avin' a barney with three thievin' bleeders out o' the Pioneers. They'd nabbed 'em pinchin' a yard or so o' pork. Well nobody noticed *me* just snitchin' a box o' grog.'

'Where's the rest of it?' asks Porta, with no little interest. 'There's usually twelve bottles in a box!'

' 'Ere,' chuckles Tiny, opening his snow-shirt. Eleven bottles of vodka become visible. They are hung round him like oranges on a Christmas tree.

'I only hope Ivan don't put a banger into you,' remarks Porta, drily. 'You'd go up like a bunch of sparklers on New Year's Eve.'

'Nothin'll 'appen to yours bleedin' truly,' says Tiny, with certainty. 'I give up my place any time to the crazy bleedin'

[5]GEKADOS: (Geheime Kommandosache): Secret matter.

59

'eroes as wants to get their names on a porous gravestone outside the barracks, an're willin' to accept a permanent leave pass just to see 'em there!'

Feldwebel Lange from Command Group comes sliding down the snow face all out of breath, and throws himself down panting alongside the Old Man.

'This whole bloody shithouse's gone for a burton,' he stammers, excitedly. 'Bloody Ivan's comin' over in *waves*. No contact with 3. Battalion. Command Group's radio busted! Direct hit! I'm the only one who got away. Last minute, it was. Baggy-arsed Ivan was knockin' on the door already!'

'*C'est le bordel*,' says the Legionnaire, working frantically at the radio transmitter. 'I can *hear* them, but I can't understand a word they're saying!'

'Use Morse!' orders the Old Man, sharply.

The Legionnaire begins to tap on the key. Heide helps him. He sends like lightning: 'Russian breakthrough. Right wing open. 2. Battalion no contact flanks and rear. Cannot hold position. 3 and 5 Company destroyed. Out. Over.'

'Sod it!' the Old Man curses, bitingly. 'That's what you get for usin' half-trained slobs to do your fightin' for you! Now what?'

Heide holds his hand up, scribbling feverishly. He hands the message to the Old Man.

'Of *course*, of *course*,' mumbles the Old Man with a bitter laugh, and takes a great pinch of snuff. 'To the last man! To the last bullet! Let's hear the *other* side for once. Get your gear on an' your garden hoses ready, boys! We're goin' to have visitors! Get me the O.C.!'

The air is full of noise. Heaven and earth seem to have opened and to be spewing fire and steel down on us. Tank tracks clatter. Heavy motors howl at maximum output. The blinding whiteness of the snow changes to violet and crimson. The whole horizon seems to be ablaze.

Albert lies beside me, tightly pressed into the snow. He has pulled his white snow mask far down over his head. He is certain that if he shows his black face he will be a perfect target.

'God what I wouldn't give for a *Heimatschuss*,[6] man! So I could get out of this shit once an' for all!' he dreams, aloud.

Machine-guns on both sides of us begin to stammer. Tracers fan out over the snow.

'What now, Oberfeld?' asks young Leutnant Braun, looking round, distractedly. He is acting platoon commander but is wise enough to let the Old Man make the decisions.

'Company attack,' answers the Old Man, shortly. 'We've got to take that sod of a village, and soon! If not we'll be gettin' a worms-eye view of the tulips!'

'Impossible,' moans the young Leutnant. 'We'll need heavy weapons to take it. There must be a battalion in there.'

'Don't cry, Leutnant,' shouts Porta, happily. 'When our shit-guns and garden hoses open up, ol' Ivan'll be rolling away on his goolies before you can say Jack Robinson!'

'Forward,' orders the Old Man, and gets to his feet with machine-pistol at the ready, and grenades hanging behind him from his belt. 'Fingers out, an' follow me!'

We storm down over the snow walls and down into the deep snow. Sweating and swearing we work our way through the white hell. Every step we take is an inhuman effort. Our feet go forward, often leaving a boot behind in the snow.

Heavy Maxims hammer from the village. Like harvesters they mow down our front ranks. Dark shapes lie like silent islands in the snow.

'*Vive la mort!*' screams the Legionnaire. He seems to fly over the snow. An attack always seems to drive him mad. He rushes forward like a crazy Arab.

From a hole in the snow a frightened Russian stares at us in horror.

The Legionnaire's Mpi stutters, and the Russian collapses in a bloody heap.

Tiny goes forward like a raging buffalo. He jabs his Mpi into the back of a frightened school-teacher, who time after time attempts to get away from his tormentor.

'Forward, you stinkin' teacher, you! This is the lovely war

[6]Heimatschuss: Blighty wound.

you've been tellin' your bleedin' pupils all about! Watch out you don't begin thinkin' 'igh treason, you bastard, or you'll be 'idin' yourself in a 'ole an' leavin' the war to us lot to win!'

The former Oberst, who is far too old for infantry attacks like this, coughs and wheezes like a leaky locomotive on it's way up a steep incline.

'Swee-e-e-e! Crack!' comes the sound of ricocheting bullets. They fly over our heads with a sound like angry wasps.

Cursing and out of breath we take cover on the far side of the hill. Death's hot breath is on the back of our necks. We slide recklessly down the slope, and suddenly, to our surprise, we are in amongst houses, half buried, with only the chimney-tops peeping up above the level of the snow.

Grenades fly through the air. Mpi's and LMG's chatter. Window frames and doors are ripped from their hinges and thrown towards us. Thousands of tracer tracks flash through the icy air and tear into the bodies of running soldiers.

Russian infantrymen vacate their holes in the snow and run to new hiding places in the snow drifts behind the huts.

We are gripped by a wild thirst for blood. Intoxicated by victory. At having taken the feared enemy by surprise.

'*Vive la mort!*' screams the Legionnaire, fanatically, smashing his rifle butt down on the head of a fat sergeant. Blood and flesh spurt all over him.

'*Njet vysstrelitj!*' moans the Russian captain, holding one hand defensively in front of him.

Leutnant Braun stops and looks, in confusion, at the wounded Russian officer. Then he dashes on, after the Old Man, who disappears round the corner of a long turnip trench.

Like a film running too fast, I see that the Russian has a grenade and is preparing to throw it after Leutnant Braun. Reflexively I smash the butt of my rifle into his face. The grenade rolls from his hand and explodes in a burst of snow and frozen earth.

A young infantryman is thrown into the air. One of his legs hangs by shreds of flesh. Blood spurts from his thigh like water from a burst pipe.

I bend over him, but it's no use. He dies, thanks to Braun's stupidity. He should have killed the Russian. Porta says: 'If we want to stay alive, we've got to be even more cruel and treacherous'n they are. There's just one second between life and death! Hesitate in firing, or throwing a grenade, and you can count yourself a dead man already.'

A skeleton-thin Russian rises to his feet in front of Tiny.

'*Millosstj*! *Millosstj*!' he screams, hysterically, jumping up and down on the spot, as if he were tramping down newly sown vegetables.

'Good Russians're *dead* Russians,' Tiny grins, triumphantly, and sends a burst as long as eternity into the Russian's body. He flops back like a rag doll against a burning fence.

Across a wrecked vehicle sprawls the body of a militiaman. The skull is split open and brain mass hangs from one side of it. An old-fashioned steel helmet lies upside down at his feet.

The schoolteacher stops abruptly, as if he had run into a wall. He stares for a few long seconds at the cloven skull. He throws down his carbine, puts his hands to his face and begins to scream like a madman.

'Split-arsed bleeder!' roars Tiny, coming on like a tidal wave. 'Think Adolf's bleedin' war's over, do you, an' the time for weepin's come? Pick up that gun an' your feet or I'll blow your balls off, I will! If you *got* any, that is!'

Like a wing-shot crow, the schoolteacher hops, croaking, in front of Tiny, who helps him along with kicks and blows from the butt of his gun.

I hasten after the others with the LMG cradled in my arms. From a narrow alley white-clad figures, with tall fur hats, come rushing. There is a sharp explosion, a hissing and ringing in my ears. Suddenly I'm stone-deaf! I drop the LMG, gripped by panic fear. The next second I feel myself leave the ground as if lifted up by a giant hand. Then I am thrown down again into the snow.

A blinding jet of fire flames upwards. Another, and another. Boots pass over me in long springing strides.

The air whines, crackles and buzzes as if millions of angry wasps were on the move.

I dig down feverishly into the snow. I have only one thought in my head. Get away from this insane hell.

A house lifts into the air, and dissolves into a rain of beams, mortar and glass.

A stove sails past, leaving a trail of sparks behind it.

The Russians at the mouth of the alley are thrown backwards and crushed against the stone walls of the *kolchos*. An antitank gun comes sliding on its tracks down the village street, crushing two German infantrymen in its path to bloody mincemeat. It crashes its way through a hut.

A Russian SMG[7] appears as the wall goes crashing down. Reflexively, I throw a hand-grenade at it.

A crashing explosion and the machine-gun is silenced.

In a few hours time the village has been cleaned out.

Some surrender. They come warily from their holes with arms above their heads and deadly fear showing in their eyes.

Mpi's chatter wickedly. We take no prisoners. We kill them all. Wounded or not.

The Pioneer company has found an entire company of German infantry, liquidated. Shot in the neck and finished off with the bayonet.

We make a circle and stare at them in silence. Some are apathetic, others internally raging. Some of the dead have been tortured. Bestially!

'*Merde*!' says the Legionnaire. 'Manure! The military muck-heap! *C'est la guerre!*'

'Only wicked men can do that kind of thing,' says Albert. '*Very* wicked men!'

'We'll do the same to them, if they come *our* way, one o' these days,' Tiny laughs, just as wickedly.

'Rally on the *kolchos*,' shouts the Old Man, gesturing with his Mpi.

A Panzer-4 comes rumbling down through the village street. Its fat exhaust glows in the grey winter light.

With rattling chains, and kicking up a cloud of snow, it stops in front of Leutnant Braun. A Major-general wrapped in a white bearskin leans out of the open turret.

[7]SMG (Schweres Maschinengewehr): Heavy Machine-gun.

'What are *you* people doing here, Leutnant?' he trumpets, dangerously.

Leutnant Braun lisps off a reply, nervously, and at such a speed that his words stumble over one another as they pass his lips.

The fur-wrapped Major-general watches him with a wickedly evaluating look.

'Are you in touch with your company?' he asks, knocking the ice from his fur glove.

'Well, General, sir,' says Leutnant Braun, in a nervous falsetto.

'The O.C. is at the hunting lodge two kilometres north of Sandova.'

'Have you been ordered to take up position here?' asks the Major-general, with an obvious threat in his hoarse voice.

'No, General, sir!'

'Then get *forward*! The road home is by way of Moscow!'

The P-4 disappears in a cloud of snow, and spouting long lances of fire from its exhausts. The General does not acknowledge Leutnant Braun's salute.

Cursing under his breath, and red in the face as a peony, Braun joins us.

'We're going on,' he says, apologetically, fiddling nervously with his machine-pistol.

'What are your orders, sir?' asks the Old Man, pushing tobacco phlegmatically into his silver-lidded pipe.

'It's probably best for all of us if you give the orders, Beier,' the Leutnant gives up, quietly. 'This isn't anything like what they taught us at officers' school!'

'Pick up your weapons,' orders the Old Man, brusquely. 'Fingers out and get out on the sides of the road! Distance between groups! Stop bunching *up*, for Christ's sake, so's one fuckin' mortar can blow the lot of you away. How often do I have to *tell* you? Spread *out*, sod it!' he shouts furiously at Tiny, who has adopted the schoolteacher and the demoted Oberst as assistants.

'Easy, Old Man! Me an' my two German 'eroes 'ere're

goin' to get us spread all over the whole o' bleedin' Russia!'

The winter morning's deathly grey changes to an ice-cold blue. The storm has stilled. A shot can be heard miles away in the killing winter cold.

Tiredly we march over the broad plain towards the threatening grey heights in the distance.

'Where the hell's Ivan arsehole got to again?' asks Porta, looking searchingly under a heap of hay. 'Just when you think he's there, down he goes into the earth. Always runnin' off, that shit is, just so's he can shoot the rotten German life out of us from behind afterwards!'

'That's somethin' the Russians've has a *lot* of experience with over the years,' explains Gregor. 'If kill-crazy, thievin' enemies like *us* ain't after 'em, then their own secret bloody police is burnin' to send 'em to Siberia an' shovel snow.'

Late in the afternoon we reach some ruins. They are full of charred bodies, tossed across one another.

After a short, furious discussion we lose interest. Porta finds a frozen pig.

'Jesus love us all,' Tiny breaks out, and begins, immediately, to build a fire. The schoolteacher and the demoted Oberst are chased out to find firewood. '*Dry!*' he howls after them. 'Or I'll use *you* two for firewood!'

The Old Man wants to continue. He shouts and screams, but gives up at last. From bitter experience he knows that only a massive enemy tank attack can get Porta away from an impending orgy of food.

With spades and hand-axes we break up the large, frozen pig.

'Shouldn't we thaw it out first?' asks Leutnant Braun, naively, holding up his hands to avoid being hit by the frozen lumps of meat which are flying all over the place.

'We ain't got the time, Leutnant, sir. If we go waitin' around, our friends over there'll be over with their old machine balalaikas and shoot our arses off,' explains Porta, and splits the pig open with the large butcher's axe.

Albert comes up from the cellar with a sack of potatoes, a whole basket of eggs and a can of frozen milk.

'Jesus'n Mary,' shouts Porta, his mouth full of quivering

pork. He is dipping it in a bowl of sweet Russian schnapps which Albert has found in the cellar with the other supplies. 'Now I'll make you some *blinis*!'

Leutnant Braun is drunk and begins to sing forbidden songs. Now and then he confides to Gregor that he never *has* liked the Führer and his party.

Heide looks at him, reproachfully. He cannot understand that an officer of the Führer's army can say such things. He decides never to have anything more to do with Leutnant Braun.

In the cellar Porta finds everything he needs to make *blinis*. Even smoked salmon. It is rather coarse and a strange colour but absolutely usable.

'I *should* use a cast-iron frying pan,' he explains, 'preferably without a handle, although that is not so important. I can make acceptable Russian pancakes anyway!'

Whistling happily he begins to mix the dough in a large pot.

'No beer, I suppose? All right, then, we'll use vodka instead.' With a flourish he breaks the eggs into the milk and flour.

Soon the entire ruin is filled with the aroma of *blinis*. Stacks of Russian pancakes mount up on the long, rickety table. Porta makes them extra thick, the way the Russians know how to. When the last one is finished we begin to eat ourselves into a stupor, as if we were preparing ourselves for seven lean years.

First a smoking hot *blini* then a slice of smoked salmon and on top of that a slice of pork. Again a *blini*. There should really be sour cream, but we have to imagine it. Instead we pour sweet schnapps over them. When all the *blinis* are gone we hardly dare to move for fear our guts will explode.

Porta draws his piccolo from his boot. Lying on his back he gives us an aria from the operetta 'The Divorced Wife'.

'Holy Agnes, have I *eaten*?' groans Gregor, letting off a long, ringing fart, which is closely followed by a double effort from Porta.

'Next time we find anything eatable I'll make us some *Bortsch*,' he promises with a dreamy look in his eyes. 'Every Russian's favourite soup. When we meet a cow we take a chunk of it and hope we meet some pork on the way. Veg' we can get hold of all right! It's a soup that'd make the Red Army capitulate on the spot!'

67

We almost have to crawl to the latrine, which, strangely enough, has avoided the total destruction of the rest of the village.

Porta is a glutton. He takes a piece of pork and a bowl of sweet schnapps with him.

'A man with his head screwed on properly never moves on the crust of this earth without taking provisions with him,' he instructs us, taking a huge bite of the pork.

Outside we hear the rattle of weapons and equipment.

'The company's arrived,' Porta states, peering cautiously through a crack in the soot-smeared wall.

'*Up!*' orders the Old Man, nervously. 'Get your kit! Löwe'll go bonkers if he finds us here eatin' ourselves senseless!'

'Yes. Let's get out an' find that ol' Red Army,' grins Tiny, stupidly drunk. 'That's what we left 'ome for, ain't it?'

'Where the hell have you been hiding, Beier?' asks Oberleutnant Löwe, red in the face, his eyes skewering the Old Man.

'Here,' answers the Old Man, waving his hand vaguely in a circle at the surrounding steppe, without knowing quite what he is supposed to answer.

Löwe looks at him suspiciously for a moment. Then he shrugs his shoulders resignedly, and orders:

'5. Company, single column after me!'

We have no more than got outside the ruined village when a mighty explosion thunders through the dawning day. Instinctively we throw ourselves down into the snow and make ourselves small.

Earth, ice and steel splinters fly through the air. The blast seems to burst our lungs, but the explosion is luckily too far away to do the company much damage. We have only three wounded. But hardly are we on our feet again, and marching, before a whole pack of white-painted T-34's bursts from the sapling forest with roaring motors and chattering tracks.

'Tea rooms,' screams Barcelona, hysterically. 'Get them storepipes forward!'

Oberleutnant Löwe lifts his hand and signals a rest to allow the anti-tank people to catch up. They are puffing and panting up the slope of the hill.

'Give us a 'and you rotten lot,' curses a Feldwebel, lividly. A 75 mm. is stuck in the deep snow.

'Not our affair, is it?' answers Porta, lifting one eyebrow.

The Feldwebel begins screaming and waving his arms about, but is stopped by the Old Man, who tells him to go to the devil and take his bloody cannon with him.

'I'll remember *you*!' promises the Feldwebel, as he disappears into the snow.

The wicked rumble of tank motors comes closer.

Porta looks carefully over the edge of his hole in the snow.

'Herr Oberleutnant, sir!' he shouts to Löwe. 'God didn't mean us to get killed here, I'm sure! Let's beat it!'

'Stay where you are,' orders Löwe, angrily. 'Get your close combat arms ready, and stay in your holes!'

'Now then! 'and me them Molotovs quick as I throw 'em under them Tea rooms,' Tiny orders the schoolteacher, knocking his Mpi barrel on the top of the man's steel-helmet as he says it. 'The devil'n 'is gran'ma 'elp you if you get out o' rhythm! I'd just as soon throw you'n your pointer under a T-34 as a bleedin' bomb! Count on it, you alphabet cracker, you!'

Silently raging, the teacher and the demoted Oberst bundle hand-grenades, and pass them to Tiny.

' 'Old on to your tin'ats,' roars Tiny, swinging a bunch of bombs round his head.

About twenty-five yards in front of him a KW-2 comes bellowing.

'It's going to crush us,' stammers the schoolteacher, in terror, preparing to run.

'You stay 'ere,' snarls Tiny, laying a hand the size of a ham on him. 'I'll tear your bleedin' balls off, if you try to run!'

Fifty-three tons of tank come to a halt. The turret turns slowly.

A crashing explosion, and a long flame spurts from the 155 mm. gun. The blast throws Tiny back onto the teacher and the ex-Oberst. The shell falls only thirty yards from their snow hole and throws an avalanche of snow over them.

69

'Funny way to open the ball,' curses Tiny, in dismay, wiping snow and slush from his face.

'Heavenly God!' screams the teacher, in panic fear. The giant belly of the tank towers in front of their snow hole.

The ex-Oberst half rises, closes his eyes, and waits for the underside of the tank to come down crushingly on top of them.

'Up you, Ivan arse'ole,' roars Tiny, throwing two bundles of bombs in quick succession under the KW-2.

There is a yellowy-white jet of flame, and a column of coal-black smoke shoots up from the tank's turret and mushrooms out above it.

'Jesus Christ!' stammers the Oberst, white with fear.

A terrible explosion breaks the KW-2 up into thousands of bits and pieces.

Tiny rolls away, as the burning remains of the KW-2 tip forward. The ex-Oberst is lying in a snow hole, screaming in terror. Fifteen tons of tank turret have slid straight over him and ripped his coat open right up the back, without otherwise hurting him. Wide-eyed and shaking all over he stares at the roaring, crackling hell of flame which only seconds ago was a deadly dangerous weapon of warfare.

'Where's the bleedin' flamethrower tank?' asks Tiny, threateningly, staring wickedly at the ex-Oberst, in whose eyes front-line madness flickers. 'The flamethrower tank, lamebrain!' he repeats, hitting the man with the butt of his Mpi.

Like a beaten dog the ex-Oberst tries to creep away. Tiny showers curses on him, his Mpi at the ready and his finger on the trigger.

'I'm gonna spread you all over Russia, you shit, an' then I'm goin' to spit on your mother's grave,' he shouts, with a grotesque grin. 'You've thrown away German Army property, an' you don't do that unpunished, *bastard*!'

Tracks clank menacingly behind the curtain of snow, threatening us with death by crushing. A long stone wall cracks open like an eggshell. The blast wave sweeps over us and throws us to the ground. The heat burns the skin, but Tiny seems not to notice the inferno around him. He sends an angry burst of shots into the snow close to the feet of the ex-Oberst.

'Flamethrower tank!' he mutters, hoarsely.

'What's up?' asks the Old Man, in his usual steady voice.

'A flock o' wild bleedin' monkeys must've been feedin' on that limppricked bleeder's arse,' cackles Tiny, furiously. 'He's thrown bleedin' Adolf's soddin' flamethrower tank away! Thinks 'e's still got 'is bleedin' pips up p'raps! Never met a shit like 'im, I ain't!'

'Where is it?' asks the Old Man, throwing the ex-Oberst a contemptuous glance.

'I lost it,' mumbles the Oberst, in a thick voice.

'Lost it?' roars Tiny, scandalised, in a voice loud enough to be heard in both Moscow and Berlin at the same time. ' 'Oly Mary, daughter of Jesus, now I've 'eard everythin'! You lyin' demoted ashcan, you! You *threw* it away, you *did*! *Threw* it away, 'cause you didn't want to 'ave to *carry* it, you bastard. An' a shit like you's been a officer in the Führer's army!'

'Go an' get it!' orders the Old Man, brusquely.

'Are you mad?' the demoted Oberst protests, angrily. 'I'll be *killed* if I go down and get that tank!'

'So *what*?' grins Tiny, wickedly. 'You won't be missed in *this* unit! Albert'll be pleased, too. Save 'im breakin' your 'ead in with 'is knobkerry before 'e makes 'ash with garlic out of you!'

'Killed!' the Old Man smiles, jeeringly. 'When you were in command you "fell for the Führer and the Fatherland"! But you're right. "Killed" is the right expression. Or "murdered"! Or "crippled"! Or "smashed"!'

'*C'est la guerre,*' smiles the Legionnaire. 'Come death, come now death . . .' he hums, softly.

'Last time of asking! Get that flamethrower tank!' orders the Old Man, swinging his Mpi, as if unthinkingly, to the ready position.

With bowed head, upright, and weaponless, the ex-Oberst slips and slides down the icy slope.

A shell explodes a few yards from him, and showers him with snow. He is thrown backwards. Loses his steel helmet. He rises, with difficulty, and staggers on through the deep snow, taking

71

no notice of the screams, the crashing of trees and the deafening explosions around him.

'Forward, No. 2!' orders the Old Man. 'Look after that old shit,' he turns and says to Tiny.

'Pleasure,' grins Tiny, satisfiedly. 'Like a bleedin' mother! But *all* mothers ain't *good* mothers!'

'God help *you*, if you turn him off!' warns the Old Man, with a hard look in his eyes.

' 'Ow could you ever believe me capable of a thing like that?' asks Tiny, with a sly look on his powder-blackened face. 'Stick to Jesus's Third Commandment *I* do: Thou shalt not knock thy neighbour off! Nor I don't forget what Moses said neither: 'Im as 'its 'is mate on the bonce with a blackjack, gets 'is own brains bashed in likewise!'

'Mad sod!' snarls the Old Man, irritably, and runs down the slope together with the Legionnaire.

The ex-Oberst comes panting back, and throws the flame-thrower tank down furiously at Tiny's feet.

'Are you out of your mind, man?' cries Tiny, reproachfully. 'You'll make a dent in Adolf's tank, you will! They'll knock it off your pay, they will! And don't forget you're drawin' coolie's pay and not officer's pay! Take you a year to pay it off. Up on your back with it, now, an' 'ang on to my arse! We're goin' out an' toast the neighbours! Where's that bleedin' schoolteacher sod got to? If 'e's run away I'll catch 'im an' stick 'is blackboard pointer straight up through 'is arse'ole!'

'Here,' pipes the schoolteacher, putting a frightened face up over the edge of a hole in the snow.

'Well *that*'s all right, then,' growls Tiny, in satisfaction. 'Be worst for you two, if you get me feelin' un'appy! Grab the bleedin' ammo'n follow your cocks! The worst as can 'appen to you lot is for you to get your arses shot off so's you can't go for a shit on the pot no more!'

'Double up, double up, you shower o' lame heroes, you!' The Old Man chases them impatiently. 'Get on! Close up, you sods! Follow the tanks!'

'You must've been eating shit, and it's gone to your head,'

72

rages Porta. 'Close up yourself, if you're tired of life! *I'm* not leaving this man's army on the end of a bullet! *I* didn't volunteer to get myself killed!'

'Rush, rush, rush! All bleedin' rush,' curses Tiny, savagely, and grabs onto a P-4's tow-hook. 'I'll soon be walkin' on me balls! Me legs are worn down nearly to me 'ips!'

The horizon flames. Rockets whine across the sky from our batteries, and heavy Stalin organs answer them fiercely.

Russian Maxim guns chatter heavily, in front of and at an angle to us. We go at them with hand-grenades and S-mines, and clean up the survivors hand-to-hand. It all goes so quickly we hardly realise what is happening ourselves.

'*En avant, marche! Vive la mort!*' screams the Legionnaire, fanatically, shoving his long Moorish knife into a Russian lieutenant. He stumbles across a corpse, the Kalashnikov flying from his hand.

Again and again the Legionnaire's Moorish battle-cry sounds through the curtain of snow.

'The sand in that war-nutty desert prick's boiling up again,' jeers Porta, spitting contemptuously into the snow.

'Mad as a hatter,' considers Gregor. 'Why the devil's he fight like that? He don't like neither Adolf nor Old Germany neither!'

'A camel probably bit him in the buttocks, when he was running round the Sahara with the rest of the Froggies'n cutting the balls of the poor Arabs,' laughs Porta.

The feared Russian field guns start up. Shells explode round about us, throwing snow, earth and frozen corpses into the air.

Cursing and swearing we struggle through the mountains of snow, often sinking down in it up to our armpits and only with difficulty being able to free ourselves from it.

We get out on the road again and literally turn cartwheels as we slip on the icy surface. Our studded boots cannot get a grip on it.

Russian machine pistols sweep the roads in long, deadly bursts. Hand-grenades explode around us in an inferno of spitting fire. We go forward in long bounds, jumping over a party of infantrymen, who press themselves into the snow fearfully and raise their hands in the belief that we are Russians.

'The Führer's 'eroes feelin' tired?' grins Tiny, sending a burst round the feet of an Unterfeldwebel.

'Forward comrades. The quickest way home's via Moscow,' shouts Porta, jeeringly.

With sharp-edged spades and bayonets the squad goes at the Russian positions. Tiny sends a long, rattling burst through the observation slit of a defence post. The havoc is terrible as bullets ricochet around inside the concrete shell. Few live through it. They are literally sawn to pieces in an undirected crossfire of misshapen projectiles.

I throw a hand-grenade towards the pill-box farthest back in the position. I throw so hard my arm almost goes out of joint. The explosion which follows throws me back with enormous force, and all the air is forced out of my lungs.

The entire post is thrown into the air in one piece, and comes down upside down. My grenade must have set off their reserve ammunition depot.

The blast wave throws Tiny and the schoolteacher into the air and drops them heavily back into the snow.

'You *mad* or somethin'?' screams Tiny, white with rage, clawing his way from a heap of snow. 'You don't 'andle explosives like that, you twit, you! Nearly got blown out o' me boots, I did!'

Two self-propelled guns come rattling past. The leading SP stops on top of a pill-box and twists on its tracks like a man extinguishing a cigarette with the sole of his boot. Wood crackles. Concrete is crushed. Men scream chokingly. The SP continues to twist and rock until the voices are silenced.

I throw a grenade towards an MG nest. Pieces of timber fly into the air. A Maxim topples, its muzzle pointing towards the earth. Over its cooling jacket hang the remains of a Russian soldier, his face a bloody unrecognisable mass.

All around us we hear the characteristic crack of tank guns.

A tall, thin Rittmeister with an officer's dress cap tilted arrogantly over one eye chases us on.

'Come on now, come on. Keep the damned pot boiling! Show you're the Führer's soldiers, lads!'

'An' you're a pile o' bleedin' chicken-shit, you are!' growls Tiny, ragingly, but not loud enough to reach the Rittmeister's ears.

'What a lot of shits there are running around in this man's war with verbal diarrhoea,' grumbles Porta, spitting contemptuously after the lanky Rittmeister. Suddenly the officer is hit. Blood spouts from his face, and he goes down with a shrill scream. His elegant cap rolls across the snow and catches on a bush.

Gregor takes the officer's weapon, one of the coveted Kalashnikovs. Barcelona breaks off half of his identification disk and puts it in his pocket.

'More dung for the military muck-heap. Come death, come . . . .!' hums the Legionnaire.

Suddenly Leutnant Braun throws down his Mpi and slumps onto some empty ammunition boxes. We stop and look at him. His eyes stare glassily at us.

'He'll soon be on his way towards the setting sun,' grins Heide, jeeringly.

'What's going on here?' asks Oberleutnant Löwe. He has come slipping and sliding down a height at the head of the Command Group.

Heide points at Leutnant Braun, laughing. 'Cowardice in the face of the enemy,' he breathes, with a cruel expression on his face.

'There 'e goes again, the bloodthirsty bastard,' shouts Tiny. 'Why can't you just put your bleedin' 'ead up long enough for Ivan to shoot it off?'

'Shut up!' snarls Löwe. 'I'll take care of this! Up on your feet, Braun! Come on. *Up* with you, man!'

Leutnant Braun stares emptily at nothing. He seems to be in another world.

'All the stuffin's gone out of 'im,' exclaims Tiny in amazement. 'Not a bleedin' bit left, there ain't!'

Löwe shakes the petrified officer, without result.

'Took the short cut to Valhalla, he has,' says Gregor, shrugging his shoulders indifferently.

'Forward, men!' orders Löwe, brusquely. 'Leave him to the medics.'

The ground slopes upwards. The strain of climbing is inhuman.

Tiny catches me by the shoulder as I slip and go sliding backwards towards a steep drop. My head reels, as I look downwards into nothingness.

Raging and swearing we struggle on and up, cursing the Army and all its ways, Germany, and the parents whose fault it was we were born at all. Many give up, and stretch out in the snow, but section and platoon leaders get them on their feet again and moving forward. Heide is extremely zealous. His piercing, icy voice can be heard far and wide.

'Just *think*! I *volunteered* for *this*!' groans Albert, flat on his face in the snow and hanging onto a bush to keep himself from sliding back down the icy slope. 'It's a punishment from God. I shouldn't never've pissed in that Bishop's wine-butt in Munich, and given him jaundice, I shouldn't. The fat pig!'

The Legionnaire's climbing irons slip, and his Mpi goes sliding down the incline. He watches it unhappily, as it goes sliding and cartwheeling away with a tail of powdery snow behind it.

We all of us know that it is statistically impossible for active front-line soldiers like us to live through this war. But we still hope, and are happy to greet each new day and still be alive.

This attack, which is carried out with a foolhardy bravery beyond anything which could be called reasonable, has nothing at all to do with heroism. It is simply a desperate fight.

Army Corps HQ has been ordered to take the heights, and our regiment has been given the job of ejecting the Russians from the OGPU prison, and holding it come what may. Whoever holds the prison on the hill dominates that whole section of the front. We've been fighting over it now for almost four weeks. Several battalions have been lost on both sides, but no German soldier has yet set foot inside it. We have reached no farther than the outer walls. Only to be repulsed. It seems that this time we really mean to do the job. Two veteran divisions have been allocated to the attack. A Pioneer battalion which has been attached to us, is pulling some strange weapons along with it. Queer things like harpoon-guns which are intended to fire

76

scaling ropes towards the prison walls. These we are supposed to use to climb the hill, which is almost a mountain. Then we break into the prison itself.

Wild rumours circulate about what goes on in the OGPU prison. Several thousand prisoners are said to be immured inside it. Our artillery has bombarded it constantly for four days now, and it is a question whether many of those inside it are still alive.

Julius Heide, who is always well-informed, says that it is an old prison, which existed even before the revolution. Now, it is used as a transit station by the Russian Secret Police, and the prisoners in it are collected from the Kiev and Charkov military districts.

After three days of bloody close combat we have a footing on the first height. Half-dead we drop in our tracks. Our lungs ache as if they had been stabbed through and through with icy daggers. We are drenched in sweat even in this freezing air.

Leutnant Braun is back with us. He lies flat on his back, his eyelids fluttering. He is dead to the world. Oberleutnant Löwe, sooty-faced, sits with his back to a tree which gives him a degree of protection from the icy wind. The Old Man stares sadly at nothing, as he fills his old silver-lidded pipe. He has difficulty in lighting it. The tobacco is damp.

Tiny lies full length on his stomach, alongside Porta. Out of the corner of his eye he watches the schoolteacher and the ex-Oberst. As usual he is puffing away at a fat cigar.

'You're pushing those two,' says Porta, with a one-sided smile. 'What've they done, anyway?'

'Done? Done?' shouts Tiny, hoarsely. He blows his nose on his fingers. 'They ain't done *nothin'*! Just let 'em *try* to do somethin'! Look 'ere now. Schoolteachers I cannot *stand*! Never 'ave been able to. Not since I got out o' the bleedin' whippin' institution! I swore then as I'd *get* every last one of them bastards I ever got me fingers on. An' that walkin' blackboard pointer over there is one o' the worst of 'em! *Oberschulrat* 'e calls 'imself! That's the bleeder as walked into company office an' said as 'ow 'e was a foot-slogger at present but 'e was really an *Oberschulrat*. For that reason 'e'd like to go to officers school quick as possible. I asked for 'im, an' Feldwebel Schluckebier, who don't like schoolteachers neither, give 'im to me. *"Officers school!"* 'e snorted at me. "I'll give 'im officers school! When I've finished with *'im*, there'll be nothing left of 'im but 'is tonsils!" '

'Well, what's with the Oberst then?' asks Gregor. 'He's not a schoolteacher, and there's a lot of all-right Obersts. Nothing wrong with our bloke Hinka, is there?'

"E's all-right, right enough,' answers Tiny, 'but this other bastard *ain't*. Not by a long way 'e ain't. My friend, Stabsgefreiter Frick of Divisional Staff's told me enough about 'im. They used to call 'im "the mad rookie killer" at Sennelager. The wickedest bleedin' trainin' depot commander in all o' bleedin' Westphalia'n the Rhineland. All of a sudden though, the list of dead rookies got too long'n they ordered an investigation. 'Fore 'e knew where 'e was, there 'e was in Germersheim with 'oles in 'is shoulder tabs where 'is pips used to be! 'E'd good connections though'n got off the mornin' walk, with twelve good friends and true armed with rifles, on the way to a wooden overcoat. 'Is connections let 'im off goin' to the boneyard'n sent 'im 'ere instead to give 'im a chance to show 'e was a 'ero really'n get 'is pips back again. Schluckebier give 'im to *me* as a birthday present. Look at 'im! Ain't no pips shinin' in *'is* eyes no more! 'E's cannon bleedin' fodder an' nothin' else. One thing 'e's learnt though. 'E's learnt what an Obergefreiter is!'

'Watch it anyway,' the Old Man warns. 'Even if he has been bust he's still got connections. And busting a shit of an Obergefreiter like you ain't much of a job!'

'I don't give a *crap* for 'is connections,' declares Tiny, grandly.

'When I've finished with 'im — well — anythin'd be worth the pleasure!'

'You're balmy,' says the Old Man, shaking his head. Finally he manages to get his old silver-lidded pipe going.

'Come on, come on! On your feet there! Move now!' shouts Oberleutnant Löwe. He pushes up a clenched fist, the signal for a rapid forward movement.

'Ivan's gone into hiding again,' states Porta, after an hour has gone by without the least sign of a Russian.

'Don't let 'im fool you,' says Gregor. 'Comrade Ivan's the wickedest and slyest bastard on the face of this earth. Just when you think he's sodded off, then there you are — looking round for half your head what the bastard's shot off you.'

'Ma-a-n I don't *like* it,' mumbles Albert. 'These goddam hills here they could hide a whole army corps, and here we are marchin' straight between 'em. 'Fore we know where we are there's gonna be a regiment of them lousy Cossacks riding their fucking nags straight up our arses! Hell, man, this place just *stinks* of them treacherous bastards' sneaky ways.'

'You don't like horses?' asks Porta.

'I just *hate* them, man,' snarls Albert, pulling back his thick lips like an angry wolf. 'Like I told you, my ol' man was a drummer in the hussars. And he used to get a ration of free meat when some horse or other keeled over'n died. We had horse-meat twice a day, and us kids we *stank* that much of horse, we couldn't go past the stables without'm whinnyin' after us. *Horses*! Jesus Christ, man! You go past their back parts'n they just fart in your face!'

Just after midnight, in a blinding snowstorm, the company reaches a large *kolchos*, which the enemy appears to have left in a hurry. Abandoned equipment lies about everywhere.

Tiny finds two heavy, triple-barrelled shotguns. He gives one to Porta with a box of bear shells.

'What the hell are you going to use those things for?' asks the Old Man, in amazement.

'You'll see,' laughs Porta. 'First we saw 'em off short, so's they don't take up so much room, and the shot spreads better. Then when *they* go off old comrade Ivan'd better duck down sharp if he doesn't want to get spread all over the landscape!'

'We can cut the bollocks off the entire bleedin' Red Army with one shot!' Tiny screams with laughter.

'Trouble-makers *they* are,' Gregor warns them ominously. 'Ivan catches you with them he'll stick 'em up your arse and blow the tops of your heads off!'

'Jesus Christ of Nazareth,' comes a scream of astonishment

79

from Porta down in the cellar. 'We've struck the Reds main supply cache!' His head pops up from a trap-door. 'We can make *bortsch*, my sons, the Red Army's favourite soup,' he laughs. 'Give me a hand with this pot, lads. It's the world's biggest, I do believe.'

'Everything's big in Russia,' Barcelona philosophises. 'Did you know that Russians *always* buy their boots two sizes too large? Makes them feel more confident of themselves.'

'You peel the onions,' Tiny orders the schoolteacher, 'and then chop 'em into thin strips. An' you, you walkin' sentry-box you,' he turns to the ex-Oberst. 'You look after the beetroot'n the cabbage. Do it *right* or, by Christ, I'll 'ave your ears off, I will!'

Porta has a flour-bag on his head, and has tied half a white sheet round his waist. He looks for all the world like the Head Cook of the Grand Hotel in Paris.

'Let us see, now,' he shouts, eagerly, waving a large knife above his head. 'First we must have five litres of water. Not a drop more, and not a drop less. Julius, you Prussian perfectionist, you must pour the water. Let us see, let us see! Here is a piece of beef. We need three kilogrammes, and then we need a kilogramme and a half of lean pork. Then, five leeks, one to every litre of water, and four hundred grammes of cabbage. *We* will use five hundred. It won't do any harm. One kilogramme of beetroot, half a celeriac, a handful of chopped parsley. Do we have that?'

'No parsley,' says the Old Man.

'Can we use kale instead? Plenty of that,' suggests Tiny, sticking his head up from the cellar. He has put himself in charge of supplies.

'Let's try,' says Porta. 'Maybe the *bortsch*'ll be the better for it. We have, for God's sake, five pieces of garlic? We can't do without *that*!'

''Ere,' says Tiny, throwing a bunch over to him. 'Give it the lot. It'll only make it better! The fur Jew's David always used to say you couldn't 'ave too much of it. Makes your prick stick up like a flag-pole on Adolf's bleedin' birthday!'

'We need sour cream' says Porta. 'I must have *sour* cream!'

'Put some vinegar in it,' suggests Gregor. '*That* ought to make it sour.'

'All we need now's butter, salt and pepper,' shouts Porta, and begins to sing the drunken milkman's song.

''Ow much pepper then?' asks Tiny, from the cellar. 'There ain't more'n one sack down 'ere.'

'*Idiot*,' hisses Porta. 'All I need's a teaspoonful!'

'The water's boiling,' shouts Heide, warningly, chasing the schoolteacher round the cauldron, at the double, five times.

'Get moving,' shouts Porta, ardently. 'The onions. The white of the leeks. The cabbage. Half the beetroot, and the celeriac in narrow strips.'

'Got it!' says Tiny. 'These two coolies of mine've done that. If it ain't good enough, say the word an' I'll cut their balls off for 'em!'

'Can it, Tiny! You talk too much. It makes me nervous,' Porta warns him. '*Now*, we brown the veg' a smidgin in good unsalted Ukrainian butter. There's no butter like Ivan's butter. If that's what old "GROFAZ"[8] is after in Russia then I'm with him all the way! In with the meat now, and while it's cooking we'll sing the Poacher's Aria from *Jägerbrauten*. Tiny'n Albert can do the baritones and Heide and Gregor the sopranos. Ready?' Porta taps his wooden spoon three times commandingly on the giant pot, and from the sooty *kolchos* the Poacher's Aria rings out over the snowy steppe.

Porta drums on his chest and his flour bag falls off his head. He places one foot on the back of the schoolteacher, who is lying on the floor polishing the SMG on Tiny's orders, and assumes the attitude of a big-game hunter.

'*Der Förster ist tot, Der Wilddieb lebt!*' he sings in a ringing voice.

'Listen to 'im,' cries Tiny, admiringly. 'Don't 'e sound bleedin' wonderful though?'

We sit in a circle round the bubbling cauldron. Porta hums a Russian harvesting song, as he shakes the garlic into it.

[8]GROFAZ: Grösster Feldherr aller Zeiten (The Greatest Army Leader of All Time) A nickname for Hitler.

'There wouldn't be a little duck lying around down there now, would there?' he asks Tiny.

'Find a duck!' Tiny orders the ex-Oberst, who does find one.

'I must explain this to you,' says Porta. 'It's a thing one *should* know. There are two kinds of *bortsch*. There's ordinary, common or garden *bortsch*, the kind the Tartars and the Muscovites gollup down by the gallon. Then there's party *bortsch*, the kind the Poles and the Ukrainians go in for. First they brown a duck, then they fillet him, take out all his bones and sinews and cut him into small pieces. Then singing a few bars of "Katerina Ismailova" the while — they let him fall piece by piece into the soup. Like this. Plop, plop, plop, *plop*! And every time the duck goes plop you can make a wish for something good.'

'Like a piece o' cunt, maybe,' cries Tiny, his eyes shining.

'Hasn't that goddam *bortsch* been cookin' long enough?' demands the Old Man, impatiently, licking his lips wolfishly.

'To a master cook,' Porta warns seriously, 'there is nothing worse than impatient guests! You may be boss of this outfit, but stay out of the kitchen. That's *mine*! Obergefreiter by the Grace of God, Joseph Porta, *Chef*! If you cannot wait until this incomparable Russian *chef d'oeuvre* is ready, then I would advise you to take a little walk outside, and take anyone else who is impatient along with you!'

Our patience is sorely tired while Porta continues, imperturbably, the operation of skimming off the soup. We find our jaws champing automatically up and down, and our stomachs rumble, as he slowly, and with a dignified air, slices the meat into cubes and drops it into the pot. Finally he pours in the beetroot juice with a sanctified air, and at the same time invokes a blessing on the soup from the God of all the Russias.

We almost fall over one another when he tells us to come along with our mess-tins. He orders them to be lined up like soldiers on parade.

Tiny almost shoots the schoolteacher and the ex-Oberst when they try to put their mess-tins alongside ours.

'Slaves to the back o' the queue!' he roars. 'In Jesus's time you'd 'ave et with the bleedin' dogs, you would. Ain't you never read the Bible, you upper-class bastards?'

Porta puts a large lump of butter in each mess-tin, and with the mien of an archbishop initiating a line of novice priests, he pours the soup over the butter.

'Dip deep with the ol' ladle, my son,' slavers Tiny, his eyes glittering with hunger. 'The best's always at the bottom!'

Finally Porta sprinkles each helping with chopped kale and pours on sour cream.

When Tiny has got through three helpings he takes pity on the schoolteacher and the ex-Oberst.

'You two duds're 'ungry too, I suppose?' he asks, graciously. 'Go on over to Obergefreiter Porta, then, with your mess-tins. If, by mistake, you find a piece of meat in *your* soup, you will report to me with it immediately, *Panjemajo?*'

'Stop tormenting those poor sods,' hisses the Old Man, irritably.

'Call feedin' 'em tormentin' 'em, then?' shouts Tiny, astonished. 'What you want me to do then? Wipe their bleedin' arses for 'em, so's they don't make shit-tracks in Adolf's army pants, per'aps?'

The first hour or so we just shovel *bortsch* into us, without much talking. When we cannot get another bit down, we lean back and feel wonderfully satisfied.

'When good old Germany has lost this war,' Porta philosophises, 'and has recovered somewhat from *this* bashing, I think it would be a good idea for me to open a restaurant in Berlin. I think I'll buy the ruins of "Kempinski". Get it cheap I'd think. I'll sell everything: New England stuffing, roast turkey American style, cockerel in the Roman fashion.'

'Do not forget *"Poulet au sang"*, from France, *mon ami*,' the Legionnaire adds to the list, lighting a Caporal.

'Wouldn't *dream* of forgettin' it,' smiles Porta, 'just as I wouldn't think of forgettin' *"Greek egg-plant au gratin"*, and cakes from the Jewish kitchen for dessert.'

'You nearly make me throw-up,' Julius Heide breaks in, furiously. 'How can you bring yourself to even speak of such Yiddischer filth?'

83

'Rather have *"lamb à la Turcque"*, would you?' says Porta, superciliously. 'I'd have that for patrons of your kind!'

'You'd have *"Venezuelan fish soup"* on your menu, I suppose?' says Gregor, licking his frost-cracked lips.

'What about *"Paelle Valenciana"*?' shouts Barcelona, from up on the window-ledge.

'What in the world's going on here?' comes a creaking officers mess voice from the doorway.

'Atten*tion*!' shouts the Old Man, jumping up in a fluster, and dropping his silver-lidded pipe.

With lips pressed tightly together, one-armed Oberst Hinka enters the low-ceilinged room. It is filled with the aroma of *bortsch*.

'What's this?' he asks, looking interestedly into the pot. There is a little of the soup left.

'The favourite soup of the Russians, Oberst, *sir*!' crows Porta.

'Give me a taste,' smiles Hinka.

Porta fills a mess-tin for him.

'And the adjutant, perhaps?' asks Porta, looking at the Leutnant standing nervously, like a laying hen, by the door.

'Don't ask silly questions, Porta,' answers the Oberst, between mouthfuls.

Doubtfully the adjutant accepts a mess-tin. He cannot conceal that he does not trust Porta's culinary art. It would not surprise him if there was a fast-acting poison in the soup.

'What a wonderful soup,' cries Oberst Hinka, handing back the empty mess-tin to Porta.

'Yes, sir, these *untermensch* know what food's all about, sir,' says Porta appreciatively. 'You ought to try *Selianka* sometime, sir. Its their salmon soup, sir. They make it on the Black Sea beaches. I got to know it when I visited a friend of mine, Sergei Smirnow, sir. Head cook of "The Grey Tomcat", the Tartar restaurant in Athens, sir. His *Selianka*, sir, why it'd draw Josef Stalin right out of the Kremlin. I've got the recipe, sir, if you'd like to have it?'

'No thank you, Porta, not today,' smiles Oberst Hinka, slapping Porta on the shoulder. 'We're off in an hour's time. Keep cool, Beier,' he turns to the Old Man. 'I think we're going to run

84

into some dirty stuff. And Porta, and you too Creutzfeldt, no plundering raids, no sniffing about after loot, you two! If I hear anything of that sort's gone on, it'll be a courtmartial for you in two shakes, and you'll get no mercy from me! Looting's a serious matter.'

'Understood, sir, understood perfectly, sir!' cackles Porta, in a servile voice. 'We've seen the warnings posted up, sir, everywhere, sir! Looting gets you the rope. Oberst Hinka, sir, beg to report, sir, we know enough to keep our fingers where they belong, sir, and not get 'em blistered. We've *seen* those posters, sir!'

Twenty minutes later Porta and Tiny have broken open a cellar door, and gone up through the floor of what used to be the mayor's office. They ransack drawers and cupboards, throwing the contents on the floor. Finding nothing of interest they continue into the next room, where they discover a bottle of vodka in a wastepaper basket.

'Let's lay the dust,' says Porta, putting the bottle to his mouth.

When they have squeezed the last drops from the bottle, they go on, laughing and skylarking, from one ice-cold room to the next. Finally they reach the bedroom, which is dominated by an ancient four-poster bed of supernatural dimensions.

Tiny sniffs around like a hound which has scented a fox. From the foot of the bed he creeps under the heavy peasant-style quilted eiderdowns.

'Here, cunt, cunt, cunt, cunt, cunt!' comes hollowly from under the bedclothes. His bowler appears briefly at the pillow-end. 'Cunt!' he repeats, and burrows in again like a ferret down a rabbit-hole.

Porta puts his head curiously under the bedclothes to see what Tiny is doing. Not seeing him he crawls in himself, and begins to grunt like a hedgehog on a warm summer night.

Tiny does not realise at first that it is Porta crawling round in there. There is a short but violent fight in which the eiderdown is ripped from top to bottom. Feathers fill the air.

They sit up at each end of the bed and look dazedly around

them. They look like two gulls in a snow storm, as feathers drift down gently on to them.

In a chest of drawers Tiny finds a pair of long red pantalettes, with lace frills, and buttoned flaps fore and aft as was the fashion at the turn of the century.

'Holy Mother of Kazan, what an arse that bint must've had on her,' cries Porta, licking his lips. 'Even a Belgian dray-horse couldn't fill *them* up!'

'Jesus love us all,' chants Tiny. 'If we 'ad that arse 'ere with all accessories couldn't we just 'ave us a pretty little old triangular tournament!'

'Cunt,' sighs Porta, dreamily, burying his face in the red pantalettes. He growls like a tomcat on his way to nocturnal adventures.

'Gimme them things,' demands Tiny. He pulls on the red pantalettes over his uniform. Porta hands him a huge brassiere.

His gasmask is in the way and he throws it out of the window. 'They won't use chemical weapons 'fore the next war, anyway,' he decides carelessly.

The brassiere is filled out with two floor-cloths. They look like young Alps. Discovery of a pair of old-fashioned corsets nearly starts a fight. Porta gets them in the end.

They admire themselves in a tall mirror. The corsets are very beautiful, and embroidered all over with roses and butterflies.

'Why butterflies, then?' asks Tiny, wonderingly.

'Natural enough,' says Porta, consideringly. 'They fly out and bring in the pricks.'

In a cupboard they find a large black hat garnished with cherries. Porta confiscates it.

'Fancy a quick rub-off?' he asks, wiggling his hips through the bedroom in an imitation of the whore's walk. 'Have it off for a tenner?' he twitters through the open window, and kisses his fingers to a group of motorcyclists, who stare up at them as if they were seeing a kind of miracle happening.

'Nick o' the arse, 'alf-price,' roars Tiny, coarsely, slapping his behind.

'Come along, now, silly boys,' Porta invites them, bobbing the cherries on his hat at them. 'Get your tickets at the door. A

86

tenner for a German ordinary. French luxury go, double price. See Sophie's arse. Only two marks a time.'

Tiny climbs up on the window ledge and waggles his hips. The red pantalettes wave in the wind.

Porta makes a chopping motion with his hand, and spits down into the snow.

'No good, dear,' he says to Tiny. 'It's true what they say in "The Crocodile", the Germans are just like their Führer. Their cocks've all shrunk up to nothing in the awful cold!'

They pull the windows shut with a crash.

Tiny stumbles, and falls into a rocking-chair which tips right over and sends him flying through a door, papered over and flush with the wall so as to be unnoticeable. He ends up in a small room behind the door, and looks around him confusedly.

'Where've you got to?' asks Porta, putting his cherry-laden hat through the broken door.

Tiny does not reply, but points silently towards a large old-fashioned safe, decorated with a red star and the hammer and sickle.

The sight sobers Porta up immediately. He runs loving, gentle fingers over the metal of the safe.

'I always wanted to meet someone like you,' he confides to it.

'Watch it,' says Tiny, doubtfully. 'That wicked bleeder Ivan might've planned a little surprise for nosey bastards like us two!'

'You've got crap between your ears,' Porta says, grandly. He commences to examine the safe, millimetre by millimetre. They try to move it away from the wall but cannot budge it. They find two iron bars but still cannot move it.

Porta spits on the red star and shakes his fist at the safe.

'Just you wait, you cold, square bastard, you,' says Tiny. 'We'll show you where Jesus got 'is beer from! Don't think we come all the bleedin' way to Russia for you to 'ave the laugh on us!'

'Hell!' says Porta, thoughtfully, looking appraisingly at the heavy box. 'We're going to have to get her away from the wall.'

'Why, then?' asks Tiny, incomprehendingly. 'The door's in the front ain't it? If you want to get into an 'ouse you use the door don't you? Don't go breakin' down the wall at the back to get in!'

'Shut *up*,' hisses Porta, irritably. 'It's different with safes! The door's for them who's in the know. The more you piss about with *that* the harder it gets to get it open. You've got to use the back door. Wish we had an oxy' cutter. That'd soon look after that bit of scrap iron.'

'What about the flame-thrower,' suggests Tiny eagerly, and is half out of the door on his way to fetch it.

'Oh, cut it out, brainy,' Porta turns the idea down. 'It'd melt down the whole box and what's inside too. We're not collecting scrap iron, and what's more we're not walking out of this war just as poor as we were when we walked in.'

'There's somethin' in that about goin' into safes from the arse-side,' says Tiny, scratching his crutch, thoughtfully, with his bayonet. 'You remember that fur Yid from 'Ein 'Oyer Strasse what 'ad a mate, as wasn't a Yid, who was a locksmith in Bernhard Nocht Strasse. Well, this bloke used to 'ave to do with safes, evenings an' weekends, like. All them as 'e 'ad to do with 'e used to take from the back. That was what sodded 'im up though, in the end. Commissioner bleedin' Nass an' 'is boys with their 'at-brims pulled down, from the David Station. They got that locksmith, as wasn't a Yid, finally. Every time a safe 'ad been give a shot up the jacksey old Nass knew it 'ad to be our locksmith. You can almost guess the rest. Early one mornin', before the milkman 'ad left the 'alf a pinta on the doorstep in crashes old Nass with a couple other dees and wakes up the locksmith, who was in bed dreamin' sweet dreams about safes bulgin' with money. It'll be nearly twenty years more fore 'e sees the outside of bleedin' Fuhlsbüttel[9].'

'But since this is our very first meeting with a Soviet safe, nobody'll ever dream it was us two German liberators who fixed it,' says Porta, unworriedly. He begins to fiddle with the combination lock.

'Reminds you of a wireless set,' says Tiny.

'Programme's a bit different, though,' smiles Porta,

[9]Fuhlsbüttel: Prison near Hamburg.

indulgently. 'With a radio you have to pay for twiddling the knobs. With this we hope to *get* paid if we find the right station.'

' 'Ave you, by the way, *tried* the door?' asks Tiny, practically. 'I remember one time when the fur Yid's David'n me was 'avin a gander at a competitor's ware'ouse'n we 'ad a lockpickin' expert along with us. After 'e'd been on the job an hour we found out the door wasn't locked at all! That expert 'e was so ashamed 'e went off'n got 'imself arrested by one of Nass's silly bleeders.'

'You're bloody well right!' cries Porta, pulling the heavy door open with difficulty.

Tiny laughs so loudly that the sound reverberates throughout the room and sends back echoes from all over the house, when he looks over Porta's shoulder and sees stack upon stack of notes.

'Millions!' whispers Porta, in rapture. 'Bloody millions! I never laid my pampered eyes on that much money *ever*! Praise the good Lord!' he intones, with eyes turned up towards the heavens. 'I'll look into your temple at the very, very first opportunity! And if I run into a heathen in this country I'll give him somethin' to really set him thinking!'

'There's a lot there. More'n we can count,' cries Tiny, washing his hands like an ancient Jew who has just succeeded in cheating an antisemite.

'Soon there will be two new Rockefellers adorning the economic firmament,' forecasts Porta, with satisfaction.

'Who's that?' asks Tiny, stupidly.

'Take a look in the mirror,' says Porta. 'You'll see one of 'em there!'

'Great Lord above! I can 'ardly believe it,' says Tiny, looking at himself closely in the mirror.

'Now all we've got to do is keep our heads cool,' says Porta running his hands tenderly over the piles of money.

'Not much chance of anythin' else in a Russian winter,' says Tiny, carelessly.

'From this moment on,' continues Porta, with an energetic expression on his face, 'we are too wealthy to take any kind of interest in Adolf's world war. Down in the cellar and find two large sacks. We're leaving, my lad!'

'Without sayin' goodbye to the others?' asks Tiny, incomprehendingly.

'We don't *know* 'em any more,' says Porta. 'If they get even a sniff of what we've dropped on we won't be rich for long! Julius'll find it to be Crown property'n get it confiscated. As I said before: Keep your head cold as ice! Our past is dead! Down in the cellar and find two sacks. *Very* big sacks, they'll have to be.'

'I'm gonna shit in Adolf's army trousers before I throw'em away'n change back into civvies,' promises Tiny, and runs off whistling down to the cellar.

'Found anythin'?' shouts Gregor, coming through the window together with Albert and his flashing white teeth.

Porta closes the safe-door quickly and moves to block their view of the broken door into the small room.

'Fuck-all,' he answers, casually, and attempts to look like a fox which has offered to keep an eye on the chickens.

Albert goes into convulsions of laughter at the sight of Porta's corsets with the roses and butterflies.

'What's *that*? Adolf's new secret weapon?' gurgles Gregor, between roars of laughter.

Albert clicks his teeth together sharply, as his eye falls on a large picture of Stalin, hanging above a desk, and looking at him with a wicked expression.

'*Kak wy pashywajetjc, Tovaritch*[10],' he roars, bringing up a clenched fist in front of him, as if he were attempting to placate the harsh Georgian stare.

Tiny returns from the cellar with two large empty sacks under his arm.

'Out on it, you shits,' he shouts, waving the sacks as if he were frightening hens. 'Don't you know it's forbidden to break into private property.'

'What you want sacks for?' asks Gregor, with interest, feeling the texture of the jute.

'We've got orders to black out the windows,' says Porta,

[10]Kak wy etc. (How are things going, Comrade?)

90

hurriedly, before Tiny can make a foolish answer.

'Whadda you think I am? Dumb or somethin'?' whinnies Gregor. 'You lot've found somethin', you have. Don't give *me* a lot of balls! I've been a moving-man. I can smell it a mile off!'

'If you don't shut up an' fuck off out of 'ere, pretty smartish an' takin' that black spook with you, an' leave us to do our bleedin' blackin' out, I'm goin' to do you *up*!' roars Tiny, furiously, beginning to swing his arms about.

'You are *on* to somethin', man!' echoes Albert, gloatingly, jumping up and down on the sofa. He throws a somersault ending in a handstand, and stays balanced, looking interestedly underneath the sofa.

'You're tempting fate, you African creeper,' snarls Porta, furiously taking a kick at a cushion which sends it up into the lamp.

'How true, man, how true!' laughs Albert, pulling out a large oil-can from under the sofa.

'Goin' to grease your goolies, maybe, an' roll 'ome to Africa an' find yourself a bed o' nails?' asks Tiny, madly, launching a kick at Albert, which misses.

'Why not?' grins Albert, taking a drink from the oil-can.

Tiny's head shoots forward like a stork going for a frog. He sniffs at the oil-can.

'Merry Christmas to all! Plum schnapps!' he shouts, tearing the oil-can from Albert's hand.

'Give me a taste,' demands Porta, grabbing the can.

'Alarm! Alarm!' The shout rings out from outside the house.

A machine-gun chatters angrily. Mortars plop away in the night. An Obergefreiter of tanks crawls up on a chair and takes hold of the picture of Stalin.

'Uncle Joe'll make a nice souvenir! This ought to look great over the family sofa back in Cologne when the war's over!'

'Don't *touch* him!' screams Gregor, in terror, throwing himself flat on the floor.

Albert is behind the sofa in one long leap, like a black cat in flight from an Alsatian. Porta is down behind an overstuffed armchair, together with Tiny, who has hidden his head like a stork. The cherry-decorated hat flaps through the air like a wounded bird.

In a fraction of a second Gregor has seen the thin black thread which runs from the picture and through a hole in the wallpaper.

The explosion breaks up the entire house. A towering pillar of flame shoots up towards the sky. The entire roof seems to balance on the tip of the flame. It is like the end of the world. Explosions come one after the other along the whole length of the street. Houses collapse as if made of cardboard. The dark heavens light up blindingly. It is as clear as day. The blast wave thunders down the street like a tornado, sweeping away everything in its path. A lorry rolls along, over and over as if it were a toy. Out through the remains of the wall comes the sofa, with Albert howling, and hanging on to it for dear life. It crashes into the wall of a house, on the other side of the road, with a nasty, splintering sound.

Albert screams like a pig on the way to the slaughterhouse. Head over heels he goes, down a narrow path, his arms and legs wind-milling wildly. His breakneck flight takes him right down to a frozen pool where Gregor has already landed.

'Jesus, man!' he chatters. 'That was enough to knock the stuffin' out of a grizzly bear!'

All around, wounded and dying men are screaming for help. Pillars of fire throw a purple glare over the boiling, filthy snow. It is like a volcanic eruption, which seems to go on and on for an eternity.

It stops!

Those who are still alive struggle to their feet. They are in a state of shock and literally stone deaf. Their ears hurt. It is as if a red-hot needle is being pushed into them.

For some minutes we are unable to understand what is happening around us. We are in a state of acute insanity. Bloody shreds of meat and splinters of bone are everywhere. Even the trees which lined the village street on both sides, have disappeared without trace. Torn up by the roots. Russians and Germans, civilians and military, are running around in circles. In senseless panic.

A Russian sergeant, in a tattered soot-blackened uniform, empties his Kalashnikov straight up into the air, throws it from him and roars '*Job Tvojemadj*'[11]. He breaks the neck of a fat Feldwebel who is taking a kick at him, with a chop of the edge of his hand.

A motorcycle and sidecar, with machine-guns and ammunition bags, is twisted around the remains of a chimney. The bloody remains of a human being hang from the sidecar.

Albert has run amok. He crawls round in circles howling like a mad dog. He returns to normal only when Porta hands him his steel helmet. The whole of the neck protector has been torn away. Albert looks at the ruined helmet for a moment uncomprehendingly. He runs a hand over his head as if to assure himself that it is still there. He looks up at the sad, black sky, and thanks God and all the known and unknown saints. Some of them he invents for the occasion. He takes the helmet with him and shows it to everybody as a proof that God is specially protecting him.

'It's because us blacks have nothing to do with this war,' he asserts. 'It's a war for the whites and the yellows.'

'What a mess! And all for the sake of a picture,' sighs Porta, staring at the remains of the mayor's house.

Oberst Hinka takes Porta to one side, when he sees the colourful corsets. Porta has forgotten he has them on.

'Where did you get those?' he asks, severely.

'Found 'em, sir!' answers Porta, which is true enough.

'*Where* did you find them? Come on! The truth now!' Hinka's eyes bore into him. 'Which house?'

Porta twists and turns. He tries to talk himself out of it with one of his usual stories. Something about a hairdressers shop in Düsseldorf whose owner always wore corsets.

'To the devil with your hairdresser friends,' Hinka cuts him off, brusquely. 'You can't pull the wool over my eyes, Porta. I thought you'd have learned that by now. What happened in that house to start the explosion?'

'Oh yes, sir! I see, sir, that's what you want to know.' Porta

[11]Job Tvojemadj!: Go home and fuck your mother.

93

smiles, falsely. 'It was one of these motorcycle fellows, sir, who was hot on a picture of Stalin, and wanted to take it with him. Nice picture it was too, sir. We warned him, sir, the motorcyclist that is, not Stalin, sir!' Porta throws his arms out in the direction of the blown up village. 'There was something fishy about that picture, sir. You can see for yourself, sir!'

'Would you recognise this motorcyclist again?' asks Hinka, distrustfully.

'He'll be gone, sir. *Totally* gone, I'm sure, sir. Might even be the rest of him hangin' up on that tileworks chimney over there! The German God is quick to punish disobedience, isn't he sir?' he adds, thoughtfully.

'Did you *see* him killed?' Hinka questions him, sharply. 'If he is still alive, I want him to find out how I punish disobedience!'

'He would deserve it too, sir!' admits Porta, sighing deeply. 'We could all of us have been blown to bits, just because one drunk couldn't leave a bit of loot alone!'

'Be careful, Porta, that you don't start growing white wings. I asked you: *Did* you see him killed?'

'Unfortunately I did not, sir. The house fell on me!'

'Who was in there with you?'

'Nobody at all, sir. I was all alone in there. Apart from the looter, sir!'

'Then you threw those pantaloons and that brassiere out of the window to Obergefreiter Creutzfeldt?' He points at Tiny, who is standing open-mouthed, with his eyes rolling around in his head, still in a state of shock from the explosion.

'Come here, Creutzfeldt!' shouts Hinka, angrily.

Tiny does not react at all. He is still stone-deaf.

'Shot his hearing aids out, sir, I'd think!' opines Porta, sagely. 'Beg to report, sir, I couldn't hear at first, but soon as I stood on my head it came back again, and now I can hear again sir, thank the good Lord. I can hear everything Oberst Hinka is saying to me, sir.'

'Get those silly corsets off,' orders Hinka, sharply. 'And I warn you, Porta. My patience is not endless! Go too far and

I'll find you a cell *some*where.'

'Yes, sir, there's always a cell free in Germersheim I suppose, sir,' says Porta, quietly, trying to look down-hearted.

'Someday I'll shoot you,' promises Hinka, turning on his heel.

'We move off in one hour,' says the Old Man. He has been at a section leader meeting with the O.C. 'What the devil are you wearing?' he snarls sourly, when he sees Porta and Tiny in their corsets and pantalettes. 'I won't have you silly sods looking like that! What the hell will the Russians think?'

'They'll forget to shoot at us,' says Porta, 'which might be a good thing, come to think of it!'

A wall of fire dances in the distance. A huge, black cloud of smoke can be seen against the flames. Thermic whirlwinds carry a thick rain of ash down on us. The ground trembles like an animal in its death throes.

Tiny appears through the thick rain of ashes, tall and broad, a living machine of muscles and sinews. His fat cigar juts out of his soot-smeared face like a glowing bowsprit. He is still wearing the old-fashioned pantalettes, and curses the schoolteacher and the ex-Oberst incessantly. They come puffing after him with the flame-thrower tank and the ammunition boxes.

The air is filled with bubbling, rasping noises. The soggy sound of a mortar shell sends the ex-Oberst into cover.

'The devil take you, you silly man,' roars Tiny. 'Didn't I tell you, goat-shit, not to take cover unless I give the order.'

The slobbering sound is there again. Tiny looks up inquisitively and follows the course of the shell with his eyes. It falls into the snow with a nasty sound and throws it up on all sides.

A splinter of shrapnel knocks a hole in one of Tiny's waterbottles. Vodka trickles down his legs.

'Dirty, 'eathen Russian sods,' he rages, pointing his sawn-off shotgun over towards the heights. 'What kind of trick's that? What's that got to do with a war?'

'Take cover, man!' shouts Leutnant Braun, nervously. 'You'll get yourself killed!'

'Nothing's gonna 'appen to me, sir,' Tiny reassures him, in his deep rusty bass. 'I'm not goin' to let myself get shot before

I've seen New York an' London, an' been on a trip to Africa together with Albert an' try 'avin' a shit on one of them fakir shit'ouses with nails in 'em.'

'No. 2. take the lead!' comes from up front. The order is passed along the company.

Slowly we get to our feet. The Old Man straddles his legs in snow up to his knees. He carries his Mpi on a short strap over his shoulder.

'Get your fingers out! On your feet!' he shouts impatiently. 'Up you get, Tiny! Take the right flank, and the evil one himself help you, if you go into a hut or start pulling gold teeth out of the corpses! You hear me?'

'You're shoutin' loud enough to wake the dead in all the cemeteries in 'Amburg! I wouldn't be surprised if all the corpses are standin' to attention now, shakin' in their bones!' Tiny rumbles, crossly, and gets to his feet slowly and provokingly.

'You sour?' asks Porta. 'You look as if you were being bitten to death by communist lice!'

'It's that bollockless Oberst, as irritates me,' says Tiny, darkly. 'A brainless shit 'e is, with no more between 'is ears than a recruit, which is to say fuck-all!'

'I won't take any more of your insults,' cackles the former officer. He tries to make his voice sharp and commanding, as it used to be when he stood in front of a regiment. Without succeeding.

'Too bad for you, you featherless budgie you,' grins Tiny, jeeringly, smacking the ex-Oberst with the back of his hand. "Cos you're goin' to 'ave to, ain't you? Got that through your bleedin' cranium? Or would you like a nice little run to liven you up a bit? Understand once and for all, you burnt out shootin' star you, you're the arse'ole o' the bleedin' Germany Army, you are. An' me? Me I'm an Obergefreiter, the backbone o' the Army! The top part, of course!'

'Do they really want us to sprint up to that fuckin' prison?' asks Porta, straightening the garter tabs on the red corsets, which are flapping against his legs.

'Want to or not, there's where we've got to go,' answers the

96

Old Man, shortly, sending a long spurt of tobacco juice into the snow.

'This lousy world war's turned everything upside down,' grumbles Porta, pessimistically, and cadges a cigarette from the Legionnaire. 'When are you going to stop smoking this black French shit you're fucking up your lungs with?'

'*Pas question, mon ami*! These cigarettes have at least the built-in advantage of my being able to keep most of them for myself,' answers the Legionnaire. 'Your pale-coloured rubbish is only for young girls not yet past their confirmation.'

'I'm getting mad enough to crack Brazil nuts with the cheeks of my arse, and spit the kernels out fast as a mortar can spit out shells,' Porta raves. He stares up at the OGPU prison, its walls illumined by the wildly dancing flames from the burning conifer forest.

'Here we're going to climb *up* hills and *down* hills, slide over frozen lakes till all the skin's worn off our arses, force our way through frozen forests like some kind of bloody bulldozers, and all just to get to that Communist fucking prison. I'm used to getting driven to prison sitting on my arse! If this ain't a case of *Human Rights*, which ought to go in front of an international court as a matter of urgency, then I'm as dumb as a lame duck from Holland.'

'It ought to be forbidden to put normal people through all this shit, just because a few twits don't know how to avoid starting a world war!' shouts Gregor, angrily.

A motorised sleigh comes rushing along in a cloud of snow. An Oberstleutnant of the General Staff shouts hysterically for the O.C.

The Old Man points over his shoulder in the direction of Oberleutnant Löwe, who is sitting on a barrel, scratching a cat behind the ears.

'Know how to stand to attention, man?' roars the Staff officer, ragingly.

The Old Man puts his heels together slowly and touches his helmet with his hand in the semblance of a salute.

'Oberleutnant Löwe, O.C. No. 5. Company, 27 Panzer Regiment, reporting, sir!' comes in a weary bark from Löwe.

'What in the name of all the hells are you sitting here picking your noses for?' screams the Oberstleutnant with the blood-red staff tabs. 'Haven't you received the order to attack? No stopping, even for a moment! Atta-a-a-ack, man!'

The echoes of 'Atta-a-a-ack!' come back sneeringly.

'Oberstleutnant, *sir!*' answers Löwe, saluting smartly, while secretly wishing the screaming Oberstleutnant into the farthest depths of hell.

Staggering like drunks, we stumble through the dense conifer forest and on into the pitch-black dark. We trip over frost-dried branches. Our faces are slashed and torn.

Suddenly a Russian Maxim hammers from the undergrowth.

Like lightning Porta throws a hand grenade and follows it up with a rain of bullets.

A Russian soldier is thrown into the air, his long cloak flapping like wings.

The machine-gun hammers again.

'Bleedin' 'ell!' shouts Tiny, and turns the flame-thrower onto the bushes. A roaring stream of ruddy fire blazes across the snow. Trees burst into flame. The machine-gun stops!

The Russians lie in a heap, their bodies, still on fire, blackening slowly, like a roast too long in the oven.

'Lucky you never know what's coming till it hits you,' sighs Barcelona, watching a Russian whose hair is on fire. 'An old soldier that one. Otherwise they wouldn't let him wear his hair long.'

'Get on, get on!' orders the Old Man, running heavily past us.

We catch sight of a Russian group, attempting to get away. One of them trips over a fallen tree, and slides a long way across a frozen stream.

'Get 'em!' shouts Heide, eagerly, bringing up the LMG he carries slung across his shoulder. His whole body shakes, as he sends a long, stuttering salvo after the flying enemy group.

Three of them are killed, shot in the back and their chests blown out. We are using a new kind of bullet. Rough stuff, which makes only a tiny entrance hole, but leaves a huge, gaping hole on its way out. Some of the wounded lie screaming heart-breakingly in the snow.

Tiny kills four survivors with the sawn-off shotgun. A terrible weapon at short range.

An old second lieutenant in militia uniform stands up against a tree with his hands folded behind his neck. He watches us with glaring, terrified eyes, as we go towards him slowly.

'A commissar,' says Heide, with a satanic smile.

'*He's* no bloody commissar,' answers Barcelona. 'He's no more'n a poor piss-scared bastard. A shakin' old bag of bones in an old-fashioned uniform. Let the poor buggar sod off back to his grandchildren!'

'You out of your mind?' asks Heide in angry protest. 'This pig's a Soviet officer, and we *kill* Soviet officers. By order of the Führer!' He lifts his Mpi and shoots the second lieutnant in the chest and head.

The head splits open. He puts a couple of shots into the stomach for good measure. 'That's that, then!' he declares proudly, slinging his weapon on to his shoulder.

A wounded infantryman gets half up, supporting himself on one knee.

'*Njet sstrjeljatj, njet sstrjeljatj, tovaritch germanski,*' he begs, desperately.

In the person of the Legionnaire, his German comrade pushes a bayonet through his back. The point comes out of the Russian at the front. Quietly the Legionnaire twists the bayonet out of the body. It falls forward into the attitude of a praying Musselman.

A Russian warrant officer pulls back his arm to throw a grenade.

Albert smashes his face with a butt-stroke. We kill the others from a distance, as we sight them. We do not go near them until we are sure they are dead, and then carefully. We bayonet them before going over them.

Their pockets are full of *machorka,* and they have vodka in their water-bottles. It is poor quality stuff — other ranks vodka. From bitter experience we know it gives us a thundering headache, and we graciously give it to the new men. Porta will provide, where we are concerned.

We go through their pocketbooks with interest. We take the snapshots of their girl-friends, and throw the rest away. The few roubles they have are of no interest to us.

Tiny is very taken by a photograph he finds in the wallet of the warrant officer whose face Albert smashed in.

' 'Oly Emma, *what* a lovely bint,' he groans, wiping a little blood carefully from the photograph. 'When you see a Russian bleedin' rose like this,' he goes on, winking invitingly at the girl in the snapshot, 'you realise that our lot's Maker must've been in a bad mood the day 'e made the standard German model, with 'er 'air in a bun, an' even the 'airs of 'er cunt tied in bleedin' braids!'

'Wow!' cries Porta, admiringly, looking over Tiny's shoulder.

'Want to swop? Three of mine for her? What a piece of crumpet! Holy Mother of Kazan!'

'Sod off, she's mine!' Tiny growls. 'The dead 'un put 'er address on the back. When Adolf's war's over I'm takin' a round trip ticket and bringin' 'er back to good old 'Amburg, I am!'

'You *must* have shit between your ears!' laughs Porta, jeeringly. 'She won't have anything to do with you, when she finds out you've knocked off her Commie boy-friend!'

'I know you think I'm some kinda nut,' says Tiny, sourly, 'but nutty enough to tell the bint that it was me as blew the other sod's bonce off I am *not*! No, no, no, *I* shall tell the little dear 'ow, with danger to me own life, I carries 'er 'alf-arsed friend on me back for twenty kilometres to get 'im to the care of the good German doctors. It'll be a lovely story, it will, just like you see at the pictures. The fact of 'er poor 'ero lover dyin', I shall lay at the door of natural causes.'

'She won't give you a tumble,' decides Porta, shaking his head sadly. 'The map of the world'll be very different when Adolf's lost this war, and the German Wehrmacht has been disarmed. It'll be no fun being German. Count on it! Anybody who feels like it'll be able to kick us up the arse, an' knock us off sharpish if we try to kick 'em back!'

'Come on, come on,' shouts Oberleutnant Löwe, impatiently. 'Forward! Forward! Get a *move* on! You scoundrels are always finding places to piss it off in! Get moving and let's get the job over with! It's *got* to be done! Oberfeldwebel Beier! Take the lead with No. 2! Scouts in advance and on both flanks.'

'Always bloody us!' grumbles Porta, viciously, kicking out at an empty Russian waterbottle. 'We get *all* the shit jobs going in this rotten army! Oh, if I was at home havin' it good in Berlin, they could fuck around here for thirty years if they wanted to!' He jams shells violently into his sawn-off shotgun, and peers testingly along the barrel. 'Come on then, for Christ's sake, let's go look for that shit of a neighbour and blow his godless, Commie, bloody head off!'

The moment the company leaves the forest we hear the hateful slobbering sound of mortars again. Followed by thunderous explosions. There is no weapon we like less than the trench mortar. It is treacherous, and gives only a short warning before the projectile reaches you, explodes in front of you. No long, warning scream like shells. Another thing we don't like is the Russian mortar crews! They are almost always women. Coarse, heavily-built peasant types.

Late one night we stormed a heavy mortar company of women. They tried to get away into the forest, and hid behind trees and bushes, but we found them one by one and killed them like rats, despite their tears and screams. The few men in the company we took prisoner. They confirmed what we already knew. These women were fanatics, and treated prisoners in horrible fashion.

'Kill the bitches!' said a captured Russian sergeant, with a satisfied grin, kicking at one of the female corpses. He could say what he liked now. *His* war was over!

One of the new men, a big lad from Barcelona's squad, has had his entire face shot off. A piece of shrapnel has cut away everything. Lips, nose, eyes and forehead are gone. Only white bone is left. His bubbling screams can be heard far and wide. He is driving us crazy.

We stand in a shivering, uneasy ring around him, watching Sani-Gefreiter Rolfe attempting to dress the wound. He is shaking his head despondently.

'Shrapnel can really do the job,' says Tiny, quietly. 'It's faster'n 'im as used to murder the pro's in Düsseldorf!'

'If he gets away with his life, and they patch his face up somehow, he ain't gonna be pretty,' remarks Gregor, thoughtfully. 'Frighten kids to death, he will!'

The horizon changes colour to a rich, rosy yellow. There is a rumbling and roaring from beyond the heights. A regiment of siege artillery takes up position along the frozen river. Two companies of assault troops join us. They stink of spit-and-polish. Steel helmets painted white, and chinstraps regimentally positioned. Belt, knapsack, gasmask. All there. Even gas-capes correctly folded. We threw ours away long ago. Their greatcoats are so neat they could go on parade with them at the Brandenburger Tor.

We watch them sneeringly, but we are also a little envious. They have everything we are short of. 27. Panzer Regiment is a poorhouse compared to them. We don't even have tanks, even though we are supposed to be a tank regiment.

'Jesus, you lot are *pretty*!' cries Porta, touching a well-polished belt. 'Brother Ivan, that old highwayman, why, you'll frighten him to death!'

'Where's the band, then?' asks Gregor. '*You* know! The old tum-ta-ta-tum boys with the drums and the fifes. Can't march against the neighbours without *them*!'

'You look like a load of tramps,' says a Feldwebel, staring contemptuously at Porta's tattered, grimy battle-camouflaged uniform.

'Just what we *are*, too, Feldwebel, sir!' grins Porta. Arrogantly he screws his cracked monocle into his eye and looks condescendingly at the Guards Feldwebel.

'What kind of a gang are *you*?' trumpets an Oberfähnrich. 'Makes you think of jailbirds just to look at you!'

'*Gang*?' snarls the Old Man, slitting his eyes and rolling his tongue round the word. 'Let me tell you, Mr. Oberfähnrich, we were fightin' before you an' your Guards Association was set up, and we've lost more men already'n your Division'd be able to lose in the whole war!'

'Yes, you do look a little burnt-out,' laughs the Oberfähnrich, acidly. He puts his fieldglasses to his eyes nonchalantly, and explores the heights. 'That the little jail up there, we've got to help you lads with? We'll fix that, while you're taking a little nap to rest your tired old bones,' he says, cheerily, taking down the glasses.

'Really?' answers the Old Man, coldly. 'Up to now that "little jail", as you call it, has cost us buckets of blood.'

'What you're in need of is backbone and the will to win,' declares a youthful Unteroffizier proudly. He stinks of Valhalla and Hitler quotations. 'What the Führer orders, the German soldier executes. These Russian *untermensch* will not stop us!'

'*Bien sur que si, sergent!*' says the Legionnaire, sarcastically, his eternal cigarette bobbing up and down between his thin lips as he speaks.

'Everybody talks about the front line,' the Unteroffizier continues gruffly. 'It has nothing to do with the question. What *makes* a soldier is iron-hard garrison service, so that the front line seems like a rest-home by comparison. What we've seen of your front line so far, is laughable to us!'

'You've weakened your brain, with wankin' too much,' shouts Porta, with a scream of laughter. 'You'll shit the creases out of your pants, when Ivan starts playing on his old machine-balalaika.'

'Before nightfall you'll be promising God you'll go to church regularly for the rest of your life,' whinnies Gregor, delightedly.

'Rubbish,' says the Unteroffizier, indignantly. 'I don't believe in any kind of God!'

'A lot of people do not believe, when they get here, *mon ami*,' considers the Legionnaire, comfortably. 'But when they are lying out under an artillery barrage, it is quite surprising to see how God-fearing they become! The most fanatical atheists become more holy than Jehovah's Witnesses themselves, and call upon Allah!'

'You'll see different,' declares the Unteroffizier in a voice of ice. 'The job you chaps've been pissing about with out here for a week, we'll have finished in a couple of hours!'

'We'll see, we'll see!' says the Old Man, with a sarcastic smile. 'I'd very much like to see you fix that prison up there in just a couple of hours. Save *us* the job!'

A rain of bullets sweeps along the snowy wall, spraying earth and ice splinters over us.

The Oberfähnrich drops like lightning, quite in accordance with regulations. Heels and boot-tips to the ground. Cautiously he peers over the edge of the cover.

'Keep *down*!' shouts the Old Man, warningly. The warning comes too late. The Oberfähnrich's head explodes like an overripe tomato, splashing those of us closest to him.

'Fuckin' stupid regulations twit.' Porta curses, wiping blood and splinters of bone from his face. 'Coming here and shittin' us up with his goddam filthy guts!'

The air fills with the slobber of several mortars. Snow goes up like a roller blind turning backwards.

Mortar bombs fall in a heavy rain, and a couple of low-trajectory guns put shells in amongst us. In a moment of time the terrain has become like a raging sea filled with all kinds of wreckage.

The heroism slowly evaporates from the Gross Deutschland Regiment. Even the Leutnant with the thin lips and the beautiful tailor-made uniform looks frightened.

'Down, damn you!' warns the Old Man, gruffly.

Despite his fear the Leutnant notices that the Old Man has not given him his service rank. He opens his tiny, cruel mouth to say something. But before he can get out a word a short MG salvo catches him, and throws him backwards against the snow wall. He falls forward again face-first splintering the ice underfoot. His legs jerk spasmodically. He lies quite still!

'*Come death . . . come. . . .*,' hums the little Legionnaire, softly.

Two Panther tanks appear out of the snow. Rattling and roaring they press past us. The enormous gun sticks threateningly from each turret like a giant index finger.

'Forward!' shouts Löwe, pushing his clenched fist into the air. '5. Company follow me!'

We run heavily forward through the deep snow staying close behind the tanks. When they stop to fire we throw ourselves down to regain our breath.

104

A party of Russians edge their way out from a smoke-blackened ruin.

A couple of Mpi's chatter, and they go down with looks of surprise on their faces.

'Half-trained!' mumbles Heide, contemptuously, kicking at the bodies. In his opinion everybody who is not a hundred per cent soldier is rubbish. Pity is, to him, the sign of the slave mentality.

A row of heavy lorries, painted with large cyrillic characters, is standing close to a *kolchos*. Potato masher grenades whirl through the air. The supply corps soldiers who have been snoozing in their driving-cabins fall out head over heels. Some are killed by the fall. It is all over so quickly that we hardly realise what has happened.

Rapidly we go over the bodies, taking what we have a use for. We are ransacking the lorries when a tiny figure in a general's uniform suddenly appears amongst us. Brusque, sharp orders crack out like machine-gun salvoes.

Oberleutnant Löwe is standing to attention, with his hand at the brim of his helmet.

'Yes sir, General sir. Yes sir!' is all he is able to stammer.

There is hardly anything else *to* say, when you are in the presence of General Baron von Mannteufel, the feared commander of Panzer Grenadier Division Gross Deutschland. This is the first time we have seen him, but we have heard of him, and that is more than enough. Even Porta and Tiny disappear silently behind one of the Russian lorries.

'To my knowledge no order has been given to stop here? Or am I mistaken?' trumpets the slim little general with the ice-cold eyes. 'We are attacking the OGPU prison, gentlemen. Look around you and you will soon realise that the prison is not *here*, but still over *there*, on height 347. Stop once more without permission and I will see to it that you go in front of a field court-martial!'

Before Löwe can open his mouth to reply the little general is gone, together with his grinning adjutant.

'Shit and corruption,' says Tiny, disappointedly, letting a single gold tooth plump into his bag. 'They've gotta be piss-poor in the Soviet. Almost all o' them's got steel in 'is bleedin' choppers 'stead of gold. Takin' the piss out of a poor German liberator, that's what *this* is!'

For the next few hours the company pushes on through the snow with the strength of despair. Sweat pours out of us as we cut our way through crackling, frost-dry undergrowth. I feel, more than see, a Russian patrol, and shoot on the fall. My burst hits a Russian officer in the mouth, and he goes down with a shattered face.

Porta sends off a long, vicious hail of bullets which lift the Russians closest to us into the air and throw them backwards like ninepins.

'Hell, man!' howls Albert, rolling suddenly sideways in a flurry of snow. As he rolls he throws two hand-grenades, which blows three Russians to bloody rags. With a sigh he catches his breath, and wipes his face with a handful of snow. 'Are you *crazy*, man?' he stammers, grey-faced with fear.

'Tea rooms straight ahead,' screams Heide, hysterically, diving almost head-first into a fallen-in trench.

'Idiot!' snarls Porta, and ties a bundle of grenades to a petrol can.

'Gimme *that*!' hisses Tiny, ripe for destruction. He tears the bundle from Porta's hands before the latter has time to protest.

With cat-like agility and speed Tiny moves towards the T-34. Quicker than it can be told he is up on the tank, both turret trapdoors of which have been carelessly left open. Small muzzle-flames spit from the forward MG. With a practised hand he slings the bundle of grenades down through one of the open trapdoors. Laughing crazily, he springs down from the tank and rolls to cover behind a large rock.

The T-34 goes up with an ear-splitting roar. Its reserve ammunition adding to the force of the explosion. We can feel the crushing pressure of the blast all over our bodies.

A Maxim barks viciously from the forest.

Leutnant Müller from No. 1 Platoon gives out an echoing scream. The first MG salvo has broken his back. He rolls around like a living rag-doll, his entrails falling out into the snow.

106

We take the flamethrower to them, and clear out the position.

We are out on the storm-whipped steppe again. Tired almost to death, we dig in, to await the artillery barrage which is to clear a path for us on the far bank of the frozen river. The motorcycle regiment has already been smashed crossing the river. Many of them drowned, as Russian mortar fire smashed the yard-thick ice to pieces. The ones who did not drown were crushed by the ice floes grinding violently together and sliding up and over one another like cliffs of ice. The noise of them is like thunder.

Porta spreads out his green cloth on the snow, and throws a few trial passes with the dice.

'Come on, you icebound birds of passage,' he challenges. 'Let's shoot craps. You take the luck! I'll take the winnings!'

Shiveringly we crawl down into a snow-hole together, and soon forget the cold in the lure of the dice dancing over the green cloth. We lose our shirts.

Gregor Martin is the first to go broke, but he doesn't lose hope and borrows a large amount from Porta at the 80% other ranks rate.

Heide is cleaned out. Shortly after that Barcelona goes. Albert refuses to believe he has gone broke. As a black amongst so many whites he cannot be unlucky, he feels. He tells us again it was his father who played the drum in the hussars.

'If you can find anything at all in those vacuum-cleaned pockets of yours I'll give you double,' promises Porta, in comradely fashion.

'If not, then we'll lend you!' offers Tiny, who is Porta's treasurer.

Albert nods, with a sad, lost look on his black features.

'But don't you forget what whites do to people as don't pay their debts of honour,' growls Tiny, threateningly, as he hands a bundle of notes to Albert.

'Hell, it's *cold*!' moans Gregor, blowing his breath up over his face. Tiny icicles are hanging from his eyebrows.

In the distance wolves can be heard howling against the icy wind, which blows in sharp blasts across the steppe.

'Too goddam right it's cold!' says the Old Man, making his point. 'But what the hell else can you expect on a winter's night in Russia?'

'*Merde aux yeux*,' mutters the Legionnaire, slapping his hands together.

'Section leaders to O.C.!' The shout passes from dugout to dugout.

'May Satan himself run up and down their throats with a roll o' barbed wire on his back!' the Old Man curses, viciously. 'A winnin' streak at last and the goddam Army sods it all up for the poor bugger of a section leader!'

'*C'est la guerre, mon ami*!' says the Legionnaire, and takes a puff at his eternal cigarette.

The spasmodic blasts of icy wind steady, and turn into one of the feared Russian snow storms. Even the wolves take cover. But for us there *is* no cover. The attack continues in the face of the storm. The wind is strong enough to push a cow along over the steppe.

The Old Man comes struggling back, on the lee side of the high snow drifts.

'On your feet, you lazy sods! Fingers out!' he shouts, while still some distance off.

Grumbling, we pick up our gear.

'Who's up front?' asks Barcelona, angrily, and takes a long, gurgling drink from the vodka can.

'114th,' answers the Old Man, slowly lighting his silver-lidded pipe.

'Let's take it easy then,' suggests Porta. 'Leave it to the foot-sloggers to cut us a path. We'll take pace from them. Cuts the danger by 50%!'

Tiny breaks open the triple-barrelled shotgun, loads for bear, and snaps the breech closed.

'Let's get on with it an' pull chum Ivan's arse'ole up over 'is ears so's we can 'ave a little peace around 'ere,' he snarls, wickedly. He moves off at a jog after the Old Man who is carrying his gun under his arm like a man on his way to a day's hunting.

The company has been issued with some strange-looking

harpoon guns, which shoot scaling ropes up the sides of cliffs.

'Monkeys on a bloody stick, that's us,' grumbles Porta, as he begins to climb up the icy rope.

One of the new men slides back down the rope, his body spinning. He almost takes me with him. In panic he lets go of the rope and winds his arms round my neck.

'Let go you fucking madman,' I scream, fearfully, and feel my hands beginning to lose their grip on the rope.

'Bite his fingers off!' shouts Porta, who is swinging on a rope alongside me.

Desperately I follow his advice and sink my teeth into the man's hands. To the bone. With a cutting scream he lets go, and whirls away down the cliff-side in a cloud of snow. He hangs for a moment on a ledge of ice, and then goes sliding on down into the depths.

At last we reach the top, and hang on for dear life with hands and feet.

A can-opener of a flare cuts the lid off the pitch-black night. In the harsh glare a village appears, as if it had jumped up out of the snow.

In short rushes we work our way in on the village. I kick open a door with my assault rifle at the ready.

A Russian officer stands up with a look of absolute astonishment on his face.

'*Germanski*!' he almost manages to shout. But gets no further than 'Ger. . .'. My explosive bullet catches him in the mouth and pushes the rest of the word back into his throat. Head and neck are blown open, the contents spattering a colourful poster showing happy bathers on the Crimean beaches. In all its horror the sight is almost comical. His body shakes, and takes two steps towards me. I fire again. The rest of the clip takes him in the middle, and slams him up into the air, where he seems to hang for a second as if he intended to throw a backward somersault. His arms are stretched out on both sides. In one hand he still holds his cap with its gold cockade and hammer and sickle emblem. His back arches violently, and blood pours out of him. With a crash he goes to the floor. A

109

bookcase is knocked over, and a rain of small trinkets comes down on the body.

A lieutenant and two NCO's come rushing out of an adjoining room. As they come an Mpi goes off beside me. A long, wicked burst.

The three Russians are thrown back against the door-jamb, and collapse like punctured balloons.

'Hey, man!' cries Albert, patting his Mpi. 'These good ol' machine-guitars do make a man feel big an' strong!'

'What the hell're you standin' there daydreamin' about?' shouts the Old Man, sticking his head in at the door. 'Get on! Get on! Speed it up! You'll have time enough to study corpses when you're lyin' in a mass-grave!'

It seems as if thousands of machine-guns are aimed at us. An umbrella of tracer tracks criss-crosses the narrow streets of the village. Muzzle-flashes come from every door and window. Hand grenades whirl through the air and explode with a sharp crack. Every bit of cover, however small, contains a Red Army soldier ready to fight on with fanatical contempt for death.

Tiny gives a high scream and stumbles, bleeding, against a wall.

'Tiny!' I shout, fearfully, throwing myself down alongside him.

He opens his eyes and looks at me confusedly.

Porta appears, on the run, from the opposite side, closely followed by Gregor. Gregor has a Russian medical bag in his hand.

'Are you dead?' asks Porta, putting his face close to Tiny's.

'No!' answers Tiny. 'The bleedin' 'eathen's shot me in the throat.'

'I'll be damned!' cries Porta, in amazement, after he has cut open Tiny's uniform collar.

'I can see daylight through you! Never seen anything *like* it! *Look!*' he points at the entrance hole. 'The bloody bullet's gone clean through him. Ought to have taken his bloody bonce off!'

'That came close to making a hurdy-gurdy man out of you,' says Gregor, pressing a dressing over the exit hole. 'Holy Agnes, but you're lucky! Just the tiniest bit higher and the atheists'd have emptied your skull for you.'

'Can you drink anything?' asks Porta, worriedly, handing him the big 5-litre waterbottle, which is filled with vodka.

'Don't ask silly questions,' says Tiny, with difficulty. He takes the waterbottle, and half empties it in exactly 21 seconds flat.

'Must be running out of the holes and getting soaked up by the dressings,' says Porta, in wonder. 'No normal person could drink that much vodka that fast.'

'*And* it went down good,' Tiny exhales contentedly. 'Made a new man of me, that little sip did! Let's 'ave the bottle! The new man'd like a drop of that 'eroes water too!'

'Well, *would* you believe it?' cries Porta, shaking the empty waterbottle.

A new slobbering fills the air, and a rain of mortar shells falls with a grating crash on the village. Fires spring up. Countless thatched cottages begin to flame.

'Let's get outa this before the neighbours begin shootin' our ears off!' says Gregor.

''Ang on a mo',' grins Tiny, gripping his three-barrelled sawn-off shotgun. 'Let me just try out this old cannon'n see what way she shoots. Maybe we can find the sod as shot a bleedin' 'ole in me!'

The whole of that night and the next day we battle our way through all kinds of devilishness. After three days we have moved forward a hundred yards. No more. Every time we try to make ourselves a little comfortable in some cover we have taken, the Russians counter-attack, more fiercely than we have ever seen them do before, and throw us back again. We go through a hell of close combat during the next few days. When we withdraw a little, for a rest, Albert is the only one of us still unwounded.

'How *do* you do it?' asks Porta, in amazement, pulling the large bandage wound round his head to a more insovciant angle.

'Bullets don't know where I'm to be found, man. 'Cause I'm *black*, don't you see!' Albert flashes his pearly teeth and rolls his eyes whitely. 'They go *round* me, an' then they just bores their little old road into you white arseholes! I tell you it's a big, big advantage bein' black in this white man's world war!'

111

That the Führer escaped from this base attempt on his life is a fiery sign from God that Adolf Hitler is our provider, who has been chosen to carry out great designs, and that no power on earth can stop his march along the predestined path which leads to the final German Victory.

'Völkischer Beobachter' 21. July, 1944.

'We have no winter equipment,' says Field Quartermaster Bauer. 'The Führer has assured the leaders of the Army that there will be no more winter campaigns, and that there is, therefore, no need for winter equipment.'

'Are you trying to make a fool of me, or what?' Oberst Hinka roars. 'We are at the beginning of November! Fourteen days ago we got the first snows. If they continue we'll be up to our necks in snow within a week!'

'The Führer's orders are that no winter equipment of any kind is to be issued. There will be no more winter campaigns.' The Field Quartermaster smiles, resignedly.

'Are you mad?' rumbles Hinka. 'Many of my men have no greatcoats, and we are short of other things, ammunition issues are at lowest level. We need winter oil, both for our vehicles and our weapons!'

'I am sorry, Herr Oberst,' replies the Field Quartermaster, shrugging his shoulders regretfully. 'I have received no winter equipment for the Army Group whatsoever. My last consignment consisted of fatigue jackets, motor goggles and contraceptives.'

'You must be mad!' Oberst Hinka rages. 'Fatigues and contraceptives! What the hell can we use those things for?'

'Come and see for yourself, Oberst Hinka. The whole consignment's still at the rail receiving point. I've signed for it, yes! But what am I to do with mountains of fatigues and millions of french letters? I don't know! I ordered what was needed! Winter oil! Furs! What have you? I've received none of the things I asked for. Führer's orders, Oberst Hinka!'

'What are we supposed to do with condoms? Pull 'em down over the Russkis' heads and suffocate 'em?' roars Hinka. It

112

almost seems as if he is about to throw himself at the Field Quartermaster.

That night German soldiers of 4th Panzer Army began to strip Russian dead of their winter equipment.

3
Fire Controller

Generalleutnant von der Hecht, Divisional Commander, screws his monocle more tightly into his eye and bends over the charts spread out over the roughly-made table. The Division's regimental commanders and staff officers are assembled in the small, low-ceilinged room.

The lanky, hard-looking Chief of Staff, Oberst von Balk, explains brusquely why one attack on the heights after another has failed.

'Nothing but excuses! Always excuses!' he snarls, angrily. He strikes the charts with his pointer. 'The truth of it is that the men have no guts, and the junior officers are spineless. *That's* got to be *changed*! No more velvet gloves! Bring on the iron hand! The smallest sign of cowardice — *or* dodging — will be punished out of hand! Mobile court-martials will be established, with summary powers! Discipline *will* be re-established! We have been attacking the sanatorium on 409, and the long mill on the far side of it, for three weeks now. The goal is the OGPU prison! Where are we? Still at the sanatorium and the mill! *And* the enemy is re-taking ground almost as soon as we have taken it!'

'Führer HQ has given Army Corps three days for this job. Here. . . .' he hammers his pointer down on a red-ringed spot on the chart, '. . . is the gate to the sanatorium and the mill! Through there and we can soon take the heights; and after that it's only a stone's throw to that long hill-top where the prison stands. Get *there*, and it's a short stroll to the Dnieper!'

'*We* are going to be the first division to reach the Dnieper!' He stands up straight, and looks at the Divisional Commander.

The General's Knight's Cross with oak leaves glitters in the white light of the carbide lamp.

The General's thin lips achieve a smile. He withdraws a very white handkerchief from his sleeve and pats his high forehead with it. His cold, fishy eyes run assessingly over the assembled officers.

'General, sir!' the infantry commander protests, weakly, 'this is going to cost a lot of lives.'

'*Every* battle costs lives, Oberst,' snarls the General, contemptuously. 'Losses don't count. The bloodiest battles are the ones which are remembered!'

'An attack will be impossible without massive artillery support,' the operations officer puts in, avoiding the General's ice-cold glance.

'Are you telling me something *new*, Oberst?' barks the General, harshly. He fills a glass with cognac, and throws it down his throat in one short movement.

An aide-de-camp fills the glass again, rapidly.

The General straightens his back with a jerk, and throws a wicked glance at the Commander of the Panzer regiment, one-armed Oberst Hinka.

'Your 2nd Battalion made a mess of things, Oberst! How could that kind of thing happen? What a pity Major Blank was killed. He would have made a fine figure at a court-martial!'

'They surprised us, sir!' Hinka defends himself. 'Anybody would have fallen into *that* trap! From only two yards away those buried Russian tanks were completely invisible. The enemy just blew 2nd. Battalion off the face of the earth. Major Blank could not have prevented it!'

'Save your excuses,' the General cuts him off, sharply. 'The remains of your 2nd. Battalion will go in as infantry. Those lazy swine could do with some exercise. All they do is sit warming their backsides inside their tanks!'

'Very good, General,' says Hinka, throwing a hopeless look up at the low ceiling.

With a crash a Rittmeister from the motorcycle regiment falls to the floor. He takes a chair with him.

The General screws his monocle more firmly into his eye and

examines the unconscious form with obvious disgust.

'My DR commander, Rittmeister Opel, sir,' says Oberst-leutnant Winkel, Commander of the 4th Cavalry Regiment.

'Get that weakling out of here,' orders the General sharply. 'Transfer him to an assault regiment immediately!'

'The Rittmeister has not slept for a week, sir!' Oberstleut-nant Winkel attempts to defend his unconscious officer.

The dry little General raises his long horsey face from the charts, and sends the Oberstleutnant a killing look.

'Do you think *I* have slept while my division has been attempting to take that bloody prison?' he hisses, hoarsely. 'Do you see *me* drop down on a filthy Russian floor? Do our soldiers collapse in their tracks? Don't give me that kind of rubbish in future, Oberstleutnant Winkel. Your sleepy Rittmeister is worthless to me. Keep him out of my sight! If he lives through the attack I want that man court-martialled for weakness and ineffectiveness in service.' He leans forward over the charts, and points with his riding-whip at the red-circled attack point. 'Listen to me, gentlemen,' he trumpets, in a voice as sharp as a knife. 'That height is to be taken, and my division is going to *take* it! The two other divisions will attack on the flanks. The reserve division will clean up behind the attack. I have been given permission from OKH[1] to take the centre with my division. Feldmarschall von Mannstein *trusts* us!' He passes his hand nervously over his shaven head. 'Gentlemen I want that height before tomorrow evening! That is an *order*! And mark my words! Anyone who fails me, irrespective of reason, will go before a court-martial for cowardice and incompetence.' He hits the chart again with his silver-mounted whip. 'That's an *order*! If it costs me the entire division I'll have those heights before tomorrow night!'

A rattling crash comes from the door. An Artillery-Leutnant has fallen flat on his face.

The General goes almost purple, and lashes his riding boots savagely with his whip.

'Any more of you want to fall on their faces?' he hisses,

[1]OKH: Oberkommando Haer: Army GHQ.

wickedly. 'Do it *now*, then, so that I can be rid of you as soon as possible!'

There is a dead silence while two medical orderlies remove the Leutnant as if he were a sack of potatoes.

'Go on Balk,' the General turns to his Chief of Staff. 'But be quick about it! Time's short!'

'The Army Corps will attack in three waves,' the Chief of Staff tells them. 'As you have been told, *we* lead the attack. It's to be a fast-moving attack. You will *not* stop, irrespective of what the enemy throws at us. We start here, at 209. Rush the ravine. We'll be supported by a barrage. It'll be laid down over the heights and will roll down the sides. It'll knock the breath out of the enemy. In front of us we've got the 39. Soviet Guards. An elite unit, led by that stubborn chap, General Koniev. They have been strengthened by 521, Panzer Division and 16. Cavalry Brigade. Their reserves will be here, twenty kilometres in the rear. They are the 731. Rifle Division, who don't mean anything. If they are sent in, one of our battalions can take care of them easily. They've neither battle experience nor bravery. A collection of half-trained peasants we can crack like lice. Oberstleutnant Winkel, you will attack from this point as support infantry to the panzer regiment, and you'll tell your people to stick close to the tanks. Have a military police command as a security force behind you. Anybody attempting to fall back will be liquidated regardless. Oberst Jevers, you are liaison to the flanking division, and follow 104. Grenadier Regiment with your No. 6. Motorcycle Regiment.'

'Very good, sir,' mumbles Oberst Jevers, shocked, staring down at the large charts. He knows the meaning of this. He has literally been given a death sentence.

With a cold smile, the Chief of Staff looks at Oberst Mullen, Commander of 114. Panzer Grenadier Regiment.

'And you, Oberst, you will attack together with the 104th. Major Zaun, you will work your way through the lines, in the course of the night, with the 76th assault battalion, and take the enemy defence points with heavy flamethrowers and explosives. Come here, Zaun. *Here* is where you will break through.' The

117

Chief of Staff raps the chart with his pointer. 'Make it *fast*! Fast as if the devil was on your back. He *is*! At H-hour you will be behind the enemy advanced posts. It will mean your head if you are not!'

'Very good, sir!' answers Major Zaun. 'Understood!' He licks his dry lips. 'A trip to heaven,' he whispers to Oberstleutnant Winkel. 'Not many of us will come back from this one!'

'Are you nervous?' asks the Chief of Staff, hearing his whispered remark. 'If you feel the job is too rough, say so! I'll soon find a replacement for you!'

The Major's face turns red as a peony, but he does not manage to reply before the Chief of Staff has gone on to the Artillery Commander, Oberst Grün.

'You, Oberst, you will command an entire artillery division. Incorporated will be a brigade of heavy "*Nebelwerfer*", and two platoons of heavy mortars. I don't have to tell you that the job will require close planning and cooperation between your various batteries. You have five hours to get them together and instruct your battery commanders. We have succeeded in getting a meteorology group attached to us, so there should be no trouble in *that* respect. If you do not trust any of your commanders then replace them with safe, experienced men. We can't afford mistakes! Everything depends on your fire! Your Fire Coordinator is your most important man. He must be a top man. Whom do you suggest for the job?'

'Hauptmann Henckel,' says the Oberst, without hesitation. He glances over at a tall, lean artillery officer in the beginning of his thirties. 'Herr Henckel has been an instructor at Jüterburg Artillery School for three years. Not long at the front but highly recommended by the school. I firmly believe that we can find no better officer for the job.'

'I hope you are right,' barks the General, looking searchingly at the tall Artillery-Hauptmann, who is standing deliberately outside the glare of the carbide lamps. 'Listen to this, Henckel, it's important. Everything depends on your understanding your orders. We have no time to repeat them! Continue, Balk,' he snarls, impatiently, whipping away at his boots. 'We're busy men!'

118

Oberst Grün takes two long steps over to his Fire Controller, and elbows him in the ribs.

'Dammit, Henckel!' he whispers. 'You're asleep on your feet! Wake up, man! Where are your fire orders? Show me what you've taken down!'

His eyes swimming oddly, Hauptmann Henckel hands the Oberst his pad with the fire plans.

'What the devil man? Are you out of your mind?' stammers the Oberst, furiously. 'You've hardly made a note! You want to get us all court-martialled? Damn your eyes, man! I never saw anything like it. Herr Pohl!' he turns to his adjutant. 'Light a fire under Henckel. And mark my words, Henckel, you're not at Jüterburg any more. A mistake here, and you won't get away with a rollocking. It'll cost you your head if *this* goes wrong! Are you sick? If so say so! *Now*!'

'No sir, I'm all right. Just a little tired.'

'*Tired*,' says the Oberst, with a sneer. 'Aren't we *all* tired?'

He returns to the chart table worriedly, and throws a nervous look at the dried-up little General, wondering who he could possibly replace Henckel with. He can think of no-one to whom he would dare give the job.

'Are you crazy, man? You're asleep again!' whispers the adjutant, annoyedly, jogging Hauptmann Henckel's arm. 'Listen, and write down what they say. If you don't you could smash up the whole Army Corps when you open fire!'

'I don't know what's wrong. I just can't stay awake,' says Hauptmann Henckel, apologetically, leaning against the wall to prevent himself falling. 'I can't remember when I last lay down on a bed!'

'A *bed*?' sneers the adjutant, with a laugh. 'Be happy if you've got a pile of stinking straw to lie on, and don't have to make do with fast-trodden snow. Beds are for high-ranking staff officers. I haven't seen a bed for two years.'

'Two years?' mumbles Henckel, in amazement. 'You *must* have been on leave? Every soldier gets three weeks leave a year!'

'Tell me Henckel, where do you come from, really? The moon or somewhere? Leave? Holy Mother of God, you're living

119

in a fantasy world! The best you can hope for is a blighty wound to get away from all this filth and catch up on your sleep. I promise you, if I'm lucky enough to get wounded all the medical officers in the Army won't get me out of bed for the first six months!'

'That's sabotage,' cries Henckel, reproachfully.

'That's what *you* think!' smiles the adjutant, superciliously. 'You'll soon change your mind. But now I'm *ordering* you to wake up. If you don't you'll run into something very, very nasty. The job you've been given, needs more than just keeping your eyes open. In front line language, your arse'll be hot enough to fry eggs on if you mess this one up!'

A thunderous explosion cuts them off. The whole building shakes and trembles. Two more bombs explode with a crash and a roar. None of the officers seem to take any notice of it. The Chief of Staff does not stop explaining the attack plan for a second.

From the darkness come piercing screams and groans.

Hauptmann Henckel looks nervously towards the blacked-out door-opening. The black curtain streams out in the blast.

'Bombers?' he asks in a whisper. His eyelids flutter fearfully. He is new at the front. There has never been an air raid at Jüterburg.

'You *could* call them bombers, I suppose,' smiles the adjutant, jeeringly. '*We* call 'em coffee-mills. They've got a bagful of them. Old biplanes with the bombs hanging down underneath, like sausages in a butcher's shop. When the pilot sees a light down on the ground, he just takes a bomb off its hook and drops it. Try and take a walk outside with a lighted cigarette in your mouth. I assure you, you'll have a bomb on the back of your neck before you can say Jack Robinson!'

A series of explosions makes the door crash open as if struck by a giant fist. A breath of icy cold air and powdery snow sweeps through the schoolroom, and blows out the carbide lamps with its last dying breath.

'Get those doors shut, and light the lights,' orders the General, irritably, lashing his long riding boots impatiently. 'Lights!' he repeats. 'Lights, damn your eyes!'

Some signalmen almost fall over their own feet, as they come running with new carbide lamps. Soon they shine brilliantly white. One of the lamps hisses and crackles loudly.

The General looks at it wickedly.

'Make that lamp shut up,' he shouts, red in the face with rage.

A Signals Unteroffizier tries nervously to adjust the burner, but the lamp continues to splutter. It is as if it has decided to tease the General.

The Unteroffizier burns his fingers, but is wise enough not to show it.

'Take that lamp away! Out with it!' roars the General, in a hoarse voice.

The Unteroffizier grabs the lamp, and rushes out of the black-out tunnel.

At the same time comes the roar of exploding bombs. The Signals Unteroffizier and the lamp come flying back through the tunnel in a rain of glass shards, strips of flesh and brickwork.

'Damned mess,' snarls the General, angrily. 'Clean it up, and let's get on with it!'

Planning for the grand attack is resumed immediately. The bombing and the dead Unteroffizier apparently of no interest whatsoever. A couple of soldiers rapidly clear up the remains.

'We are to hold down the enemy with a short, violent barrage?' asks the Artillery Commander, Oberst Grün, uncertainly.

'Yes, yes of course!' answers the General, irritably, and screws his monocle more firmly into his eye. 'What else would you expect? Your fire falls in no-man's-land and creeps forward in front of the infantry advance, which must keep tight up to the barrage. We'll lose some fools, but that's unavoidable. The enemy will never dream our people are that close behind the barrage. They will be shocked, and will not have time to get their automatic weapons into position. Their *heavy* weapons will have been smashed by our shells. The moment of surprise must be *used*! Surprise, gentlemen, and don't forget it. And you, Oberstleutnant Winkel, will attack over the open steppe. I *know* this will be costly, but I feel sure you can do it. I trust you. But do *not* forget to keep in touch with both flanks. Lose that contact, and we have *had* it! Our opponent is a genius at counter-attacking through weakened connecting lines. The least mistake here,' he slashes his riding whip down across the plans on the table, 'and we are in the biggest mess of all time!'

The briefing of the individual regiments continues for a further half-hour. Every so often threats of court-martialling and military prison can be heard.

Finally, the General emphasises again the strengthened artillery's grave responsibility. He lays his hand heavily on Oberst Grün's shoulder.

'Grün, promise me now that you *will* replace anyone in whom you do not have full confidence. One dunce amongst your officers can be of unforseeable importance!' He brings his hand up to his cap. 'Thank you, gentlemen. I wish you all possible good luck! If the attack does not succeed, none of you will be officers when it's over! Keep that in mind!'

'My God, *again*!' whispers Oberst Grün, exasperatedly. Hauptmann Henckel is again asleep on his stool.

'I'm sorry sir!' mumbles Henckel, ashamedly. 'I can't understand what's wrong with me, I feel as if I'm two different people!'

'What am I to do with you?' asks the Oberst, worriedly. 'I haven't *got* a replacement Fire Controller. Any other time I could use an experienced Wachtmeister, but I can't do that this time. You *must* pull yourself together. Damn your eyes, pull yourself together, man!' he repeats, stiff-arming the sleepy officer savagely. 'You *have* taken everything down?'

'Yes, sir, everything is on paper, sir. It's nothing very difficult. You can trust me, sir!'

'By God and all the devils. I hope you're right. But don't fool yourself that this is going to be an easy job. Go through it, for safety's sake, once more with the adjutant.' The Oberst takes his long fur coat from a hook.

Servilely, Henckel moves to help him on with it.

'Cut that shit *out*,' the Oberst repulses him, angrily. 'You are not in the officers' mess. Use your time to go through your instructions. The devil, God and all the saints help you, Henckel,' he mumbles as he moves out of the door, tightening his belt. He takes his pistol from its holster, and slips it into his coat pocket where it is easier to get at.

Hauptmann Henckel stares strainedly in front of him. The long schoolroom moves in front of his eyes, like a ship at sea. He only wants to throw himself down on the floor, and sleep, sleep, sleep. . . .

'I must take a shower, an ice-cold shower,' he thinks, and treads on his own toes until he can feel the pain right up to his knees. It does not help him. The pale faces of the officers in the room whirl around him in circles. Far away somebody is saying something about synchronising watches.

A major from the 'Nebelwerfers' punches him in the ribs and says something to him, but all he catches is the word 'wait!'. What he is to wait for he doesn't recognise.

'Are you sick? What the devil's up with you?' asks the major, sharply.

'Just a little tired, sir.'

'I hope to hell, man, you're not too tired to do your Fire Controller job properly? If you are, you'd do best to go sick immediately. They'll jail you, probably, but better that than make a cock-up of this job! Do that and you'll get a court-martial. And lose your head, my friend!'

'I'll be all right in just a minute, sir,' Henckel assures the Major in a thick voice.

'I damn well hope you are, too! Have you got the time intervals down right?' asks the major, suspiciously, staring at Henckel with cold, slitted eyes. 'If I burn off my rockets too soon — or too late for that matter — the whole bloody shoot-ing-match'll go up in smoke! Let me see those time intervals!'

Silently, his hand trembling, Henckel hands the major his large message-pad.

With lips pressed tightly together the major runs his eyes over the columns of figures and calculations. He sees, to his relief, that the figures are correct where his own 'Nebelwerfers' are concerned. What he does not know is that these are the adjutant's notes, which Henckel is to copy but has hardly yet looked at.

123

'Get a couple of hours sleep,' the major advises him, slapping him on the shoulder. 'You've got to be fresh, and lively as a cricket, when this little lot starts. You'll be balancing along the edge of a razor tonight!' He tips the peak of his cap with one finger, and saunters over to the howitzer commander.

Tired, and strangely dizzy, Henckel goes over and sits down at the rickety table alongside the adjutant. Together they go through the timetables and the various targets for the guns.

'One thing I'd recommend you to do,' the adjutant advises him seriously, 'is check your telephone network. Don't leave anything to chance. The Chief of Staff will be in contact with you, on the two-way instrument, if anything goes wrong. If you're in doubt about anything at all, say so *now*!'

'I'm not a *complete* fool,' answers Hauptmann Henckel, angrily. 'Not many people know as much as I know about fire control. In my opinion everybody's making a mountain out of a molehill. We used to *play* at this kind of job at Jüterburg.'

'Good God Almighty,' mumbles the adjutant to his driver, as he creeps, shivering, into his Kübel. 'That jumped-up garrison stallion doesn't realise he's already got one leg in front of a firing-squad. *Jüterburg*! A kindergarten compared to this! It wouldn't surprise me in the least if that sleepy fool didn't break his neck tonight. Regiment!' he orders, brusquely, pulling a blanket around him. 'God, but it's *cold*!'

Several times the heavy Kübel slides, and is close to going into one of the deep ditches which run on either side of the road.

'Those of us who get through this one alive,' growls the adjutant, thoughtfully, 'will not forget the battle for that damned OGPU prison in a hurry.'

'Know what, Rittmeister, sir,' remarks the driver, Unteroffizier Stolz, pulling the wheel round to avoid an electric pylon, 'if I was the General, I'd let Ivan keep his bloody prison, *and* his sanatorium, *and* his mill too. There's plenty of room on both sides to go round it.'

'But you're *not* the General, Stolz,' grins the adjutant, sarcastically. 'When this lovely war is over, you'll go home and pick up being a lorry-driver, whether the prison is taken or not. But, you see, our Divisional Commander is a General-leutnant, with only one little golden star. He would very much like to have three more tiny, little golden stars before the war is over. That is what Generals consider wars to be *for*. If we take the prison our General-leutnant will be General der Kavallerie, and, who knows, maybe a bit of coloured ribbon round his neck. And from General der Kavallerie it's a short step to General-oberst. Apart from this, if he doesn't take the OGPU prison, he could lose his command. New little, shiny stars all gone away. Pension sized accordingly!'

'Well, I'm sorry, Rittmeister, sir, but it sounds crazy to me that us squaddies have to go and get shot to bits and piss blood, just so's a general can get a couple more stars on his shoulders.'

'Quite right, Stolz, but these are the rules of the game. You are lucky to be a staff driver. Thank the good Lord that you are not one of those poor, little devils in the assault regiments.'

'Yes, thank God indeed!' groans Unteroffizier Stolz, feeling a shiver of fear run down his spine.

The Artillery Commander's heavy Kübel is standing at the wide crossroads. He, himself, is standing by the side of the road talking to Hauptmann Henckel.

'Stop here!' says the adjutant, jumping out of his vehicle before it has finally drawn to a halt.

'Everything in order?' asks Oberst Grün, sharply, taking shelter from the icy wind behind the Kübel.

'All in order, sir,' answers the adjutant, knocking his hands together. 'I've been through everything with Hauptmann Henckel.'

The Oberst nods, satisfied, pulls his fur collar up around his ears, and looks worriedly out across the dark steppe. Low-hanging, black cloud masses rush headlong across the sky.

'I shall be with Divisional Staff for a time,' says Oberst Grün, stamping in the snow. 'You can get me there, if you're in doubt of anything. Henckel, if you've got any questions, let's have them now!'

'Very good, sir,' answers Henckel, his voice shaking notice-ably. '*Am I* to give the fire orders, or will they come from Division?'

The Oberst stares at him in stupefaction. He cannot believe his own ears.

'Now I've heard it all!' he foams, furiously. 'Haven't you understood a word of what has been said? Of course it's you who gives the bloody orders. That's what a Fire Controller's job *is*! Controlling the fire of the guns!' The Oberst slits his eyes suspiciously, and stares at him. 'You haven't lost your mind, have you?'

'No sir, no. I'm all right, sir. My head's going round a bit, and I feel very tired and dizzy. I haven't slept for the longest time,' he adds, shamefacedly, after a short pause.

'There are plenty more of us who haven't slept either,' the Oberst says, coldly. 'You, of all people, have no reason for complaint, Hauptmann. You have enjoyed a pleasant period of three years garrison service at Jüterburg, while we've been living like rats out here. And now you're crying like an old woman with a rheumatic backside, just because you're short of a little sleep! If you don't feel you can do the job then spit it out before it's too late! I can always use you as a runner!'

'Oberst, sir, I am specially trained as a Fire Controller, and I do not regard this particular operation as being specially difficult,' answers Henckel insultedly.

'That sounds promising,' laughs the Oberst, acidly. 'Make a mess of it, and the General will tear your liver out up through your throat! Get on and get your connections checked out. This has *got* to work properly! *Hals und Beinbruch*, Henckel!' he adds kindly, swinging himself into the Kübel. It disappears in a whirling cloud of snow, closely followed by the adjutant's vehicle.

'Self-centred idiot,' mumbles Henckel. 'Without the war that fool'd never have made Oberst. The best officers are kept back home as instructors. Good instructors make good officers. I know more about fire control than you do, you self-important front-line pig! Took you twenty years to make Oberst and I've made Hauptmann in three! When this is over with, I'll be called back to Jüterburg with the rank of Major!' With an insulted mien he gets into his own vehicle, and pulls his fur coat more tightly round his shivering body.

126

'Jesus, Hauptmann, sir! Listen to 'em bumpin'!' groans his driver, an old Obergefreiter of Tiny's type.

'Keep your cheeky remarks to yourself, Obergefreiter,' trumpets Henckel, rebuffing him, 'or I'll take care of *you!* Speak when you're spoken to!'

The Obergefreiter lifts one eyebrow, in wonderment. 'Conceited shit!' he thinks. 'We're the ones, who have to look after you! We've knocked off better blokes'n you by the dozen!'

'Herr Hauptmann, sir, Obergefreiter Schwarz requests permission to request your destination instructions, *sir!*'

'You *know* where we're going,' snarls Henckel, angrily.

'No sir. No idea, sir!'

'To Fire Control Centre, you fool!'

'Which one, sir? There are a lot of them, sir.'

For a moment it seems as if Henckel is going to explode. He clenches his gloved hands, and gives the cheekily smiling Obergefreiter a killing look.

'The Artillery Fire Control Centre! Where did you think?'

'*I* don't *think,* sir. They taught me not to do that when I was a rooky. Leave it to the horses, they said. Their heads are bigger, anyway!'

'You think that, do you?' Henckel spits out, ragingly. 'Leave me at the Artillery Fire Control Centre, and report yourself as returned to duty with the battery. I never want to set eyes on you again!'

'Very good, sir,' grins the driver, carelessly. He sets off with a great clashing of gears, and with his foot on the floorboards, he drives at breakneck speed over the uneven road. He takes the snowdrifts at an even higher speed, but despite the wild, boneshaking ride Hauptmann Henckel falls into a deathlike sleep.

Obergefreiter Schwarz looks at him out of the corners of his eyes. A humorous expression appears on his face, and he begins to sing full-throatedly:

> *Es geht alles vorüber,*
> *es geht alles vorbei,*
> *das Ei von Dezember*
> *kriegst du im Mai!*

Zuerst fällt der Führer,
und dann die Partei![2]

At one spot the Kübel goes into a slide, swings round twice on its own axis and slips sideways down a long slope.

Schwarz laughs loud and long and seems to think it all highly amusing. He glances over again at Hauptmann Henckel who has slipped down on to the floor of the vehicle, half unconscious.

'You think you can fire me, do you, you puffed-up stowaway? You'll find out! Even if you stand on your head and blow orders out of your arsehole, you won't get rid of old Obergefreiter Schwarz!' He brakes the vehicle violently outside the Fire Control dugout.

'Beg to report, sir, we're home and dry, sir! Wake up, mate, you've got to get out an' start throwin' scrap iron at old brother Ivan you have! Bang off wrong and they'll fill *you* up with iron!' He shakes the heavily sleeping officer roughly, but it does not seem to help. 'Wake up, Goddammit, you gold-braided arsehole! The taxi's *got there*! Hi, Herbert!' he shouts to a Gefreiter, slouching in the entrance to the dugout with a carbine slung nonchalantly over his shoulder. 'Come and gimme a hand. Here's a shiny leather bastard wants to sleep the rest o' the war away!'

'Kick him in the balls,' suggests Herbert, uncaringly, and takes a huge bite of a frozen sausage.

'Can't do that, mate. This is one of the big chiefs,' grins Obergefreiter Schwarz, happily.

'Where'd you find it?' asks Herbert, sauntering slowly over to the Kübel.

[2]*Es geht etc.* (freely translated)
All things must pass over,
All things *must* pass away,
An egg from December
You catch in May!
First off goes the Führer,
Then the party! Hooray!

'It's the new Fire Controller! cast iron, and got a sabre blade for a backbone!'

'Shit'n haemorrhoids,' growls Herbert, pulling Hauptmann Henckel out of the Kübel as if he were a sack of potatoes, and letting him roll down the snowy slope.

'Where am I? What's happening?' shouts Henckel, in confusion, waking up as he rolls into a snowdrift.

'Beg to report, sir. You're in Russia, sir!' shout the two soldiers in chorus, saluting with mock clumsiness.

'Russia?' mumbles Henckel. He looks nervously up at the sky. A 'Coffe-grinder' is buzzing on its way up there. On the horizon multi-coloured flares go up. An automatic cannon thunders viciously. In the distance grenades explode with a hollow sound. Away in the forest the meteorology unit is just visible. Shadowy forms move busily about. A beam of light goes straight up into the air, measuring the height of the clouds.

On feet which seem far, far too heavy, Henckel wobbles, drunk with sleep, into the Fire Control dugout, and salutes the two Leutnants who receive him.

'Everything in order?' he asks, arrogantly. Here he feels at home. This he knows. Along one wall are the large telephone switchboards, served by four signalmen. The fire chart, with target points marked on it, lies across a broad table.

Together with the Leutnants he takes out the coordinates and notes the necessary time intervals.

A runner brings the meteorologists report.

Henckel complains. The report is carelessly written. He demands it rewritten.

'Regimental two finger margin too, *if* you please!'

The two Leutnants look at one another, and keep their thoughts to themselves.

'I'll lie down for a while,' he mumbles, sourly. He throws himself down on a bench, and pulls his fur-lined hood over his face.

All present look at him in amazement. They do not believe their own eyes.

'He must be crazy,' whispers Leutnant Rothe. '*Sleeping* just before the big artillery attack! The chap must have nerves of steel. He hasn't even bothered to check the telephone network!'

As he speaks a telephone shrills alarmingly.

'If it isn't the Chief of Staff or the C.O. then let me sleep,' mumbles Henckel, in a sleepy voice, pulling his fur hood even further up over his head.

'Very good, sir,' answers Leutnant Rothe, uncaringly, picking up the jangling telephone. 'SNOW HARE here. Leutnant Rothe. Yes, Oberstleutnant, sir! All in order. As you wish, sir! Over and out!' He replaces the receiver. 'Howitzer boys,' he says to Leutnant Hassow.

For the next fifteen minutes the telephones ring incessantly. The various artillery units are reporting themselves cleared for action.

Three clerks are working furiously preparing the orders for all sub-units. The Fire Control Centre is a scene of feverish activity. The two Leutnants are working like horses to get the complicated work of preparation ready in time. Only the Fire Controller himself sleeps on peacefully, as if none of this activity had anything to do with him.

'God save us,' says Leutnant Hassow, lowing up from the piles of fire tabulations lying in front of him. 'What a *bang* this is going to make. Enough to frighten the bravest. Thank God *I'm* not Fire Controller, with responsibility for this lot. It's unbelievable what they've dragged together here. Two brigades of "*Nebelwerfers*". That's twelve sections with four batteries in each section, and each battery's got four "*werfers*" with ten pipes to each of 'em! Then there's the 210 mm howitzers. Four guns to each battery gives thirty-six in all. Then there's the heavy section with three batteries. Nine guns altogether. And our own lot with ninety-six 105 and 150 mms.'

'Not forgetting the specialists with four batteries of 280 mm peashooters,' Rothe puts in. 'That's another twelve! We're going to make some noise in the world,' cries Leutnant Hassow. 'And there's *mountains* of ammunition!'

'It'll feel like the end of the world,' mumbles Rothe, 'those poor sods that lot's going to drop on. Even their lice and the rats won't live through it!'

'Won't be much left for our infantry to do,' laughs Hassow. 'Do you realise? Just under five thousand shells'll go off in the first six minutes! Frightens you to think of it. Then the next salvoes at three minute intervals. Good Lord above! And there *he* lies fast asleep! He must be stark raving! Do you realise what could happen if something went wrong somewhere?'

'Don't need much imagination for *that*,' answers Rothe, laconically. 'We get *him* to sign everything, so *we* don't have to carry the can! I've got a nasty feeling about what *might* be going to happen!'

Henckel feels as if he has not been asleep for more than a few minutes when Leutnant Rothe shakes him awake a couple of hours later.

'Hauptmann! Wake up! Division's on the line. Wake *up*, sir!'

Confused and yawning, Henckel finally gets on his feet.

Rothe looks at him doubtfully. 'You're not sick, are you sir? You were so far away I thought for a moment you were dead.'

'Why the devil did you wake me? What's up? Can't you manage the tiniest thing yourselves without coming running to me for help? It's necessary I get a *little* sleep before the attack starts.'

'Sir! Division demands you come to the telephone immediately!'

'Division?' mumbles Henckel, still in a state of confusion. Suddenly he realises where he is, and straightens up so quickly that he crashes his head into a beam supporting the low roof. 'Hell!' he shouts, putting his hand to his head on which a huge lump has already risen. 'What damned fools made this place with such a low roof? Have it changed tomorrow, Rothe. Blasted incompetence is what this is! Bring the man responsible before me at 09.00 hrs. Understand, Leutnant!'

'You're a nut,' thinks Rothe. 'You ought to be glad you've got a roof over your head at all, when most others have only got a hole in the ground.'

Henckel takes the telephone and gives his code-name sleepily. A wide-awake voice at the other end says: 'Justa moment, sir. I'll put you through to the Chief of Staff.'

In quick time the Chief of Staff's cutting voice sounds on the line. Henckel finds it hard to understand what is being said. Something about attack timings and connections.

'Very good, sir,' he answers automatically, doodling meaninglessly on his pad as he replies.

'Understood?' snarls the Chief of Staff, after a short pause.

Henckel sways on his feet as if he is about to fall. He listens with closed eyes.

Leutnant Rothe grips his arm and shakes him violently.

'Hell! Wake *up*, sir!'

Henckel looks at Leutnant Rothe, his eyes swimming in his head. Rothe continues to shake him, until the Hauptmann pushes him away, irritably.

'Not understood, sir,' he says in a voice that sounds as if he were speaking through cotton-wool.

'Are you stark, staring mad?' roars the Chief of Staff, fiercely. 'I'll repeat the times again! God help you if you don't get down every single one of them!'

He rattles off a series of figures into Henckel's ear at lightning speed.

'Repeat them back!' hisses the Chief of Staff when he has finished. He drums his fingers impatiently on the table.

Luckily for Henckel, Leutnant Rothe has been listening on the line. He pushes a pad with the timings in front of Henckel.

In a hollow, unreal voice Henckel repeats them to the Chief of Staff.

'Henckel, you sound as if you're asleep on your feet? What's the matter with you?'

'I'm very tired, sir!'

'So bloody well am I,' the Chief of Staff's voice explodes in Henckel's ear like the roar of a hungry carnivore. 'The General's tired! We're *all* tired! I don't want to hear any more of that shit from you! You're an officer and you'll do your duty like one!' He cuts off with a noise that crashes in the sleepy Henckel's ear. He stands staring at the telephone for a moment, then turns and staggers back to the bench.

Hardly has he pulled his hood up over his face, before he is again called to the telephone. Cursing he gets to his feet and snatches it up to his ear.

'Write this down, Hauptmann,' comes the adjutant's pleased voice: 'H-hour BERTHA HELGA LUDWIG ADOLF BERTHA. Repeat! Over!'

'H-hour BERTHA HELGA LUDWIG ADOLF BERTHA. Over!' replies Henckel, tiredly, wishing the adjutant and the entire staff were roasting in hell.

The connection is broken. Sleepy as he is he thinks it is the adjutant who has rung off.

His hands trembling, lying half across the chart table, he writes down the message. He has heard nothing of the time comparison.

'Let me sleep in peace, now!' he says, throwing himself down again on the bench.

The two Leutnants look at him and shake their heads at one another.

'Queer that call was cut off,' remarks Leutnant Rothe. 'I've got a feeling there's something missing.'

'My God! I'm more dead than alive,' groans Hauptmann Henckel when Leutnant Rothe wakes him again half an hour later. He pours a bucket of ice-cold water over his head to come to himself. It helps only briefly.

A Feldwebel brings him the latest reports. Together with the two Leutnants he checks the various connections and time-tables. Slowly the timings are gone through again.

'Come on Rothe, you read 'em out,' Henckel orders, sleepily. He throws himself into a chair with his hands folded behind his head and his eyes closed.

'Fire command to be given 05.06 hours.' Rothe reads out, loudly. '05.12 hrs. Heavy artillery opens fire with 75 mms. Plus two minutes panzer and infantry attack. Barrage lifts over them and creeps forward to ready ground for assault troops following.'

'Mere routine. Nothing difficult in that,' remarks Henckel, indifferently, stretching his long, booted legs. He yawns, noisily, until his jaws almost go out of joint. 'The devil, I nearly dropped off again! If I didn't know better I'd think I'd got sleeping sickness. Give me a large vodka. It freshens a fellow up!'

Looking askance at Leutnant Rothe, a Feldwebel brings him a glass of vodka.

Henckel throws the spirits down with a flick of his wrist. It goes down the wrong way and he goes into a spasm of coughing. He jumps to his feet to avoid choking.

'Wouldn't you rather have a cup of coffee, sir?' asks Leutnant Hassow, carefully. 'We're going to have to keep our heads cool, and I wouldn't call vodka the best kind of cooling mixture!'

'Don't tell *me* what to do, Leutnant,' roars Henckel, harshly. He demands another glass of vodka, and swallows it greedily.

Leutnant Hassow pushes over some documents for signature. Henckel signs them with a flourish, without reading them.

Rothe looks relievedly at Hassow, as if to say: 'There goes the can!'

'Let's try our connections,' orders Henckel, slapping the Signals Feldwebel on the shoulder. He looks at his watch. It shows 04.45 hours. 'Put me through to the "*Werfers*". Those part-time soldiers always need more time than anybody else.'

After a short conversation with the '*Nebelwerfer*' commander he asks for the fire charts and memorises the targets. Together with the Leutnants he runs quickly through the Army orders. Then he asks to be connected with the advanced artillery spotters. There seems to be some disagreement with the spotter at 104. Infantry Regiment. Henckel puts him in his place, brusquely, and cuts off the connection. Satisfied, he leans back again in his chair and orders a third glass of vodka.

'Do you think that is wise, sir?' asks Leutnant Rothe, worriedly.

'If I want your opinion I'll ask for it, Leutnant!' Henckel rejects the advice, sharply, and hangs a long Russian cigarette with a cardboard tube between his lips. He swallows half the vodka, and stretches until his joints crack. He looks at his watch again and notes that it is eight minutes to H-hour. For a moment he considers taking another nap before the fun starts. The vodka has made him optimistic. He is looking forward to unleashing his own private hell of fire. It is the first time he has aimed at live targets. 'I'll make 'em open their eyes, those stuck-up fools,' he thinks, with satisfaction. 'Who knows, I might even win an Iron Cross for perfect fire control. Why not?' He throws the rest of his vodka down his throat, and looks contemptuously at the two young Leutnants standing bent over the target charts. He selects another of the long Russian cigarettes. They look well, he thinks, just right for a man in uniform. Before he manages to light up the telephone shrills impatiently. With a self-satisfied mien he takes the receiver from Rothe's hand.

'What the devil are you up to?' comes in a furious voice from the Chief of Staff. 'Why have you not opened fire as ordered?'

'Opened fire?' answers Henckel, nervously, looking at his watch in astonishment. 'There's six minutes yet, sir!'

'Are you mad?' screams the Chief of Staff, his voice cracking. 'You damned fool! The time is exactly 05.10 hours. I have had to wait several minutes getting through to you. *You* are the most useless sod I've ever had to do with. You, you, you. . . .' The Chief of Staff cannot find expressions strong enough to express his opinion of his Divisional Fire Controller. 'Hauptmann Henckel, do you *know* what has happened?' he asks, at last, in an icy voice. 'All three panzer regiments have rolled, and the infantry is attacking. No power on earth can stop them. Wait . . .' his voice is suddenly cut off. Only a distant buzzing can be heard on the line.

'Hello, hello, hello!' screams Henckel, furious and afraid at what might happen as a result of his time error. His eyes roll wildly in his head. He looks around desperately. All his arrogant self-confidence has deserted him. 'Wait . . .' the Chief of Staff had said. What did he mean? Wait at the telephone? Or was it the beginning of a threat of what he could expect to happen to him for failing in his duty? No it couldn't be that! It must be that he should wait for a new call!

'What's up?' asks Leutnant Rothe, uneasily, staring at Henckel in fear.

'My watch is slow,' says Henckel, tonelessly, staring at it blankly. 'We should have opened fire several minutes ago! The tanks are already attacking!'

'*We* should have opened fire?' asks Rothe, emphasising the

'*we*'. '*You*, sir, should have given the order to open fire! Not Leutnant Hassow, and not me! But how could your watch be wrong? Surely you all synchronised your watches before leaving Division? It's standard procedure!'

'I was asleep on my feet,' Henckel admits, in a dead voice. 'Must have missed it!'

'Good God!' cries Hassow, shocked.

'You *must* have known that you hadn't synchronised your watch with the rest of the staff!' Rothe puts in, in a reproaching tone.

'I remembered it as soon as I was outside,' sighs Henckel, wiping the sweat of fear from his forehead.

'Why didn't you go back and do it then?' asks Hassow, blankly.

'My watch has always been exact to the second!' answers Henckel, darkly.

'But not *this* time,' says Rothe, in a dry voice. 'Expensive minutes, those!'

The telephone jangles again.

'Joint line to all artillery units, sir!' says Henckel's telephonist, handing him the receiver.

Henckel stares for a moment at the instrument in the man's hand. What in the world is he to do? His head feels empty. 'Wait . . .' the Chief of Staff had said. Of *course*. He meant I was to wait until the joint call came through.

'Take the bloody 'phone, man!' shouts Rothe, disrespectfully. 'The guns are waiting for your orders!'

'Orders?' mumbles Henckel, confusedly. He stares numbly at Leutnant Rothe. He tears open his stiff uniform collar, and bares his teeth in a death's-head grin. 'Give me another vodka,' he orders, hoarsely. Greedily, he snatches the filled glass from the Feldwebel's hand. '*I'll* show 'em!' he thinks. Resolutely he grabs the telephone connecting him to all units. He takes a deep breath. His eyes begin to shine eagerly: 'Target number one! Open fire!' he roars into the mouthpiece. He grins horsily, as he replaces the receiver. 'Jüterburg training, understand! Know what it's all about!'

'*That* was a clear and firm decision,' cries Leutnant Rothe, in

136

amazement. 'Ought to wake 'em up all right on *both* sides of the front!'

Every gun in every unit tilts its barrel, the black muzzles pointing up at the darkness of the winter sky.

The gunners stand ready with lanyards in hand. Gun commanders stand tense, listening for the battery commander's order. The '*Nebelwerfer*' crews are in their dug-outs behind the batteries, fingers on firing-buttons, ready to despatch their deadly rocket. Second-hands seem to race madly round. It is very quiet, a sinister-seeming silence reigns in the pitch-black winter morning.

The silence is broken by a terrible roar. With a single deafening crash the guns open up! They send their shells in salvoes into the dawn. The terrain is lit up by the intermittent flash of exploding projectiles. Flames begin to dance out there.

The morning is filled with a roaring, crashing, thundering howling. As if a continuous line of express trains were rolling across the sky. The noise of the guns threatens to split the eardrums of the men in the Fire Control Post. A long, sinister organlike sound makes itself heard through the thunder of the guns. It rises to a nerve-shattering howling scream.

' "*Nebelwerfers*",' mutters a Feldwebel, with fear in his voice.

'Heavenly Father!' moans Leutnant Rothe, throwing a frightened glance out over the terrain.

'If I wasn't seeing it, I wouldn't believe it! Both heaven and earth are ablaze! God help the poor devils who're on the receiving end of *that* lot!'

A wild, ungovernable feeling of gladness fills Hauptmann Henckel, as the fire of the heavy howitzers shakes the Fire Control Post. The heavy roar of the 320 mm guns hurts the ears, and sends shudders of fear running up and down the spine.

The grey winter morning is lit up like the sunniest of summer days. All round the horizon the muzzle-flashes of guns can be seen. The crash of exploding shells goes over in the noise of the firing in one long roar of sound. Shell after shell thunders from the gun muzzles.

Sweating gunners push the heavy shells in on the loading rails. Then ram in the various loads.

In the distance a wall of fire dances. As if the earth is spewing up an inferno of flame. Each thunderous salvo is followed unbelievably quickly by the next, in one long continuous, stormy, roll of thunder.

The howling and roaring of the shells becomes even more insupportable. The surface of the earth is splintered like glass. Buildings collapse like houses built of playing cards. Multi-coloured flames shoot up towards the heights. Blast waves press human bodies into the boiling, bubbling slush. On the horizon the fire-fly flashes of the guns dance. The specialist batteries are brought into the battle. A new sound cuts through the thunder of guns. Incendiary shells fall, splashing burning, liquid flame out to all sides. Even the air seems to have caught fire.

Hauptmann Henckel lights another Russian cigarette, with a self-satisfied air, and sips a fresh glass of vodka. He feels pleasantly relaxed. His sleepiness has gone away. 'This is fine,' he thinks. A good, firm decision. He slaps the Signals private condescendingly on the shoulder. At a great moment like this one loses nothing by showing the lower ranks a little friendliness, he feels.

The shrilling of the field telephone interrupts his pleasant meditation. With a pleased smile on his face he takes the instrument, satisfied that he has done what was expected of him. 'Child's play, really,' he thinks. Trained in it hundreds of times at Jüterburg Artillery School.

'Fire Controller here!' he barks, harshly, into the mouthpiece, setting his face in severe folds.

'That you Henckel?' comes the controlled voice of the Artillery Commander, Oberst Grün.

'Yes, sir! Henckel here!'

'You gave the order to open fire?'

'Yes, sir!' answers Henckel, proudly, certain that praise and the promise of the Iron Cross are to follow.

There is a short, noticeable pause. The Oberst's calm voice comes again.

'*When* did you give the order to open fire, Henckel?'

'Exactly six minutes ago, sir?' replies Henckel, happily.

138

'Six minutes ago! I see! And you gave the order to all units?'

'Of course, sir! The Chief of Staff thought my watch must be a little slow!'

'Is that so, *Hauptmann* Henckel?' The Oberst emphasises Henckel's rank sharply. That emphasis alone should have been a warning to Henckel.

'I was sure the Chief of Staff was wrong, sir. I trusted my own watch, which has never let me down, and gave the order to open fire by it. You could say, perhaps, that I made a snap decision, sir,' Henckel laughs, assuredly.

'*You* made a snap decision!' says Oberst Grün, with a noticeable pause between each word. 'What were the Chief of Staff's orders to you, when you spoke to him on the telephone? What was his last word?'

Henckel's blood seems to freeze to ice in his veins. He feels as if he would like to throw down the telephone and run. Run away over the steppe. Run over to the Russians. To be hidden and forgotten in a concentration camp until the war is over. He feels as if death itself is on the other end of the telephone line.

'The Chief of Staff's last word, sir? That was — Wait!' he stammers. Suddenly he understands everything.

'Yes! *Wait*!' screams Oberst Grün, wildly. His former calmness has disappeared completely. '*Wait! Wait!* You impossible fool! *Wait!* Do you realise what you have done? The panzer troops and the infantry attacked at the time ordered. No power on earth could stop that. As they drove through the first assault target, you, you opened fire! *Six minutes too late!*' he roars. 'You smashed our own assault troops into the ground! *You* took a snap decision! You've massacred our own men! The Russian artillery couldn't have done it more effectively! I don't know what they must be thinking over there! Your clever snap decision has blown the whole Army Corps to *hell*! You admit hearing the Chief of Staff's clear order? *Wait*?'

'I must have misunderstood him, sir,' comes weakly from the miserable Fire Controller. 'I thought I was to wait by the telephone!'

Oberst Grün takes a few deep breaths. If Henckel had been with him he would have strangled him.

'Wait at the telephone!' The Oberst laughs, coldly. 'Do you think you're an errand boy? Jüterburg recommended you as Fire Controller. They'll pay for that! Listen closely Hauptmann Henckel. I don't want any more misunderstandings. You will immediately hand over your command to Leutnant Rothe. Don't interfere with anything, whatever happens! Place yourself under arrest, and sit in a corner and wait for the adjutant, who is on his way to your post! Hand over your pistol to Leutnant Rothe! Remember you are under arrest! *Don't* try to take the easy way out with that pistol!'

'I am an officer, sir,' Henckel defends himself. 'Allow me to take the consequences of this terrible occurrence myself, I am an *officer*!'

'Yes, more's the pity,' snarls Oberst Grün. 'But you will be surprised when you hear what the infantry commanders think of you. The Panzer Regiment's C.O., Oberst Hinka, has just been on the telephone to me. He wants your head! You've murdered two thirds of his regiment. But *I* want you in front of a court-martial. You impossible fool! Give me Leutnant Rothe!'

Silently Henckel hands the telephone to Leutnant Rothe.

'Yes sir!' he says, and, 'Yes, sir!' and again, 'Yes, sir!' He replaces the receiver quietly.

Petrified he stares at Hauptmann Henckel, who is sitting on a stool with his head in his hands, rocking his body from side to side.

'Rothe, I have been relieved,' he says, tonelessly. 'I am under arrest. You are in command. Here is my pistol.'

'Those were the Oberst's orders,' mumbles Rothe, unhappily. 'But, but! What has happened?'

'We fired on our own troops! I massacred the whole Corps!'

'God have mercy on you,' cries Leutnant Hassow, in horror.

'Rothe, help me! Give me back my pistol,' begs Henckel, stretching his hands out, pleadingly.

Leutnant Rothe looks at him, uncertainly, and is about to

140

hand him his pistol, when the door crashes open and the adjutant storms in. His usual, cynical smile wreathes his lips.

'Well, well! And here we have the great fire control specialist from Jüterburg!' he shouts, sneeringly, as his eyes fall on Henckel. 'The Divisional Commander is longing to meet you again, and tear strips of hide off you! Why the hell couldn't you wait for the order before you opened fire? Even the slaves know enough not to open fire six minutes late! My God, but what a mess you've made of everything! I hope you're away from the division before the infantry and panzer officers get hold of you. They'll pull your guts up through your throat!'

'It wasn't my fault! It was a misunderstanding,' mumbles Henckel, despairingly, bursting into tears.

'You'll have a time explaining that one when you're in front of a court-martial,' laughs the adjutant, coldly. 'Your one chance is the head-shrinkers. If *they* don't save you, you'll be shot ten times over!'

'Give me my side-arm,' begs Hauptmann Henckel, catching at the adjutant's arm.

'Like that, wouldn't you?' laughs the adjutant, jeeringly. 'I never before wanted to see a man go before a court-martial. Where you're concerned it's my dearest wish!'

Shortly afterwards Oberst Grün arrives with two MP's and an Oberinspektor from GEFEPO[3].

'Remove him!' orders Oberst Grün, with loathing. 'The very sight of him sickens me!'

Handcuffs click around Hauptmann Henckel's wrists. He leaves the Fire Control Post hanging between the two stalwart MP's like a bundle of rags above a pair of staggering riding boots.

[3]GEFEPO: Geheime Feldpolizei (Field Secret Police).

Soldiers are citizens of death's grey land.

Siegfried Sassoon

The OGPU captain slid from the chair and landed in a sitting position, with legs wide apart, in the middle of the large pool of blood. His dark glasses had slipped down on his nose, and his eyes were crossed weirdly. His cap, with its blue band and large red star, was hanging crookedly over one eye. His left arm dangled uselessly at his side, blood running down it and dripping from his fingers. With his right hand he fumbled for his Nagan. He got hold of it, lifted it, and sniggered. In the enclosed space the shot sounded like a howitzer going off in a ballroom.

Porta whirled, and shot on the turn. All four bullets went home into the OGPU officer's body, making it jerk spasmodically. His cap fell off and rolled across the floor. Strangely his glasses rode up his nose and back into place.

Porta and the Russian's guns went off again simultaneously. A large blue vase splintered to pieces, water streaming out over the floor. Porta's pistol clicked, and the OGPU captain sniggered again.

'Job tvojemadj!' he whispered, and lifted the Nagan.

Porta kicked out at it, but slipped in the blood and slid across the floor.

Again the Russian sniggered. A rattling sound came from his throat.

Porta lay on the floor, and stared, paralysed, into the muzzle of the Nagan.

Tiny leaned across the desk. He had to lie on his stomach to press the muzzle of his 08 against the OGPU officer's grey, crew-cut hair. He pressed the trigger. The officer's head exploded like an overripe water-melon. Brains, blood and bone spattered the ceiling and ran down the walls. The dark glasses sailed through the air and landed by the door. A prisoner in a grey smoking jacket crushed them under his boot.

'Hurra!' shouted the prisoners. One by one they went over and kicked the dead OGPU officer's body.

4
OGPU Prison

'Gear ready?' asks the Old Man, looking down the position. 'Open your ears, now, you soaking sacks, you, and don't interrupt. The section follows up, right straight behind the barrage. It'll sweep everything away in front of us. If the artillery *hasn't* smashed in the positions and softened up the opposition, then *we* roll up what's left with grenades and automatic weapons. The first few minutes after the barrage lets up, the neighbours won't know whether to shit or get off the pot! So we take him *fast*, and pull the ring of his arse up over his ears. See that funny-looking bush over by the bushy-topped tree, there?' He hands Porta his binoculars, but the odd-looking bush can be seen with the naked eye. It has the shape of a horse sitting down.

'What *about* the funny bush, then?' asks Gregor, taking the binoculars from Porta.

'They've got a 50 mm gun there, depressed to ground level,' explains the Old Man, puffing away at his silver-lidded pipe. '300 yards further back there's an 80 mm group, dug in. Women. But make no mistake. They're pro's from a line brigade. So blow 'em away! Leave 'em, and they'll have you from behind before you can say Jack Robinson!'

'We'll blow 'em to hell and gone!' says Porta, decisively.

'A bit in front of the bushy-topped tree,' the Old Man goes on, 'there's four dead 'uns lying. See 'em? You can use 'em for cover while you're waiting for H-hour. If the opposition there see any movement they'll think it's the bodies getting thrown about by blast.'

'What about if these 'ere bints in uniform, ain't fooled though?' Tiny breaks in. 'If they get the idea them bodies are full o' German life, what then?'

'You get yourselves a pass to the Heavenly Kingdom, don't you?' declares the Old Man, snappishly. 'You won't be able to go either forward or back from that position!'

'Its gonna be *some* trip. Enough to make an ostrich sweat blood!' mumbles Gregor, doubtfully. He examines the terrain carefully with the binoculars. 'But those lads certainly picked a good spot to turn up their toes. They might have had us in mind when they did it!'

'This rotten army, man! It gets its money back all right!' says Albert, sourly. 'Even when you're dead an' gone they *still* ain't finished with you!'

'They chase *us*, all right. Fast as a bucket of hot shit,' says Barcelona. 'Kick up the arse, one on the side of your head, and keep your trap shut!'

'Peace you get, nearly, when you're cold and stiff, man!' continues Albert, indignantly.

'When you're six feet under, pushin' up the daisies, they get the violins'n flutes out, and start singing your praises,' sneers Porta, throwing out his arms widely. 'When you're alive they don't sing your praises. Only when you've been dumb enough not to get out of the way, when a bullet's coming at you and've got yourself killed!'

As H-hour for the grand attack gets closer, the company is caught in the grip of that strange deathly feeling which always precedes an attack. We scowl wickedly at one another, start nervously without the least cause. Our lips are compressed to thin lines. Eyes empty, and glassy. Stomachs filled with cramping fear.

The Old Man looks at his watch incessantly, and examines the ground in front of us with his binoculars.

'Has everything I've been saying got through?' he asks, checking his flare pistol.

A mumble of indistinguishable sound is all the reply he gets.

'What about giving the bones a roll?' Porta offers, rattling the dice in his cupped hand.

Nobody bothers to reply. We look at one another, knowing well that for many this will be the last morning of life. Which of us will it be this time? We put the question wordlessly and let

144

our eyes wander around. Of course it won't be any of our lot, we think. We always think that. And are surprised when it happens to one of us.

The list of the men who have caught it is a long one. Very long! A few of us have been together for a long time, and seem, somehow, to have learnt how to edge our way between the knife-edged bursts of shrapnel. We live only fractions of an inch away from death.

A long shrill whistle make us jump. An inch-long furrow appears across Gregor's forehead. He cries out and falls backwards. For a moment we think he has bought one, but after a few anxious moments his eyes blink open again.

'Bloody hell, chaps,' he mumbles, his face twisted in pain. 'I *hate* gettin' shot!'

'Close one that,' says Sanitäts-Unteroffizier Jarmer, bandaging the wound with expert hands. 'You were lucky! That bullet was nearly spent when it kissed you.'

'Feels as if it's still knocking around inside trying to find a way out,' groans Gregor, putting his face in his hands.

Major Zaun comes up, leading his engineers. They are cursing and swearing under the weight of their heavy equipment. The special-type flame-throwers are enough in themselves, but they also carry boxes of high-explosives and large rolls of special wire.

An Obergefreiter with a brutal face breaks open a box of plastic explosive. Porta and Tiny get a handful each.

'What that, man?' asks Albert, curiously, bending over the open box which is filled with small packages. They look for all the world like packets of soap.

'Blow you out of your black skin, they would,' grins the Obergefreiter. 'Try treadin' on 'em. Turn even *you* pale, mate!'

'Shit, man!' growls Albert, moving gingerly away from the boxes.

'Minus five minutes H-hour,' a Major confirms. His harsh features tell the story of many desperate encounters. His mouth is twisted, as if it had been put through a grinder.

The Old Man brings out his whistle, adjusts his chin-strap,

and pushes a couple more potato-masher grenades into his jackboots.

'Ready, sir!' he mumbles.

'Don't let us down, Oberfeldwebel,' snarls the Major, gruffly. 'Our lives depend a lot on you!'

The engineers ready their long pipes of explosive. Second hands flash round the dials of watches.

'Where in the devil's name are those guns?' asks Barcelona, looking uneasily over his shoulder.

'The usual,' laughs Porta. 'The flayed dog's wrigglin' on the pan. Nothing *ever* goes right in this damned army. The gun coolies'll be lying about fast asleep, not giving a fuck for us foot-slogger sods!'

'What the hell's going *on*?' asks the Major, uneasily. 'H-hour plus one to H-hour plus seven's the barrage. Now it's H-hour plus eight.' He compares his watch with the Old Man's and Feldwebel Brandt's. 'Correct,' he confirms, thoughtfully. 'Something's gone wrong, but why in the name of hell don't they send a message?'

The thunder of 122 mm and 150 mm guns comes from the OGPU prison. Shells howl over us and crash down into the forest.

'Ready for attack,' the Major commands, harshly. He unslings his Mpi.

'We can't go over without artillery support!' protests Leutnant Gernert, angrily.

'If I need your advice, Leutnant, I'll ask for it!' snarls the Major, wickedly. 'It's H-hour plus ten! We attack as ordered! Forward!'

'It's madness,' the Leutnant still protests. 'They'll slaughter us like cattle! We can't get up to that goddam prison without artillery support. We've tried it countless times.'

'To God and the Prussian Army nothing is impossible,' Porta grins, phlegmatically. 'Fingers out and let's roll. *Für Führer und Reich, Heil!*'

'I often wonder whether God was in a good mood or a bad mood when 'e let us march into the bleedin' world as Prussians?' laughs Tiny, noisily.

146

'You should be proud of being German,' proclaims Heide, patriotically, striking his chest.

'I hope for you that you will continue to be proud,' smiles the Major, bitterly.

Heide sends him a contemptuous look, and mumbles something uncomprehensible.

'Time!' orders the Old Man, sharply, shrilling on his whistle.

White-camouflaged shapes seem to appear from everywhere in the snow. They move forward with long, fast strides.

'Get on, get on!' roars the Major, in a shrill voice. Despite his fifty years he takes off like a youngster. He storms forward through the deep snow with Mpi in one hand and an explosive charge in the other.

Harpoon ropes shoot, hissing, up the cliff-face. The first of the assault troops commence their climb. Flares rise in the dark night. Muzzle flames spit from all sides.

'*Allah-el-Akbar, vive la mort!*' screams the little Legionnaire, fanatically, gripped with battle madness, as always when we attack.

I stumble over a roll of barbed wire. I get caught on the sharp metal thorns. They tear into my long winter greatcoat, through it and into my skin. Feverishly I rout around after my wire cutters, but cannot find them. I must have dropped them somewhere. Terror gets hold of me. Desperately I peer around for the others. They have disappeared, bending forward, into the darkness. The worst thing that can happen to you in an attack is to lose contact and be left behind on your own. We have the initiative just now, but that can change any time. In minutes. Then God help the man who's cut off. A bullet in the back. Or maybe worse!

'You're in a mess all right,' laughs Barcelona, bending over me. He cuts me loose quickly. The wire snaps out to both sides.

Head over heels I land in a hole together with Porta and Tiny.

'Gregor's a bit up front,' says Porta, pointing into the pitchy darkness. 'Get on up with him. You've got to open the door with the grenades!'

147

We are no more than a hundred yards from the depressed gun, which has been beautifully camouflaged. We can't see it, even in the brightness of the flares.

'They're fast a' bleedin' *sleep*,' whispers Tiny, scandalised, stretching his neck. 'Cheeky bleeders don't think fuck of us any more.'

'*Throw*,' orders Gregor, hoarsely, taking back his arm. The grenades whirl up in a high arc and drop down into the Russian position.

Porta and Tiny ready them and hand them to us.

My arm pains me. A special throwing technique and a lot of strength is needed to throw a grenade as far as Gregor and I have trained ourselves to do. Your whole body weight has to go into the throw. It is particularly difficult when you are throwing from the lying position. It is as if your body went part of the way with the grenade.

Our two first grenades must have struck an ammunition pile. The explosion is violent as a volcanic eruption. The long-barrelled gun goes whirling up into the air together with its crew. The Old Man appears out of the blinding snow at the head of a party.

'On your feet, damn you,' he shouts, madly, pushing on into the remains of the smashed gun position.

At a breakneck pace, we rush through the deep, powdery snow and throw ourselves down on the far side of the position. We have to get on before the survivors pull themselves together and turn everything they have left onto us.

Tiny is like an elephant run amok. He swings his sharpened entrenching tool above his head, slashing and cutting in blind rage.

We are through the protective wire in the first five minutes, throwing grenades into dugouts and fox-holes. Like a runaway storm we roll up the enemy position.

By the light of a flare I see the Major of engineers and his flamethrower group attack the artillerywomen, who come rushing from their dugouts.

The women put up their hands and stare in horror at the onrushing snow-camouflaged devils. Flames roar out in long fiery tongues. There is a stink of burning oil and charred meat.

We take a short rest in the enemy position. We feel as if our chests are too narrow for our lungs. Despite the icy cold, we are soaked with sweat. We tear open our uniform collars, one thought only in our minds. 'Air!' The snow around us is scattered with broken, blackened, bloody bodies. The flames bubble and sizzle, with a sound like meat burning on a spit.

'Where the hell's the guns?' shouts the Old Man, angrily.

'Eleven minutes over time, now!' mumbles Leutnant Gernert.

'All it wants now's for 'em to open fire while *we're* in the neighbours' positions,' forecasts Barcelona, darkly.

'They couldn't be *that* crazy!' cries Gregor, fearfully.

'They must know we're through 'em now!'

A creeping terror moves up our spines. To be smashed under our own artillery fire seems the stupidest thing that could happen to us.

'*Merde aux yeux*, let's get out of here *quick*,' suggests the Legionnaire, looking questioningly at the Old Man.

A company of motorcyclists appears through the choking, poisonous vapours which rise from the ground. Their O.C., a grey-haired Hauptmann, waves us on, and screams something we cannot understand.

'Fuck that cunt!' snarls Tiny. '*Any* pistol-packin' piss'ead can't order *us* around. It ain't *that* bad yet! We're still bleedin' us, *we* are!'

'Get on, get *on*!' shouts the Hauptmann, feverishly, putting his clenched fist up in the sign for double time forward.

We laugh openly at him and pretend not to understand his signals. From bitter experience we know that we might as well give up if we get mixed up with a strange lot. We'd get all the dirty jobs, stinking of heroism and Valhalla.

'I don't move out of here without artillery support, *panjemajo*?' decides Porta, categorically. He fishes the rest of a black pudding from his knapsack. 'Even GROFAZ at the head of all his psychotic cases couldn't make it to that commie jail without supporting fire!'

An explosion of enormous force cuts him off. Concentrated

fire hammers down in front of and behind us.

In the course of a few seconds the gunfire increases to a veritable typhoon of steel and flame. It seems as if the whole earth is thrown up towards the heavens and falls back with an enormous concussion. The whole horizon burns from the Northeast to the Southwest.

Blast throws us around as if we were footballs. We clutch at the snow with hands and feet.

A huge salvo falls on the signal command dugout. Timber, planks, telephone cables and flayed human bodies are strewn in a horrible hotch-potch across the battle-ground.

Yet another direct hit roars down into the destroyed position, smashing it up even more. The area is like some terrible, tumbled rubbish-tip.

A little further back a large shell hits the orderlies dugout. It becomes a boiling cauldron of blood and crushed bone.

Shells fall incessantly. Where the flamethrower company was there is now a landscape of smoking holes and smashed material, spattered with human blood. With unbelievable force the concentrated gunfire ploughs up the heights. Human bodies are thrown into the air, and smash to unrecognisable messes as they hit the ground.

A new sound drowns out the roar of the guns. A blanket of fire rolls towards us like a steamroller.

Panicstricken German soldiers flee shoulder to shoulder with the Russians, but are caught in the all-consuming, crushing rain of shells. Torn-off parts of human bodies geyser towards the burning sky. Wounded men scream heart-breakingly, but nobody helps them. The whole terrain has become a boiling, indescribable inferno. The end of the world.

A deafening roar from the 105 and 150 mm's brings us down on our faces in the snow. In a continual chain of explosions fire rains down on the assault companies, turning them into a porridge of blood and mangled flesh in the course of seconds.

I lift my head carefully and begin to get up.

'Down!' screams the Old Man, warningly, rolling into a smoking shellhole.

A new rain of shells makes the earth shake as if in the throes of a violent earthquake. The air is thick with red-hot shrapnel. Shells are falling on every inch of ground.

The Old Man snatches the flare pistol from Leutnant Gernert and fires off a red flare. The barrage continues without pause. The Old Man sends up another red signal light, and curses our artillery. We all realise by now that it is our artillery which is firing on us.

The pulverising fire moves slowly forward, smashing Russian positions which the German troops have already taken. Shells hail down on the backs of the terrified front line soldiers. Bodies are tossed up out of the snow again and again. The dark clouds open themselves and reveal a long, seething sea of flame.

In the course of only a second it seems as if a giant fist has pounded trees and houses to a sickening mush.

Our nerves are set vibrating by a long, fearsome, howling whine. In terror we peer upwards as long flaming trails drive like comets across the sky and explode thunderously on the heights. A forest of redly glowing mushroom clouds rises from the earth. Rockets bore into the snow.

The Russian heavy artillery joins in the hellish concert. The icy air seems to ring with the sound of steel on steel. Shells hail down. Nothing is spared. The frost-bowed forest along the rounded height is shaved off the cheek of the earth, in one long sweep, by the razor of the guns. Only a stubble remains.

Slowly the hell of fire creeps forward, destroying everything in its path. Nothing escapes destruction.

The terrain is unrecognisable. Tumbled. As if an idiot with a plough had driven back and forth across it. Everywhere bodies. And screaming wounded.

Just as we are about to rise to our feet, there is a new sound in the sky. It is as if millions of empty oil-drums come rattling across the heavens.

A colossal sheet of fire shoots upwards and a deafening explosion shakes the earth.

Julius Heide shouts, and digs his way into the snow alongside Porta.

Feldwebel Brandt dives from the half-crushed dugout, blood

fountaining from his face. Without a sound he goes down in the middle of us.

An entire infantry company, seeking cover, is thrown up into the air. It falls back in a carnage of blood and shredded flesh.

'God in Heaven have mercy on us,' sobs Leutnant Gernert, hysterically. 'Those damned fools have opened fire too late!'

A grating whistle cuts him off. His helmet is torn open, as if by a giant can-opener. Half of his face is gone. Like a punctured rubber balloon he sinks down in his own blood.

'Russians! The Russians are coming,' a party of Grenadiers shout fearfully. They come down from the heights as if the devil himself was at their heels.

Barcelona sends a long, chattering burst into something he thinks is a Russian. I tear a grenade from by belt, pull the cord and sling it from me.

The antitank gun barks poisonously, joining the long rattling fire of the SMG's.

'Now it's cookin',' moans Porta, glassy-eyed, pressing the butt of the LMG into his shoulder.

In front of us star-decorated helmets loom through the poisonous mist.

'*Uhraeh! Uhraeh!*' the shout comes, hoarsely, as the khaki-clad hordes spew out of the mill on the brow of the height.

Feverishly we ready our automatic weapons. Mpi's hammer at shadows. Hand grenades rain down on the closely-packed attackers.

A signaller works at his apparatus, screams into the mouthpiece. The line is dead. Every wire has been cut long ago. He kicks the silent telephone, viciously.

'We need the guns to cover us,' says Oberst Hinka, who has come up to the front with his entire staff, armed with carbines and machine-pistols.

'Let's send the schoolteacher, that inky-arsed bleeder,' suggests Tiny, laughing noisily becuse he thinks he has said something funny.

'You nuts, or something?' answers Porta. 'He wouldn't stop going till he was halfway out in the Atlantic!'

'He's dead,' laughs Gregor, looking at the schoolteacher's slumped body half under a rock.

'You dead?' roars Tiny, jabbing at him with a bayonet.

'Leave me alone,' pipes the schoolteacher, desperately.

'Dear God, what have I done to have to go through all this? Help me, comrades. Help me!'

'Shut your trap, you cowardly swine,' orders the Old Man, harshly.

As he speaks the skies open. It is as if it were the gates of hell! Fire from the heavy artillery sweeps roaring down over the earth. 210 mm shells drop so closely together that it is unbelievable anyone can survive them. Slowly the shelling increases to a deafening, angry roar which takes away our breath.

The attacking Russian columns are blown away in a rain of fire and steel. A Russian soldier comes staggering out of the glowing cloud of sulphur fumes. His whole stomach is ripped open. His entrails drag behind him. He disappears in a fountain of flame.

Groups of weaponless soldiers press themselves, screaming, into the ground. One terrific suck of air and they are scattered like chaff into the sweeping tempest of fire.

'Forward!' roars Oberst Hinka, signalling with his only arm.

We wade through dead bodies and screaming wounded, slipping on pieces of raw meat and the remains of human beings. We throw ourselves down for a moment behind a heap of bodies. It grows from minute to minute.

'Forward!' shout company and platoon leaders, but uselessly. Get on your feet and you're smashed immediately to a pulp.

The mad rain of high explosives rolls on up over the heights, like a volcano in eruption. An unbelievable concentration of artillery fire smashes down on us, pulverising everything to dust and ashes. Hell kisses the earth! Poisonous, sickening gases rise from bubbling, steaming holes and craters.

The giant prison on the hill is pecked at unceasingly by innumerable shells from the heavy guns.

I don't know how long I have been lying alongside a camouflage-uniformed soldier, before I realise he is a Russian. We have huddled close together, seeking protection and consolation from the fiery rain of metal. It is as if all the powers of evil have been unleashed in one mad, uncontrollable raging convulsion.

The mill on top of the first hill disappears in a cloud of snow, earth and fire. Literally pulverised. When the artillery fire moves on, only its five huge chimneys are left pointing accusingly at the sky.

I look nervously at the Russian, and he looks, fearfully, back at me. He is a little, fat man wrapped in a greatcoat much too big for him. We smile, carefully, at one another. Weak, frightened smiles. Without saying a word we promise one another: 'If you don't kill me, I won't kill you either!'

For a short moment there is a terrifying silence. It is as if the guns are taking a deep breath, before readying themselves for a new attack.

In front of and behind us flames shiver in a crazy devil-dance. From all sides come the groans and cries of the wounded. A roaring sound commences, far off in the distance. It comes quickly closer. It is as if the earth is being turned inside out. Bodies whirl up into the air and come down again with a loud, final slap.

No. 4. Section is sucked up in a spiral. High in the air they seem to explode into a mist of flesh, bones and blood. The river boils like a kettle. The yard-thick ice is long since gone. Large sheets of it lie far out from the banks. The lower part of a man comes running out of the orange-yellow smoking hell. Where is the rest of him? In all its horror the occurrence seems almost comical. A pair of boots and trousers rushing along all on their own through the snow.

'It's the nerves,' says Julius, who always knows it all.

'*Für Führer und Reich, Heil!*' crows Porta, ceremoniously, watching the legs, which have sunk down in a bloody bundle into the snow.

A giant shell explodes in the middle of the long, white house. The house disappears in the blast.

154

The company which has been taking cover behind it is blown away. Along the entire street houses are cut across the middle. Suddenly the streets are filled with blood-spattered civilians, milling around and screaming in horror at their plight.

In the midst of the smoking ruins a platoon of shocked German infantrymen sit staring with dead glassy eyes. Dead, yet still alive.

'New lot for Giessen, there!' nods Porta.

Tanks and armoured sleighs pour out from the prison hill, and descend the slopes, each in its cloud of snow. With a crash they land, and bounce forward over the cleft. The tracks of many of them are broken. Shells whine over us and explode behind us like brilliant red poppies.

From the forest an increasing roar can be heard. It is the remains of the German tanks starting up. They have been held back in readiness. They sweep past in broad arrow formation.

From a shell-hole and a half-destroyed dugout a group of machine-guns fire on anything which moves. Even the dead do not escape. Bodies jump at the impact.

'Take *them*!' roars Oberst Hinka, pointing with his Mpi.

The flamethrower crew creeps forward through the tumbled snow. Two men cover a wicked looking Obergefreiter, who has the heavy equipment on his back.

A spear of flame shoots towards the battered position. A scream of terror is heard. Burning shapes appear. Fall to the ground, writhing. Two more jets of flaming oil pour over them. Rags of flesh and uniform spurt from firing-slits as if from an exploding powder-keg.

The MG's fall silent.

The Obergefreiter with the flamethrower looks around him for a new target.

Like red lightning the flame pours over another machine-gun nest. Even in death the Russians continue firing. The tongue of flame returns. Rolling like a coloured ball, it seeks out every hiding-place in the shell-hole.

A filthy stench of burnt meat hits us like a clenched fist.

I feel as if the sweat on the back of my neck is beginning to boil. The terrible smell sickens us.

All around us we can hear the crack of tank guns. Burning tanks send up great mushrooming clouds of oily smoke.

Slowly, our section works its way forward. We have advanced a good way up the hill. We jump over twisted skeletons of steel, our feet slip on the remains of dead humanity.

The ground opens again in a sea of flame.

'Stalin organs!' roars Barcelona, going head-over-heels into a hole which is still smoking from a shell-burst. In the distance we hear a mad howling which changes to a cyclonic roar. Then the third movement. Strike and explosion. A long, monstrous, rolling roar, louder than any until now.

Time after time we are buried in mountains of snow. We fight madly to escape before we are suffocated in it.

'Forward! Come on! Up with you!' shouts Oberst Hinka.

We crawl, run and slide towards the prison, which towers threateningly in front of us.

We storm into the Russian defence positions.

'Roll 'em up!' comes the order.

We wipe them out in no time. With uniforms soaked in blood we rush onwards. We begin to be able to see details of the long prison building.

The dark skies open, and Jabo's[1] appear, cannon fire jetting from their wings.

We try to find cover in the ruins of the mill. Clouds of flour and bran almost choke us. It is as if our throats are stopped with lumps of dough.

I slide down a long chute. I glimpse a Russian with a lifted spade. I let off a whole clip at him. He jack-knifes, screaming, and falls into a boiler filled with a heavy gruel. A few bubbles form on the surface and burst.

'I can't! I can't!' groans Leutnant Haase from 3. Platoon. His voice is choked with tears. His eyes stare wildly. A terrific blast wave throws him back against a concrete wall. He creeps back, screaming.

'No! No!' he babbles. He pushes forward his Mpi and

[1]Jabo: Jagerbombemaschinen (Fighterbombers).

156

sends bullet after bullet into a bloated corpse. It explodes, gassily.

'Shell-fucked 'e is!' growls Tiny, dropping on him with all his weight.

'Knock him out!' orders the Old Man.

Tiny swings his enormous fist. It hammers into the Leutnant's face with a heavy thud. He crumples like an empty sack.

A P-2 tank comes flying through the air and crashes through an outhouse. It bounces onwards like a huge rubber ball. Trees, ruins, snow, even the river, seem to flame where the Stalin organ's rockets have fallen. The flames lick the heavens, dancing through the spectrum from sharp yellow to violet and blood-red. The heat strikes us, like a glowing blanket falling down on us from the rose-coloured clouds.

We stare, fascinated, at the unbelievable sight. A thundering rolls through the winter night.

'Full *cover*!' screams the Old Man, rolling down like lightning into a depression in the ground.

A party of shocked Russians appear from the uneven ground, closely followed by an equally terrified party of Germans. Far behind us we hear a howling, whistling sound.

'It's *them*!' cries Gregor, in terror.

'280 mm's! Jumpin' Jacks by Christ!'

The entire salvo drops in the middle of the fleeing Russians and Germans. Their bodies explode into an enormous pink cloud. It falls on us like a heavy rain. That salvo should have dropped two hundred yards in front of us. Half an hour ago! Now it drops straight on top of us, killing both Germans and Russians. They promised us massed artillery support. A fire concentration of which we had never seen the like. They were right! They were not exaggerating. Their fire has completely destroyed our own men. At least eighty per cent of our attacking force is lying out there smeared into the snow.

'That Goddam artillery's *killing* us!' groans Porta, forcing his way into cover beneath some charred beams. 'How little do you have to *make* yourself to get through this lot alive?'

All around us great lumps of frozen snow, earth, rock,

snapped-off tree trunks, and twisted metal are blown towards the sky. Terrified men are pinned to the earth by long spears of steel which come flying through the night. Arms and legs are torn from quivering bodies and thrown to one side like rubbish. The whole area becomes a giant dump of human spare parts in the course of seconds. It steams with blood and ripped out entrails.

'It's our own fuckin' artillery shootin' us down,' screams an Oberfeldwebel, desperately, getting up to run to cover. A blast throws him up against the remains of a stone wall. He is crushed like an egg-shell.

The ex-Oberst jumps to his feet, and emits an echoing scream.

Gregor grabs at him, and pulls him half under cover. The next second his head leaves his body. Cut off as if by a giant knife. Startled, Gregor lets go of his ankle. The headless body sits up, with a thick stream of blood spouting from its neck. The head, its eyes widely open, rolls along over the hard-packed snow.

We avoid the rolling head, automatically lifting our feet to let it pass. Tiny, who is consuming the remains of a frozen duck he has liberated from a dead commissar, does not notice the head, which rolls on and stops at his feet.

'Well I'll be?' he cries, in surprise, forgetting to bite into the duck. 'Who do you think *you're* starin' at, you silly sod? It ain't *my* fault you've lost your body, now, is it? Gerrout on it!' he snarls, waving the hand holding the frozen duck. He gives the head a kick which sends it flying out over the snow.

A major of Panzer Grenadiers screams hysterically at Tiny and threatens him with a court-martial. But the major disappears in a sea of flame. Only his steel helmet is left behind, rocking desolately in the snow.

By my side lies an elderly Hauptmann whose whole side has been torn open. It resembles the offal bin of a slaughterhouse. Splintered bone and shreds of flesh. His face is a mirror of pain and horror. War is a hell of agony and shredded nerves, fear and terror. When will it be me? Me who will be thrown up into the air. A geyser of smashed bone, flesh and blood.

Flames shoot up from the earth. Glowing fragments of weapons, houses, animals and human beings rain down over the positions.

A cook-waggon, spouting soup and potatoes, comes flying through the air. The horses whirl, screaming, head over heels together with the waggon. A storm comes rushing over us, followed by a piercing howl. The next second the earth shakes to renewed colossal explosions.

A sleigh company is caught on its way into the gulch and paints the steep sides of it with a slick of blood and crushed bone. The heavy motor sleighs are reduced to heaps of twisted metal scrap.

The OC of 2. Company has both legs torn off, just above the knee. He crashes down with a shrill scream. He reminds us of a torn rag doll, lying there. Nobody goes to his assistance. There are too many wounded and dead. We cannot interest ourselves in their fate.

'*C'est la guerre!*' says the Legionnaire. 'More garbage for the military muck-heap!'

Obergefreiter Lamm gets hit just as he is taking a huge bite at a Westphalian sausage. With a completely astonished, lost look on his face, he slumps against the wall of the entrenchment. A piece of shrapnel has left only a tiny hole in his forehead. Hardly any blood issues from it.

'By all the devils of Castile,' cries Barcelona. He grabs at his throat. Blood trickles out between his fingers.

'You're 'it!' shouts Tiny, in dismay, bending over him. 'Jesus'n Mary it's gone right through you! Lucky you weren't eatin' at the time. That Commie bullet'd 'ave took your grub with it!'

'This is what comes out of going to war with generals who shave their heads and wear monocles,' says Porta, applying dressings to the hole. 'They've got only one thing in their heads, those boys. That's getting their names in the history books. We lot foot the bill by getting ourselves shot to bits!'

'Want to go back?' asks the Old Man, jogging up from the far end of the position.

'No, I'll stay here,' answers Barcelona, decidedly. 'I don't want to get separated from the boys!'

'Think you'll be all right?' asks the Old Man, doubtfully, staring at the entry hole. 'You can see your feet through that!'

'I'm *stayin'*,' mumbles Barcelona, firmly. 'There's something tells me if I leave you lot I'll never come back!'

'The God of Germany's pissin' on us,' Tiny explains to a Russian corporal who just jumped down to us by mistake. '*Panjemajo?*'

'*Nix panjemajo,*' answers the Russian, handing Tiny a *machorka,* in the belief that he has asked for a cigarette.

Tiny accepts it and offers the Russian a swig from his water-bottle.

'We ought to've run into one another on the Reeperbahn,' he says, with a broad grin. 'Might've 'ad some fun together. I could've got you bags of 'Amburg cunt cheap, and between times we could've taken the piss out of Commissioner bleedin' Nass. Bleedin' pity we 'ad to 'ave a war 'fore we could meet one another. Specially when its 'ere, where a bloke can risk gettin' killed forty ways from Sunday!'

'*Nix panjemajo!*' grins the Russian, sheepishly. He fishes a snapshot from his tunic pocket. '*Nevaéssta*[2]' he explains, kissing the greasy photograph. It is dog-eared from having been looked at so often.

'Be all right on a sheet, she would!' Tiny says appreciatively, laughing like a Cheshire cat. ' 'Aven't got them yellow monkeys quartered on *your* village I 'ope? They say them Mongol bleeders fuck 'em that fast even the rabbits go dizzy watchin' it!'

'*Nix panjemajo!*' says the Russian, putting the photograph back in his pocket. '*Vaernútssa, dassvidánya*[3].' He gets up suddenly and shakes hands all round.

We help him up over the lip of the trench. Just before he disappears from sight in the snow, he turns and waves to us.

'Think he'll get through?' asks the Old Man, doubtfully.

'They'll shoot him,' says Porta, knowledgeably. 'It's high

[2]Nevaéssta: Sweetheart.
[3]Vaernútssa, dassvidánya: I'm off home, goodbye.

treason to exchange two words with us capitalists.

'We ought to 'ave given 'im the schoolteacher to take back as a prisoner. 'E'd 'ave been all right then,' says Tiny. '*And* we'd 'ave got rid of the whinin' little shit. 'E's that bleedin' dumb 'e can't find 'is own arse'ole even when 'e uses both 'ands!'

The bitterly cold wind has now turned to a raging blizzard. Huge clouds of snow and crystals of frost sweep across the icy, shivering earth. Snowdrifts move like waves in a storm-tossed sea, burying tanks, guns, horses and soldiers irrespective of uniform.

The murderous gunfire continues incessantly. Countless horses are stuck fast in the snow. Teamsters' whips crack, but the animals only kick themselves deeper and deeper into the snow. Their screams cut through the thunder of the shells. Roads have disappeared, buried in mountainous drifts. We try to mark them by pushing long sticks with wisps of straw tied to their ends, deep down into the snow.

Dragging our feet we force our way forward, leaving many behind in the white hell. The frost soon finishes them off. The catastrophe is complete. Our artillery has certainly done a good job — on us!

A Russian colonel, the tails of his open greatcoat flapping behind him, comes running through the snow. He rushes on, fully convinced that everyone is trying to kill him. He stumbles and rolls a long way.

'*Germanski! Germanski!*' he screams with mouth agape. He is swallowed in a fountain of flame which shoots up from the earth and takes the shape of a giant, violet mushroom.

Now the barrage rolls along the ground like a carpet of steel. Every battery is engaged. What has been happening previously is as nothing to the destructive fire which roars down on us now.

Six runaway horses come bolting over the frozen snow with a 100 mm field-gun bouncing behind them. Three gunners hold on for dear life. One of them loses his grip and is crushed under the heavy wheels of the gun-carriage. The gun bangs up and down like a toy cannon.

A Supplies NCO is hit by a ricochet and falls from his horse. His foot catches in the stirrup. With a loud crack his head smashes against a rock.

Three P-4's come roaring from the remains of the shot-riddled village. The leading tank suddenly spins on the icy surface, slides backwards and to one side, and rolls, crashing and clanging, down a steep slope. The flame of an explosion spurts from its turret. Coal-black smoke mushrooms up. Another P-4 goes into a skid. The commander in the open turret hatchway tries to get out. Halfway, the steel hatch cover snaps down on him, crashing his hips. The heavy tank rolls over on him, crushing him to a bloody pulp.

A party of unarmed German infantrymen comes sliding down a slope. They have only one thought in their heads. Escape. Escape anywhere. If only they can get away from this thundering, flaming inferno which is ploughing up the heights.

A Kübel, with a G-staff flag, brakes on the icy snow and goes into a long sideways slide. It is a wonder it does not crash down onto the wrecked tanks.

An Oberstleutnant with carmine G-staff tabs jumps from the Kübel with Mpi at the ready.

'Back, you cowardly dogs!' he roars, swinging a punch at a Leutnant in a uniform filthy with blood. 'Back to your positions, you dirty deserters!' He lifts his weapon and sends several short, well-aimed bursts into the troops crowding down from the flaming heights.

'Kill the bastard!' screams a Feldwebel, furiously, attempting to wrest the Oberstleutnant's Mpi from him. 'First they smash us up with our own guns, now they're tryin' to mow us down with their machine-pistols!'

'To hell with you, you war-mad sod!' shouts a Jaeger Unteroffizier. He throws himself on the Oberstleutnant, foaming at the mouth with rage, grasps him by the throat and strangles the life out of him.

The driver of the Kübel snatches up an Mpi and sends a long, barking burst into the mob of furious soldiers who are stamping the Oberstleutnant's body into the snow.

'You fuckin' sons of bitches,' he shouts, in a white-hot rage. He throws a grenade into the crowd. Panting at the exertion he drags the body to the vehicle and throws a greatcoat over it. He threatens the fleeing mob. 'Die then, like the shit you are!' he screams, with tears of despair choking his voice. 'You don't deserve any better. Arseholes of the Army *you* are!' He edges under the steering wheel and takes the Kübel off in a cloud of powdery snow.

Now the Russians send a new hell of flame down on us. Rockets whine from the clouds, hammering down into the fleeing troops and smashing men and material to pieces. Salvo after salvo of rockets, with long fiery tails, come shooting across the skies.

'Stalin Organs,' groans Gregor, pressing himself further down into the snow.

A pair of T-34's comes from the narrow gulch, thundering over the heaps of dead and sending a spray of blood, flesh and bone to all sides.

'Flamethrower tanks!' screams Barcelona, furiously. He drops down behind a tall rock.

Albert rushes round in circles, trying desparately to find cover from the rapidly approaching flamethrower tanks.

'Where's there a hole? Where's there a hole?' he screams, jumping about like a shot rabbit.

'Come on down here,' shouts Porta, hospitably. 'We'll throw out the teacher and make room for you!'

Albert dives headfirst into the deep shell-hole.

'Jesus Christ!' he pants, in a fearful voice. 'This ain't no place for human bein's. Black *or* white!'

'Don't get big-'eaded, now,' says Tiny, with a broad grin. 'The 'uman race starts at Leutnant. The rest's nix an' nothin'! That's *us* lot!'

'I've never been much of a one for infantry field service,' confesses Albert, throwing away his white snow mask. 'And there was nothing that prepared you for this at Sennelager and Grafenwöhr!' He grinds his teeth together so violently that he almost puts his jaw out of joint.

'Life *ain't* much fun up front!' says Tiny, in a melancholy voice. He ducks quickly as a grenade falls just in front of the lip of the hole and sends a storm of shrapnel whining across the terrain.

We can hear the threatening approach of the flamethrower

tanks, even through the roar of the guns.

'We *must* have artillery support,' says the Old Man. 'If we don't get it we'll end up in the lap of the Devil!' He rolls the Signals Officer's body off the telephone, and settles the rubber-cushioned earphones on his head.

'The code, dammit!' mumbles the Old Man, irritably, leafing through the message pad.

'Here,' says Heide, handing him the code book.

'Fire support!' orders the Old Man in a harsh, commanding tone.

'Who is speaking?' comes the question, in the arrogant snarl of a higher-ranking officer.

' "Newt" here!' answers the Old Man. He spits a series of orders into the apparatus.

Soon after, shells come howling over us, and hail down on the heights.

With a few sharp words the Old Man corrects the short-fall. Heide works feverishly, drawing lines on the chart and calculating distances with the help of the spotter's instruments.

Snow and steel spurt up from the shell-bursts. They are now closer to the gulch in which the Stalin Organs are positioned.

'T-34's, for fuck's sake!' says Porta, excitedly. 'Blow 'em quick, or we've *had* it!'

At least a battalion of flamethrower tanks are operating. Moving in curves like a herd of wild boar. Jets of flame spurt from their turrets turning everything living in their path to charred, smoking lumps.

Crowds of cheering Red Army soldiers storm from the OGPU prison. Mpi battalions first. Then infantry, with bayoneted rifles as if they were parading across the Red Square. Behind the infantry, column after column of prisoners, in grey uniforms, armed only with clubs. As they advance they pick up the weapons of the fallen. Finally OGPU special troops, with Kalashnikovs aimed at the backs of the prisoners. Their job is to liquidate anyone attempting to break for cover.

'God in Heaven,' cries Oberstleutnant Löwe. 'They'll *crush* us, smash us completely. We *must* retreat!'

A barrage of incredibly concentrated fire falls behind us. It is as if the Russians have guessed we are thinking of flight, and intend to defeat our purpose by laying down a barrage through which we cannot possibly break. It stretches on each side of us for as far as we can see.

'Re*treat*!' shouts Oberst Hinka. 'By companies, re*treat*!' He turns, in astonishment, to see what is occasioning the deafening howl approaching from behind us. From the German lines.

'Rockets!' he cries, in surprise, throwing himself down behind a wall of snow.

Next moment, the feared rockets fall right in the middle of the flamethrower tank formation, throwing the heavy vehicles about as if they were no more than toys.

Cool and collected, the Old Man gives his corrections to the high-ranking artillery officer far to the rear.

'Two degrees less,' he orders. 'Sixty yards more length.'

Fire and steel fountain into the air.

'Got 'em!' cheers Barcelona, wildly.

Flames fountain up from the T-34's. Pieces of the tanks fly through the snow-laden air. Coal-black mushrooms of cloud, streaked with crimson, form high above the ground. The battle-field seems to dissolve in the rolling thunder of the guns.

From the redly glowing blanket of smoke, large, formless shapes come flying. It is as if the devil were playing bowls with tanks. The organ note of the heavy explcsives changes from second to second, rising to a nerve shattering howl. We huddle together, shivering.

'Explosives and incendiaries,' the Old Man demands. 'Rapid fire 460 yards right.'

Soon, heavy high explosive and incendiary shells begin to fall on the attacking Russian infantry forces. Chemicals splash out on all sides. Even the air begins to burn.

'Thirty yards back,' orders the Old Man, coldly.

The blast from the explosives throws us back against the snowy walls of our shellhole. The ground in front of us is a boiling, bubbling, poisonous porridge. The snow melts into rushing cataracts, which pour down the slopes, carrying everything in their path with them into the depths.

165

More and more artillery units are coupled in, as it becomes obvious that an expert is spotting for them.

'Who's the spotter?' asks a sharp voice. 'Name and rank damn you? Is it *you*, Eberhardt? Heard you'd fallen! Masterly, Eberhardt, masterly!'

The Old Man does not reply, even though he has recognised the Commanding General's knife-like voice. Without permitting time for interruption he continues to give corrections.

In a giant drumfire the rain of shells follows the retreating enemy battalions. Mercilessly they are being cut to shreds.

'New correction,' the Old Man demands.

'Here you are,' says Heide, with a sadistic grin. His military heart sings with happiness at the bloody results of the well-directed artillery fire.

Soon, the guns reach down into the ravine and smash the mobile Stalin Organs. Their attempts at escape do not succeed.

The remains of the regiment attack through the mess of carnage, at the heels of one-armed Oberst Hinka. Heavy Maxim MG's still fire from the ruined positions.

'Radio Group, centre,' screams Oberst Hinka. 'Forward to prison walls!'

Yellowy-grey clouds of smoke from the high explosives hang like a huge, horrible umbrella above the prison. Every second they grow in size.

Quite close by I hear the crack of a tank gun. Close behind me a machine-gun spatters the snow with bullets.

'*Panzer*!' I shout, throwing myself into cover. I see the huge underbelly of the tank ride up over a partially destroyed wall. It balances there for a brief moment. Rocks over and forward with a clang of metal. The motor roars at maximum revolutions.

Slowly the turret swings in my direction. Flame jets from the long barrel of the gun. Firing, impact and explosion come almost in unison.

My head feels as if an iron rod had been passed through it from ear to ear. Porta comes sliding over to me. The bazooka slips from his grasp and slides over the icy ground. Fascinated I stare at the gun on the Stalin tank, which is slowly sinking towards me.

'About time,' mumbles Porta, grabbing the 'stovepipe' and putting it to his shoulder. He gets the tank in his sights. 'Enjoy life, dear neighbour, there may not be a lot of it,' he grins, sardonically, and pulls the trigger.

A hollow, thunderous explosion, and the red star on the turret disappears abruptly. A human figure is thrown from the hatchway on the tip of an enormous yellow flame.

'That was close,' I say, letting out the deep breath I have been holding.

Two T-34's roll into cover behind some ruins. Their turret machine-guns sweep the whole length of the road. Spent bullets ricochet over our heads.

'We're not meant to die here, God tells me,' shouts Porta, rising to his feet with his 'stovepipe' at his shoulder.

Tiny rushes in with a heavy T-mine in his hand. He slides like a toboggan across the road towards the tank, roaring loudly in a mixture of rage and fear. He holds on to the mine tightly, but loses both helmet and machine-pistol during his rapid passage.

Like an acrobat he regains his feet and swings the T-mine up under the turret rim.

The hatch of the rearmost T-34 crashes open. A leather-clad form comes to view with a Kalashnikov at the ready.

Bullets plough up the snow around Tiny. He runs for dear life towards the burning ruins, trying to reach cover.

'Death and damnation, man, how they do *shoot*,' roars Albert, coming jumping through the snow with a Molotov cocktail in his hand. Fast as an old tom-cat caught stealing herring, he is up on the T-34. He drops the Molotov cocktail down inside the tank behind the T-34 commander. The Russian turns and stares in amazement at Albert's black features and pearly-white rows of teeth, showing in a happy grin.

'*Panjemajo*, man!' yells Albert, turning a back somersault down into a smoking shellhole. The tank goes up in fragments, before its commander has had time to recover from his astonishment.

Tiny races across the snow with one of the tank's heavy caterpillar track rollers coming trundling after him.

I hold my breath in terror. If it hits him, he'll be crushed to death. But by some miracle it strikes a stone, jumps into the air, and passes above his body. It rolls on across the road and crashes into a machine-gun nest.

The flamethrower section hurries past. Infantry storm up towards the closed prison gates.

From the barred windows MG fire hammers at us. Flares hang in the sky like brilliant umbrellas, throwing a ghostly light down on the prison. Black smoke pours from its roof.

The engineers place explosives along the walls.

A Russian officer appears suddenly in front of me.

A short burst from my Mpi throws him back against the prison gates. He falls forward, smashing his face into the ground. Desperately I run on, and collide with a half-crazy jailer, who is swinging a huge bunch of keys in one hand and a pistol in the other.

The first bullet from my Mpi hits him in the heart blowing it to pieces. He is dead before he hits the ground.

A huge stone comes flying through the air and hits me with enormous force in the chest. All the air is knocked out of my lungs. I fall forward, my face buried in the snow. How long I remain lying there I shall never know. I hear guttural Russian voices, when I come to myself. One of them kicks me brutally, but I manage to remain silent, despite the pain.

They run on, while the machine-guns continue to chatter.

I know it is dangerous to lie there too long without help. I could freeze to death. Or die of shock. My chest is burning like fire, and the pain comes in steadily increasing jabs. Everywhere dark running shapes. It is impossible to determine which are Russian, and which German.

Long, fiery tongues of flame lick out from the barred windows of the six-floor tall buildings of the women's wing. In the light of the flames I can just make out human beings gripping the red-hot bars of the windows. Heavy window-glass melts like wax. It takes only seconds to transform a human being to a blackened, charred mummy.

'What the hell are you lying here for, basking in the glow of

Russian Communism,' asks Porta, with a wide grin, bending over me. 'Where'd they shoot you?'

'Chest,' I gasp.

With sure fingers he examines me.

'Lucky,' he says. 'All you can see's your pale skin goin' the colour of Albert's.'

'It was a stone. A huge stone,' I groan.

'Hell!' cries Porta. 'Ivan must be runnin' short of ammo' if he's startin' to throw stones at us.'

'What's wrong?' asks the Old Man, stopping. He has Heide with him.

'He says Ivan's thrown a stone at him,' grins Porta, unworriedly, 'and there he lies moaning like a sick cat!'

'Come on! On your feet, son!' orders the Old Man, harshly. 'Don't go thinking you're on a winter sports holiday!'

'I've got to see the M.O.,' I groan. 'I — I think my ribs are broken, and it feels as if they're going into my lungs.'

'Take a couple of deep breaths,' suggests Porta. 'You'll see! *That'll* straighten out the timbers in your old hull for you.'

'I want to see the M.O.,' I demand, stubbornly.

'You *do* not think that pox doctor's clerk's hangin' around out here in the heavy rain, surely?' says Porta. 'Get up on your pins and keep with us. Stay here and old Ivan'll give you *his* treatment. A dose of *his* cough mixture and you'll need a magnifying glass to find any ribs at all!'

Groaning with the pain, which is enough to drive a man mad, I hobble on after the section. A strange medical orderly gives me a handful of pills.

We throw mines into the great reception hall. The thick walls crumble as if made of glass. Heavy iron-bound doors crash through walls. The blast throws us backwards, but we are soon up and storm into the prison. Mpi's chatter at anything that moves.

Great piles of bodies lie in the hall, all with the same red, blown-up faces. Blast makes you look like that when it has killed you. Many of them are only youths with soft, downy cheeks. Lives lost before they even knew the value of what they are losing. Killed in acts of meaningless heroism.

Silently we stand amongst the mounds of bodies and look around us at the terrible sight. Bodies lie thick on the staircases. Six floors of them. Many of the cell doors hang by one hinge. In the cells the bodies of prisoners lie broken like blood-splattered dolls. Apparently killed by grenades which the jailers have thrown into their cells, before fleeing.

'Just like home,' says Porta, sadly. 'Prisoners killed to prevent their falling into enemy hands. It's *dangerous* to think independently.'

'There's one alive 'ere!' shouts Tiny, who has kicked open the door to one of the offices.

Behind a desk sits a giant of a man, dressed in the green OGPU uniform, with gold stars embroidered on his arms.

'Aja *tovaritch*,' shouts Heide, happily. He jabs the highly-placed officer with the muzzle of his machine pistol. The officer watches us with hate-filled eyes.

The Legionnaire picks up some papers from the desk.

'Execution orders,' he says, smiling, and hands the documents to Oberleutnant Löwe.

'Take him away,' orders Löwe, shortly, 'but God help you, Unteroffizier Kalb, if anything happens to him! I will hold you responsible for killing a prisoner.'

'*Par Allah*, I shall look after him as carefully as if he were a hair of the Prophet's beard,' promises the Legionnaire, with a wicked grin. 'Come on,' he snarls at the OGPU Commissar, giving him a brutal blow in the back with the butt of his Mpi. 'May Allah grant you, in His mercy, the curse of a lingering death, you heathen dog of a Russian! And may small flames melt away the fat from your bones for all eternity!'

A crowd of strangely-dressed people totter and stumble down the steep stairs, women and men. One of them is wearing a suit of blue-striped pyjamas, another the uniform of an Esthonian major. One is wearing pale riding breeches and a black smoking jacket topped off by a scarf which was once white. Most of them are, however, dressed in rags and tatters of clothing. Here and there a blue OGPU cap can be seen.

We keep our machine pistols at the ready. The sight of this

strange collection of people makes us nervous. They look as if they are ready to spring at our throats at any moment.

'You goin' to give us food?' shouts one of them, menacingly, and spits on the floor.

'Keep your trap shut!' shouts another.

Suddenly they seem to be afflicted by a communal rage. They all begin to shout at the same time.

'Bonysov is here!' almost in chorus.

'Kill him! Trample him flat! The stinking pig!'

'What the devil are they up to?' shouts Oberleutnant Löwe, nervously. 'Break 'em up! Then get 'em into line! Any trouble put 'em back in the cells. Then at least they can't murder one another!'

'*C'est indifferent,*' grins the little Legionnaire, cynically. 'All they want to do is to get hold of their dirty jailers.' He points with his Mpi to a bloody corpse, stamped almost flat. In the middle of the mess lies a blue cap.

The prisoners stare at us, and we stare questioningly back at them. We are a little scared of these skeleton-like creatures with their deeply sunken eyes.

'Hell of a pong, isn't it?' mumbles the Old Man, holding his hand to his nose.

'From there,' says Tiny, pointing with his thumb.

'Hell and Tommy!' cries Barcelona. 'That's the biggest an' longest latrine I ever *did* see.'

'Try looking down into it,' suggests Porta. 'There's something else down there you never saw either.'

A little man, with ratty eyes, wearing an OGPU uniform, comes towards us with his hands folded behind his neck to show he is unarmed and finished with the war.

'Herr Kommandant, sir,' he barks in fluent German, clicking his heels together in front of Oberleutnant Löwe. 'I hereby hand over to you the prison reception department, and place myself under your command.'

Without hiding his contempt Oberleutnant Löwe looks at him carefully, his eyes like slits.

'What is that?' he asks, pointing to the long wooden beam.

'Prisoners latrine,' answers the OGPU man, with a crooked

171

smile. 'We can't manage one any better. We have our regulations, and we follow them. The prisoners are pigs. They are allowed to go to the latrine at certain specified times. This is not a luxury hotel. But they cannot wait for the proper defecation time. They shit in their cells. Then when they sit on the plank they fall asleep and fall down into the latrine. There they drown. It is not the fault of the jailers. We follow orders like other soldiers.'

'Let's drop *him* in the shit!' suggests Porta, with a wicked smile.

'Take him away,' answers Oberleutnant Löwe, turning on his heel. 'Let's get out of here! We have no more to do here. We are a fighting unit, not jailers, either for one side or the other!'

Over at the great wings of the prison fighting is still going on fiercely.

'Just like our lot,' says Porta, pointing at a huge pale-blue sign which can be seen from all the prison buildings.

FOR OUR FATHERLAND, FOR STALIN

it says in large red letters. In slightly smaller black letters:

WE LIQUIDATE WITHOUT HESITATION
ALL ENEMIES OF THE PEOPLE
ALL IDLERS, ALL TRAITORS

On the wall of the great machine workshop, in yard-high letters, is written:

WORK IS THE GREATEST
PRIVILEGE AND BENEFIT
OF THE SOCIALIST STATE

'Come! Forward! Over *here*!' shouts the Old Man, signalling 2. Section to collect on him.

We throw outselves into cover under a long ramp.

'We're going through here,' explains the Old Man. 'Prepare the charges! These swine have barricaded themselves inside, and are using the prisoners for cover!'

A long, gurgling scream cuts him short. It is a woman. She is

172

screaming with a horrible intensity, as if in her death agony, under terrible torture.

'God preserve us,' cries Barcelona, aghast. 'What *can* they be doing to her?'

'Pinching her with hot irons. That's what the priests used to do in the old days,' says Porta, drily, snapping his fingers.

The scream is cut off sharply, as if the woman had suddenly been gagged.

'Let's get it over with,' orders the Old Man, his face hard. With an agile spring he is up on the ramps. Stooping he runs along it, followed by Gregor and the Legionnaire with the ammunition box full of explosives.

Tiny slings three or four of the heavy boxes up on to the ramp.

'You too, teacher,' he says, throwing him up after the boxes. 'God 'elp you, you scraggy bleeder, if I catch you skulkin'! I'll use you to pack the charges with, an' send you straight into the arms o' baggy-arsed Ivan!'

'Why are you always chasing me?' whines the schoolteacher. He tugs at one of the boxes, but cannot budge it.

'Keep your mouth shut! Both when I'm talkin' an' when I'm thinkin',' Tiny cuts him short. 'Take this pickaxe. Go an' make a 'ole for the powder, you walkin' son of a' inkwell you. When I'm finished with you you'll either be a corpse, or the best soldier in the German army an'll goosemarch all the way back to that village school o' yourn!'

'Get *on* with it,' shouts the Old Man, impatiently. 'Five yards between charges. Heide, you connect up the cables!'

'I'll blow 'em!' shouts Tiny, eagerly. He loves setting off explosions.

We work at feverish speed for the next half-hour.

'Do you realise how thick these walls *are*?' asks Barcelona. 'They're thicker than the walls of the fortress at Brest-Litovsk, and you wouldn't call *them* stage decorations exactly!'

'Can that *crap*!' scolds the Old Man, irritably.

He pushes Tiny's shoulder. The big fellow is intently pushing a triple charge into one of the holes.

'There's plenty of it,' Tiny defends himself, pointing at the

173

filled ammunition boxes. 'Besides, what we use we don't 'ave to carry back with us.'

'You want to go up with it, seems,' growls the Old Man, viciously. 'We're not packing toffees in there, you know. This is dangerous as hell!'

'Ready,' shouts Heide, strutting proudly back to the Old Man.

'Let me!' shouts Tiny, rushing to the pump, to which Gregor is connecting the last cables. ' 'Old on to your 'ats an' your arse'oles, my sons. We're gonna make bang-bang,' he laughs gaily. He grasps the handle firmly with both hands and leaning all his weight on it presses it home.

The explosion clears the ramp. We feel the pressure of the mighty blast-wave all over our bodies. The crushing power of it knocks all the air out of our lungs. A 20 foot high wall crumbles in a shower of crushed stones and mortar. A few seconds later the entire outer wall goes down. The whole building seems to sway for a moment, and then collapses in upon itself. Two tall chimneys by the boiler house fall in over the women's wing. The crashing seems to go on for ever; the dust cloud over the buildings to grow and grow.

There is a moment of complete silence. Flames shoot up from all sides, spreading with terrible speed. They look like a carpet being rolled out by a madman.

Walls fall. Great chunks of building material rain down.

'You silly sods!' curses a Feldwebel of engineers, wiping blood from his face. 'In hell's name! You haven't left a rat alive in there. I'd shove off if I were you. That'd worry *me*!'

'Jesus'n Mary,' cries Tiny, getting up on to his knees. 'That's what I call a bang! The 'ole bleedin' cage 'as gone for a burton! Be a bit 'fore they can 'ave it ready for the next lot o' slaves, wunnit? The Prisoners Aid Association'll give us a medal for this lot, in gratitude! Lord save us, what a *loverly* bang that *was*!'

Albert gets to his feet quite grey in the face, and lifts clenched fists above his head.

'Red Front!' he screams, idiotically.

'Get on,' orders the Old Man, rising to his feet. His Mpi is ready in his hands.

174

The flamethrower sections take the lead. Wherever there are fire-openings they send in a jet of flame.

I spring down, together with Porta, into the nearest defence post, and send the beam of my flashlight round the inside.

Everywhere charred bodies stretch fleshless hands out protectively in front of them. Many are nothing but shrunken mummies. The flamethrower has killed them in one fiery blast. Those who have not been hit directly look unnaturally large beside all the small mummies who have.

'Cruel war's quick war. Says so on the propaganda posters, anyway,' says Porta. 'But it's a lie, like everything else in this war. This one's the cruellest of the lot and it looks like being a hell of a long one.'

In a long, narrow yard, between two tall soot-blackened prison buildings, bodies lie in heaps.

'Neck-shot, the lot,' confirms Barcelona, turning a few of the bodies over with his Mpi.

'It's not true,' cries Gregor, unbelievingly, bending down to look more closely at a body in tattered rags.

'Too true it's true,' sighs Porta. 'The OGPU boys have been busy getting rid of the unbelievers, with us liberators knocking on the door. Don't need to have gone to detective school with the KRIPO's to see what's happened here. One in the neck! Little hole at the back and whole face blown off.'

Shots crack wickedly over on the other side of the building.

'Our lot,' explains the little Legionnaire, with an indifferent shrug. 'SD Special Troops. They are blowing away all the commissars!'

We stop for a moment, and stare from between two burnt-out lorries. The long, chattering burst seems to last an eternity but it is really over in a few seconds. The lanky commissar's body jumps about in the rain of bullets. First up into the air, then back down to the ground. His body still jerks spasmodically, even when all life has been shot out of it.

A boyish Untersturmführer, his cap, with the skull badge, rakishly over one eye, goes over to the body and points a P-38 at the head. Three shots and the face is smashed to an unrecognisable pulp.

The prisoners, who are hanging out of the windows of the laundry, cheer and clap, mad with enthusiasm.

The next one is pushed out from a narrow doorway. He is an elderly, white haired man in khaki with the green OGPU shoulder straps. With fear in his eyes he stands against the wall. A chattering salvo knocks him to the ground.

The prisoners cheer and whistle, as a party of uniformed and half-uniformed men and women is pushed out of the laundry.

'Come on! Come *on*!' rages the young SD-officer, impatiently. 'Let's get this over with quickly!'

With butt-strokes and kicks they are chased over to the wall. They stare, apathetically, at the killers with the death's-head emblem on their caps.

'Fire!' screams the SD-officer, mouth agape. The Mpi's rattle their death-song. The sound echoes back and forth between the buildings.

A long, vicious burst of MG fire comes from a window on the top floor.

The Untersturmführer sinks down. The execution squad is thrown backwards, writhing in the slowly reddening snow. The machine-gun traverses, ploughing furrows in the laundry walls. Glass smashes. Prisoners are blown away from the windows, faces smashed in.

We get down behind cover, and crawl hurriedly away. None of our business.

The flames make crazy patterns on the sooty prison buildings.

As we move round the long store houses, we are stopped by the sound of concentrated fire from automatic weapons. Shrill screams of terror come from the isolated bathhouse.

'Let's take a look in there,' orders the Old Man. 'You and Sven first,' he says to Porta, throwing a bag of grenades over to us.

Between the remains of broken-off trees we run towards the bathhouse. A figure rises up in front of me. Automatically I press the trigger, and a burst from my Mpi shatters his spine. He rolls over and over, arms and legs jerking.

Porta kicks the door, which flies open with a crash. A fat, little officer stares at us in amazement and fumbles confusedly for his Kalashnikov, which is lying on a table in front of him. A pistol bullet ploughs through his throat, sending his whole neck splashing back against the wall. His cap with its blue band rolls like a wheel across the floor, and settles softly alongside a heap of empty bottles.

I empty my gun in one long, concentrated burst, down a passage along which I more sense than see dark forms coming at us. The first shot from the Schmeisser hits the leader in the mouth. He falls without a sound. Our Mpi's seem to run amok.

Two soldiers in ankle-length greatcoats are lifted into the air and thrown against the wall. They slide down it, and collapse into sobbing, bloody ragheaps.

Grenades whirl into a dark room. We take cover against the wall and sweep it with Mpi bursts.

The screams subside slowly to a hoarse rattle.

'Get on,' commands the Old Man, taking a Kalashnikov from one of the dead.

A long snarling salvo of machine-pistol bullets whips at us. Albert jumps high in the air, gives out a shrill war-whoop and throws a potato-masher grenade. A thunderous crack comes from the far end of the corridor, a blinding flash, and three twisted bodies lie on the floor.

'Hell, man,' he groans, holding his hands to his ears. 'Was I shit-scared, man?' He looks about him, with a lost expression, and lets himself go down slowly to the floor, which is covered with torn human remains and broken glass. 'To hell with the whole rotten German Army,' he moans.

'Yes, one must admit you *do* seem to have got yourself into the wrong army, don't you?' laughs Porta, taking over the hand-grenades.

The fire, which no-one is fighting, has almost consumed the north wing of the women's prison.

We approach the glowing ruin carefully. It looks ready to fall on our heads, at any minute.

Whole rows of bodies hang around the women's wing, festooning it like horrible garlands, swinging and rotating in the air currents.

'Business as usual despite all difficulties,' says Porta.

177

'Executed five minutes before closing time!' He spits against the wind.

'They should have kept in step and held their silly, bloody traps,' says Gregor. 'There they are, now. Swinging. What good were all their protests. No. Better to go with the current and let *them* think and talk who have been given the job. You live longer that way, and life's short enough as it is.'

The fighting has almost ceased. From the main block the sound of automatic weapons and the sharp crack of grenades can be heard, sometimes broken by the thump of a mortar. But that's not our job. That's infantry and engineers' work.

We sit on the floor in the kitchen block, together with a party of prisoners, and talk about methods of interrogation.

A sixteen year old boy, arrested straight from school and accused of counter-revolutionary propaganda, had lost an eye during interrogation. He describes his experience in a few words.

We look silently at his face. It is far too old for his years. His eyes seep pus. There are no doctors in transit prisons.

An elderly man shows us his crushed toes, sadly.

'There's worse things,' cries a woman, who has been shot through the knee-caps. She will never walk properly again.

'We ought to shoot them jailers. The *lot* of 'em,' says Tiny, decisively, playing with his triple-barrelled shotgun.

'That's what they're doing,' says Porta, pointing with his thumb towards the yard, from which Mpi bursts, and unintelligible screams, come continuously.

The schnapps which Porta has liberated from the Commandant's cupboard is sweet and warms us beautifully.

A fat prison jailer, who was called 'Hell's Angel' because he was a friend of the prisoners, is sitting back to front on a chair and singing:

A snowstorm is sweeping over the plain.
Behind it wanders my heart's true swain. . . .

'Soon as we got in that bathhouse, man, she was breathing down my neck and *gnawin'* away at it,' Albert tells us, with a happy grin. 'Black men give me butterflies in the stomach, she says, an' then she starts playin' around with my balls!'

'Jesus on the Cross!' groans Tiny, his eyes wide, and scratching at his crotch. 'Go *on* then! Keep *talkin'*!'

'She takes off my summer tunic, then,' Albert continues, 'opens up my flies, an' pulls the old boy out. He was standing up there, right on the tips of his toes.'

'Don't you let go of him, now, I says. You drop *him*, an' I'll get all my toes broken! Well, she was down there in no time, suckin' away like a little ol' filly-foal goin' at its mammy's teats. Then I swung her up on the bench, and climbed her. In that steamy old bathhouse, man! The bells were ringing so hard in our ears, we thought it was Sunday. There ain't nothing like a Blitzmädel[4], who don't give a shit for the Führer and the final victory, but just wants to get fucked. When she fell asleep, off I went naked up to the convalescent huts. I met another of 'em on the way, an' *man*, we had it off up against a tree! Ice-cold birch tree, it was. *It* must've thought it was spring already 'cos it started buddin' two months too soon. After that I thought I'd take a little rest, but dropped right off to sleep. Well, what woke me was somebody feelin' me up, very gentle like. I opens my eyes an' it's two nurses from surgery. We made us up a nice little triangular tournament right on the spot. We done it German, French and Swedish, and we was just going on to Japanese when a staff doctor, with swastikas where his eyes ought to be broke up the party. I don't know what they did to the two nurses but they declared me fit for duty *on* the spot. Then they threw me in the clink, charged with racial defilement an' rape. They usually shoot a man for *that*! But that ol' Kriegsgerichtsrat, an' his two military judges, who sat on my case, they had a bit of difficulty when it comes to sayin' "Heil Hitler!". So, 'stead of shootin' me full of holes, they gives me three months in Germersheim.' Albert throws himself over backwards, roaring with laughter.

'When I left Germersheim to go to Paderborn, I spent the night at a soldier resthouse, where I got talkin' to two Navy girls. I was red an' blue all over by the time those kids'd finished

[4]Blitzmädel: Woman Telephonist (Signal Corps)

with *me*! They knew about massage, an' they massaged me just 'bout everywhere a man can *get* massaged. One of 'em had her breasts hanging down over my face, swinging backwards'n forwards till I was near out of my mind. The other one chewed away at my balls till my ol' man was that big he could've been used as a lighthouse any place on this earth. An' just every time I was gonna come they'd stop me comin' one way or the other. They was *real* professionals, them girls! When I finally *did* come it was if the sun and the stars and heaven'n hell an' the whole fuckin' earth fell down on my head!'

'Stop it! Bleedin' *stop* it!' pants Tiny. 'You'll 'ave me out there takin' the maiden'eads o' the dead fuckin' 'orses if you don't!'

Porta pours boiling water on some coffee he has also found in the Commandant's office. In the desk.

'Coffee,' mumbles a prisoner in a Lithuanian uniform, 'where'd you get it?'

'I have an uncle in Brazil,' whispers Porta, confidentially. 'He sends me a sack now and then.'

'If only we'd got 'ere a bit earlier,' says Tiny, glumly, looking through the smashed window.

On the far side of the broad yard a row of women are climbing up into lorries, for which a road has been cleared.

'We could've had a good fuck if we'd been quicker off the mark,' grins Albert, salaciously, wiping his mouth with the back of his hand.

'You crazy or something? They'd've screamed and resisted us,' says Gregor, with pretended horror.

'Only makes it better,' says Tiny, licking his frost-cracked lips.

'The penalty for rape is death!' snarls Heide, harshly. He straightens his belt and pistol holster.

'Rape?' Tiny laughs, noisily. 'Nobody's talkin' about *rape*? We fuck 'em first, then we knock 'em off afterwards. That's what you do in wartime.'

'When they had me cuttin' out paper dolls in Germersheim,' puts in Albert, 'I *did* hear about some of these war-stallions who'd fixed some women without asking. When they'd finished with 'em they put 'em all in a hut and fixed up some H.E. charges to give the girls a good send-off. That story got out an' the watchdogs came and got them. Well, *man!*' He throws out his hands expressively. 'The next we saw of them was one morning when they got driven over to the Engineer Parade Ground to get the final kick in the arse. One-way!'

'Let's change the subject,' says Porta, blowing on his coffee. 'It's no doubt wisest to pay for your cunt, if you can't do without it, and avoid all that nonsense afterwards.'

There is a whistling howl and a large section of brickwork falls down into the prison. We are half-buried in bricks and mortar.

The coffee-pot flies out of Porta's hand, straight up into the air.

'Outside fast!' screams the Old Man. 'Ivan's attacking!'

A flare goes off straight up above our heads. An automatic cannon hammer quite close to us. Large pieces fall from the sooty walls.

I slide a good way down the slippery road and end in a shell-hole from which Porta and Tiny are already firing. The MG is almost glowing.

Albert and Heide appear, moving like greased lightning.

'Don't shoot, man. It's only us,' shouts Albert, at the top of his voice, crossing a wrecked T-34 in almost one leap.

But Porta fires anyway. At the party of Russians who are chasing after them.

'No, stop man!' screams Albert. 'The neighbours are after us with all kinds of shit!'

'What do you think I'm shooting at, you silly, black sod!' snarls Porta, clipping a new drum on the MG.

'Come down here,' I shout, waving to them. I take over the MG and send covering fire at the women's wing.

'Hell, man,' pants Albert. 'You trying to cut our arses off?'

The firing ceases. We hear the pound of running feet. The earth shakes at a fall of shells. In front of us.

'They ours or the neighbours'?' asks Heide, fear in his voice.

'Who the hell knows,' answers Porta. 'Let's get out of it, anyway! I'll take this pointy-eared sod with me,' he says, picking up the Russian MG. 'The neighbours don't care what they get killed with.'

I jump down into a long dip, and sense figures at the far end of it.

Porta turns 'pointy-ears' on them and empties the drum.

We rush on, fast as ever we can move, run as if the devil himself were at our heels.

I stumble, somewhere, over a body. Head over heels we slip and slide down into a position. Our weapons fly from our hands. I hammer my face into a wrecked Maxim MG.

'Hell's bells, man! Ivan's coming,' howls Albert, twisting round in the air as he jumps with the agility of an acrobat. His Mpi chatters off a long burst at a party of white-camouflaged Russians who come rushing out of the forest.

'The neighbours,' shouts Tiny. 'The bleedin' neighbours.'

'Let's get out of here,' says Porta, getting up and putting the Russian MG on his shoulder. 'I have *no* desire to die for Führer, Folk and Fatherland!'

The cutting wind howls through the gulch, blows icily over the open plain, and is now almost a storm. Its howl makes it impossible to talk to one another. Nobody in his right mind would stay out in it longer than absolutely necessary. But who asks a soldier when he's in the line. In reality we should have frozen to death long ago. The frost cuts at us, and seems to be slashing out our very lives.

> *'Tell us miserable life,*
> *How can you grow, and flower, upon the ice?'*

sings Porta, as we rest for a moment behind a storm-battered hedge.

'What in the name of hell, man, is the highly praised German infantry doing?' curses Albert.

'Lying in holes, letting their arses get a look at the Russian full moon,' answers Porta, sending a long burst out into the curtain of snow.

'Let's get on!' says Heide.

'By the seven devils, man, but it's shit-cold,' grumbles Albert, his teeth chattering like an entire orchestra.

'Plop! Plop!' mortar bombs drop around us.

Bending forward we run on down a winding track.

Suddenly I get caught in a blast of wind, which spins me round and sends me over the edge. Icy storm winds hit me like fists. Desperately I catch at a ledge, but my gloved hands slip on the ice-clad surface. I go on down, in a raging storm of snow and ice crystals, which whip at me, stinging like scorpions. It feels as if I am moving at terrific speed through a maelstrom. Everything spins around me in a crazy whirl. A flare goes off close to me, blinding me completely. Tracer tracks speed by, both above and below me. I feel as if I am falling endlessly, down, down through the icy-cold air. Crystals of ice fill my mouth, threatening to choke me. Suddenly I realise I am falling head downwards. Trees and rocks projecting from the snow come rushing towards me with express speed. Desperately I try to remember what they taught us at the guerilla warfare school. 'When falling from a great height, spread out your arms, glide like a bird!' I kick out with my legs and strike out with my arms, but cannot change my direction of fall. Helplessly I rush on down to be crushed on the great rocks, which seem as if they were coming up at me. I scream, am stiff with terror, hope only that it will be all over quickly.

With a long, gliding movement I land softly as if on a giant sack of feathers. A whole mountain races past me. A row of trees follows. These too I pass at high speed. All the wind is knocked out of my lungs. I feel a burning pain lance up through my right side. My sight dims, but I come to myself again, surrounded by snow, snow and more snow. I realise I have landed in an enormous snowdrift. Above me tower huge cliffs. In some way I must have turned in the air, landed feet first, and then tobogganed for many yards on my back through the soft snow.

My Mpi is gone. My P-38 too. All I have to defend myself with is my combat knife and two plastic grenades.

The storm howls deafeningly above me. A machine-gun chatters viciously from somewhere in the forest.

I shout desperately, but shouting is hopeless while the storm continues. Even someone standing next to me would not be able to hear me. Now, I suddenly feel the cold. A merciless, killing cold. I must move. It is not possible to stay alive for long in this inhuman frost. Round about me trees burst with a noise like rifle shots.

A long drawn out scream sounds, not far away. When I turn, in alarm, I see a pair of eyes shining in the darkness, and can just see the outline of a snow wolf. I hit out at it with a branch. It snarls, but stays where it is. Gently I draw my combat knife from my jackboot.

'Get away,' I shout, lashing out with the branch.

It turns and slinks away. From the concealing curtain of snow it howls its hatred at me.

I cannot remember how I get out of the deep snow. I remember walking a long way on an icy, slippery track, which I continually slip and slide on.

A sharp, commanding '*Stoi*!' sends me to cover behind the roots of a tree. I throw one of my grenades at the shape. The explosion rings through the woods. The Russian is thrown into the air. He lands again and remains still.

His Kalashnikov has almost been thrown into my arms by the explosion of the grenade. I grasp it, and work my way towards him, silent as a snake. His stomach has been torn open. The blood has already frozen to ice in the hard frost.

Then I see the four others. All killed by Mpi bursts. They have obviously walked into a trap. The man I have killed is the only one who has escaped. If he had kept quiet, and hidden behind a tree, it would be me who was dead now. He was probably crazed with fear. Its no fun running around in a dark, frost-cracking forest with all kinds of mad killers sneaking about in it.

I leave the track and force my way through the snow and in between the trees. I have readied the Kalashnikov and am fully-prepared to shoot anything that moves.

An arm goes round my throat and cuts off my breathing. A battle knife is at my throat.

'One more'n you're dead, Fritz,' snarls a voice, in Russian.

I am completely paralysed. The blood in my veins turns to ice. The pressure of the knife against my throat increases

184

slightly. I wait for the unavoidable end. With a quick movement he will slash open my throat.

There comes a roar of laughter. A hard push in the back, and I fall on my face in the snow.

'Scared you, didn't we?' laughs Porta.

I feel as if I would like to go straight for him, I am so furious.

From between the trees come Tiny and Albert, grinning broadly. They seem to think they have perpetrated the joke of the year on me.

'Lucky for you it was us you ran into,' says Porta. 'Now maybe you'll know better than to walk around in these parts as if it was peacetime.'

'Shut up you shit,' I snarl, viciously, picking up the Kalashnikov. 'Hell, I was *scared*!'

'You must be mad as a bleedin' 'atter to go walkin' along like that in the middle of a Commie forest in wartime,' says Tiny, reproachingly.

'Maybe you ain't understood it yet, but the neighbours are ripping chunks off our poor bleedin' arseholes!'

'Let's go home,' says Porta. By 'home' he means the front-line.

We have only just got through the ruined village when we meet the remains of the Company. Oberleutnant Löwe is covered in blood, and talking from a hole in a heavy bandage which covers his head and goes down onto his chest.

In a long column of single file we march out over the frozen lake. What is left of the regiment musters at Bajkanskij.

Lips compressed, Oberst Hinka receives the strength figures from his company commanders. Losses are very great, due to the late commencement of the artillery covering fire.

5. Company: 19 men, reports Oberleutnant Löwe. 98 fallen, 36 wounded, 51 missing. By 'missing' he means those who have been blown to unrecognisability, left dying, or taken prisoner. It is doubtful if any of them will ever be heard of again.

A thunderous, whistling sound becomes audible. With a long roar a salvo explodes amongst us. In seconds Bajkanskij is a sea of flame.

A torn-off leg, still wearing its boot, hits me in the back and knocks me to the ground.

'Thank *you*, man,' says Albert. 'That guy must've been real mad at you to throw his whole leg at you like *that*!'

We run through the flames, firing as rapidly as we can. The Russians are following a plan they often use. A sudden, violent artillery attack, followed by a madly fanatical attack by the infantry, who have been lying in wait close in front of our positions. We can usually beat them off with our automatic weapons, but this time is different. They are superior in strength and continue to press their attack.

We withdraw. Fleeing for the second time through Bajkanskij with grenade-thrower and mortar fire at our heels.

'Follow me!' says the Old Man, raising his Mpi above his head.

Above all, we have learnt about death, at an age at which it is more natural for us to regard ourselves as being immortal.

P. Caputo

Porta draws his P-38 from its holster, and moves carefully up towards the wide main door, which is standing half open.

'After you,' he suggests to Tiny, standing politely to one side.

'You believe, maybe, that my 'ead is filled with Russian earth?' answers Tiny. 'I 'ave been takin' part in this war long enough to 'ave discovered years ago never to go through a door first unless you are desirous of a 'ell of an effective an' sudden death.'

'The devil!' Porta swears, staring at the wide door, so temptingly open. An open door could mean a lot of things. There could, for example, be some sneaky type standing behind it ready to knock a chap on the head with a T-34, if a chap were dumb enough to put his head inside. 'To hell with it,' he mumbles, throwing himself through the door. Before he has finished sliding across the floor he has turned and is shooting at the place behind the door. No-one is there! He rolls over, and sends a bullet through another door. 'Empty as a politician's head,' he shouts, looking up cautiously over the edge of a table.

'Bleedin' right,' roars Tiny, coming thundering into the hall, and sending a couple of bullets through a door, for the sake of good order.

We are about to open the hatches when a long chattering Mpi burst sounds. The man who comes rushing out on to the landing of the staircase disappears in an explosion of scarlet drops. His head flys off, like a tall hat in windy weather.

First comes Tiny rushing down the stairs. With a leap of Olympic dimensions he lands in the Kübel. Porta follows at a speed which appears to be no more than two yards slower than the speed of light. He dives headfirst into the Kübel's driving seat. He backs, then shoots forward, in between all kinds of tanks, followed by the startled looks of both Russian and German tank commanders. They almost fall out of their turrets to see what is happening.

187

5
War Debris

Hot blood drips down on me, melting the snow which has covered my face. Both his legs have been torn off at the knee. This is where the blood is coming from. Every tiny movement I make makes me scream with pain. After a while I manage to edge my head out of the steel-helmet, and turn it slightly to one side, so that the drip of blood from the man hanging across the beam above me just misses my face.

Over by the empty ammunition boxes lies Porta, rolled up like a dog. Beside him lies Barcelona in a pool of blood. After a while I find them all. Tiny is sitting with Albert, on the remains of what was once a tank turret. The gun barrel has been opened up like a banana skin.

'I wish I was a hen'

sings Albert, in a hoarse voice.

I cannot remember what has happened, excepting that the earth seemed to open and throw out fire and steel.

A Hauptmann walks, stiff-legged, down through the litter of bodies. His Mauser swings in his hand. He gives orders to troops he no longer has.

A bare-headed Padre appears, like a spectre, from a hole. He quacks something un-understandable, and gives out a mad laugh.

'Get thee behind me, Satan,' screams the Hauptmann, and shoots the Padre through the head. With a shrill laugh he staggers on over dead and wounded. He does not even see the T-34 which comes up over a rise in the ground and comes rattling towards him. He is thrown up in the air and lands with a hollow thud on the turret. His body slides down over the back of the tank, and is crushed under the broad tracks of the T-34 following it.

'Another damned *Germanski* less,' laughs the tank driver, as he feels the tracks bump over, and crush, the Hauptmann.

The Old Man bends over me. His helmet is cut open, as if by a can-opener. Shrapnel has gone in through the neck-piece and out at the front.

It is one of the new helmets which are supposed to be proof against shrapnel.

'You're still alive,' he smiles, comfortingly, and wipes the blood from my face. 'Where are you hit? Doesn't seem anything wrong with your head.'

I point upwards.

'It's *his* blood.'

'Yes. Well, we won't have to bother about him,' says the Old Man, glancing up at the legless body hanging across the beam.

'I must have got it in the guts,' I say, painfully. 'Hell, but it hurts, and I can't move at all.'

'Take it easy, now,' says the Old Man, patting me on the cheek. 'It's almost never as bad as you think it is.'

'What about the others?' I ask, worriedly.

'They've had a rough time of it, too,' answers the Old Man. 'Albert's gone mad, I think. Singing all the time. The whole load dropped right in the middle of us. I was thrown miles away. The infantry in front of us were simply blown to atoms. Not even a button left.'

'Are my legs still there?' I ask, fearfully. 'I can't feel them at all.'

'They're still firmly attached to the rest of you,' smiles the Old Man. He lights his silver-lidded pipe and blows a cloud of blue smoke out into the cold air. 'But you took a hell of a trip through the air. Stay quite still now. But we'll have to get on the move before the neighbours come running.'

'Devils in hell,' groans Barcelona, his voice full of pain and horror. 'I've been to the gates of both Heaven and Hell, but neither place'd have me. How can that be? I don't understand.'

'Natural as Creation,' mumbles Porta. His eyes are on Gregor,

189

who is lying in the barbed wire talking to a Russian body.

A line of infantrymen appears from the forest. An Oberfeldwebel glares sourly at us.

'Got both your arseholes an' your guts shot out of you, looks like,' he comments and is about to continue on his way without helping us.

'Take us with you,' shouts the Old Man. 'We can't manage on our own.'

'All right, then. Cut the cackle, chum!' growls the Oberfeldwebel with a wicked grin. 'You wanna play big white chief? There's two of us can do that, then!'

'Up *you* brother,' snarls the Old Man. 'You take us with you! If you don't I'll find you again sooner or later! Your arse won't like it, then!'

'That's what you think,' the Oberfeldwebel gives out a confident peal of laughter. 'We're the last, son! Rearguard you might call us! After us're the neighbours'n the end of the world for you lot. However, I'm in a friendly mood today so we *will* take you with us. But no further'n till the neighbours catch up. Then it's the sailor's farewell, chummies! Pick up these poor sods!' he orders his men. 'If one of 'em dies on you drop him off!'

'What the fuck've these shits to do with us?' protests an Unteroffizier with a flamethrower fuel-tank on his back.

'Shut your trap,' snarls the Oberfeldwebel, brutally. 'Get movin'!'

'We can't take 'em all,' shouts a Gefreiter. 'Some of 'em'll have to stay here'n hope Ivan's in a Sunday mood when he gets here!'

'Those farthest back in the queue get left,' decides the Oberfeldwebel, shortly.

Roughly and unwillingly they pull us to our feet, taking no notice of our groans.

A young Leutnant who is only slightly wounded, but completely exhausted by dysentery, begs and pleads to be taken along. He offers a wrist-watch and a valuable gold cigarette case in payment.

An Obergefreiter weighs it thoughtfully in his hand, then

190

puts it in his pocket. He and another man get hold of the Leutnant and drag him along between them like a sack of potatoes.

'God, but how he can shit,' says the Obergefreiter, with disgust, as yellow liquid, streaked with blood, spurts from the Leutnant.

'Stinks like Hell's own shithouse,' whines the other soldier.

'Won't 'urt you two, then!' grins Tiny. 'You're nothin' but a coupla walking shit'ouses yourselves!'

'This catchin' is it?' asks the Obergefreiter, who has been smeared with bloody excrement.

'Believe you me it is,' says Porta, enthusiastically. 'I'd give you two weeks at the outside before you're dead of typhus and dysentery! Terrible death it is!'

'You bastard!' curses the Obergefreiter furiously, as a great flow of excrement leaves the young officer. He is now unconscious and his breath rattles in his throat like that of a dying man.

'Can't we get him emptied out in some smart way or other?' asks his pal, looking shiftily around.

'Let's knock him up against a tree?' says the Obergefreiter, stopping thoughtfully. 'That ought to send it through him!'

'We can try it,' grins the other, cynically. 'Kill or cure sometimes works. Empty him out and he'll likely feel better.'

They swing the unconscious officer's body several times up against a tree.

'You two dirty bastards'll pay for that,' shouts the Old Man, furiously.

'Shut your trap,' warns the Obergefreiter, sending the Old Man a look of hatred. Scowling, they go on after the column with the Leutnant hanging between them. They have not gone far before they discover he is dead.

Carelessly, they sling the body into a ditch and saunter over to the Oberfeldwebel who is marching at the head of the party.

'Leutnant's shit himself to death,' reports the Obergefreiter, shamefacedly. 'He's up there now in the Heavenly Mess, playin' casino with Saint Peter!'

'I should think he *is* dead,' shouts the Oberfeldwebel, angrily.

'Anybody'd be dead the way you treated him. Try that sort of thing again and I'll have your heads for it! Understand!'

They drop us outside the Field Dressing Station, where many are lying already. They don't even bother to report us in.

The short day turns to night. Units of different kinds pass by continually. Three white-camouflaged P-4's come noisily sliding and slipping down the icy road. A frozen body smashes like glass under the tracks of the leading tank.

'Take us with you,' shouts Porta, waving wildly at them. 'Take us with you. We're from 6 PD.' He has seen the 7. Panzer Division tactical sign on the tanks. An elongated Y in yellow.

They go past without stopping. The commanders are up in their turrets, swathed in leather. They don't even glance at us. They are too busy racing for safety while there is still time.

'And that's our sister division,' says Porta, bitterly. 'Mates, take it easy! I'm going to get help!'

'They're shutting up shop,' comments the Old Man. 'The neighbours'll be here soon and clean up the remaining stock.'

'Good-night. Mary. Your maiden'ead's 'angin' on the nail!' coughs Tiny, contemptuously.

It is late at night, before a worn-out assistant doctor, followed by a couple of Sanitäts-Unteroffiziere, staggers down the long rows of wounded and dying. Every now and then he stops and bends over a stretcher, adjusts a bandage, and shrugs his shoulders resignedly.

A Sanitäts-Feldwebel pushes a hypodermic into each of us. He works like an automaton.

'Tetanus,' he mumbles, as he moves on to the next.

'Where's the sawbones then?' asks Tiny. 'Ain't they goin' to operate? I got 'alf the second world war's steel in me, I 'ave!'

'Operate? No chance!' grins a medical orderly. 'We'll have to leave that to the neighbours. They won't be long!'

'Shit-eater! German swine!' Tiny shouts, furiously, throwing a large piece of ice after him.

A General-major, with his whole face wound about with bandages, comes from one of the long buildings. He presses a Staff doctor's hand solemnly. They salute one another and click their heels. The General edges into a Kübel, which disappears in a cloud of snow, barely avoiding running over some of the wounded.

'The good generals know the way to safety,' grins Porta, sneeringly. He slaps the inside of his elbow, lifting his fist at the same time. The international sign for 'up you!'.

Some medical officers in thick fur coats, and with suitcases in their hands, leave the long buildings at a run. They tumble into ambulances with the Red Cross emblem, which are waiting with motors turning over.

'What about the wounded?' asks a Sanitäts-Feldwebel uncertainly, saluting foolishly.

'You can stay with them if you wish,' suggests a white-haired medical officer, with a cynical grin, jumping into a Red Cross Kübel.

The columns of soldiers, hastening past us as if the devil were at their heels, begin to thin out.

Three field MP's, with the headhunter badge on their chests stop their heavy BMW motorcycles. The machine-gun in each sidecar seems to point, as if accidentally, at us. A Stabsfeldwebel, with a head which reminds one of a mad Alsatian dog, looks at us with cold, considering eyes from under the brim of his steel-helmet.

'What the hell are you wet sacks lying around here for?' he barks, showing tobacco-yellowed teeth in a snarl. 'On your feet, you lazy swine, or I'll see you swing!' He points his machine-pistol at the nearest man, who is lying on a bed of branches. 'Get on your feet!' he hisses, 'or I'll blow your brains out for you!'

'Blow the breath outa that lousy watchdog,' roars an Obergefreiter in a blood-stained uniform.

Two shots ring out. Loudly and viciously.

The well-fed MP springs backwards, and sweeps his Mpi barrel round in a searching half-circle.

A new series of shots kick up snow and ice in front of him.

'Are you all mad?' he protests, in a hoarse voice, taking cover behind a motorcycle. 'You can't shoot at *us*!'

'Don't you bleedin' believe it,' roars Tiny, snatching the Mpi.

193

'Kill 'em! *Murder* the bastards!' comes in a mighty chorus from the wounded.

A fusillade from all kinds of hand weapon smashes at the heavy motorcycle. It explodes in a burst of flame. The Staff Feldwebel rolls burning in the snow. He rolls himself into a ball like a piece of charred paper.

'Sounds like an overweight sow sizzling on a hot plate,' grins Porta, pleasedly.

The two other MP's attempt to run. Five or six hand-grenades go whirling after them and explode hollowly. They fall into a snowdrift already packed with dead, frozen bodies.

Like a gift from heaven a convoy of heavy lorries stops beside us. Swearing supply soldiers jump from the backs of the lorries and protestingly begin to pack us into them.

'Only the living,' orders a Rittmeister. He chases the supply soldiers impatiently. 'Come on! Come on! We must get on!' he cackles, slashing impatiently at his long fur boots with his whip.

'Gawd but I'm goin' to kick your bleedin' piles up into your throat when I get well again,' Tiny promises a supply soldier who has dropped him twice on the way to the lorries.

'If you don't shut up,' answers the supplies man, a giant as big as Tiny, 'I'll let you lie here an' get your head blown loose! Ivan'll *take* anybody as ain't Russki. Count on that!'

'We gotta take that black *untermensch* with us too?' asks an Unteroffizier, pointing with a grin at Albert, who is lying in the snow grinding his teeth.

'Now I've seen everything,' shouts a Feldwebel, in surprise. 'A cannibal in German uniform! Are you a secret, or does the Führer know about you?'

'Shut your arse, man. You ain't *that* funny,' sneers Albert, contemptuously. 'I'd ten times rather be me than I'd be a stinking sausage-eating white German like you!'

'Watch your tongue, you abnormal Zulu, you! Or back you go to the trees with the other apes!' the Feldwebel warns him, with a sinister look on his face.

'We takin' him?' repeats the Unteroffizier impatiently,

194

looking as if what he'd most like to do was give Albert a kick in the backside.

'We'd better,' answers the Feldwebel. 'If Ivan finds *him* here he'll use it as propaganda, and say we've called up the monkeys from the Zoo. But put him at the open end of the lorry, so's we can tip him off at the first muck-heap we come to on the way.'

'That's it!' shouts the Rittmeister, 'off we go. We've no more time. Let the rest lie where they are! The Russians'll have to look after *them*!'

A shout of protest goes up from the wounded who are left. Those who can do so, get to their feet and hobble after the lorries.

'Move! Move!' shouts the Rittmeister, jumping up into the leading lorry.

Many hang on to the lorries, and allow themselves to be dragged after them. Fear of the Russians gives them the strength of despair.

We manage to pull some of them up into the lorries, but most of them fall off and end under the wheels of the lorry behind. The drivers have no chance of avoiding them on the icy roads.

'A good example of how much the life of an ordinary soldier is worth,' says the Old Man, bitterly.

'No more than the shit a plumber rakes out of a stopped-up sewer,' snarls Porta, lighting a cigarette.

'Shit on the army muck-heap,' confirms the Legionnaire. '*C'est la guerre!*'

'Look at the fat fellow there,' the Old Man breaks out, pointing with the stem of his pipe at a dying ski-soldier. 'He has a wife at home twisting floorcloths, and a big nest of snotty-nosed kids. And the kids'll end up on the shit-heap just like their father. Queer we still *take* this sort of thing!'

'We ain't worth any better, man,' philosophises Albert. 'I've often thought about what we're really doing in the Army. Why don't we quit and leave it all to the owners. To the officers and the fat-gutted civilians at home. The ones who need *us* to protect *their* riches, so they can sit fartin' in their soft armchairs!'

'Now you keep your black trap shut,' shouts Heide, trem-

195

bling with rage. 'You talk like a fucking Communist!'

A stream of tracer spits from the forest, and stops all discussion. A lorry crashes down a slope. The wounded are thrown about in wild confusion. At the bottom of the slope the lorry explodes, and disappears in a burst of yellow and red flame.

'Get on! Get on!' shouts the Rittmeister, hysterically, waving his Mpi. 'Don't *stop*!'

Another lorry rolls over and bursts into flames. It burns out, together with its load of sick and wounded.

'Hell but it stinks here,' curses Barcelona. 'Worse'n a Chinese shithouse after an orgy of spring rolls.'

'It's them five sods in the corner lyin' there shittin' their bleedin' typhoid germs all over us,' shouts Tiny, red in the face. He kicks out at a moaning heap of sick humanity in the corner.

'Throw 'em off,' suggests an artillery Unteroffizier. 'Let 'em shit their typhoid on the fuckin' neighbours!'

'Are you crazy, we can't do that,' protests Porta, 'they'd accuse us of starting bacteriological warfare, and we've not gone that far yet, despite everything.'

'Any of you believe in this new wonder-weapon?' asks a Gefreiter with sharp mousey features.

'Now I've seen *you* I do,' answers Porta, bending double in laughter.

We rumble on all night. At a reckless speed we roar through a village where a row of hanged shapes dangle from the telegraph poles.

'Partisans,' mumbles Heide, his face crumpling in rage.

'Think so?' jeers Porta. 'More likely some murderous sod who's finally got the chance to show his power. Partisans don't come out and ask to be hanged. They're like snakes. A quick strike and out again like lightning.'

Our lorry goes into a deep hole and gets stuck fast. A tank motor roars out in the darkness. Tank tracks rattle ominously.

Panic spreads amongst us. Those who can, jump from the lorries, and take cover behind snowdrifts.

A VW-Kübel comes struggling up the hill, and smashes with a crunching sound into the wall of a house. Four soldiers hang from it like lifeless puppets. It begins to burn. Small, dancing flames spring up.

Three grey-white T-34's push out from the forest. Trees snap like matchsticks. There is an earsplitting report, followed by a long, thundering noise, as if a goods train were rushing over a steel bridge. The leading T-34 rolls across the ice with its turret blown off, like a bucket somebody has given a kick. There is a new fearful explosion. A tank gun going off. A giant, orange-coloured bolt of lightning, and a thunderous explosion. A glowing fireball lights up the scene.

The other T-34 stops short and bursts into flames. The commander in his black leather equipment, tries to escape from the turret at the last moment. His left leg is torn off at the knee and whirls, spinning, up above the tongues of flame.

A Panther appears on the top of a rise. Its long gun swings towards the last T-34. A jet of flame shoots from the muzzle and two terrific explosions make our ears ring. The T-34 has fired at the same second as the Panther. Flames and black smoke pour from both tanks.

Two crew members jump from the turret of the Panther. Coughing, and fighting for breath, they roll in the snow.

Three of the crew of the T-34 are thrown from it, burning like torches as they fly through the air. The classic death of the tank soldier.

'Keep your heads down, lads,' warns the Old Man. 'They'll blow up any minute now.'

Some shapes run around the burning tanks, spectrally illuminated by the light of the flaming inferno.

'Ivan,' says Tiny, pointing. 'Some lamebrain commissar must be kickin' their arses.'

'They are, perhaps, tired of life,' grins Porta, unsmilingly. 'When the ammo' goes it'll make a bang'n a blast that'd lift a one-legged monk's backside up high enough to shit the devil in the face!'

The next second the burning tanks explode. The terrific blast wave tears up trees by the roots and sends them, like javelins, through the air. Nothing remains of the inquisitive Russians.

197

'Gone with the wind,' cries Gregor, throwing out his arms, 'just simply gone!'

'They've been blown to the other side of Kolyma, and can discuss how they got there with a couple of elks,' comments Porta, making himself comfortable in the snow. 'Be kind enough to wake me, please, before I die!'

'Hell, man, haven't you got any nerves at all?' Barcelona rages. 'You can't just go off to sleep and wait for the neighbours to come an' knock you off!'

'What do *you* think I ought to do, then?' asks Porta, hotly, lifting his steel helmet. 'Don't imagine Ivan's boys are ready for a cosy chat just now. You can count on it they've been given a powerful Ilya Ehrenburg injection of propaganda piss. Kill the *Germanski*, tear them from their mothers' wombs, crush the skulls of the capitalist plague rats of the west!'

A P-3, with its long 75 mm gun angled up towards the skies, comes to a rattling stop alongside us.

'Want any help?' asks the commander, leaning out of the open turret.

'Yes, mate. Specially if you got a couple o' thousand spare parts with you. '*Uman* spare parts, that is!' comes Tiny's voice from a deep hole in the snow. 'We're short of everythin' from arse'oles to elbows!'

The commander, an Oberfeldwebel, jumps down from the tank, together with the loader.

'Give us a hand with the wires,' he shouts.

'We can't manage it,' answers Porta, 'we're all wounded. We can hardly crack a fart without help!'

'*Forget* you're wounded,' says the tank commander, pulling feverishly at the frozen towing cables. 'We're in a hurry. Ivan's right on our heels.'

Cursing with pain some of us get on our feet to help out with the recalcitrant towing gear. Finally we make them fast and the P-3 begins to pull.

'Slow'n easy does it,' warns the commander. 'We don't want it to break. Steel's brittle as glass at these temperatures!'

Quite slowly the lorry begins to move. For a moment it looks as if it is going to fall over on its side. The front part of it balances on the edge of the hole, with wheels in the air. With a crash, and a great creaking of springs, it rocks forward, remaining, by some miracle, on the road. The towing cable snaps and whistles through the air, taking off the face of an infantryman who did not manage to duck in time.

A tongue of flame comes from the hill-top, and the characteristic sound of a tank gun going off throws echoes back from the forest.

The P-3 begins to burn immediately. Black, oily smoke mushrooms above the trees. With uniforms on fire the crew jumps from the open hatches. Screaming they roll in the snow, slowly blackening in the violent flames. Nothing can be done. We cannot help them. They are drenched in petrol from the two large fuel tanks, which are poorly protected in the P-3.

Our lorry roars at breakneck speed along the icy road. It slides sideways down a steep hill and smashes an amphibian in which are two SS riflemen. At a bend we whirl round three times in our own length. Three telegraph poles go down with a splintering sound. Four men are thrown out over the tail-flap, but we drive on. The driver is afraid to stop. It would probably be impossible to get the vehicle started again. We must keep going all the time.

Well into the night, we stop at a medical unit, which seems to be getting ready to move out. A long row of ambulances are standing waiting with engines running. They are not only being loaded with wounded, but also with boxes and suitcases.

After an eternity of waiting a nervous assistant M.O. appears. He examines the closest of us superficially. We soon realise that there are only two categories of patient. Those who can be moved, and those who cannot. He examines only the dressings. Too much blood and pus, and you are out. He disappears as suddenly as he appeared.

The roar of war comes steadily closer.

An Oberst, wound in so much bloody bandage that he resembles an Egyptian mummy, demands to speak to a doctor.

'That's an order,' he shouts, hoarsely, when he realises he is being ignored.

'Yes, sir,' answers a medical orderly, carelessly.

199

'Why doesn't the doctor come?' repeats the Oberst.

'Don't know, sir,' says the orderly, hurrying on to the next man.

When a Sanitäts-Feldwebel comes dashing by, the Oberst stubbornly repeats his demand.

'The Staff M.O.'ll be here soon,' promises the Feldwebel, pulling himself from the Oberst's grip.

But the Staff M.O. does not come. Instead two orderlies arrive and silently move the Oberst away from the growing queue.

'You lazy sacks,' shouts Tiny, furiously, after an orderly, 'what a way to bleedin' treat us after the blood we've shed for Führer'n Fatherland! We're Germans! 'Uman beings!'

The orderly stops, and looks at him with a superior smile.

'Did you say human beings? With those two bits of scotch mist you've got on your arm you're not as much worth as a pimple on an elk's arse. An Oberst's lapdog's higher up the ladder'n a stinking cooley like you! If we'd *had* an Oberst's lapdog here, wounded, we'd have operated on *him* before we got to shit like you!'

'Arsehole of the army, we are, man!' sighs Albert. Apathetically he pulls his greatcoat collar up around his ears.

'When we clear up after the war, the first to get it'll be you medical shits,' promises Porta, waving his fist threateningly at the orderly, who moves away, laughing heartily.

In the course of the night we are carried inside. A stench of gangrene hits us. The wind whistles icily down long corridors, blowing powdery snow in great clouds before it.

The wounded Oberst, still calling for a doctor, is inside too. Querulously he demands the windows closed. There *are* no windows to close. Blown out long since. He tries to get up. Threatens the orderlies. Groaning, he falls back on to the blood-spattered stretcher.

His eyes follow the many stretchers which are taken past him and return empty. It is only when his own stretcher reaches the far end of the long corridor that he realises what is happening. It ends in nothing. The wall is gone, and, far below, the frozen river can be seen. That is where the contents of the stretchers end. An easy way to dispose of the dead. Room, and stretchers, are needed for those still living. Those who are well enough to be transported onwards from here. Sometimes some poor chap is not yet quite dead, and begins to scream when he realises what is going to happen to him. His protests do not help him. Out into the river he goes with the rest. If he does not die on the way down the frost will soon finish him.

'Get me out of here,' roars the Oberst, furiously. 'I demand to speak to a doctor! I am an Oberst and commander of a regiment!' Nobody bothers to answer him.

An elderly medical officer bends over him.

'We'll soon be getting to you, sir,' he promises, tiredly. 'You are to go on the next transport.' He turns to a Sanitäts-Unteroffizier. 'A hopeless case,' he whispers.

The Oberst hears him and begins to scream and roar. The entire staff of doctors and nurses would have come running if it had happened anywhere normal. But in this enormous slaughterhouse, where panic spreads from minute to minute, the Oberst is merely left to scream himself into exhaustion. In a mad rage he lifts a bayonet and jabs it into his throat. Blood geysers up.

Shortly afterwards an orderly looks at him.

'Finished,' he comments, without interest. 'Gives us another stretcher!' With a practised movement he sends the Oberst down into the river after the others.

A Leutnant with crushed legs gets the stretcher.

We are pushed on, right into the large operating theatre, which steams with blood and entrails.

'That one,' decides a Sanitäts-Feldwebel, pointing at a stretcher on which a blood-spattered engineer is lying.

'Don't you think he'll die?' asks an orderly, covered in a long rubber apron.

'How the hell do I know? Think I'm clairvoyant, or something?' the Feldwebel flares at him.

'Looks like a well-preserved corpse already, to me,' comments the orderly.

'Very clear diagnosis,' hisses a stressed assistant M.O., lifting

201

the engineer's eyelid. He knocks a fat louse from his nose, and crushes it under his boot.

'My leg! Oh, hell! My *leg*!' groans the engineer as he is placed on the operating table, and strapped down. 'I can't stand it any more. It's burning. Burning like hell!'

'Double morphine,' says the surgeon, commencing to cut away what passes for a dressing. There is a huge gaping wound below the knee, right in to the bone. The leg is swollen and almost black. Gangrene has spread right down to the foot. The toes are like small overblown balloons.

'Leg'll have to come off,' says the chief surgeon, brusquely. 'Anaesthetic!' he orders.

'None available,' answers the assistant, laconically.

'Morphine,' snaps the chief surgeon. He reaches for the instrument the operation room orderly is holding ready for him.

A sickening, sweetish smell fills the air.

An orderly cleans the gaping wound quickly, and the surgeon opens up the skin. The operation proceeds rapidly. Everyone works in silence. Only the chief surgeon talks. Continually. The operating-room orderly passes the various instruments to him, with trained economy of movement, as they are required. The knife bites deeper and deeper into the rotten flesh.

The engineer begins to scream.

'Put something in his mouth,' the surgeon orders, angrily. He begins to cut through to the bone. The clips applied to the main artery open up, and blood spurts onto his face. 'Saw,' he snaps, holding out an expectant hand. With a terrible rasping sound the saw eats through bone.

The anaesthetist shrugs his shoulders, resignedly. The chief surgeon attempts to hurry. The saw whines on the leg-bone. The amputated leg falls to the floor with a thump.

'Next!' he says.

A Leutnant, whose stomach has been ripped open, is placed on the table.

'Transport ready,' roars a Feldwebel. His voice echoes down the long, windy corridor.

When Albert is pushed into the ambulance, the last man of the party, he pulls his greatcoat collar away from his face and growls at the orderly. The man starts at the sight of an ebony-coloured face.

'What the hell?' he cries, in amazement. 'Germany still got colonial troops?'

'No, man!' grins Albert. 'Ah'se American, boss! Gran'son of Ol' Uncle Tom, ah am, man! Yes, siree!'

The ambulance drives at a breakneck speed which throws us about inside it until we feel that every bone in our bodies must be broken. We grumble and rage, but the driver couldn't care less. All he wants is to get as far away from the front line as possible.

'If you don't like the speed I drive at, then jump off'n walk,' he yells, banging the window between us shut.

'I'll tear 'is bleedin' prick off, I will!' promises Tiny, furiously, trying to get to his feet. He has to give up. There is too little room between the stretchers.

After a couple of hours of dangerous driving, the ambulance stops. We hear petrol cans banging against one another. With a noisy rattle the back doors of the ambulance are thrown open, and a Sanitäts-Feldwebel, with an appearance reminiscent of an overfed pig, stares at us with a pair of cold, blue, Germanic eyes.

'Anybody dead speak up now? Plenty waiting in the queue!'

'Come in and check,' suggests Porta, with a hoarse raven's caw of a laugh, 'you'll soon find out how much life's left in us!'

'I'll see to you later, Obergefreiter,' grants the Feldwebel, slamming the door to with a reverberating crash.

'Let's get goin' ' shouts a Jaeger with fear in his voice. 'Ivan's tanks're right up our backsides!'

As the cold, sad day wakens from the night's chill darkness, we drive out onto a rickety bridge, which hangs, swinging from rusty cables, looking ready to fall at any moment. It creaks and groans and grumbles in every part. Under normal circumstances no person in his right mind would risk crossing it, but now everybody rushes across in panic.

The Russian tanks, with mechanised infantry support, are after us, and represent a much greater danger than the rickety bridge.

A party of engineers, under the command of a Leutnant, are

getting ready to blow up the bridge. Anxiously they chase along the hundreds of soldiers pushing and shoving in an unruly mob to get down to the river.

A tank column comes roaring, recklessly, forcing the men in its path to jump for their lives.

'Stop! Stop!' shouts the Engineer-Leutnant, waving his arms. 'Do you want to commit suicide? That bridge can't take tanks! You'll have to cross somewhere else!'

A tough-looking Major stares down at him from the turret of the leading tank.

'Be so kind as to shut your trap, Leutnant! *I* am going to cross that bridge with *my* tanks, whether *you* like it or not! Get out of my way or I'll flatten you!'

The Leutnant steps aside, shaking his head, and sits down resignedly on an empty petrol drum. What can a Leutnant do when he is up against a mad Major?

'One at a time,' shouts the Major, waving his tanks forward. 'Speed up and take it *fast*! And God help any fool who smashes up that bridge before the last waggon's over!'

'Major, sir, I hand over responsibility for this bridge to you,' protest the Leutnant, angrily.

'Do that, then, if it makes you happy,' barks the Major, indifferently.

The bridge gives out creaking and cracking sounds. It swings like a hammock as the first tank rolls over it. The cables sing like overstrung violin gut. As soon as the first tank is across the next is on its way.

'Goddam, bloody idiots,' curses the Engineer-Leutnant. He holds his breath when one of the centre cables breaks, with a crack like a whip. Pieces of it whistle through the air. The next to last of the tanks rolls onto the bridge. What the Leutnant has been expecting, and fearing, happens. The driver is nervous. The heavy vehicle hits the supports at the middle of the bridge. They break like cotton. In a rain of steel girders and cables the whole bridge collapses. The tank turns a somersault as it whirls on its way down into the depths below. Part way down it strikes some projecting rocks on one side of the gorge, and hangs for a moment before continuing straight on down. It crashes through

204

the ice and into the river. Faster than the words can be written thick ice floes close again over the spot where the tank has broken through.

'God help us,' groans the Leutnant. 'I *told* 'em what'd happen. I told 'em and would they listen? Idiots *never* listen!'

'It looked like the gates of hell, opening and closing down there,' cries Porta, fearfully, staring down at the crashing ice-floes below.

A blinding flash of light illuminates the grey day. The ambulance is thrown, tumbling over and over, out above the remains of the bridge, which are swaying and thrashing in the air. A gout of flame comes from it. Two stretchers fly from its open doors. It goes into the river and is swallowed in the roiling screw of ice-floes smashing over and on top of one another.

'Tanks! Tanks!' comes the alarm. White fingers of light search the darkness for prey.

Panzerfausts[1] roar, hollowly. Splintered metal crashes. A jet of flame goes up as the first T-34 explodes with a thunderous roar.

'My leg! My leg!' groans Heide, dragging himself through the snow to cover.

I get hold of his shoulder and pull him along with me. We force our way under a lorry lying on its side on top of a number of frozen bodies.

A T-34 comes roaring straight through a house, which collapses behind it. Two heavy beams hang, see-sawing, on the front of the tank. A blue blanket waves like a flag from its double antennae. The remains of a crushed perambulator whirl round in its tracks. The characteristic whining roar of Otto motors can be heard from all sides.

They come rattling down the snowy slope. Across the double track of the Kiev-Moscow railway. Thick clouds of snow whirl out over the low houses, creating great drifts in the streets. The streets are too narrow for tanks. Houses crash down in clouds of stone and mortar.

A horde of Cossacks come, on the run with sabres drawn. They

[1]Panzerfaust: Bazooka.

slash at the fleeing soldiers.

'*Uhraeh Stalino! Uhraeh Stalino!*' The victory scream rings from the throats of the bloodthirsty Siberian infantry. They storm forward, machine-pistols chattering. Inflamed to madness they slash, stab and batter at everything which is not Russian. "Kill them in their mother's womb! Drown them in their own blood!" Ilya Ehrenburg's scream of hatred sounds continually in their ears.

We withdraw slowly, fighting desperately at close quarters the whole time, to the half-burnt village, and take up position in the ruins. We forget the pain of our wounds, think only of staying alive. We fight like madmen. Combat knives cut into entrails. Infantry entrenching tools split open skulls.

In the middle of this inferno of battle a small crowd of civilians assembles on the little square, at the foot of the statue of a horse jumping. A woman commissar with the insignia of a major gives guttural orders to them. She speaks so quickly that her tongue seems to stumble over the words. The civilians, who appear paralysed with fear, huddle closer together. She takes a few steps backwards. Her Kalashnikov spits death. The civilians fall, in a kicking, screaming heap, at the base of the statue of the jumping horse.

'Well hell!' cries Porta. 'Aren't those bloody neighbours even satisfied with wiping *us* out?'

The woman commissar gives out a neighing laugh, and kicks viciously at one of the bodies.

'What the hell can they have done?' asks Gregor.

'*Rien!*' answers the Legionnaire. '*C'est la guerre*! The lady with the golden stars is extending her collection of bodies before the war ends.'

Three terrified German nurses come running across the square. A party of grinning Siberian Cossacks are at their heels.

'Somebody there lookin' for a fur coat for 'is old John Thomas,' growls Tiny. He presses the butt of the LMG into his shoulder and sends a couple of short bursts at the Siberians. They are knocked backwards as if hit by a club.

'Prickteasin',' he grins clipping a new magazine on the MG.

With a wild roar, a giant Russian grabs the two nearest

nurses, picks them up as if they were chickens and brings their heads together with a hollow thud. He throws his arms around them and presses them in to him in a brutal bear hug. With his free hand he draws his Nagan from its yellow leather holster and presses its muzzle into the neck of one of the girls. Three shots follow in rapid succession.

'That's what I call a perfect liquidation,' cries Porta, amazed. 'Those bullets went straight through the one and into the other. What happened to the third though?'

'Knocked off the one over by the tree,' answers Tiny, pointing.

The big Russian looks around him. With a brutal laugh he kicks at the two bodies.

'He's lived too long,' says Porta, raising his large calibre combat carbine.

'Shove 'is bollocks up in 'is throat,' suggests Tiny, vengefully.

Porta takes careful aim. The carbine gives a dry crack. The Russian is hit. His entire chest is torn open by the special bullet. It is sheathed in hardened steel and can tear through armour plate.

'Say hello in hell, *tovaritsch*,' mumbles Porta, lowering the carbine.

'The commissar cunt's mine,' says Tiny. He sends a burst of explosive bullets at the woman, without hitting her. Like a witch on her way to a Sabbath, she disappears between the smoking ruins.

'Let's get out of here,' says the Old Man, decisively.

The Russian have found a supply depot, and for a short while think of nothing but looting. The scene resembles a lunatic asylum in which all the patients have run amok. Boxes and bottles fly about. Two Siberians have got hold of a sack of flour and slash at it with their bayonets. Soon they look like a couple of lumps of dough.

Slivovitz and vodka flow in rivers. They do not waste time opening the bottles. They knock off the necks, open their throats, and put back their heads. The spirits flow down their gullets like Niagara. Nobody bothers about us. We sneak along

207

close to the soot-blackened walls of the houses. A few miles from the village we run into the arms of a Russian mortar group.

Grenades fly through the air. Automatic weapons chatter. It takes only a few minutes to defeat the mortar group.

In a half-destroyed stable we huddle against the charred bodies of cattle. Porta finds a smoked ham hidden up under a tie-beam, but nobody feels like eating. Except Porta. He fills up on it, gluttonous as always.

Tiny is lying in a pool of blood, groaning miserably. During the encounter with the mortar group a ricochet has torn open his hip lengthwise.

'Good Lord in Heaven,' cries the Old Man, worriedly, when he has cut open his trousers. 'It'll need a hundred dressings to fill that hole.'

Tiny howls in protest as the Old Man pours a pint of alcohol down into the wound.

'Shut it!' snarls the Old Man. 'You'll be rotten in two days if we don't get that hole cleaned out.'

'A lorry,' shouts Gregor, alarmingly, getting up to move out onto the road, where a large Büssing lorry has coughed to a stop. It is full of badly wounded, smothered in bloody bandages.

'All over,' shouts the driver. 'The motor's gone for a burton. You'll have to get back best you can!' He puts his Mpi under his arm, and pulls his greatcoat collar up round his ears.

'You can't just bloody leave us here,' protests a wounded Wachtmeister indignantly. 'It's your duty as a medical orderly to help us.'

'Duty,' grins the orderly, sardonically. 'Stick it up the Führer's arse!' He slips an extra Red Cross bandolier on his left arm. He has discovered that there are *some* Russians who do not shoot at the Red Cross.

'Lay down out in the snow, it'll be over quicker,' he suggests, springing over the deep ditch. Soon he is swallowed up in the flying snow.

'If I ever get 'old of 'im, I'll tear 'is prick off an' push it down 'is throat an' choke 'im with it!' groans Tiny.

'You never catch that kind of a shit,' says Barcelona, darkly. 'They live through any war!'

'Lord, but I'm *sleepy*,' moans Gregor, almost yawning his jaws out of joint. 'I don't care a damn what happens, if only I could get some sleep.'

Porta stretches out on the packed earth floor, pulls his greatcoat around him, and lays his head on a dead cow. 'Hell, I could sleep till way into next year!'

'Sleep's funny, man,' mumbles Albert, tiredly. 'It's really only a nice kind of dyin'!'

'There's nothing a man longs for like sleep,' says Gregor. 'Beats even food and fuckin'.'

'When I sleep,' says Albert, in an unclear voice, 'I always dream about a lovely place where everybody is nice an' don't get after niggers like me, an' I'm always rich as all get out. Once I dreamt I was in court, an' the judge give me a fine of 100 Reichsmarks, but that didn't mean nothing to a rich man like me. Here, boy, I said, handing him five hundred smackers. Keep the change your honour, an' buy yourself some nice black pussy with it! And I lifted my shiny silk hat and off I went!'

'Were you going to a party, since you had a top-hat on?' asks Porta, in surprise.

'I always wear a silk topper, and a black cape with a white silk lining, when I'm dreamin',' answers Albert, smiling happily.

'Do that to a German judge'n 'e'd put you inside for a 'undred years,' comments Tiny, with a world of experience behind his words.

The deep bellow of a lorry engine breaks off the conversation. We crawl eagerly to the door. A heavy eight-wheeled Puma stops, and an arrogant Leutnant peers down from it.

'What the devil do you lot want?' he shouts, irritably, wiping snow from his face.

'A lift,' answers the Old Man, curtly.

'Get up on the back then,' growls the Leutnant, unwillingly, 'we're in a hurry.'

'Most of us can't stand up on our own,' says the Old Man.

'Damn your eyes,' the Leutnant curses, viciously. He gives his crew orders to help us. 'But hurry, *hurry*!' he shouts, impatiently. 'We're not a bloody Red Cross unit. We're tank clearance.'

His crew have just as little pity for us as their chief. They sling us up onto the back of the waggon, in a heap behind the turret, without taking any heed to our cries of pain.

'Couldn't you lukewarm shits've died a bit sooner?' shouts an Obergefreiter. His brutal face glares at us from the background of a heavy fur collar. 'If the neighbours blow us away it'll be *your* doin'!'

'Wait'll we catch you in the same position, matey,' Porta threatens him, blackly. 'We'll throw you on the shit-heap, where the rats can get at you.'

'Better keep your trap shut, son,' the Obergefreiter warns him, wickedly. 'We just might happen to forget you when we drive off!'

'Humane sods, aren't they?' says Gregor, tiredly.

'You think so, do you?' laughs the Obergefreiter, sourly. 'Just wait till we start this thing. I'm the driver and I'll do what I can to see you get shook off!'

'I shall see to it that you go on report,' shouts Heide, angrily. 'You hear me, Obergefreiter!'

'You will, will you?' grins the Obergefreiter, treacherously. He winks at a little, sharp-nosed Gefreiter with "Gross Deutschland" flashes. 'Grab the good Unteroffizier's flat feet and let's be careful nothing happens to him. It *would* be a pity if he didn't get us put on report!'

'Shut up, dammit,' rages the Leutnant. He seems to radiate an almost murderous degree of energy. He is one of the dangerous kind who always get their own way. Cross him seriously, and he will draw his pistol, and use it.

'The Unteroffizier here's goin' to put us on a charge,' grins the Obergefreiter, sneeringly.

'Leave him then,' orders the Leutnant, curtly. 'He can make his report to the Siberians. They'll be here soon!'

The two transport men drop Heide. His head cracks against one of the heavy springs. He gives out a scream. Blood pours over his face from a deep hole in his neck.

'The shit dead?' asks the pointed-nosed soldier, with a pleased gleam in his eye.

'No, not yet, unfortunately,' answers the Obergefreiter. 'But we'll put the kind Unteroffizier here on the outside, where he might fall off quite soon.'

'Finished,' shouts the Leutnant. 'No more time for that! The rest'll have to go on the next waggon.'

'It'll be Russian,' laughs the Obergefreiter noisily. He sidles through the driver's hatch, and pulls it down after him.

'Hang on with your teeth'n stick your pricks into the ventilation slits,' shouts the pointy-nosed man. He disappears into the turret with a cackle of laughter.

The Leutnant throws an irritable glance down at us, and adjusts his throat microphone.

'Panzer! Full speed ahead! March!' he orders. He disappears into the turret and pulls the hatch to with a clang.

We have not gone far before the first of us has frozen to death. It is a slim young infantryman whose right arm has been amputated.

'One 'ere gone to Val'alla,' comments Tiny. He pushes the body over the side, leaving more room for the rest of us.

The armoured Puma races down a steep declivity. A Feldwebel is thrown out onto the hard-frozen road surface, where his head is crushed like an egg-shell against a pointed rock. Without anyone noticing it, two of the badly wounded have been suffocated by exhaust gas. They were unlucky enough to be at the bottom of the heap directly over the engine ventilation openings.

'Stop, stop you mad sods!' screams Tiny, furiously, crashing his Mpi against the hatchway.

The hatch remains closed. Even if they hear us inside the vehicle they do not react at all.

'Filthy gang of murderers is what they are,' rages Heide. He has returned to consciousness and has a scarf bound round the open wound in his neck.

'Be glad they took you along,' says the Old Man, tiredly. 'They could easily have left you back there, because of your crazy threats of reporting them. All six of 'em are cold and callous as a Russian winter.'

A mighty explosion cuts him off. Splinters of steel fly around our ears. A corner of the turret has disappeared, and we can see down inside the vehicle.

'Anti-tank hit,' groans Gregor, fearfully, huddling against the turret.

The heavy armoured vehicle swings round, and roars over the anti-tank gun emplaced between winter-naked bushes. The gun is crushed.

Two Russian anti-tank soldiers, in clumsy, quilted winter uniforms run headlong over the frozen fields. The Puma's forward MG's spit tracer after them.

The leading soldier is thrown forward, and lies, his body twisted, in the snow. The other is crushed under the Puma's giant wheels. The Puma stops with a jerk and reverses at full speed towards a corporal who has given up and has his hands in the air. When he realises that the armoured vehicle intends to run him down he goes completely crazy, and begins to run round in circles. The murderous vehicle plays cat and mouse with him. Every time the armoured car has almost reached the poor Russian the driver stops and revs up the motor in neutral.

'What the devil?' shouts the Old Man, bitterly. 'We've been given a lift with a travelling madhouse!'

The fleeing Russian falls down in the snow. He raises his hands towards the Puma in a prayer for mercy. It stops and seems as if it is preparing to spring on him. The engine howls at maximum revolutions. The heavy eight-wheeled vehicle roars forward and crushes the Russian, leaving only a bloody smear on the snow.

'I'll report 'em, devil take me if I don't,' shouts the Old Man, furiously. 'Killing one another's all right out here, but this . . . this is going too bloody far!'

'Don't you think it might be wise of you to stay well away from Torgau?' asks Porta, with a broad grin. 'You can bet your life Iron Gustav's[2] found out who it was drank his cognac and filled the bottle up again with horse-piss!'

'Iron Gustav's not at Torgau any more,' says the Old Man, to our great surprise. 'He's Hauptwachtmeister at Germersheim now!'

At a sharp bend the driver of the Puma loses control of the

[2]See 'March Battalion'.

212

vehicle. It begins to wobble, roars over the edge of the road, and down a steep slope. With a crash it breaks through the thick skin of ice covering the river. Freezingly cold water splashes up over us. Rapidly we are sheathed in ice. With a short cough the engine stops.

'Now I'm *really* tired of this world war,' rages Porta, when we are safe from the ice floes. 'I want to go home and shit on a porcelain water-closet again, and enjoy the benefits of all modern conveniences. Let the sodding Russians shit on rough, iced-up beams, and drop their turds down into holes in the ground and wipe their arses with a handful of gravel!'

'Home,' says the Old Man, pessimistically. '*We're* never going home!'

With inhuman exertions we reach the road and surmount the remains of the low stone protecting wall through which the armoured car has crashed. A motor sleigh picks us up. The driver, a lanky Obergefreiter with a long horsey face, is alone with the dead, frozen body of an Oberst on the back seat.

'What about throwing Chiefy there out. There'd be more room,' suggests Porta. '*He* probably wouldn't care.'

'Can't do it,' answers Horseface. 'He's my pass. I've already gone through five headhunter road checks. I tell 'em it's our Chief of Staff, an' I've been ordered to take back for a real German, Christian hero's burial! Flags, drums, trumpets'n all that shit! What goes on when a big man's bein' sent off to Valhalla.'

'Where you thinking of going to?' asks Gregor, edging himself in alongside the frozen body.

'Cologne,' answers Horseface, with a whinny of laughter.

'You must've swallowed a commissar,' considers Porta. 'They'll string you up long before you get to Cologne. And your frozen old Chief of Staff'll get strung up alongside you as an awful example to others.'

'Don't you believe it,' answers Horseface, in an assured voice. 'A Chief of Staff, with red tabs and bits of shiny stuff, opens all doors. Even when he's dead. The watchdogs become quite human.'

'Was he really your Chief of Staff?' asks the Old Man, looking

213

askance at the frozen Oberst's frost-blackened face, which is set in a grin of death.

'Course he was,' answers Horseface. 'We were out looking at artillery positions when the neighbours threw a shell down alongside us an' blew the life out of the old 'un there. The Divisional Commander told me to see to it that his Chief of Staff got a Christian, German burial. That I can't do in this land of the godless, can I? So I'm driving the old boy to Cologne, where I know there's a Catholic piece of earth, which has, indeed, been blessed by the present Pope, Pius XII.'

'You bring that one off,' cries Porta, admiringly, 'and I'll take off both my hat *an*' my socks to you!'

'Can't be done,' says Gregor, darkly. 'It just ain't possible. Somewhere or other he'll run into some checkpoint where the headhunters begin to ask questions and then there'll be a rope round his neck in no time. Goodbye Cologne!'

'Hell'n Tommy!' cries Porta, fearfully. An MP checkpoint with red lamps and stop signals looms up ahead. Stopped vehicles are lined up at the side of the road, soldiers can be seen in flight across the fields. Bodies hang swinging from the trees. The MP's are armed to the teeth. Their commander is a nasty-looking Hauptmann. His Mpi is at the ready in his hands and his ability to use it is very apparent.

'Where are you from and where are you going?' he asks, in a crackling machine-gun of a voice. 'Movement orders!'

'Yes, sir,' says Horseface, in a tone which reflects long experience in cases of this nature. 'Beg to report sir! Proceeding under orders from Divisional Commander, sir! Our fallen Chief of Staff to be carried to Heroes Graveyard, sir! For state funeral, sir!'

The MP Hauptmann seems to consider the matter. He stares suspiciously at the frozen Oberst, and does not notice Porta, who has quietly left the sleigh, and appears shortly after behind him.

'Beg to report, sir!' crows Porta, exuding strict military zeal. 'Trouble over here, sir! Behind us, sir! Corps General, sir! Held up with all his gear, sir!'

The MP officer spins round, and glares furiously at Porta,

who is standing stiffly at the salute with his hand to his bandaged head.

'What's that to do with me?' he barks. 'What General's this you're talking about?'

'Don't know, sir! Sorry, sir!' answers Porta. 'Just know, sir, there's a high-ranking General, sir, sitting in his Mercedes-Kübel, sir, shouting, sir! You there, Obergefreiter, he says to me, sir! Get your arse over to that MP Hauptmann at the crossroads there, sir, an' tell him from me to get over here and bring his men with him, sir!'

'Hell's bells!' curses the MP officer, angrily. 'Where *is* this bloody General? Can you sit on a motorcycle? *You*, Obergefreiter!'

'Sorry, sir, no sir, can't be done, sir! Cheeks of arse shot off, sir! By the Russians, sir!'

'Stupid bastard,' says the Hauptmann, curtly, and thunders off on the powerful motorcycle, with all his men following him.

Porta doesn't even look back at them, as he takes his place in the sleigh again.

'Shit, but he'll be *mad*, when he finds a little twit of an Obergefreiter's took him for a ride!' Horseface screams with laughter. 'If ever he finds you again he'll kick your arse fifteen feet in the air!'

'He won't find me,' Porta assures him, spitting in the snow.

Several miles on, they catch up with a seemingly endless column of heavily loaded lorries, stuck helplessly in the slush.

An Oberst stands in the middle of the road, waving a machine-pistol.

'Out!' he roars, furiously. 'Out! Only drivers stay in the waggons!'

Nobody moves. None of them will leave their waggon.

'What's going on?' asks Gregor, inquisitively, craning his neck.

'A war-mad sod, playing hero. Wants to set up defence positions,' answers an Unteroffizier, from the cab of a Büssing. 'Going off about oaths on the flag, and all that shit. Defend the Fatherland to the last man'n the last bullet.'

'Won't they ever have had enough?' rages the Old Man.

'Aren't we ever to hear anything else but "oath on the flag" and "fight to the last bullet"?'

'Yes,' sighs Porta. 'The oath on the flag.' He gestures with one hand. 'The German sickness. Soon as three Germans get together, they start makin' oaths to the state'n the German God. And the worst of it is, there's always some lamebrain ready to lead us straight up the arsehole of hell!'

'That's enough, now!' screams Heide, insultedly. 'Lamebrain! I'll bet I've guessed correctly, when I say it is the Führer you are referring to?'

'For it is he!' laughs Porta, easily. 'But there's plenty more in this country, who've just as much shit between their ears and are ready to play "*Niebelungen*", so's all us German's can get their backsides browned to a turn in the national frying-pan!'

'That load of Middle Ages shit only a nationality-crazy German's capable of thinking up,' says Gregor, contemptuously.

Julius Heide is struck dumb. He has never heard anything like it. To call the national masterpiece '*Die Niebelungen*' a load of shit. He notes down the date, time and names of all present on his message pad.

Tiny looks inquisitively over his shoulder, and sings in a high, falsetto voice:

Wenn alle untreu werden,
dann bleiben wir doch treu. . . .[3]

The motor sleigh rushes at full speed over the steppe, away from the mile-long convoy stuck in the snow, and the Mpi-waving, suicidal maniac of an Oberst.

A broad row of tanks comes roaring over the steppe, alongside the hills, closely followed by armoured troop carriers and armed sleighs.

'We're in the middle of a counter-attack,' cries the Old Man, fearfully. He stares at the long lines of self-propelled guns roaring past us.

From the lowering clouds Stukas appear with a nerve-

[3]Wenn alle etc.: When all others are unfaithful,
we will still be true. . . .

shattering howl. They drop bombs in the midst of the Russian units, which begin to flee in retreat. By battalions, they throw down their arms and put their hands in the air. Only to be crushed under the tracks of the tanks, which rage through the snow in one long, seemingly endless, killing line.

Outside a forward field dressing station, overflowing with sick and wounded, we leave the motor-sleigh. Horseface won't take us any further, certain that he can manage better with only his frozen Chief of Staff for company.

With a bit of bribery we manage to stay together. If we get separated we may never see one another again. Our division is smashed, and may never be re-formed.

'Berlin, Berlin, here I come!' Porta dreams aloud. He grins hollowly. 'There'll be some people shitting themselves, when I turn up again!'

Two infantrymen are lying on a heap of dirty straw. Their heads are covered in bandages. Only a thin slit has been left for their mouths.

'Necked,' says one of them, in a hoarse voice, gesturing with a frost-charred finger.

'Necked?' asks Barcelona, in astonishment, getting up on one elbow. 'Can you live through *that*?'

'I'm the proof you can,' comes from a bandage-swathed head. 'They took us prisoner just after we left our position. They were all right in the beginning. All they took was our watches. Ivan's got watches, bikes and women on the brain. Don't give a shit for anything else. But then up turned a limping *Pallkóvnik*[4]. One of them dangerous bastards with a Nagan in a open yellow holster. He took two SS-men off straightaway, himself. Bang! Bang! One in the guts, then their arses blowed away. Then he yelled a bit at the rest of us, and promised us we'd go the same road. Everybody outside in a straight line, and off we marched towards the east. Some got away in the confusion. The Russians didn't like it when they found the tally didn't fit. They knocked us about a bit, an' three fellows who'd dropped from exhaustion they cracked their skulls, after they'd give 'em a bayonet in the

[4]Pallkóvnik: Colonel.

217

gut. The limping *Pallkóvnik* had disappeared, and we thought we were gonna be let live. Soldiers usually ain't too bad with soldiers, even when they're wearing different uniforms. Well, we halted in a place with thick cover, and we could hear engines going all round us. The Ivans started puttin' their heads together an' lookin' funny at us. We were thinking the engines sounded like Maibachs, and there was most like a counter-attack going on. But it looked as if the natives were brewing up somethin' nasty for us. They kept on babblin' away in some queer Asiatic dialect, and sending round a big jar of German schnapps they'd got hold of. After a while they were pretty sloshed, and started to sing so's you could've heard it miles away. Every now and then they'd threaten us with their Kalashnikovs, and promise us a quick trip to the Pearly Gates, and no more war.

'In the morning they ordered us up in a long row, single file, and marched us further into the woods. In a clearing, where there was a couple of wrecked guns, they called a halt. I felt a cold pistol muzzle on the back of my neck.

' "*Dassvidánja*, Fritz," the bloke behind me shouted, happy as a pig in shit.

'Then everything disappeared in a roar an' a bright light. But I must've turned my head, somehow, the very second the gun went off. Anyway I wasn't killed by it and woke up a bit later when somebody started pulling me about. It was one of our follow-up units who'd found us, but only me'n my mate over there had got out of it alive. All the others'd had their heads blowed off. A Nagan ain't no lady's gun. Well, as you can see, I stayed alive, but my eyes were gone.'

'Might've been better they'd killed you dead, then,' says Porta, looking at the bandaged head.

'Might indeed,' nods Barcelona, and sighs deeply.

The long corridors are packed with wounded, moaning and calling for a doctor or an orderly. Nobody attends to them. They must wait their turn.

A constant stream of dead bodies comes from the operating theatre. After a while we begin to think that most of the wounded die on the operating table.

218

'The Party bosses are going to have a busy time in the next few weeks,' says Porta, his eyes following five bodies which are being carried away by Russian prisoners. 'Heil Hitler, Frau Müller, the Party feels with you in your proud sorrow. Your son has fallen for Führer and Fatherland! The Führer thanks you! Heil Hitler, Frau Müller!'

'Cut it out, sod it!' The Old Man swears angrily. 'Isn't this enough, don't you think?'

Young doctors, in blood-stained gowns, bend over us and discuss with professional interest: Angles of penetration, lung perforations, broken jaws, smashed-in faces, shot-away eyes, gut wounds, crushed ankles, burns of various degree, and countless other mutilations. As if we were objects of study to them. When they are in agreement they share out points like examination results. Those who get over five are put to one side and a red label is attached to one of their ankles. They are the ones who are not worth operating on.

Where I am there seem to be nothing but red labels, all around me.

Porta waves to me as they carry him into the nauseous operating room. Gregor follows him. He manages a brief glance in my direction. Tiny tries to push his stretcher closer to mine, but before he can manage it they come for him and carry him into the big room where busy doctors are ceaselessly amputating legs and arms, opening stomachs, cutting into craniums. A constant whirl of activity.

Orderlies, covered in long rubber aprons, race excitedly to and fro in a continuous fight against busy death. This is a room in which there are no differences of rank. Officers and other ranks lie together. A heap of human debris. Harsh Prussian faces have long since fallen into the folds of men pleading for survival. Those who have anything to pay with: currency, jewels, watches, spirits, tobacco, almost anything, attempt to buy their way to a green label. Prices go up and up continually. The exchange is in a panic. Green tickets give a man the right to transport, far, far away from the shelling, and from Ilya Ehrenburg's fanatical, victory-inflamed Siberians.

I feel like a tiny boat in a raging sea. Everything is moving up and down. Now it is not only pain which is maddening me, but also thirst. A burning thirst, which makes me long for ice-cold water. A face looms mistily above me.

'Take this one,' says a voice.

I feel the stretcher lifted up. Want to protest, but cannot.

I am tipped over a plank wall, and fall with a bump, onto a heap of frozen bodies.

Another body lands on top of me. An unspeakable stench of rotting flesh fills my nostrils. To my horror I realise that they have thrown me onto a heap of corpses in the belief that I am dead.

An amputated leg flies through the air, and hits the wall on the far side with a soggy thud. A naked, blood-stained body follows it. There is a huge hole in its back, from which the lungs dangle like a pair of perforated bladders.

I attempt to scream, but no sound crosses my lips. I must get out of here, I think desperately. They'll bury me, together with all these bodies. The Russian prisoners, who make up the burial squad, certainly cannot be bothered to see if there might be anyone alive amongst all these dead. Like all prisoners of war they do what they are ordered to do, apathetically. I clutch at my chest, get hold of my identity tab. Half of it is missing. There is no doubt of it. I am already registered as dead. Desperately I feel for something I can use to pull myself up out of the heap of corpses. I get hold of an icy hand. It comes loose as I pull on it.

Shivering I throw it from me, and fumble around in the darkness, but my hands touch only the stiff features of the dead. I push and pull myself up through the mass of torn and twisted bodies. I am on top and can see light above me. My fingers push into an open mouth. I feel as if I am sliding down a chute. Far, far, far away from this hellish slaughterhouse.

I remember no more, until I feel a pair of strong hands grip me and pull me up and out into a brilliant white light.

A man's voice shouts, in guttural Russian. He pulls me further out of the pile. Somebody laughs, noisily. German voices mix with the Russian jabbering.

'Well, now I've seen it all! The man's still alive!' A

220

Russian, in a tall fur hat, lifts me, and carries me back into the warm corridor, where a Sanitäts-Feldwebel is waiting.

'Hell, man!' he shouts. 'You must be more careful! It's a bad show, putting people in the lime-pit *before* they're dead. I will not *permit* that kind of slackness!'

'*Da gasspadin*,' answers the Russian, with complete indifference.

'Put him in the queue with the others,' orders the Feldwebel, impatiently. 'Things are easing off a bit in operating. They ought to be able to look after a stubborn fellow like this, who flatly refuses to die!'

They drop me on a straw mattress, and go on their way. I throw up, and almost choke on the bitter gall. The pain seems to be tearing me to pieces.

The medical station shakes and trembles. A long roar of artillery fire commences. When I turn my face towards the window I see the flash of an explosion. Whether Russian or German I cannot tell.

A yellow hand appears from beneath a dirty blanket. I put out my own hand but cannot reach it:

Morgenrot, morgenrot,
leuchtest mir zum frühen Tod[5]

cackles the man on the stretcher next to me, blue lips stretching wide in an animal grin. He gets half up, and stares at me, with strange, dead eyes. He falls back with a sigh. His head hangs over the side of the stretcher, lolling helplessly on the far too long, thin neck.

A fat M.O. with tired, burnt-out eyes, and a white death's head of a face, looks down at me. He seems to be counting points, wondering what to do with me.

'You're the fellow who refused to let himself die, eh!' he says, taking a shiny instrument from an orderly standing waiting at his side.

A needle jabs into my chest. My arms are pulled back. I feel

[5]Morgenrot etc. Rosy morn, rosy morn, light me to an early death.

as if they are tearing my body apart, crushing my bones, pressing my insides out through my back.

'Shut up,' snarls the surgeon. They press something down over my face.

When I wake up, a long time afterwards, I find myself lying in a room in which there are a great many other wounded. Down the whitewashed walls lice are marching in columns. They veer to the left and fall on the three patients alongside me. They do not seem to find me attractive. It is a bad sign. I am freezingly cold. My stomach burns. The whole room seems to swim about me.

A fat, bald-headed rat is sitting, nibbling at something, a little way out on the floor. A steel helmet comes flying through the air and hits the corpse-rat. Squeaking, it disappears in the direction of the mortuary.

A medical orderly, in white drill, asks me how I feel.

'Like hell,' I answer, weakly.

'We'll give you an injection,' he says, taking a green label from his pocket. 'You're a lucky fellow. The Staff M.O. was in a good humour today. When we fished you out of the corpse pile, you were wearing a red label. Where are your things? You owe me something. But for me you'd have been buried in quick-lime now. Believe you me, buddy!'

'I haven't a thing,' I answer, in a tired voice.

'Useless sod,' he snarls, angrily. '*Trouble*, that's all you pigs are, to anybody.' He goes through my pockets and finds my watch. An antique timepiece, given to me by my grandfather.

'I'll take this,' he says, coldly. 'Your lousy life's worth an old watch, I suppose?'

He opens it and puts it to his ear. 'Funny watch,' he goes on. 'I'll look after it well for you. Now don't create problems. You're not on the train yet. We can easily forget you here, and Ivan's T-34's are on the way, with the neck-shot specialists riding on their backs.'

I let him take the watch. When a Sanitäts-Feldwebel turns up, he vanishes, as rapidly as the corpse-rat disappeared earlier.

'They've done *you* up all right,' says the Feldwebel, an elderly, white-haired man, with many years of active service

222

behind him. 'I'll see you get an injection before you leave for the train,' he promises.

I thank him, and wonder what he will want for that.

'Don't thank me,' he smiles, in friendly fashion. 'It's only what Army Medical Regulations allow you. But I'll give you a bit of advice. *Don't* groan. Grit your teeth, and don't make a noise. Look as if you feel fine. If you don't, they won't take you, even if you're wearing *ten* green labels. The ones who make noise, make work!'

I doze off, wondering where the others are. Dream about Porta, sitting in a steamy kitchen preparing the 'Soup of all Russians'.

'Will you sell your green ticket?' asks a fat Quartermaster, in the bed next to me. He shows a handful of glittering stones. '*Diamonds*,' he says, in a tempting tone of voice.

I stare at him. He must be mad. Nobody would sell his chance of leaving here when the Russians are almost knocking on the door.

'Hope you choke in your own shit,' he hisses, furiously, turning to try some of the others. Soon he is offering them his block of flats in Hamburg. 'It's a big building,' he says, stretching out his arms to show *how* big. 'Forty-eight flats, with good, solid tenants who pay on the nail. Nine shop premises at top rentals!'

'Stick your building, *and* your tenants straight up your arse,' they laugh, jeering at him. 'Try doin' a deal with Ivan when *he* turns up. There's sure to be some Russian who'd like to own a block of flats in Hamburg.'

'I don't think you realise what I'm offering you,' he continues, stubbornly. 'A block like this, in a central part of Hamburg, is a fine thing to have when the war is over. People who own land and buildings, will always get by. Money you can wipe your backside on, when your country's lost a war.'

'That's all *right* then,' laughs an engineer over against the wall, 'you're a lucky shit, man! All I've got is a bicycle without any tyres, if it hasn't been pinched. But I *do* have a green ticket!'

The house-owner with the diamonds begins to weep. He sud-

223

denly realises how poor he is.

'I want to get away from here,' he shouts, hysterically.

'You will, too,' a mousey-looking Gefreiter promises him. 'But it'll be in the other direction. To Siberia!'

Everybody with a green ticket laughs maliciously. They make as much noise as if they were sitting drinking in a beer-parlour.

A party of medical orderlies, with full packs, rush excitedly up and down the corridors.

'Come on, speed it up,' an aged Staff M.O. brays, hysterically. 'The Russians may get here any moment!'

The orderly, who stole my watch, comes over to me and jabs a needle into my arm.

'Come on, buddy-buddy,' he grins, straightening the straps of the bulging knapsack on his back. He puts his arm around my shoulders and helps me up.

'Can you stand on your legs?' he asks.

'I believe so,' I answer, biting my lip.

'You'd better believe it,' he growls. 'It's the only chance you've got. If you can't stay on your pins, they'll leave you behind. Even if there's *fifty* green tickets tied to your prick!'

I hang on to him, and try to make myself as light as possible. If he feels I'm too much trouble he'll drop me, as carelessly as if I were an empty cigarette packet.

The street is one mass of filthy slush. Abandoned stretchers and equipment lie everywhere. Groaning wounded, in blood-soaked bandages, crawl, like half-dead lizards, along the ground. In the distance a heavy roar of engines, and the thudding noise of 'coffee-grinders' can be heard.

In the middle of the road a P-4 is burning. The charred bodies of the crew hang from open hatches. Their empty eye-sockets glare at us.

'Time to get out of here,' grins "my" orderly, nastily, kicking a crawling patient, both of whose legs have been amputated, out of his way. 'Why can't these dopes stay in bed?' he snarls, irritably. 'They won't let 'em get on board the trains. All he'll get out of it's he'll get himself squashed flat by some tank or other!'

Great, greasy, mushrooms of smoke hang over the railway

station. A blast of hot air meets us. Earth, asphalt, tiles, corrugated iron, and steel splinters, hail down on us. A complete carpenter's shop comes sailing through the air and smashes to pieces amongst the ruins of the houses. A huge boiler falls, with a scream of torn metal, straight down on to a party of wounded. Twisted human forms hang on the lamp-posts. Bodies without heads. Bodies without backs. The blast removes them, and replaces them with other bodies.

'We've made it,' says the orderly. He pushes me up into a packed goods waggon.

'Here's your buddies, buddy,' he grins, patting me cheerily on the back. He disappears into the crowd with his bulging pack.

They are all there. Albert embraces me. Tiny waves from the far corner. Porta is, of course, sitting close to the glowing stove, baking potatoes.

'You were hard to find,' says Gregor, 'but we got the orderly who brought you to help us. He cost a pretty penny.'

'That lad's worse than all the sharks in Germany put together,' says Porta. 'A real body-snatcher!'

'I pray to the God of the black peoples, that that pig doesn't manage to get away before Ivan drops his heavy hand on his shoulder,' says Albert, vengefully. He folds his hands, and elevates his eyes piously towards the dirty roof of the cattle-waggon. As if he expected the African God to be enthroned up there.

The long train jerks violently. The two heavy engines, which are to pull it, give out long, shrill whistles.

At the back of the waggon somebody begins to sing:

Zu mir zu kommen ist nicht leicht für dich,
und bis zum Tod sind es bloss vier Schritt. . . .[6]

Porta pulls a thick, black notebook from his knapsack, licks a stump of pencil and writes for a while in silence.

'What *is* it you keep on writing in that book?' asks the Old Man inquisitively.

[6]Zu mir etc: (freely):
   To come to me is not easy for you,
   when death has only four steps to go. . . .

225

'Totting up who hasn't paid his 80% while I've been off fighting the world war. Looks as if I'm going to be busy when I get to Berlin! There's one or two boys who may get their balls shot off!'

'Are you *sure* we're going to Berlin?' asks Gregor, disbelievingly.

'Sure I'm sure. I've bought a ticket for Berlin for our lot. A Staff Grefreiter, who's Chief Clerk at the RTO here's a good friend of mine. I let him off an 80% man's loan. *That's* guarantee enough for *us* getting to Berlin!'

'He'll twist you,' decides the Old Man, quietly, leaning tiredly against the frost-coated side of the waggon.

'Not him!' says Porta. 'He's a swine all right, but not a *rotten* swine!'

For nineteen days the hospital train zig-zags through the Ukraine and Poland. Then into Czechoslovakia. A trip around Eger and Hof, and then northwards with the remaining wounded. Late one evening the train stops, with a screech of brakes, at Berlin/Anhalter Bahnhof.

'Damn my eyes,' cries the Old Man. He shakes his head in silent admiration. 'You're the king of 'em all, Porta! The eight wonder of the world, you are!'

'Didn't I *say* we were going to Berlin?' answers Porta. He makes himself appear to be far more sick and suffering than he really is, as the doors slide open and a party of medical orderlies enters the waggon to off-load us.

'Where you from?' asks a Hauptfeldwebel, in a stern barrack-square voice.

'The arsehole of the universe,' answers Porta, with a broad grin.

'Don't you be cheeky with me, Obergefreiter,' barks the Hauptfeldwebel, nastily, straightening his offensively clean tailor-made uniform.

'Berlin, Berlin so sehen wir uns doch wieder. . . .[7]

hums Porta, as two assistant nurses, breathing heavily, carry him along the platform to the waiting ambulance.

[7]Berlin etc: Berlin, Berlin, now we meet again. . . .

*When quite ordinary young soldiers begin killing,
it is very difficult to stop them.*

Killing had become an everyday occurrence to us. There was no weapon we were not experts in the use of. From the garrotting wire, to heavy machine-guns and cannon. Most of us could also kill with our hands alone. A sharp blow with the edge of the hand. Two stiff fingers. At the age of twenty we were already older than our seventy-year old grandfathers. We knew more about life and death than they had learnt in all their years of life. We never passed a body without putting a bullet into its head. A grenade always went through the door before we entered a house. We were bereft of every illusion for always and forever. Nothing could surprise us. We had experienced far too many psychic shocks. Our normal emotional life had been shattered by hundreds of treacherous ambushes, by sudden artillery attacks. Rape amused us. Particularly if we were a whole company with only one woman. We took what we could get. We hadn't much time, and death was always close beside us.

227

6
Eighty Per Cent

'Sally's in *Berlin*,' shouts Porta, happily, 'and he's at *GHQ*!'

'The War Ministry,' the Sanitäts-Feldwebel corrects him.

'Even *better*!' Porta grins like a Cheshire cat. 'It's what I've always said. If God loves you, the sun is always shining! Sally in Berlin! Sally at the War House! *This* is the kind of thing that strengthens a man in his faith!' He laughs, loud and long. The Chief Medical Officer, an Oberst, enters the ward, at the head of his staff, at that precise moment.

'You seem to be recovering at a most wonderful rate,' comments the CMO, rapping Porta's chest with his stethoscope. 'Yesterday you were totally paralysed, with a burning fever! I'd like you to tell me more about this lightning cure you seem to have achieved in the course of one night. It might be of use to me in the future, when treating *other* hopeless cases!'

'Sir, Oberst, sir!' smiles Porta, happily. 'It seems to have happened to me, sir, like it says in the Bible, sir! With the fellow in Palestine, sir. And Jesus said, sir, "take up thy bed and sod off". And off went the crippled chap with his fartin' bag on his shoulder!'

'It *does* seem as if it must have been some occurrence of that nature,' says the CMO, drily. 'We'd better discharge you, straight away, to the convalescent battalion. Let you get a bit of healthy exercise.'

'Beg to report, sir! Obergefreiter Creutzfeldt there, sir! He's also become cured in the course of one night. All the pains in his back have disappeared.'

Tiny shakes his head furiously behind the CMO's back, and throws up his arms in bewilderment. He doesn't understand a

228

word of it. The plan was to drop anchor in the Berlin Hospital until the end of the war.

'It's good to hear that Creutzfeldt has also been struck by this case of acute health!' smiles the CMO, sarcastically. 'Then we'd better let him go as well! We'll discharge you both to convalescent battalion!'

'Beg to report, sir,' crows Porta. 'We are soon to be posted to special duty at the War Ministry, sir!'

'I'll believe it when I see it,' answers the CMO, with a short laugh. 'In any event you both go to the convalescent shop.' He points to the crutches leaning against the bed. 'Hand those in to the stores. Anybody can see you won't be needing *them* anymore.'

'Dummy,' whispers the orderly to Porta, as he checks them out.

'Think so?' laughs Porta, slily. 'In a couple of days time you'd give your arse to swop with us! We'll be lying back in the War Minister's chair despatching Generals and coolies hither an' yon, as we feel the urge!'

It is a noisy reunion, when Porta and Tiny, after negotiating countless check-points, reach Oberfeldwebel Sally's office in War Ministry Department A.W.A.[1]

'This is *nice*,' cries Tiny, overwhelmed, hopping up and down on a springy sofa.

Porta lounges in a deep armchair with a large cigar in the corner of his mouth. He opens his uniform at the throat and pulls his cap down over his left eyebrow. This is the way he likes to sit. Makes a man look as if he *was* somebody, he believes.

'What about a drop of something to wash the hospital bacteria out of your throats?' suggests Sally, taking a bottle from a cupboard marked GEHEIME KOMMANDOSACHEN.[2]

'With the greatest of pleasure,' answers Porta, puffing out a great cloud of smoke. 'Might just as well fill the glass right up while you're about it. Don't want you over-exerting yourself having to fill 'em up all the time!'

They toast one another, bowing arrogantly from the hips in

[1]A.W.A. Allgemeine Wehrmachtsangelegenheiten: General Army Affairs.
[2]Geheime etc: COMMAND FILES — SECRET

officer fashion. They are, after all, at the War Ministry.

Porta takes the whole glass down in one, and licks out the glass afterwards.

'I hear you had a lot of fun with that wildcat I sent you[3]' laughs Sally, heartily. 'What about another one? I've got two vicious bastards in stock, and you can take 'em over anytime, if you want to teach a "friend" a lesson!'

'No more wildcats,' protests Tiny, in horror, showing the scars of his meeting with the first one.

'You *must* post us immediately to special service,' says Porta, seriously, pushing forward his glass for a refill. 'We've got one leg in Russia, already.'

'Can do,' considers Sally, confidently. 'What branch would you like?'

'Sittin' plannin' somethin' or other with you, an' drinkin' Slivovitz,' suggests Tiny. He breaks out into a great roar of laughter.

'What about HDv,' asks Sally, 'nice and comfy there. No dangerous Valhalla aspirants, longing for the thunder of warfare.'

'What's HDv?' asks Porta, suspicious as always.

'*Heeresdruckvorschriftenverwaltung*[4],' explains Sally, with a superior air.

'One of those places where they eat regulations raw, and send 'em out again fast as a turn 'o the shits after Christmas,' nods Porta, understandingly. 'Sounds just right for us. Put us on the payroll quick as you can, so we can start fucking up the plans soonest. I am greatly worried,' he goes on, leaning forward confidentially across the desk, which is about the size of a helicopter landing space. 'There are some people here in Berlin who think they can piss on me. Just because I have been engaged for a while in Russia looking after the progress of this bloody war. I've been sniffing about a bit, and have discovered, to my great sorrow, that nobody gives a shit for me anymore. They laugh at me, and spit on my boots. Even in "Greedy

[3]See 'Court martial'.
[4]Heeresdruck ... etc: Army Service Regulations Directorate.

Minna's" knocking shop they pretended not to know me. Minna got a pain in her gut laughing when I reminded her I had 80% due. She was fresh enough to demand payment in advance if I wanted to get across one of her skull-faced whores. So now I've reached the stage where a man can only drink and fuck, and get depressed in between times. Until I heard you were back in Berlin and that brought my pecker up again. Before then I was already standing on a chair with the noose round my neck.'

'You made the biggest mistake of your life, when you turned down my offer of the job of keeper of the files at Paderborn Command,' says Sally. '*You'd* rather drive a tank. More fun it was, you said.'

'I didn't know then that Grofaz was going to get me mixed up in a war,' Porta excuses himself.

'But he *did*,' smiles Sally, 'and off you went, together with all the other dopes, into the fiery rain of shells. Those few of us who kept our heads cool remained behind to weather the much less dangerous rain of documents and typewriters. We're keeping business going as usual until one day peace breaks out and a new sun shines down on us.'

'I was foolish,' admits Porta, sadly, taking a critical look at himself in the mirror behind the desk. 'Get yourself sorted out, Porta!' he barks at his mirror image. He twists his head, so that with an effort he can see himself in profile. 'You *look* clever enough,' he nods to his mirror image, with an air of satisfaction. 'Those limp pricks'll find out all right that taking the arse of an 80% man don't go unpunished.'

Oberfeldwebel Sally leans back smilingly in his swivel chair. 'Did you know, by the way that "Egon the Poof's" pinched your pitch? He's going round telling the world you're nothing but a cleaned-out rabbit's head, stuffed with sauerkraut, and if you're lucky enough to get back from the front he's going to see to it you get deported to a cowshit-stinking hole in South Bavaria, where the entire population consists of village idiots.'

'Jesus,' exclaims Tiny, with pretended fear. He claps his hands over his head, which is quite difficult since he is lying flat on his belly on the carpet. 'It was *time* we left Adolf to look after 'is war 'imself, so we could straighten up on the home front!'

'Well hell,' cries Porta, indignantly. 'That's a pretty coarse kind of joke coming from that poof, a pretty coarse joke. Unless it was an attempt to commit suicide, or something very personal of that kind.'

'Let's go out now an' do 'im up with a sandbag,' suggests Tiny.

'Don't rush things, now, and you won't risk doing something you might regret,' warns Sally, filling up their glasses again. 'Take a leaf out of my book. You can see it pays dividends. Always proceed according to a well-thought out plan of action.'

Porta looks thoughtfully out of the window. His eyes follow a loaded barge sailing slowly up the Landwehr Kanal with a fat woman at the rudder and a thin one on watch at the bow.

'Egon's a dirty bastard,' he declares, viciously, banging his fist on the window ledge. 'I'll shoot the sod straight through the heart and blow it to pieces. He'll be dead before he knows it.'

'I know some people, who now and again like to dress up as parsons,' says Sally, mysteriously. He lights a large Brazilian cigar, and blows a cloud of smoke across the desk.

'In vestments?' asks Porta, not understanding. He sinks into the armchair. 'Some of that holy clobber they climb into when they want to have an intimate chat with Jesus and God?'

'Parsons' walking clothes,' says Sally, pleasedly, puffing strongly at his cigar. 'Those fellows know what they want. They carry the Book of Moses in their left hand, and look holy when they come out into the light. Jesus knows all about *you*, they say when you meet them, and then they pull a "soul-remover" out of their holy uniform, and everything's over in under a minute. Their fee's $33\frac{1}{3}$ % of everything they collect!'

'How does a fellow meet those boys?' asks Porta, interestedly. 'They're not any of these spaghetti-eating Eyetie sods, are they? Never see any chips *they* collect!'

'Absolutely not,' laughs Sally, heartily. 'They're tougher. Wicked men from Berlin/Moabitt. Good friends of mine!'

'How good friends?' asks Porta, filled with healthy suspicion.

'Good enough to meet you, if I ask 'em to,' smiles Sally, slily, showing a row of beautifully white teeth with gold edges.

'You've a good dentist,' sighs Porta, enviously, sucking at his only remaining tooth. Which is, also, black.

'I do,' answers Sally. 'Lives just round the corner in Prinz Albrecht Strasse.'

'I suppose he's S.S. Heini's dentist too?' asks Porta, with a lop-sided smile.

'You're right,' answers Sally, with a happy laugh. 'I found a couple of blots on his family escutcheon, while I was running through some old documents from the Weimar days. So I never have to make an appointment, and I never get a bill either!'

'Watch out they don't hang you one day,' warns Porta, darkly. 'I wouldn't let an SS-man fix my teeth! When all this world war piss's over, it could be they found out the gold in your teeth came out of a Jew's jaw'n the bloke who owned it before had gone up the chimney in smoke!'

Sally laughs, loudly and heartily, and passes a hand down over his elegant tailor-made uniform. 'You two'll have been knocked off by the liberators and your bodies pecked to bits by the crows, before anybody even thinks about me. And by then I'll have become irreplaceable. They'll need some "clean" Germans to kick last year's heroes in the backside!'

'And you think they'll use you for that?' smiles Porta, with an air of overbearance. 'They're not that silly!'

'I don't just *think* so, I *know* so,' boasts Sally, with self-confidence, pushing a button under his desk. 'But let's get down to *your* business, so that we can tear the heads off the villains who're bustling about on your territory.'

There is a cautious knock on the door. A dry-looking Gefreiter, wearing an unhappy expression on a face decorated with gold-rimmed, schoolmasterish spectacles, edges nervously into the large office. He makes a hopeless attempt at clicking his heels in military fashion. It sounds more like a sick hen tap-dancing in a bowl of lukewarm water than a German soldier coming to attention.

Sally leans back in his chair, and regards the Gefreiter commandingly. The man stands stiffly in front of the desk, with doggily devoted eyes, awaiting orders.

'Listen to me closely, Lange. I am making you responsible for ensuring that Unteroffizier Hartnacke is present in "The

233

Three-legged Goose" at 18.00 hrs., and that he has with him his special equipment. Two Obergefreiters from the panzer arm will contact him.'

'Very good, sir!' pipes Gefreiter Lange, again attempting to click his heels.

'Oh hell, man,' groans Sally, resignedly. 'You'll *never* learn it! Look at your arms, how they flop around! Get those thieving fingers along the seams of your trousers! Elbows forward, and tighten the cheeks of your arse! *Your* arms hang down as if you were getting into position to scratch your backside! I think I'll do it, after all. I'll send you off to brother Ivan. Perhaps *he* can teach you how a soldier stands to attention. You're a nothing, a cow of a man. What *are* you then, Lange?'

'Beg to report, sir, Gefreiter Lange is a nothing, and a cow of a man, sir!'

'Get out of here,' commands Sally, flicking his hand at him as if he were knocking a fly off a piece of bread and jam!

Gefreiter Lange backs away, and, of course, falls over the threshhold. Sweating profusely he gets to his feet, bows in a civilian, unmilitary manner, and closes the door cautiously behind him.

'Jesus'n Mary, what a circus clown,' sighs Tiny from down on the floor. He hands up his tumbler for a refill. 'What we sorely-tried Prussians have to put up with in these times of war.'

'He was a professor at some university or other down south, before we got him,' explains Sally, in a pleased voice. 'After he'd nearly wiped out a whole company on the firing range they sent him to me. He's completely useless as a soldier, but he's good with erasers and pencils and things like that.'

'It's nice to have people like that around, sometimes,' admits Porta. 'A couple of words removed, in the right place, from a black document, can soon turn it into a welcome communication.'

Shortly after six o'clock in the evening Porta and Tiny sneak into 'The Three-legged Goose', where Unteroffizier Hartnacke is already enthroned at the bar with a large bowl of mixed salad and garlic sauce in front of him.

Tiny takes two bar-stools, as usual.

'One for each cheek,' he says to the sour-faced barmaid, laughing noisily. She looks plump, but only because she is wearing a dress which is too small for her.

They pour a shot of Slivovitz into their beer.

'Good for the humour nerve, this is,' grins Porta, emptying his glass in one long, gurgling draught.

'Another?' asks the barmaid, in an insulted tone. She pokes about in her hair with a fork, then rolls it up, together with a knife, in a paper serviette, and lays it by the side of a guest's plate.

'If you ask every time, you'll soon get 'oarse,' remarks Tiny, in friendly fashion.

Porta turns and winks at the large man. 'I hear you can do a quick job without making a lot of noise about it,' he says.

'They call me "Happy Release",' answers Hartnacke, laconically, shovelling garlic sauce into his mouth, as if he were pitching hay.

'And nothing ever goes wrong?' asks Porta, with healthy suspicion.

'They go off quickly, the people you look after? Like, *very* quickly, without even having time to say toodle-oo?'

'I was born in Chicago,' says Hartnacke, proudly. 'My mother's from Palermo. My father was sent back again to Greece. You can guess the rest.'

'Jesus'n Mary!' cries Tiny, enthusiastically. 'That sounds really promising.'

'What's your M.O.?' asks Porta, professionally. 'I've heard something about dressing up like a parson. Hallelujah! The Lord be with you! All that kind of thing?'

'You buyin'?' asks Hartnacke, pushing forward his empty glass.

Porta gives the barmaid the international 'fill-em-up-again' sign.

'See here,' whispers Hartnacke, in a conspiratory voice, slapping a large parcel which lies beside him on the bar. 'When one of God's chosen walks in people are usually friendly and just a little bit uncomfortable. Even the worst villains don't go for a parson *straight* away. Another big advantage, when the job's

235

over, is that the bulls from Alex[5] are runnin' round lookin' for a Holy Joe and not a plain German Unteroffizier.'

'*Do* these Kripo creeps do much about the kind of small jobs people like us do?' asks Porta, looking searchingly at the mottled picture of Hitler hanging behind the bar.

'Not really,' Hartnacke admits, wiping up the last of his garlic sauce with a piece of bread. 'They chase about a bit for the sake of appearances, but they're too busy with saboteurs, an' political criminals who're against Austria takin' over dear old Germany, to bother much with us. An' if some zealous bastard does stick his long nose out too far, then War Minister Sally pushes one of his row of buttons, an' before the bloke knows where he is he's findin' a new use for his energy chasin' dangerous guerillas in the Polish forests. We're all right long as we keep away from politics. If, now, you should want a Gauleiter sent to heaven with a stick of gelignite up his jacksey, *don't* come to me! It creates problems. The Alex boys just come burstin' out from every openin' in the buildin' and they do not desist from their efforts until they find somebody they can persuade to confess.'

'I begin to understand,' says Porta, thoughtfully, craning his neck to get a better look at a woman in a brown calfskin cape, 'you walk up in your phony parson's uniform with a smarmy grin on your face, and ask the target when he last set foot in church. Before he's had time to think about it, you sew him up with lead thread! Goodbye and give my love to the Old Boy!'

'Somethin' like that,' admits Hartnacke. 'What do you say to a hot steak? Horse they'll give you without coupons!'

His suggestion sets off a furious argument with the barmaid, who does not want to serve hot food at the bar. She gives in when Tiny draws his combat knife from his boot, and placing it confidentially between her legs asks her if she's ever had one as sharp as that.

'Ain't nobody never got wise to that parson trick of yours?' asks Tiny, his mouth stuffed with bloody horse-meat.

'Yes it *is* funny,' Porta puts in. 'If I heard about a mate of

[5]Alex: Alexander Platz Police Station.

236

mine getting put on the heavenly bus by a sky-pilot, I wouldn't let a black cassock get anywhere near me. Not without taking the stuffing out of it first anyway.'

'Most grown-up people're stupider now'n when they came into the world,' explains Hartnacke, 'and you must *not* forget that the only guy who *really* knows it was a blackbird who knocked him off is not talkin' much any more. He's dead!'

'How *do* you knock 'em off, usually?' asks Porta, interestedly, ordering another steak.

Hartnacke keeps silent until the barmaid has served their beer and Slivovitz.

'I use only tried and true methods. Garrottin' wire or a silenced hand-gun. Nothin' that makes a mess. Messes're repulsive. Learnt the trade at Fort Zittau, where I went as a volunteer. Knew they taught you things there, you'd never be able to learn anywhere else in peacetime.'

'What things?' asks Porta, waving a prostitute away irritably, as she is about to sit down alongside them.

She opens her mouth to say something, but closes it again quickly when her eye falls on a knife and a set of spiked knuckle-dusters.

'We learnt the kind of tricks a gentleman of the old school would absolutely *not* have anythin' to do with,' continues Hartnacke, shovelling the remains of his horsemeat steak into his mouth with a motion like that of a man cleaning out a pig-sty.

When they saunter out of 'The Three-legged Goose', a couple of hours later, Porta says in a low voice, elbowing Hartnacke confidentially in the ribs, 'I want Egon the Poof changed from being alive, alive-o, to being frozen mutton. But I want that twisted little cocksucker to know it's me that's turned him off! And when you've blown his dirty little soul to hell I want you to leave an 80% card on the body. That's to show Berlin what happens to people who think not paying their debts to an 80% man is a big, big joke!'

'Isn't that bein' a bit careless?' asks Hartnacke, cautiously. 'Everybody knows *you're* an 80% man, and even if the Alex bulls aren't exactly Berlin's cream of crime-solvers, they wouldn't have to knock their brains out to get to that one. The Poof's got a whole fleet of pavement pounders too. Couple of those girls get talkin' and the Alex lot'll be tearin' at the seat of your pants in no time.'

'It's no fun, if Egon doesn't know it's me that's put out the contract,' laughs Porta, noisily. 'The pleasure alone's worth a bit of risk.'

'OK, it's your neck,' answers Hartnacke, uncaringly, '*I'll* keep *my*self in the clear, anyway!'

'Too right,' smiles Porta, 'and when they find that 80% card on the body, there's a lot of people here in Berlin who'll start shittin' themselves, and rushing out madly to pay off their just debts.'

'Our patience is not inexhaustible,' bellows Tiny, his voice echoing between the houses. 'They're gonna *know* we're back from the wars. When the Poof's 'ad it, we'll take the bleedin' dwarf.'

Porta rings Egon from a telephone box to give him the glad news of his return to Berlin.

'Love us all, dears! Is that really you then, Porta? What a nice surprise,' cries Egon. 'There hasn't anything *nasty* happened to you while you've been away in that cruel, cruel war? There's such a lot of *awful* things one *does* hear about from out there! Just when you think a dear, good friend's still in the land of the living, then suddenly somebody says he's *dead*!'

'Don't cry then,' Porta comforts him. 'There's more life in this old dog than you, and some others, dream of. You might just find that out, if what you owe me for the last two years isn't paid up by 8 o'clock this evening!'

'Dear *dear* Porta, everything's *changed* since you went off out there to pick up a bit more of that nice *lebensraum* for dear, old Germany. I'm really, really sorry to have to be the first to tell you about it, but some other people have taken over *all* your business affairs. Nasty dark-looking men, they are. Can't *ever* get a smile out of them!'

'Fuck *that*!' roars Porta, losing his self-control. He blows smoke into the mouthpiece as if it were Egon's face. 'You come at the time I've said and hand over my coppers. And you can

238

stuff your dark-looking men up your shitter if there's room for 'em!'

'But Porta, darling *man*,' says Egon, in a fat, self-satisfied voice, 'you *don't* think I want to get myself *killed*, now do you? Especially just now, when the future's beginning to look a little brighter?'

'Listen to me and listen closely, you stinking little monkey's arsehole, you dirty rotten son of a Zulu whore, you sneaking, treacherous jackal, you,' roars Porta, into the telephone. 'If you don't turn up here with a big, heavy chinking sack, something *bad's* going to happen to you. Something very, very bad. Something that'll put you out of touch with ordinary human beings very effectively and for *ever*!'

'Oh you *wouldn't*,' whines Egon, nervously, knocking the telephone against the wall in fear.

'Think it over, you little maggot, and sort out for yourself just who it is who's boss around here!' Porta leaves the earpiece dangling from its cord in the telephone booth. Well down the street they can still hear Egon's excited piping.

' 'E was really scared, was Egon,' grins Tiny, in a satisfied tone.

' 'E'll be there.' But Tiny is wrong. Egon does not turn up.

The following day Porta and Tiny are walking down Sperling Strasse, together with Unteroffizier Hartnacke, to have a personal conversation with Egon the Poof. As they turn in through the gates of Egon's apartment building, 'Viola Ballbreaker' comes rocketing out of it and knocks Tiny over.

'What the 'ell,' he shouts, angrily, picking his cap up out of the gutter. 'Can't you look where you're goin', you blubber-gutted sow, you?'

'Who're you callin' blubber-gutted?' screams Viola, insulted, kicking him in the ankle.

'What you think you're at, you seventh-rate two mark whore, you?' explodes Tiny, furiously, hopping up and down on one foot and rubbing his painful ankle. 'I'll *do* you, I'll split your lousy, fucked-up gorilla cunt open from arse'ole to breakfast-time!'

'Blow, you village cocksucker, you,' hisses Viola, beginning

239

to work herself up. 'I'll tear your *balls* off. If you've got any to get a hold on, that is!'

'You must've got fucked by an octopus,' roars Tiny, throwing a punch at Viola which would have killed her, if it had landed.

She avoids it by taking a quick step backwards. She kicks out at him, and hits him on the knee. As he doubles up with a howl she sticks a finger in his eye. He whirls, and snatches up one of the overflowing fish skips outside the fishmonger's shop. In the same movement, he raises it and its contents of stinking fish offal above his head, and brings it down on her with all his strength. Pieces of fish fly up into the air.

'Stop larking about,' shouts Porta, irritably, vainly attempting to separate them. 'We haven't time to play games. We're here on business!'

But Viola is now as mad as a March hare. She grabs a huge catfish and swings it round her head a couple of times to build up momentum. She lets go of it, but misses her target. Instead of hitting Tiny, the catfish hits the fishmonger, who has come roaring out of his shop, full in the face. With a piercing scream he falls backwards. His false leg, from the first World War, flies through the air and hits Viola in the face. She thinks it is Tiny who has kicked her. Her fingers are like the claws of an eagle. Ten painted nails tear at Tiny's cheeks. Blood spurts.

He grabs the fishmonger's false leg and brings it down on Viola's head. It breaks in two.

Viola is not beaten yet! She is in training, and used to having bottles broken over her head. Breathing stertorously she attacks Tiny's private parts. Her trained fingers find their way through his greatcoat and three pairs of stolen Army winter underpants.

His mouth gapes, redly. A long, agonized jungle cry rings down the street. Both knees fly up over his head. For a moment he is without contact to the ground. He would have got a great round of applause at Circus Kranz. He rolls out into the road, where a delivery tricycle, loaded with sacks of corn, runs over him. He is in such agony that he does not even notice it. When he comes to his senses again his only thought is for Viola. She has disappeared, as if swallowed up by the ground.

'My *leg*!' screams the fishmonger, surrounded by smashed boxes of fish.

' 'Ere then, limpy,' cries Tiny, throwing the smashed leg down into the middle of the mess of fish. His eye falls on Viola's blue hat sticking up from behind a cask of fish offal. '*There* you are, then! You fuckin' cock-swallower!' he roars. He catches hold of her by the breasts and slings her through the door of 'The Green Hen'.

She flies through the air like a bullet, takes Porta with her and crashes into a heavy hatstand, which is made of shell-casings from the first World War, and weighs almost half a ton. With a deafening crash it topples on to the painters' special table, and crushes it to kindling. Beer, pork, horsemeat, sauce and sausages splash up into the air and run down the walls.

'It's the *Russians*,' howls an invalid from the first World War. He gets his false legs entangled and is unable to move. 'Red Front!' he just manages to groan, before he faints. He has forgotten to take off his party badge, which shines, revealingly, in his left lapel. From that day onwards he never wears it again.

Unteroffizier Hartnacke, who is in the process of unpacking his parson's habit, is thrown over the bar and takes three dishes of *sauerkraut* and *Eisbein* with him. He emits a hoarse, owl-like groan and goes amok. All former plans are cancelled. This is no time for caution and undercover action. Straight into the attack! With a diabolical grin he rips the Nagan from his shoulder holster.

'All right Egon, you're on the way *out*!'

He knows that Egon is sitting in his office, with an overheated adding machine, just waiting for a purposeful killer to blow his head off.

He takes an agile leap over the bar, barely avoiding Viola and Porta, who are lying on the floor chewing on one another's ears. He wipes the *sauerkraut* from his face and thunders on through the bar-room. This, he thinks, is going to go down in the history of Berlin. It's never happened before. When old Fritz and all his fucking generals are dead and forgotten they'll still be talking about 'Happy Release' and what he did to Egon in the Second World War.

Egon is sitting in a deep, upholstered chair, feeling happy about the figures he has arrived at on his adding machine, when the door is kicked open so violently that it is left hanging from only one hinge. His first impression is that a whole regiment is coming in through the door opening. He glares down the black barrel of a heavy pistol. A cry rings in his ears, making the few hairs he has left on his head stand up, quivering with fear. It is Leo, the cook, attempting to warn him of rapidly approaching danger and sudden death. The dwarf, Olfert, who is only four feet ten inches tall, but almost the same across the shoulders, goes down like lightning behind Egon's chair, flapping his arms like a turkey with its head chopped off.

Egon opens his water-blue eyes wide in terror, and begins to make noises like a drenched cat on a rocking ice floe.

'You've *had* it! You miserable whoremonger, you!' roars Hartnacke. 'I'm goin' to shoot the last of your rotten wits out, I am!'

'Can't we talk about this,' begs Egon, who is an expert at talking his way out of difficult corners.

'You've talked enough in *your* life,' Hartnacke cuts him off with an icy laugh. 'You're gonna *get* it!' He presses the muzzle of the pistol against Egon's nose and presses the trigger.

An enormous explosion echoes from wall to wall of 'The Green Hen', and makes the fishmonger in the street crawl to cover behind a herring barrel.

Egon rolls over and over, still sitting in his chair. The dwarf, Olfert, sits in the middle of the floor, screaming for the police and the SS to come. He is one of the party founders, and always remembers it when his life is in danger.

Hartnacke stands glaring in amazement at the remains of his hand. Blood drips from it onto the documents on the desk. In his hurry he has made a fateful mistake. Unforgiveable even for a recruit who has just picked up his uniform from the QM. He has the bad habit of always carrying two different types of pistol, a Russian Nagan and a German P-38. And ammunition in his pocket for both. Viola's knocking over of the hat-stand, and the resulting confusion, has caused him to load the Nagan with P-38 ammunition. No weapon in the world can stand up

242

to being loaded with the wrong ammunition. The Nagan has been blown to pieces, peppering the walls with pieces of itself and Hartnacke's fingers. In shock he rushes out of 'The Green Hen', and never remembers, afterwards, how he got back to the War Ministry. Sanitäts-Unteroffizier Steinhart sews his hand together clumsily, in a way no surgeon would ever accept.

'Don't show your nose outside the War Ministry for at least a month,' rages Sally furiously.

'I hope you're cured of carrying two different weapons, at least! You madman, you! You *do* realise you're mad? Stark, raving mad? The whole of Berlin knows already it was you, you halfwit, who shot up "The Green Hen"! Even a starving Jew wouldn't be that dumb! After this I know your mother must have been paralysed in the head when she dropped *you* in the gutter!'

Hartnacke scowls and whines in miserable resignation. He swears silently to himself that when he sees Egon again he'll knock him a yard into the nearest wall.

In the inner sanctum of 'The Green Hen' Egon is still sitting, touching his face cautiously. Very, very slowly he realises that there is no blood, that his features are still all there. An unbelievable feeling of joy streams through him.

'I've come back from the dead,' he says, sobbing and laughing confusedly at the same time. He begins to thank God, and in the next second to curse Him. 'Revenge!' he screams furiously, 'revenge! I want that bastard "Happy Release" brought to me in twenty-five separate pieces. And I'll put him through the mincer and sell him for dog food, off the ration!'

With Olfert the dwarf in the lead, Egon's gang go through Berlin looking for Hartnacke. Egon is so furious that he cannot eat for three days, despite the fact that he is a great glutton.

Slowly, the hunt eases off. Late one afternoon, when Egon is enjoying himself with two of his favourites, Porta and Tiny enter the room without knocking. Egon has just slipped into a set of lacy, silk women's underclothes. He likes the feel of them.

Tiny presses a sawn-off shotgun roughly against his ear.

'Thought it was all over, didn't you, then?' he hisses, wickedly.

'It's not! It's just beginning! Those cultural sods who go to the opera say the end's the best part of it!'

'We *did* ask you to drop in on us, didn't we?' asks Porta, gently, bending over Egon. He smiles, and pinches the man's cheek, gently. 'You don't seem to want to hear what we say to you, so *we've* decided you can do without ears. Altogether! And now we're going to shoot them off! You're going to have the pleasure of hearing it, of course. We wouldn't deny you that! It'll be the biggest bang you've ever heard! It'll make you feel as if your *whole* head's being blown off. Maybe it *will* be! And those ears of yours, that you don't like using! They'll go *with* it!'

'You can't *do* that,' cries Egon, in a heartbroken voice, holding his hands out in front of him.

'No?' laughs Tiny, noisily. 'You'd better believe it, you broken-down brown'oler!'

'Its *murder*!' whispers Egon, hoarsely. He attempts to scramble away.

'*Folie de grandeur*!' Porta laughs, in a pleasant voice. 'Let's call it pesticide, shall we, you little rat? When we cut off your prick and hand it in to "Alex" they'll give us a medal! Into the cupboard, you two!' he orders the Poof's two, half-naked, companions, who are sitting trembling on the sofa. 'Make any more noise than a tiptoeing tomcat chasing after kitten cunt and we'll fuck your arseholes up through your brains! Know what *that* feels like?'

'Know a prayer, do you?' asks Tiny, with gruff friendliness, slapping Egon with the back of his hand. 'We're good enough fellows at 'eart, you know. Wouldn't like to send a bloke off on 'is last flight without givin' 'im a chance to sob a prayer first.'

'Let's talk this over,' begs Egon, in a hoarse voice. 'I've got the money. Not coming to see you, that was only a misunderstanding!'

'Yes, yes, of course. Mistakes and misunderstandings! They're the cause of 'alf the troubles of the world,' sighs Tiny, feelingly. 'Let's 'ave your prayer now, just to make sure St. Peter'll be glad to see you.'

'I don't know any prayers! I ain't religious!' cries Egon, unhappily.

'No, I don't suppose you are. It's only good people as are religious, an' you just ain't *good*!' says Tiny, tapping him on the back of the neck with the cold barrel of the sawn-off shotgun.

'*You* pray for him, then!' shouts Porta, locking the door behind Egon's playmates.

'Our Father who art in Heaven,' intones Tiny, with eyes turned up towards the ceiling, 'stay where Thou art an' leave us down 'ere to fix up this little job ourselves so it won't 'urt Thy reputation!'

'Come on then, Egon, let's go for a little stroll together,' says Porta, throwing a raincoat at him. 'Put it on! We can't have you running around in ladies underwear on the streets of Berlin. We'd have the Vice Squad after us!'

'No screamin' mind,' says Tiny, severely, as they descend the stairs. 'Not if you don't want your prick an' balls chopped off an' pushed down your throat!'

With Egon between them, they walk down Friedrichs Strasse to a War Ministry amphibian, which Oberfeldwebel Sally has provided.

A Schupo watches, interestedly, as they push Egon into the vehicle.

'Deserter?' he asks, looking at Egon with inquisitive contempt.

'Right you are,' answers Porta. 'Due for a squad, this sod is. That's the way of it. The bastards who're scared of the enemy shootin' 'em, *we* do it!'

'That's the way it *should* be,' nods the Schupo importantly. He inserts his thumbs behind his highly-polished belt.

'They're going to *murder* me,' shouts Egon, desperately, thinking he might still have a chance.

'*Execute's* the word,' the Schupo corrects him, sharply. He pats his pistol holster, with a speaking gesture. 'I hope they beat you up proper before they turn you off, too! You traitorous bastard!'

'No,' smiles Porta, falsely, 'no! We don't do that in the army. We're humane. We aim at the forehead. And *bang!*' He lifts his hand to the brim of his cap, in a nonchalant gesture. The Schupo returns the salute, in regimental fashion.

They move off down Friedrichs Strasse at top speed.

'I can promise you a quite unique experience,' says Porta, as they turn down Charlottenburg Chaussée. 'You're going to be the first person in the world to fall off *Siegessäule*!'

'Let's talk it over,' whispers Egon, faintly. 'You don't *know* the worrying time I've had. You've only got the *war* to worry about, and *that's* going as bad as can be!'

'And don't we know it,' says Porta, slapping the steering wheel with one hand. 'It's worrying makes this rotten, lousy world totter, and take all the miserable worriers down into the black hole with it. Optimistic blokes like me, we just cruise along on top of all that shit. From the first day I came into the German world I've been a respectable business-man, dealing honestly in all the goods everybody else wanted.'

'For example,' Tiny puts in, knowledgeably, '*cunt*! And you've never, ever asked more'n a very reasonable 80% on top!'

'*You* must be nuts, Egon,' continues Porta. 'Even if you *have* got a civilian haircut, don't imagine you can pull the carpet out from under *my* feet!'

'Barmy, that's what 'e is,' cries Tiny, angrily. 'Thought 'e could tip the 'ole bleedin' shit-bucket over, an' take *us* for a ride!'

'Bit of a shock for you, I suppose? Us comin' back to Berlin!' says Porta, shaking his head sadly.

'I've always been a good pal to my friends,' whines Egon, miserably. 'Be nice, now, fellows, let's drive back to "The Hen". All your 80%'s are lying there in bundles waiting for you. They're all in the account books. Maybe there's a little error here and there in the addition, but that's understandable enough in this terrible time of war. Don't believe everything they say about me. Down inside I'm a *good* person. I deserve thanks for what I've done for people, but I never hear a *word* of it!'

'What *you* deserve is to be knocked on the head by the great globe of the world, time and time again,' declares Porta, slapping the wheel. '*I* know, for example, that it was you who whopped "the Bike-Stealer," and it was you was the cause of "Charlotte the Whore" getting her nut blown off.'

'It's a *wicked, wicked* lie!' protests Egon, clapping his hands to his face. 'My hands have never, never been stained by blood.' He holds both his hands in front of Porta's face, in proof of his statement, with the result that Porta barely avoids hitting a newspaper-woman in a blue dress. She sends a volley of Goethe's vulgarisms after him.

'No, you're too cowardly, *and* too clever to do it yourself,' smiles Porta. 'The dwarf looks after that part of the business for you. He was up there with Charlotte, and the Stork was with him. They told her they were going to throw her two kids out of the window head-first if she didn't fork out 60% of her earnings at "The Owl". When she didn't pay up, they came back and minced her face up a bit. That didn't help either, because she thought Bike-Stealer could fix your arse, you little shit, you. So both her and the nippers went out of the window headfirst.'

'You don't really believe I could do anything that *wicked*?' asks Egon, in a shaky voice. 'Find Bike-Stealer, and he'll *tell* you it's all a lie!'

'That's a great comic act you've got there,' Porta jeers. 'If anybody sees Bike-Stealer outside Moabitt ever again, after what they sentenced *that* boy for, he'll be wearing a long white beard and be past 97. From what they tell me he already looks like a cross between Frankenstein'n the Mummy.'

'You must *listen* to me,' shouts Egon, anxiously. 'What've you got going with Stealer? He was a *terrible* man and tortured ladies!'

' 'Ow you *do* talk,' Tiny cuts him off, irritably. 'Be a bleedin' German man for once. Look death bravely in the eyes. You're one of the Führer's old SA lot, as used to go round wavin' clubs in '33.'

'No hanging around in the corridors, as the executioner said when he marched number ten in,' grins Porta, noisily, whipping the vehicle round and into the park.

'Don't make yourselves into contemptible murderers for my miserable sake,' babbles Egon. 'I was only joking when I said you were out. Ain't you got *any* sense of humour, man? You must have a good laugh now and then, in these horrible times!'

'Laugh, then,' suggests Porta, laughing heartily himself. 'That's just the reason why we're on our way to *Siegessäule*, so we can have a good laugh on a miserable day. Tiny and me, we've seen all kinds of quick death in our time, but we never *did* see anybody go off the top of *Siegessäule*. I seem to remember once you told me your greatest wish was to learn how to glide. Well, now you're going to get your wish. Don't forget to spread your arms out wide, and do like the gulls. All *we're* going to do is get you started, and I can promise you you're going to get a good send-off!'

'It'll be a *lovely* sight,' cries Tiny, jubilantly. '67 metres up, and when you land it'll be in the middle of a bed of roses!'

'67$\frac{1}{2}$ metres,' Porta corrects him, 'but don't forget to waggle your feet Egon, or you'll nosedive, and I don't think that softened-up head of yours can take that!'

'Yes, flatten out, the way they say in the glider clubs,' Tiny advises him. 'Use the risin' air currents!'

A crash drowns out his voice. Porta leaves the amphibian abruptly and goes through the air in a great arc, ending well out in the lake. Ducks and swans flutter wildly into the air, wings flapping madly. Tiny rolls across the asphalt in a ball, but is quickly on his feet again. He rushes across the grass, attempting to get away from the amphibian, which comes rattling and crashing after him.

Flames rise above the tree-tops as the vehicle bursts into flames.

Cursing and swearing louder than the protesting babble of the ducks and swans, Porta arrives back on land.

'That blasted little worm,' he rages. 'He tricked us. Where'd he go?'

' 'E got in the taxi that banged into us,' explains Tiny, waving, his arms about wildly. 'I seen it before. It was over there, waiting for us like a bleedin' grave-snatcher. I thought it was just standin' waitin' for a fare. Then I saw it was the dwarf at the wheel, but too late to do anythin' about it.'

'In a way he *was* waitin' for a fare,' snarls Porta, wringing the water from his cap. 'Not an ordinary fare though!'

'If you want my opinion,' says Tiny, in an outraged tone, "e's got a bleedin' nerve, deliberately runnin' into a peaceful vehicle from Adolf's Army right in the middle of the park! Maximum speed 20 it says on all the signs, an' 'ere that little pig comes at 100! Where's the bleedin' traffic police when you want 'em? Never there!'

'*Now* I really *have* heard everything,' rages Sally, when they get back to the War Ministry, and report the taxi incident. 'Never heard of dynamite? Stuff a couple of sticks up that skinny little bugger's backside, why don't you? One thing's certain, now! You've *got* to kill that little rat if you want to stay alive yourselves! His jailbirds'll be all over the place now, waiting to blow your heads off! And here you sit like a pair of soaking-wet alley cats, drying off on my government radiators! Oh, I ought to-to-to-to *spit* on you!'

'This case is going to end in a stiff sentence,' growls Porta, with a nasty look in his eyes. He wrings some more water out of his great-coat. 'The Poof's gonna suffer for this! When I've decided he's goin' to take a header off the Siegessäule, he can't get away with taking off in a taxi!'

'I can't understand 'ow they knew we were goin' to the park?' wonders Tiny, with a thoughtful look on his face.

'The two you locked in the cupboard,' explains Sally, throwing his arms out in disgust. 'They heard everything you said, and where you were taking him. Doesn't need Einstein to work out *your* clown of a plan. The dwarf's little grey cells began rattling round in that big head of his, and you know the rest. Come on, get your arses out of here, and fix this job once and for all. Egon'll be sitting in "The Owl", shooting his mouth off. Go through the yard and get in by the cellar window, so you can take him from the rear. It's easier from behind. That's why Stalin's commissars always neck-shoot people when they're to be liquidated!'

Porta puts his favourite Nagan into his shoulder holster. He puts ten clips of ammunition in his pocket.

'Think it'd be better to take a "piano" with us?' he asks,

putting his P-38 in another pocket where it will be easy to get at, if problems become acute.

'*Don't*,' says Sally, drily. 'You're in civilized Berlin now, where they don't like people to go around with machine-guns smashing the windows!'

'Let's go,' decides Porta, his face hard. 'This time we keep it simple. We'll string him up the way they do with horse-thieves in Texas!'

'Be careful, now,' warns Sally, as they leave the room. 'Expect surprises. Egon's not some peasant from Schleswig, remember! He's a real Berliner, and knows what's needed here to stay alive!'

When they crawl through the cellar window, to come up on Egon from behind, Tiny gets stuck in the frame. Porta has to use a jemmy to get him loose.

They tiptoe carefully up the stairs to the first floor, from which loud voices can be heard. The first two rooms they come to are empty, but the third is packed with people.

Egon is behind a huge desk, which makes him look even smaller than usual. He is dressed all in black, with a blindingly white shirt which he believes looks well against his artificial sun-tan. He believes that a sun-tan gives a man a look of power and success. On each side of his chair stands a broad-shouldered bodyguard, staring alertly about the room. In the shaded lighting, two other goons can just be seen, standing guard on the door leading to the restaurant. The sound of drums and saxophones can be heard in the distance.

'Bow-wow!' barks Tiny, bending over Egon, 'you look as if you'd been mixin' it with a fleet o' wasps, but maybe you've only been 'avin' a little taxi-ride round the Zoo?'

'You boys were going to *kill* me,' drawls Egon, slowly. He blows smoke in Tiny's face, in approved American film gangster manner.

Tiny laughs long and loud. He thinks he has to do this to save face.

Suddenly a lot of things start happening all at once. Porta said later it was the nearest he had seen to a really big earthquake. The whole gang goes at them. The goon closest to Tiny hits him across the face with a plank, so hard that the plank breaks across the middle.

'*Kill* 'em!' howls Egon, happily, launching a murderous kick at Tiny.

The two guards at the door get hold of Porta, and start trying to tear his head off. Knuckle-dusters flash, and land on his face. He twists and kicks upwards, connecting with something soft. One of the guards jumps away screaming, both hands pressed between his legs.

Tiny rolls like a ball, and is back up on his feet in a flash. He grabs a chair and brings it down on the neck of the nearest of his attackers. It shatters to pieces and the man goes down with a weary grunt.

The remaining goon rushes at Tiny waving a blackjack. Tiny goes at him head-on with all his 260 pounds. He hooks a foot behind one of the man's legs, and they go down, with a crash like a ship's boiler falling down through the house. Tiny hammers a blow into the killer's throat, which crushes his larynx like an eggshell. He makes a horrible, inhuman sound and falls to the floor, the blackjack falling from his hand.

Porta grabs it and showers blows on his two attackers.

Egon soon sees the turn events are taking, and, since he is not the kind of person who feels comfortable as the centre of a scene of violent action, he grabs his well-cut black overcoat, and rushes out of the door.

'After him,' shouts Porta, cracking the blackjack down on the head of one of the goons, in almost friendly fashion.

'You're breaking my 'eart,' shouts Tiny, swinging his pistol from side to side. 'We're lettin' you off this time, but someday I'm gonna blow you lot away! We don't usually murder people except by agreement. Up against the wall! Spread your legs and lean your 'ands on it! Get your paws up 'igher! Anybody can see you shits've never been to 'Amburg!' He runs practised hands over them, emptying everything, keys, coins, cigarettes, wallets, pistols, out of their pockets. The wallets he stuffs in his own pocket. The rest goes out of the window. He goes backwards out of the door, locks it after him, and pushes a chair up under the handle.

Porta spurts through the restaurant, knocking over a waiter in passing, and out into the street. He starts off down it, then stops, realising Egon has most probably gone the other way, and runs back the way he came.

Tiny rushes out of the gate, his pistol still in his hand, and looks round him in confusion.

A crash comes from behind him.

'I'm gonna *get* you,' rages one of the body-guards, August, who has broken out, and taken up the pursuit. 'I'll *smash* you!' he howls, and waves the blackjack Porta has dropped, to show he means what he says.

A bullet comes screaming from the darkness. It whirls him round and throws him against the door, which crashes inwards in a rain of broken glass and wood splinters. For a moment he has the look of a man thinking of stepping to one side, and then he sinks down slowly like a sack of grain with a hole in it.

'Watch out,' screams Porta, more sensing than seeing a dark figure step out from behind some garbage-cans. It points something large and black at him. In a flash of light he notices that the hand holding the menacing object is grimed with dirt. He throws himself behind a pile of potato-sacks, together with Tiny. A volley of shots sounds, murderously. Bullets whine over their heads. Their own pistols are ready in their hands. The dark figure has vanished. All is quiet. Dangerously quiet. Cautiously they rise to their feet.

'Hell, hell, *hell*!' curses Porta. 'Everything we try goes *wrong* on us! Who the devil *was* that sneaking Nazi pig who took a shot at legally-inducted army personnel?'

'Couldn't of been Egon,' considers Tiny. ' 'E'd break in two if a gun of that size went off in is 'and. They're only for old soldiers'n real men!'

They move along, close to the house walls, with well-trained caution. Tiny is just about to peer round a corner, when a terrific explosion splits the night. The roar of it echoes, from wall to wall, along the blacked-out streets, but not a corner of a curtain is lifted for an inquisitive peep. Every Berliner knows that unnecessary inquisitiveness can shorten people's lives considerably. If it was not the Gestapo out for scalps, it could be something even worse, and, in any case, not in the least healthy to witness.

Cat-footing, and with pistols at the ready, Porta and Tiny step lightly on down the street. They look into, under and behind every parked car, and lift the lid of every refuse-bin.

It is Tiny who first picks up the sound of footsteps, moving fast in the darkness of the night. Soon after, they catch sight of a figure flitting across the street.

'Goddam!' shouts Porta happily, squatting and holding the Nagan out in front of him with both hands, in approved New York Police fashion. He sends off five shots, so fast that they sound almost like one. None of them find the target, which surprises him considerably since the shots the New York Police fire always do! 'An Mpi would've done the job,' he rages. 'That pig's got away without a scratch. Just wait, you. . . .'

'That boy's shit-scared,' says Tiny, with a sneer. ''E's runnin' like a rabbit with its balls cut off. 'Ere an' there an' not gettin' anywhere. We've *got* 'im. We'll soon've put a 'ole in 'im! Take 'em one at a time'n you can knock off an entire army without gettin' a scratch.'

'Step the light fantastic over on to the other pavement,' orders Porta, 'and I'll waltz along this one. Soon as we see that wicked monkey, then bang, bang, and off the map of Berlin he goes!'

'Neither that boy, nor nobody else neither's *ever* gonna blow *me* away. Not even with dynamite and pincers,' says Tiny, grinding his teeth. 'By all the dirty 'eathen devils and the 'oly body of Christ at the same time, I'll give that bleedin', atheist sod what for!'

Porta rounds the half-ruined statue, across from Franken Strasse, like a bulldozer and runs straight into the arms of the gunman, who is now carrying a machine-pistol. It is impossible to say which of them howls loudest. The screams alert Tiny. Without hesitation he fires across the street. Shop windows, and the display cases outside the closed cinema, disappear in a rain of glass and splinters which shower out onto the road.

'Thank Christ we're still fit from Russia,' groans Tiny, taking cover in the gutter.

The gunman races down a narrow alley. Porta is right on his

heels, with the Nagan held out in front of him. Windows and plate-glass shop fronts are smashed on the way. Now and then a car windshield is shattered.

At the tram terminus Porta stops, panting, to allow Tiny to catch up with him. He comes thundering down the street, his hob-nailed boots striking sparks from the cobbles.

'Jesus,' he cackles, excitedly, as he comes to a stop alongside Porta. 'That rotten civilian's sure got 'is tail on fire! Think we managed to get a chunk shot off of 'im? 'E was spoutin' blood up to the rain-gutters when 'e beat the lights at Bellevue Strasse.'

'I do believe I *did* nick him a bit,' says Porta, peering up and down the street with the light of the chase gleaming in his eye. Heads are beginning to poke out cautiously from doorways.

The sound of a police siren becomes audible, approaching from Link Strasse. Flashing lights hasten towards the area where the shooting started.

'Never there when they're wanted, those Schupo shits,' grumbles Porta, reloading his Nagan. 'May the holy German god cut off the cheeks of their arseholes with a wooden knife!'

'Know who it is who's bangin' off at us?' asks Tiny. 'You were close enough to 'im to be treadin' on 'is 'aemmorhoids. Even a fly, with 'is little eye, ought to been able to recognise 'im!'

'It's a fellow called "Strawberries'n Cream",' says Porta, thoughtfully, blowing into the muzzle of the Nagan and eyeing the cross-filed dum-dum bullet in the chamber. 'When we've finished with him they'll change his name to "Strawberry Jam".'

'Why'd they call 'im "Strawberries'n Cream"?' asks Tiny.

'Red hair, white chops. Looks as if they'd dipped him in flour. Soft in the head, too!' answers Porta. 'Looks just like what they call him!'

'Must be batchy,' considers Tiny, craning his neck to look down the street. 'Runnin' round in the public streets, and bangin' away like a bleedin' madman, where other people can see it. Don't 'ave to be a bleedin' trick-cyclist to find out as 'e's got shit where 'is brains ought to be, an' 'as got 'is brains tucked up 'is arse'ole!'

Thoughtfully, Porta tilts his cap, and scratches his head with the sight of his pistol.

'Let's piss off down Koester Strasse. If I'm not very much mistaken he's on his way to the docks to find himself a hidey-hole in amongst all them packing-cases.'

As they turn into Hafenplatz a rain of bullets comes at them from the far side of the road. They whine off the walls behind them, and send chalk and cement dust down over their heads.

Tiny's P-38 roars, tearing half a brick out of the corner of a building and blowing a window in. Glass rain's over one of the occupants.

'Come on out, you rotten helping of strawberry flan,' howls Porta, wild with excitement. He lets go with his Nagan, so rapidly that it sounds like a machine-gun.

'Stick your 'ead up, so we can get a shot at it,' roars Tiny, hot for action, and reloading his P-38.

The gunman loses his head, unfortunately for him. He races across the square, swings himself up and over a tall fence, and falls into some dustbins on the other side with a noise like a T-34 going through a china shop.

'That sour strawberry's 'ad it for sure now.' Tiny is jubilant. He takes off, in Olympic Games high jump style, over the fence, only to go straight down into the stinking contents of one of the tall dustbins. Snorting with rage he puts his head up over the edge. Six feet away his eye falls on 'Strawberry' sitting on a sack of onions and banging at his Mpi. The magazine is stuck and he cannot cock it.

'Jesus Christ,' he howls, throwing the Sten on the ground, desperately. *Now* it works. The whole magazine goes off in one burst. Bullets shower the house-tops.

Cautiously, Porta puts his head up over the top of the fence. He takes in the situation at a glance. He jackknifes over onto the other side and fires as he is still in the air. Bullets whine and ricochet all round Strawberry, who throws himself, screaming, to the ground. He thinks he is already dead.

It is all over. Porta and Tiny stand over him, each aiming a gun at his head.

Strawberry closes his eye and waits for the shots. To his great surprise nothing happens. If he had been in their position he would have fired long ago. Experience has taught him the wisdom of that.

'That all you've got to show us?' asks Porta, in a disappointed tone, giving him a kick. 'Up you get, you green strawberry, and tell us where Egon and the dwarf are hiding out! Don't try pulling the wool over our eyes. We're not going to let a rotten berry like you take *us*! Open your stinking mouth to warn 'em and your tiny little brain'll get splattered all over Moabitt! And when we let you go, make tracks for the setting sun, *panjemajo*?'

'Why don't we kick 'is arse all the way to Egon's an' the dwarf's 'ide-out?' asks Tiny, longingly.

'You're one of these cunt-crazy bastards who like girls with riding boots on, *aren't you*?' asks Porta, jabbing his gun-barrel into Strawberry's ribs to stimulate his mental activity.

Strawberry nods sheepishly, and wipes garbage from his face. He was on the receiving end when Tiny displaced the contents of the tall dustbin.

'If you don't do exactly what we want, and tell the truth,' cackles Porta happily, wagging his finger under Strawberry's nose, 'you'll never, ever, see another pair of riding boots on a girl's legs. Your next set of footwear'll be the concrete ones we fit you for before we toss you off one of the Spree bridges. Now then, where do we find Egon the cunt-wholesaler?'

Strawberry looks round desperately, like a drowning man searching for land. He cannot see any, and decides that it would be wisest to answer Porta's question truthfully, and to hope Porta will have shot Egon before the latter discovers who has given away his hide-out. He draws a couple of deep breaths, and attempts to put an honest expression on his face.

'Egon'n the dwarf are at the crazy zoo keeper's, waitin' for word you two've been shot!' he whispers secretively, looking around on all sides.

'Is it that mad sod who buys all sorts of dead animals and stuffs 'em?' Porta drills at him. He slaps him about a little to clear his mind.

'Yeah, yeah!' answers Strawberry. 'You get a shock when

256

you go in there first. He's got 'em full of clockwork'n they roar and move about like they're alive!'

'It's Egon and the dwarf as'll get the shock, when we turn up,' grins Tiny, delightedly.

'Don't you move from here till half an hour after we've left,' warns Porta, as they climb back over the fence. 'Do, and you'll be a very dead son of a bitch, but smartly!'

They sneak through the garden and up to the keeper's house.

'Now,' orders Porta, when they arrive outside the door. They are dripping wet from a fall into a swimming pool in which the keeper washes the dead animals before he starts operating on them.

They meet an obstacle in the shape of an oversized house-keeper, who has a chain on the door.

'Good-day, mum,' nods Porta, smiling at her and saluting politely.

She wrinkles her forehead and looks suspiciously at the guns in their hands.

'What do you men want here?' she asks, in a 'Prussian' voice. 'The Chief Keeper is in conference, and does not wish to be disturbed.'

'I'm 'is brother, 'ere on a visit,' grins Tiny, cheekily.

'Are you now?' she asks, with obvious disbelief in her voice. 'I've never heard the Chief Keeper had a brother. Is your name Taut, too?'

'Brothers usually do have the same name,' smiles Porta, in friendly fashion.

'Get out of the way,' roars Tiny, suddenly losing his patience and putting his P-38 half-way down her throat. 'Maybe you want a lead pill to steady your stomach?'

'Oh God! No,' she stammers, putting her hands to her face.

'Get that chain off, and keep your mouth shut, and nothing'll happen to you,' says Porta. 'We don't want to do anything, to a nice, sweet lady like you; that'd be painful, and cause a lot of writing back and forth to the insurance people!'

With shaking hands she takes off the chain, and moves away from the door.

'*That's* better now,' grins Tiny. He pushes her into the toilet and locks the door.

As silently as great cats stalking their prey they move through the Head Keeper's house. Tiny is in a furious rage and overflowing with incontrollable force. He is ready to go straight through a concrete wall to get hold of Egon and the dwarf. They look under sofas. Open cupboards. Tiny even opens the windows and looks down into the garden.

They find them on the first floor together with the mad keeper and two streetwalkers. The girls are lying on separate sofas, doing things which would make any film censor faint clean away.

The dwarf has a pistol in his hand which is nearly as big as himself.

'Stop, or I'll shoot,' he crows, waving the pistol about, as if he were shooting hens out of a flower bed.

'You'll piss, is what you'll do,' laughs Tiny. He catches him by the chest in one giant fist. 'On a point of order, I'd say you've got your bollocks caught in a rat trap.'

'Head first out the window,' orders Porta, firmly.

' 'Ow far'll I throw 'im?' asks Tiny, using the dwarf's head to smash the window pane. Glass rattles on the cement below.

'Far as you can,' snarls Porta, 'and make sure he drops on a big, sharp rock.'

Tiny holds the dwarf above his head in up-stretched arms. He takes a pace back to give more power to his throw.

The whores hide their faces and pitifully begin to whimper.

'Goodbye, then, you pygmy prick,' bellows Tiny, and throws the dwarf straight through the window. He takes frame and all with him down into the garden.

The dwarf lands with a nasty-sounding thud, but he is a long way from being dead. Quite the opposite. Like an arrow from a bow he dashes through the fruit bushes, and disappears over the sopping fields, taking an unwilling trip through the keeper's swimming pool for dead animals on the way.

'Now then, you've hailed your last taxi,' shouts Porta. With a practiced movement he slips a thin cord round Egon's neck.

One of the girls goes into action. The girl in the black dress.

She jumps on Porta's back and gets her teeth into his ear. With a scream he lets go of Egon. The Poof is on his way through the door when Tiny drops on him. They roll down the steep staircase, wrapped tightly in one another's arms, making a terrific noise in the process. They crash into a large stuffed orang-outang, which is full of clockwork and which begins to move. It opens its enormous red mouth, and swings its arms from side to side. Tiny cannot believe his eyes. He fumbles for his pistol, gives out a shout of horror, goes straight up into the air, like a cat on a red-hot spring, jumps out of the window and stumbles through a series of deep puddles. Water and mud splash up around him. He passes through the keeper's swimming-pool once again. This time he does not even notice it.

Egon, who is lying on his face, rolls over with difficulty, to see where Tiny has gone. But instead of Tiny he sees a huge, hairy monster approaching him, rocking from side to side with huge yellow fangs protruding from a gaping red mouth. From the depths of the brute come two terrific roars. Egon, who is half-way up on his feet with the intention of running, falls back in a light coma. Life comes back into him with a rush when the orange-furred monster, with glowing eyes and gnashing fangs, falls on top of him. He attempts to roll from under it, but becomes paralysed with fear from top to toe when he feels its fangs brush against his cheek. He screams twice. The second time is when he finds that his head is inside the gaping mouth of the orang-outang. It is the last thing he ever feels in his short, stormy life. He does not even have time to be really frightened. His heart breaks down completely. One spasm after another constricts it. He dies on the spot from shock, with a scream, and a deep, deep intake of breath.

'Hell,' shouts Porta, shaking off the girl in the black dress. 'We'd all better get out of here pdq. The yokels who've come to the big city for a bit of excitement are already crowding the street down there. They've heard there's a "Berlin happening" going on in the house. The Schupo's'll be here in a bit, and *they* use guns!'

'Will they shoot *us*?' ask the two girls, in chorus.

'You bet your life, they will,' answers Porta. He drags them after him down to the street, where they mix with the expectant rubber-neckers. They look as if they have come straight from the train, from Silesia or Westphalia.

'Jesus on the Cross,' cries Porta, taking a long, long breath, as he sits in Sally's office a little later. 'Now I've just *got* to relax a bit, so I can think clearly like a normal person again.'

'I'll tear that fuckin' dwarf's ears off for him,' promises Tiny. As usual, he is lying face-down on the floor. 'We just *can't* let 'im get away with things like *'e* 'as. 'Im as 'as got the mental equipment of a back-arsed gorilla, that's knocked its 'ead on a tree gettin' born!'

'First of all we need some new irons, which can't be traced,' says Porta thoughtfully, scratching his pigeon chest. 'Can't be lice again, can it?' he asks, trying to look down himself inside his uniform.

'What you want new irons for,' asks Tiny, without understanding. 'I got my *own* iron, as I can 'it a fly between the eyes with, on a night black as the 'ob of 'ell itself. New irons you've got to get *used* to!'

'You're stupider now than the day you were born,' shouts Porta irritably. 'Can't you understand, man, that when you're out shootin' people, outside the war, you need a cannon they can't trace back to *you*! *That* makes for painful problems, and a lot of silly questions. If you get caught, and the prosecutor's standin' there with a peashooter they can prove is yours and it's been used to blow some dope away with, it would be a source of great wonder to all if the jury didn't find you guilty. Do you understand *now* why we've got to get hold of some new hand-artillery that belongs to somebody else and don't have our name on it?'

'I'm on my way to organise some,' grins Tiny, happily. 'It's easy as kiss me arse. I can pick 'em up from the guards in *this* place. All their shit's 'angin' on 'ooks down there. Only got to put your 'and out'n take 'em!'

'No, I protest,' shouts Sally, shocked, jumping up from his officer's desk-chair. 'No War Ministry fire arms! Our escutcheon's blotched enough already!'

'All right, then, I'll go over to Prinz Albrecht Strasse,'

declares Tiny, unworriedly. 'I know a dog's 'ead over there as runs on rails like a bleedin' train! When the bulls from Alex find out the soddin' dwarf's been blown out of 'is boots with SD cannons, they'll call it a legal execution an' drop it like a 'ot brick!'

'*Not* so stupid,' admits Porta, with a touch of admiration.

When Tiny returns with three large P.P. 7.65 Walthers which he's picked up at Gestapo HQ on Prinz Albrecht Strasse, Sally almost has a stroke.

'How did you get 'em out?' he enquires, open-mouthed. 'Didn't they search you on your way out?'

'As I said before, I know a bloke over there as runs on rails,' answers Tiny, superciliously.

'Himmler in person, maybe?' asks Porta, with a crooked smile.

'I know 'im too,' grins Tiny, in a state of reckless happiness, 'but luckily 'e don't know me. I picked up some "greens" too, while I was over there. They're enough to give a eunuch a jack on,' he goes on, taking a box of green pills from his pocket.

Porta and Sally immediately take two each, while Tiny takes three. He says, he feels a bit down. They wash them down with Sally's whiskey.

'Those greens're fantastic,' says Porta. 'They start working halfway down your throat already. I don't know how they take you, but right now I feel like a *panzer* division with auxiliary weapons going all out to roll a village flat. That dwarf'll be more than lucky if he lives through today, and I'd like to see anybody get nasty with *us* about it when they hear he's departed this vale.'

On their way through Berlin they look into 'The Golden Pig', but nobody there has seen the dwarf for some time.

'That place is usually hopping,' says Porta, as they cross Gendarmenmarkt. 'At a Christmas party there once, some camel driver or other who was working at Siemens sticking cartons shut, got himself crippled for life, and a couple of his dark-skinned mates got knocked *right* off. That was a real good Christmas party, that was. Or so they say. The place's been shut down for three months, by the way. Some big, fat

261

Commissioner, who sells pigs, came along and said "We're closing now, boys!" '

'And did they do it?' asks Tiny, amazed.

'They *had* to,' smiles Porta, 'this fat commissioner had all the Schupos in the world with him, and they had their guns out!'

They look into a lot of places. In 'The Wooden Leg' they meet an acquaintance of Porta's. He is sitting on a tall bar-stool, wearing hat, fur coat and sun-glasses, despite the darkness and the heat inside.

'You seen the dwarf?' whispers Porta, conspiratorially.

'I don't know you anymore,' says 'Sun-glasses'. 'You've had it in Berlin.' With a movement not to be misunderstood he slips his hand inside his coat.

There is a loud thump. Sunglasses and hat hit the ceiling, and their wearer is rotating in the swing-door. Tiny has given him a tremendous kick in the backside.

'And him a member of the "Ring" too,' Porta spits contemptuously.

'Ring?' asks Tiny, doubtfully.

'Yes "the Ring". All members of it have been behind the fence for at least three years.'

'You lookin' for the dwarf?' asks a prostitute in a red dress.

'You must be clairvoyant,' laughs Porta, happily.

'Take a peek in "The Transvestite",' she smiles slily, batting her long false eyelashes fascinatingly at him.

'Funny him being in "The Transvestite",' says Porta thoughtfully as they go back across Gendarmenmarkt. 'Usually its only crazy sods, with cream-puffs instead of bollocks who come in there, wearing high heels and stinking of whore's petroleum!'

The dwarf *is* in there. Sitting right at the back of the room. He is extinguishing his cigarette on a prostitute's naked breast, to make her remember to pay her protection money next time.

'I've been looking forward madly to meeting you again,' whispers Porta, who has come up silently behind him and is pricking the back of his neck with a pointed combat knife.

The dwarf gives out a shrill scream and falls down off the bar-stool. He bangs his head on the wall, picks himself up, and rushes through the door, only to find Tiny alongside him. He emits another shrill scream, and dives head-first through a closed window, without considering the fact that he is up on a high first floor.

'Plop, plop!' goes Tiny's silenced Walther.

'You can sleep a week with me for nothin' if you shoot the balls off that sadistic little sod of a gnome!' the girl the dwarf has been using as an ashtray promises.

'*Sleep?*' grins Tiny, waggling his ears. 'You've got it all wrong. I've been in 'ospital, an' won't *need* to sleep for at least a week!'

'You *are* a nice girl,' Porta says in a tone of gallant flattery, slipping his hand between her thighs. 'You're pretty enough for old Odysseus to have sailed the wrong way for.' He cranes out of the window. 'Where the hell's the pygmy got to?'

'You'll find him in the Tiergarten,' says a girl with silver stockings, and a red garter round her thigh. 'When things get hot for him, he always hides out with one of the keepers. You can't mistake it. A round, white house, there when you get a bit into the park where the riding paths start and the place stinks of horseshit!'

'We're on our way,' shouts Porta, eagerly. He takes the staircase in two jumps, with Tiny thundering after him like an avalanche.

A pimp, standing in the doorway keeping an eye on his girls, is knocked down and tramped almost flat.

'Is it the Russians?' he shouts, in confusion, gazing in terror after Tiny and Porta as they go roaring down the street.

A few yards into the Tiergarten they catch sight of the dwarf. He sees them at the same time and with a long, penetrating death scream, sprints down the path leaving a cloud of dust behind him. Then he makes a tactical error and dodges into the deserted water tower.

'*Got* him,' chuckles Porta. 'We *are* going to see somebody fall from a high place. This is *much* better than *Siegessäule!*'

Tiny puts his head back.

'Bleedin' 'igh, it is,' he says, admiringly. 'When 'e goes off of that, 'e ain't gonna get away with just *one* limp. What about if 'e

263

won't jump though? 'E's got to get up over the railing an' 'e's that little a shit 'e can't even reach the top of it with 'is 'ands stretched up an' standin' on tip-toe!'

'We don't want him to strain himself,' says Porta. 'We'll *lift* him up!' He grins delightedly, already seeing, in his mind's eye, the dwarf whirling down from the water tower.

They force open the iron door, the clang of it sounding hollowly inside the empty tower. The dwarf has pressed a shovel up under the door-handle. They hear his feet drumming on the metal stairs.

'He's in a hurry to get up there,' laughs Porta.

'Be in more of a 'urry comin' down,' answers Tiny, with a broad grin. 'Oh, but won't it be lovely to see that little bleeder droppin' like a Anglo-American bomb on its way down after the Führer's HQ?'

They reach the topmost platform on the heels of the dwarf, who is whining and screaming with fear. They circle the platform four times, before Porta turns and goes round the opposite way with the result that he and the dwarf run into one another head on.

'You've *had* it, lover-boy,' roars Porta jubilantly, reaching for the little man's throat.

'No, no!' howls the dwarf, jumping back, and kicking out with a size twelve hob-nailed boot.

Porta dodges too slowly, and the boot catches him on the shin. As he doubles up in agony the dwarf's stiffened figure arrows into his face. He makes a bound, dodges between Tiny's legs, and, spinning round like a top, lands a terrific kick between the big man's legs.

Tiny screams like ten wretches being stretched out on a mediaeval rack all at once, and grabs at his crotch with both hands.

'You've *had* your fun,' roars Porta, aiming at the dwarf with pistol arm outstretched. He gets off three rapid shots, but without getting a hit.

The dwarf springs up onto the top of the platform railing, and stands there, wavering dangerously, for a moment.

Porta lowers his pistol and stares, open-mouthed, at the tiny man, who stands there, thrashing his arms to keep his balance.

'Jesus'n Mary,' cries Tiny, forgetting the pain in his testicles. 'That pygmy shit don't seem to realise 'ow far down it is there!'

'Holy Mother of God,' yells the dwarf, desperately. He rocks backwards, but regains his balance with a flailing of arms.

'If he lives through this, he could make a packet in a show,' says Porta, thoughtfully. 'Wonder if we could sell him to a travelling circus?'

Tiny puts out a hand to give the dwarf a push, but a gust of wind gets there before him. The little man leans out from the platform at what seems an impossible angle. He stretches his hands out in front of him, but there is nothing he can take hold of. He topples, and falls straight down through the foggy air.

Porta and Tiny lean out over the railing and watch him go.

'Use your arms,' shouts Tiny, 'use your arms like the seagulls do. Then you'll land soft an' not crack open your napper!'

A Schupo, standing talking high treason with a park-keeper by the entrance gate, looks up and catches sight of the dwarf on his way down. He gives a grunt, and his legs give way under him. They called him 'Gutsy Peter', and he had a reputation for bravery earned in the roll-up units at the end of the twenties, where he was one of their best men with a baton or a rifle-butt.

The park-keeper goes down flat behind a garbage container. He thinks the dwarf is a new kind of Allied bomb on the way down.

The dwarf's size twelves, sticking up through the broken roof of one of the Tod organisation's sand-coloured VW's, are all that remain visible of him. The rest of his body is mixed up with the steering wheel and the gear lever, or splattered over the instrument panel.

'*Think*, he did it himself,' shouts Porta, wildly, as he and Tiny run down the iron staircase, their footsteps echoing. '*We* are completely innocent!'

'Our 'ands are as clean as the spaghetti feller who nailed Jesus up on the plank said 'is was,' crows Tiny. He is moving so quickly, he almost falls over his own feet.

A few minutes later a whole row of telephones begin to ring at the Alex Station. The Commissioner, 'Murder' Schultze, who got his name from being second-in-command of the Homicide Squad, can hardly believe his ears.

'*What* did you say? Jumped off the water tower and smashed up one of the Fatherland's vehicles? Must be a foreigner, or a Jew, or something. No true German'd be that stupid. Sweep up the pieces. I'll take a look at it. Be there immediately!'

As soon as he arrives 'Murder' Schultze has 'Gutsy' Peter and the park-keeper arrested for not preventing the madman from jumping off the tower and damaging government property.

When they find out it is the dwarf who has taken a dive, 'Murder' lights a big cigar and begins to think hard. The little swine's been pushed, he says to himself, blowing out a cloud of blue smoke. If I knew who did it I'd shake hands with him and offer him one of my good Brazilian cigars. The air of Berlin's a lot cleaner now *that* little shit's turned up his toes.

The good result is cause for a celebration in Sally's office.

'A drop like that — seventy-five and a 'alf metres it was —,' laughs Tiny, noisily, 'can certainly fix things up. They'll be queuin' up now to pay their debts! We'll 'ave that much cash I don't even know what the figure's called!'

'Hurry up and collect,' advises Sally, looking over at Porta. 'You'll be going back to the cruel war on Sunday. I can't hide you away here. They've already traced one of the shooting-irons to us, and asked some painful questions. You've got to be off before GEFEPO takes over the case from KRIPO. Our boss, an empty-headed Oberst, has begun to make noises with his brains for the first time in ten years. He rang me a little while ago and asked if any of my department's people were going around shooting other people.'

'Blessed be the fruits of the earth,' intones Tiny, solemnly. He pushes a fat leg of goose into his mouth, and washes it down with a great gulp of wine.

'And all, who partake thereof,' continues Porta, scooping up a whole handful of prunes from the dish.

'Amen,' sighs Sally, drinking from the neck of the bottle.

Your laughter is an interrupted song,
and death found you friendly and cheerful.

Siegfried Sassoon

When he awakes Porta's head feels as if a hand grenade had exploded inside it. He looks about him in confusion. He is in a strange bedroom. The entire colour scheme is in red, a colour Porta likes. To his amazement he discovers there is another person lying beside him. A black-haired girl, with almond eyes.

'What the devil?' he cries. 'Am I dead, and gone first class to heaven?' Slowly he begins to wake up and to think like a soldier. He reaches out of bed, picks up the vodka bottle, and takes a couple of long swigs at it. 'You are alive,' he says to himself. 'You're not in heaven at all. You're in fat Natasha's knocker, and you've paid 500 reichsmarks for this bed, service included.' He feels for his wallet. It isn't there. Heaven's a damned expensive place, he thinks. He reaches out again for the vodka bottle.

The almond-eyed girl wakes up and looks as if she is wondering what a strange, naked man, with his cap still on, is doing in her bed. She stretches herself, and yawns.

'Germanski, you want fuck, you fuck now! You pay only 8 o'clock. One quarter hour go you bugger off to hell with you. Panjemajo, Mr. Germanski soldier?'

'I've got a headache,' answers Porta. 'But thanks for the offer, anyway!'

'You no want,' answers the girl, turning over on her side, 'then me go sleep. You put lock on door when fuck off, Mr. Germanski!'

7
The Boxing Match

'I 'ave no doubt of where we are,' says Tiny, with an unhappy laugh. 'So *this* is Russia! I just found me first louse. The poor bleeder was dead. 'Ard luck!'

'*You* were lucky,' grins Porta. 'The family that's staked a claim on me's a real lively lot!'

'I thought I was lucky too,' sighs Tiny, sadly, 'but eight 'undred guests came to the funeral, an' they seem to 'ave made up their minds to settle down 'ere!'

'I'm off,' says Porta, 'I've more important things to do than stand here discussing the funeral of a louse.'

A moment later he stops and examines, with interest, a large, bright-yellow, sign. It says, in large black letters:

GEHEIME SONDERKOMMANDO IV/3 z.b.v.
ADMISSION STRICTLY FORBIDDEN FOR
UNAUTHORISED PERSONNEL

As usual he is completely convinced that he is authorised. He struts airily in, and salutes, in passing, Chief Mechanic Wolf's favourite cat, which has been promoted to Unteroffizier and sits washing itself on the radiator of an Army vehicle. He saunters down a long, narrow corridor, and stops outside a heavy door with a white sign:

COMMAND OFFICE
ADMISSION STRICTLY FORBIDDEN

The word 'strictly' has been underlined. He cocks an ear, then kicks the door open with a crash, and enters. He finds himself in a large elegantly furnished office, which would make even a

Prussian general of aristocratic birth lick his lips.

'What the *hell* do *you* want?' asks Chief Mechanic Wolf, the army's uncrowned emperor of supplies and equipment. He is standing in front of a full-length mirror enjoying the sight of his own image.

'Can't you see I'm gettin' ready to go out?' he says, without a trace of friendliness, as he pours half a bottle of eau-de-cologne over his shiny black hair. He pulls back his lips, and admires the sight of his gold teeth. 'How'd you get in anyway?' he asks, obviously displeased. 'Didn't you see those signs, "Admission Strictly Forbidden"?'

'Get in?' smiles Porta, superciliously. 'Through the door, of course. How else? What're you putting all that "Whore's Dream" on for? Going after Russian cunt, are you?'

'It's so I don't have to smell you, shithead,' answers Wolf, sourly.

'You *are* a nice-looking fellow,' Porta flatters him. He tries to snap his fingers, but does not succeed.

'Well, what'd you expect?' asks Wolf, with celestial superiority. 'You don't expect a Chief Mechanic like me to go round lookin' like you lot of coolies, the dregs of society, do you, then?'

'Just my opinion,' smiles Porta, falsely, keeping his own council. His real opinion is that Wolf looks for all the world like a braying donkey. '*You* are an exceptionally elegant person. Smell your rose-water five miles away against the wind you can. Nobody seeing you could be in any doubt about your being well aware of your own worth.'

'You are *right*,' answers Wolf. He does not attempt to hide the fact that he really enjoys Porta's obvious admiration. 'If you want to reach the heights, where high finance suns itself, you *must* carry with you an aura of respect. It don't help one bit to go round lookin' like *you. You* look like a feller who spends his time pushin' oil drums around. You'll not get far lookin' like that. *Class*, you must understand, *class* is what it's all about. If you've *got* it then the dummies'll kiss your arse!'

'I cannot deny it,' admits Porta, smarmily. 'They *all* say Chief Mechanic Wolf's a really handsome man!'

'*And* I bloody know it,' answers Wolf, preening himself, and putting his head on one side to see himself from a new angle.

'We're having trouble,' says Porta, miserably. He smears jam on his bread and cheese.

'What?' asks Wolf. 'Won't those shit-eaters buy tickets?'

'It's not *that*,' explains Porta. 'They've *all* bought tickets, but now they've begun to sell 'em on the black to the division alongside us. We're oversold!'

'Put in more seats then,' says Wolf, indifferently. He throws out one hand. 'Do you *have* to bother me with that sort of thing?'

'Well its "Old Leatherlegs" that's making all the trouble,' sighs Porta. 'He'll only let us have that little hall where he's got his fucking tractors. Those Russian Commie tractors. There's only room for *our* lot in that place.'

'Let's think,' says Wolf, taking a cigar, and sniffing at it like a Greek shipowner who has started at the bottom of the ladder. 'Take one,' he invites Porta.

They light up for one another, exhale great clouds of smoke, and *think*! They are both men of affairs, who regard the war as a kind of high risk business. For them, front lines and enemies do not exist. At most, 'difficult' business associates.

If anybody thinks they are going to let an opportunity pass they are wrong. To these two everything has its price, one way or another.

'What about a little Enzian,' suggests Porta, pointing at a large decanter, standing bombastically on a French table alongside Wolf's personal steel helmet with the silver eagle. 'One of those little mountain schnapps makes a man *think* better!' He gets up and takes a swig straight from the decanter.

'You'll never learn manners,' growls Wolf. 'Not even if you get rich.' Sourfaced, he takes two tiny schnapps glasses from a drawer.

'You don't have any smaller?' asks Porta, pointedly.

'Unfortunately no,' answers Wolf, pretending not to understand him.

The first three glasses go down in one gulp.

'As I was saying,' Porta begins, 'it's going to be a real big match. Our publicity people've properly gone to town on it.

270

Every single dope in the entire Army Corps has bought a ticket, and they'll be loaded when they come. *Heavily* loaded! With *real* money! Not just wooden army chips. But this silly sod "Leatherlegs" is plain stupid. A squareheaded dope, who wants to keep inside the law. He keeps on telling me that *he* is responsible for administering Army Defence Regulations.'

'He's that careful he never uses a strange shithouse without ringing to HQ in advance to find out whether its permitted! It's not long since his whole unit got nothing to drink, and couldn't wash themselves or brush their teeth for four days, because he hadn't got written permission to turn the water on! The worst thing about him is he listens to what other people say, and *believes* it. I get that mad when I see him bring his shoulders up round his ears and make a face like a prize pig that can't get an "oink" out quick enough.' Porta bends forward, his own eyes taking on a piggy look. 'Why don't you let those Chinese gooks of yours play with him a bit. It just might be he could get to understand that a friend in need is a friend indeed, and find out who he owes a favour to. I can't *stand* these people who're always making waves, and won't take life as it comes!'

'I'll go an' have an understandin' talk with him,' promises Wolf, his eyes glittering. 'We'll take the boys with us. They can tell him what the Chinese an' the blacks do to people they don't like. We'll let Albert start by breathin' on him a bit!'

Together with Tiny, Albert and Gregor, Wolf and Porta march, noses in the air, down through the huge ordnance storehouse, which is packed with all kinds of heavy pieces of artillery. Guns stand, side by side along the walls, barrels angled up towards the skylights. Stubby, thick-barrelled howitzers fill the middle of the floor space.

Field Ordnance Master Kunze, 'Old Leatherlegs', sits behind his desk, fat and broad, and literally oozing power and authority. He is wearing a wooden, *Herrenvolk* expression.

'What do you want?' he asks, trying to look severe, but with a total lack of success.

'I imagine it's only a rumour I've heard, that you are refusin' to move all your shit?' Wolf opens the conversation. He blows smoke past the ordnance man's ear. 'Or have I heard wrong?'

271

Kunze passes a fat hand over his totally hairless head, and stares at Wolf with doggy eyes.

'I'm just saying,' he says in a whining, angry falsetto. 'Not you, and not Porta, can come in here and tell me what to do. You've no business here at all. Everything here's mine. Note that!'

Porta claps his hands together, and doubles up in a spasm of laughter.

'Cut it *out*, you puffed-up twit! You don't own one bit of this ironmongery. You don't even own the studs in your boots. The Army's lent 'em to you. It's the Army's lot. The Army owns you, too, and who's the Army. If you want to know, the Army's *us*!'

'I'll report you to Corps HQ,' threatens Kunze, furiously. He gets up from his chair, panting and with considerable difficulty. 'Then we'll see what the QMG has to say. He's tough! Tough as Krupp steel!'

'We piss from a great height on your QMG,' grins Wolf, looking superior. He pushes a stiffened finger hard into Kunze's chest. '*You* are gonna do just what we tell you to. Otherwise something nasty's gonna happen!'

'Set the bleedin' dogs on 'im,' suggests Tiny, wickedly.

Gregor spreads some large drawings out on the desk.

'This is what we suggest,' he declares, with the air of a promoter, pointing at the plans.

'I won't *have* this,' says Kunze, in his whine of a voice. He falls heavily back into his chair, somewhat deflated.

'*You* don't have to have anything,' declares Porta. '*You* just do what we tell you. All these bloody guns'll have to be got out of here!' He looks, searchingly, through the small windows, and his eye falls on 'Timberwolf', Kunze's special duty labour squad boss. Timberwolf has served four years inside, at Torgau, for negligence with firearms. He and a friend from the Unteroffizier School, went into the Dresdener Bank, at Bielefeld, to get a quick loan. They had guns in their hands at the time. Instead of a loan they gave them four years imprisonment, broke them to special labourers, and posted them 'unworthy ever to carry arms'. 'Come here, jailbird,' orders Porta, waving grandly at Timberwolf.

272

'Don't get big'eaded, yokel,' explodes Timberwolf, angrily. He stands where he is, provocatively stiff-legged, and Porta has to go out to him.

'Listen to me, tortoise,' Porta begins. 'We want seats along all these walls, and everything, I repeat *everything* spick'n span and in place by 12.00 hours on Saturday.' He pauses artistically before continuing, almost solemnly, in a low, threatening voice. 'That's when the spectators'll be comin', and they won't be a very patient bunch!'

'What've you *got* up there?' asks Timberwolf, spitting contemptuously on the spotless concrete floor. 'It's Wednesday today,' He counts on his fingers. 'Only three days to Saturday!'

'Count the nights too. That makes six,' says Porta. '*Whatever*, the spectator accommodation's *got* to be ready by midday Saturday, when the greatest boxin' match *in history* comes off. If not, then you'll be out sweeping mines before you know what's hit you! That's a bit more dangerous than waltzing about with a worn-out Russian broom, like the job you've got now!'

'What's Kunze say?' asks Timberwolf, cautiously, looking across at the little office, from which voices can be heard. Field Ordnance Master Kunze's shrill whine is overborn by Chief Mechanic Wolf's harsh, barrack-square roar.

'Who cares *what* he says?' rages Porta. He opens his mouth wide, very wide, determined to drop a whole load of Army adjectives on Timberwolf: 'You fuckin' woodcutter you, you do what I tell you! Get hold of your shit-shovellin' squad of crap-eaters! Get hold of some tools and get your arses *movin'*! Quick about it, now, before I lose my temper'n get *really* rough!'

'I don't think you know our Mr. Kunze,' warns Timberwolf. 'You ought to know he's got connections. High-up connections. Higher'n you'll ever get! Squashin' an Obergefreiter like you ain't anything for Kunze. He's broke the back of an Oberst who came here tryin' to piss on *us*!'

'Close it,' shouts Porta, furiously, 'and carry out my orders. Otherwise you'll soon learn what connections I've got!'

Chief Mechanic Wolf struts down the great ordnance hall, enjoying the jingle of his non-regulation spurs!

He lifts his feet like a fighting-cock, and brings them down sharply, so that the sound echoes between the steel supporting beams of the huge roof. There are guns everywhere, camouflaged in brown and green, artillery tractors, brand-new trucks, ammunition carriers, tracked and half-tracked vehicles. All lined up in long, perfectly straight rows.

Wolf spits contemptuously on an 88 mm A.A. gun, and lights a fat Brazilian cigar, striking his match on a sign which says:

SMOKING STRICTLY FORBIDDEN

'What's that bell-wether standin' there scratchin' his balls for?' he asks, pointing at Timberwolf with his British officer's swagger-stick. 'Got nothin' to do has he?'

'Stupid, that's all! Stupid as a cow's arse!' says Porta.

Kunze comes rushing out of his little office, his legs creaking like a harness factory, and sweating with nervousness.

'Get out of my gun-shed!' he whines furiously, almost losing his false teeth in the process.

'I think, you know, you'd do best to obey orders,' says Porta, his eyes drilling at Kunze.

'This shed's gotta be empty as a vacuumed out whore's cunt on Christmas morning,' he adds, threateningly.

'But, but *listen*,' whines Kunze, unhappily, his false teeth clicking. 'I *can't* put all these guns just *anywhere*! D'you know what only one of 'em costs the German people? They're *valuable*! And they'll be needed, too, when the big offensive they're talking about just now, at Führer H.Q., gets started. An' anyway they're not *my* guns. They're 4. Panzer Army pieces!'

'Well that's all right then,' thunders Chief Mechanic Wolf, in satisfaction. '*We're* 4. Panzer Army! 4. Panzer Army's *us*!'

'What do you mean?' mumbles Kunze, in amazement, staring open-mouthed from Porta to Wolf and back again. They are standing like true Prussians, bobbing up and down from the knees like a pair of Fieldmarshals.

'I *say*,' says Wolf, with a superior smile, 'that *we* are 4. Panzer Army!' He taps Wolf on the nose with his pay-book.

'Says here, in black and white, we belong to 4. Panzer. So, as you said yourself, this iron junk's all ours, and we want it out of here, you dusty storeman, you!'

'And if you don't get movin' sharpish,' continues Porta, triumphantly, 'you can come outside'n make the acquaintance of Chief Mechanic Wolf's Chinese. They'd love to play with you. But *you* wouldn't like the games *they* play!'

'You threatenin' me?' asks Kunze, making an abortive attempt to pretend he is still making the decisions.

'You're a quick one,' sneers Porta. 'People who get their legs screwed off, like you, usually lose some of their brains. Oozes out through the holes in their thighs!'

'Those guns stay where they are,' says Kunze, severely. He slaps one of his Army artificial legs with his ruler. 'And I'm *telling* you Obergefreiter Porta. Don't you come into my storehouse puffing yourself up. I am a military servant, mark me! I'm not just a louse, like you, that any stray dog can piss on.' He slaps his narrow green shoulder tabs, proudly. 'I'm a kind of an officer, I am!'

'Holy Agnes,' grins Porta, superciliously, 'breaking boys like you's easier'n plucking the hair off the arsehole of a lame Russian cow.'

'I won't stand for that,' howls Kunze, insultedly. 'You'll speak to me in a proper manner!'

'You must understand that we have to get these guns out,' Wolf attempts a diplomatic approach. False friendliness oozes from him. 'Be sensible now, Bernt. Take off your government face and get back to normal! We are promoting a boxin' match the world's never seen the like of. People've paid for *seats*. We can't ask 'em to sit up there balancin' on a gun barrel, can we, now? Sittin' up there, they'd look like a loada fuckin' lovebirds chatterin' an' watchin' a parrot havin' a fuck at a wanderin' llama!'

'It's not because I'm not co-operative,' wheezes Kunze, weakly, 'but it just won't do! Soon as we put the first gun outside, Russian Intelligence'll know all about it. And who's the *silly* bleeder then? *Me*, Field Ordnance Master Kunze! It's *me* who gets courtmartialled, and maybe shot! Now you don't want that to happen, do you?'

'We're not really worried,' answers Porta, cheerily. 'All we want is this junk out of here, so's we can get ready for our fight!'

'I'm tired of all this talk, talk, talk,' roars Wolf, in a sudden rage. 'This shitheap's gotta be emptied, so we can get organised.' He blows a thick cloud of cigar smoke at Kunze, who coughs protestingly. 'If you don't want your leather underpinnin' jammed down your throat'n your ears cut off, you'll get these guns rolled outside, quick!'

'You *must* be sensible,' almost weeps Kunze, twisting his hands on his ruler. 'What'd *you* say if I was to come and demand you move all your trucks!'

'Not a thing,' grins Wolf, 'I'd let my Chinks cut you about for as long as they felt like it. They don't usually tire easy!'

'There, you see,' says Kunze, victoriously, 'I take the same stand, even though I've got no Chinks. The guns stay with me. Inside the shed where it's nice and dry.'

'Put your nose outside, man,' shouts Wolf, impatiently. He waves his British swagger-stick in the air, irritably. 'Out there it's dry as the Gobi Desert, where water's something they've only heard about. The Commie bloody sun's shinin' down as if it thought it was up above a highly-developed capitalist country. It'd do your guns good to get aired a bit!'

Deep inside Kunze's aching head, a woolly cloud begins to form. It seems to concentrate in a knot behind his forehead. He opens his mouth and screams, but it does not help. Then he begins to knock his head on a shell casing which hangs, swinging, on a wire. That helps a little. He begins to shout out a confused stream of orders.

'Invited guests will sit there,' decides Porta, in a loud voice, pointing at the space taken up by thirty-five heavy howitzers. 'Come on, you lot, get moving,' he shouts, at a group of work soldiers. They are sitting on a gun-carriage, drinking beer, as if nothing had anything to do with them.

'Get that military junk out of here! Civilisation's coming in! Make room for Western culture, as the Russian peasant said when the liberators burnt his house down!'

'You don't give the orders here,' says a labourer, who resembles an overgrown gorilla with a head too big for its body. 'Nothin' gets moved in here. This is a shed for guns, an' what's in here *stays* in here, 'less we get orders in writin', stamped and with four copies!'

'Jesus'n Mary, are we goin' to stand 'ere listenin' to that kinda shit?' roars Tiny, his arms beginning to swing. 'The man's bleedin' barmy. Acute attack o' superiority complex, *'e's* got. Let me kick some sense back in 'is German bleedin' jacksey!'

'Hang on a mo',' says Porta, catching Tiny, who is already on his way over towards the man. 'These coolies haven't found out yet that I don't like complications. I prefer the straight road!'

'This is a shed for guns,' says the gorilla man, stubbornly, 'not a playground for sportin' idiots! You wanna fight, go an' have yourselves a coupla rounds on the muck'eap outside!'

'No bleedin' labourer's gonna get away with talkin' like that to me,' raves Tiny, savagely. He gives the man a kick in the stomach which makes him double up with a grunt, grabs him by the hair and smashes his face down on a metal sack-truck.

The labour squad begins to get moving. Particularly after Tiny has thrown another of them headfirst out of the window into a muck-heap buzzing with flies.

The first of the howitzers begin to roll out into the open air. Kunze runs round in circles like a confused hen.

'Be careful of them! Be careful of them!' he babbles, nervously. 'Line them up nicely in rows, and keep the calibres separate, or we'll never be able to sort 'em out afterwards.'

When a long-barrelled 105 mm gun slides into the nearby river, Kunze sinks down, in despair, onto a pile of shells.

'Don't take it so hard,' Porta comforts him, handing him a sausage sandwich. 'What's one gun? We're going to lose the war anyway!'

For the next three days nothing but the sound of hammering and sawing is heard from the ordnance stores. Between times the Match Committee holds meetings at Chief Mechanic Wolf's, where 'Heavenly Apples' and Jewish pastry are served, washed down with 'poor man's champagne' — Slivovitz and beer mixed.

277

' 'Oo's the winner goin' to be?' asks Tiny, inserting a large piece of 'heavenly apple' into his even larger mouth.

'The winner, of course,' answers Porta, his mouth stuffed with Jewish pastry.

'Why?' grins Tiny, cunningly. 'When David'n me used to fix up matches for the sports-barmy, back in 'Ein 'Oyer Strasse, we used to know the winner long 'fore we started!'

'So *that's* what you mean,' laughs Porta, slily. 'That's all fixed up. People'll play the right bloke, so's we come out winners. There'll be *such* a lot of nice, nice coppers for us.'

'What about if we get caught, man?' asks Albert, his brow wrinkling.

'Only one way for us, then. Over to the Russki's, fast as we can go!'

'We ain't African banana-eaters, here,' jeers Wolf. 'We got six bouts before the main one, son, an' in them six the marks'll get a fair crack o' the whip. In the main bout, the heavyweight championship fight between the Soviet an' German champions, we go to town!'

'And Greater Germany will win, of course,' declares Heide, with patriotic self-assurance. He smiles the smile of a victor.

'No, my lad, that's just what Greater Germany *won't* be doing,' grins Porta, digging his elbow into Chief Mechanic Wolf's ribs in conspiratorial fashion. 'All the suckers, dropped by a German bint complete with swastika an' salad dressin', will be backing old Germany to win, an' all the cash they can scrape together'll be riding on the German twit!'

'An' they lose the *lot*,' shouts Wolf heartily, ' 'cause the sub-human Soviet specimen's gonna knock the *shit* out of the noble representative of the German *herrenvolk!*'

'Aren't you afraid there'll be trouble?' asks the Old Man, worriedly.

'Not a bit of it,' answers Porta, his eyes sparkling. 'The only ones who'll have problems, are the dopes who've backed the German. When the first six fights are over, they'll be giving out German victory whoops an'll be that far gone in superiority complexes that by the time the main show comes on they'll pawn their arseholes to get a bet on. Convinced that the Germans are unconquerable.'

278

Wolf hammers the table, in glee, so hard that the 'heavenly apples' bounce about on the dish, and a blob of jam lands on his cigar.

'They'll be wild,' says the Old Man, darkly, 'and then there'll be trouble — with a capital "T"!'

'We'll be gone by then,' grins Albert, his whole face splitting open in a snowy grin.

'How can we be sure the fighters won't get together, and do *us*?' asks Barcelona, who was born suspicious. 'Somebody might just point out to 'em that it could be worth their while?'

'Something in *that*,' admits Porta. 'We'd better take out some insurance against that, just to be on the safe side. But how?'

'Cages!' says Tiny, his mouth full of jam.

'Cages?' asks Porta, blankly.

'Monkey cages,' shouts Tiny, grinning all over his face, 'pulled up under the roof. There's a pet shop bloke on Paljma in town's got bags of 'em. 'E's got a real good 'un, with a black panther in it just now, a wild-lookin' sod with yeller eyes. 'Im after you, an' even a broken-down nun'd beat Jesus Owens's world record!'

'*No* panthers,' protests the Old Man, excitedly, 'that's an order! *No* panthers!'

'Why not?' asks Porta, blankly. 'You can have a lot of fun with a pussy-cat like that!'

'You're off your rocker,' shouts Barcelona, siding with the Old Man. 'Do you realise what they *eat*?'

'People,' admits Tiny, happily. 'I know plenty of people I wouldn't mind feedin' to a black panther.'

'*Quel bruit pour une omelette*,' remarks the little Legionnaire, drily. 'Let us buy the cage without the panther.'

' 'E's got some o' them execution cages too, like they 'oisted Jew Süss up in,' explains Tiny. 'Bloke gets a noose round 'is neck. Up 'e goes in the cage, out goes the bottom of it, an' down 'e goes till 'e gets to the end of the rope. Then 'e stops up sharpish with 'is neck broke!'

'I don't see how we could use 'em,' says Porta, thoughtfully. 'We don't want to *execute* the boxers.'

'Sometimes you're dead slow,' shouts Tiny, impatiently.

'They don't get no rope round their necks. We just 'oists 'em up under the roof *in* these cages. Then nobody can get at 'em, an' talk 'em into doin' us in the eye. Soon as the bell goes, we open the bottoms of the cages, the two shits flop down into the ring, an' start 'ammerin' away at one another!'

'Might be a good idea,' admits Porta. 'Be something new in the fight game, having two heavyweights drop from the sky!'

Chief Mechanic Wolf takes out a cigar, and ignites his gold cigarette lighter with an expensive sounding click. He holds the cigar between the thumb and forefinger of his left hand, and takes a couple of deep draws. He blows out smoke in a heavy cloud across the table.

'We'll buy the cage *with* the panther,' he says, consideringly, 'but only if we can get another cage exactly like it. We put the German in the one cage, the *untermensch* in the other.'

'What do we do with the panther?' asks the Old Man, thinking with trepidation of other animals No. 2 had taken on strength.

'We can probably find a use for him,' laughs Porta, taking one of Wolf's cigars without asking.

'I won't have him inside the tank,' says the Old Man decisively, and realises too late that he is half-way to having given in.

'You couldn't. Not without takin' off 'alf the turret,' Tiny grins, noisily. 'I've *seen* 'im. Even though 'e still is a kind of a cub, that ain't learnt 'ow to bite proper yet. When 'e *does* find out, the war'll speed up rapidly.'

It is late when we break up and go down to the pet-shop.

Tiny falls hard for an old gorilla, which can imitate all kinds of laughter and drink beer like a human. The pet shop dealer won't sell it, however. He regards it as one of the family. A brother, almost.

'What you goin' to use them cages for, then?' asks the pet-shop man, blankly, when the deal has been completed, and we begin to carry the cages out.

'We've started slave dealing,' whispers Porta, secretively, 'but you mustn't tell anybody.'

'Well, now?' cries the petshop dealer, opening his eyes wide. 'Is there money in *that*?'

280

'Queer looking animal,' thinks Porta, peering through the bars of the cage at the panther. 'His legs are too long and his feet are too big.'

'He's only a cub,' answers the animal dealer, 'no more'n eight months!'

'He looks, though, as if he wouldn't mind chewing my hand off,' says Porta. He jumps back, as a great furry paw, with claws like curved knives, bangs against the bars.

'Don't be afraid of him,' the pet-dealer says, soothingly. 'He's very easy to deal with. Put a joint of meat in front of him, and he forgets everything else. He's a little bit scared of humans yet, but just wait a couple of months. Black panthers are notorious for going at anything or anybody they come near. They're more dangerous than ten Gestapo men with machine-guns.'

Around midnight loud screams and roars sound down the *Umanskaja*. Inquisitive heads peep from doorways, but not for long. The doors are soon banged shut when Tiny comes along, dragging the cage with the protesting panther inside.

Cursing and shouting loudly, he tugs and pulls the cage into Wolf's office. It is hard on the furniture and various packing cases and sacks. Finally, he manages to get it into an empty room behind the office. He takes an entire ham from a meat hook and pushes it through the bars to the panther, then pulls the door to, and bolts it.

'A puss like that can really go to town,' cries Porta, admiringly, as he bandages Tiny's countless, deep scars. 'And he's only *playing*, so far. He'll really be something when he grows up, and realises what he's got teeth and claws for.'

' 'E ain't doin' too bad just at present,' says Tiny, trying to open an eye which the panther's last attack has closed completely.

'Only bring trouble, he will,' says the Old Man, blackly. 'Oberst Hinka'll jump clean out of his boots when he hears about him. Since we had that bear[1] he's forbidden the keeping of animals of all kinds!'

Before we leave Tiny throws a large bagful of chopped meat

[1]See THE BLOODY ROAD TO DEATH

in to the panther. It looks up at him with golden, glowing eyes. Two overlarge paws catch the bag in the air. The contents go down in one gulp.

'Jesus,' cries Tiny, pleased. 'See that? Just wait till we start givin' 'im *people*.'

The last plank has not yet been nailed in place when the fans start crowding in. The atmosphere is animated. Sports maniacs commence arguing, both with one another, and with others who couldn't care less. German patriots scream 'Heil'! People from the Rhineland whistle with their fingers, in the French fashion.

A watchdog[2] unit, not wearing the provocative steel helmet, do their best to keep the crowd in order. The thump of batons is heard, when an Unteroffizier from the Tyrol pushes a sausage, covered with ketchup and strong mustard, into the face of a watchdog-Gefreiter and calls him 'a noisy Prussian swine'.

The witches cauldron quietens down a little when the bell goes for the first round of the first bout. It is between a skinny-looking little Bulgarian and a sour-faced, sinewy Westphalian. The match is over in the second round. The Westphalian wins on a knock-out, decided on in advance by Porta and Wolf.

When the second and third encounters also end in a victory to the national colours, it seems as if the patriotic roar will never end. When the fourth match goes to Germany they go amok, and begin to sing '*Deutschland, Deutschland über alles*', and '*Wacht am Rhein*'. They embrace one another, stand to attention, salute and roar: 'Germany for ever!'.

'Must've been like this when they got back from France in 1871,' says the Old Man. 'God love us, they're stone, staring crazy!'

The fifth match is between a Greek, Konstantino, who is middle-weight champion of his village, and an Austrian from Salzburg whose name is Rudolph, and who looks as if he deserved it.

'Wanna say a prayer 'fore I kill you?' asks the Greek with a wicked grin.

[2]Nickname for Military Police

'You don't have to take that,' howls Oberzahlmeister Saul, from Corps HQ.

'Flatten 'im!' roar the Italian *Alpinos* from the back row, forgetting that the Greeks are their hereditary enemies.

With an animal roar the Austrian rushes the Greek, and hammers his fist into him well below the belt. A dangerously low blow, which can put a man out of a fight immediately. The Greek doesn't seem even to feel it. He butts Rudolph in the face. Also a foul. At the same time he trips him. This last foul brings the referee into action, with wildly waving arms. The Greek manages to give Rudolph a left, a right and a hook, before the Austrian can get to his feet. The crowd demands the match re-started, which is done. The Austrian wins by a knock-out in the 18th round.

'This's made this whole damn World War worthwhile, man,' shouts Albert. He joins in with the jubilant roar of the delighted crowd, despite the fact that he has no time for Austrians, as a rule.

'Wait'll we get to the main bout,' says Wolf, lighting a Brazilian cigar with his usual aplomb.

Three times as many people have been packed into the ordnance stores than it can hold. By any form of calculation. They have come from far and wide, and a lot of petrol, much-needed in wartime, has been burnt in the process. Men sit on beams high up under the roof, balancing like hens roosting on a perch. And still they keep coming. Punters push and shove and pant to get into the small concrete cell where Porta and Wolf sit taking the bets. Through the small openings they can see only hands. Hands pushing money at them. Hands grabbing receipted betting-slips. Hands of all shapes and sizes. Fat hands, thin hands, pale hands, tanned hands, clean hands, dirty hands.

All eyes are fixed on the two cages which hang, swaying, up under the roof.

A roar erupts, seemingly endless, when the trapdoors in the bottom of the cages swing open, and the two boxers drop almost twelve feet through the air to land with a thud in the ring. The Russian from the Caucasus is on his feet first, and lifts a pair of club-like fists confidently above his head. The German, hairy as an ape, moves round the ring with hands hanging down lower than his knees. He looks like an ape waddling about with knuckles to the floor. He roars out his challenge: the Caucasian *untermensch* is going to get smeared all over the hall before the end of the first round.

The Caucasian's mouth splits open in an animal grin. He draws the edge of his hand, speakingly, across his throat, so that everybody can see what he is thinking of doing to the German. An excited roar goes up from the crowd. Several rows of seats breakdown under the concerted tramp of feet.

The bell sounds and the two monsters go at one another slavering and frothing. Iron fists hammer into taut stomach muscles and crack against heads which are equally as hard. An uppercut lands cleanly. It would have torn the head off an ordinary man, but seems not to have any effect on the recipient.

'Hell's bells,' mumbles Barcelona nervously. 'Those two dumb-bells *do* know who's supposed to win, don't they? The way they're goin' at it they look like they're plannin' a double suicide!'

'Take it easy,' grins Wolf, sure of himself. 'They ain't that thickheaded they don't know what's best for themselves. It'll be in the last minute the dumbum from Leipzig lies down. We got to give the crowd somethin' in return for all the lettuce they're handin' over, or they just might start wonderin', an' then anythin' might happen!'

In the first two rounds it looks as if the Caucasian is not looking to get hit too often. He fights on the defensive, goes into clinches to avoid the German man-killer's attack. Then, suddenly, in the third round, he goes over to the offensive, dances forward and sinks two lightning-fast punches into the German's midriff.

The crowd holds its breath for a second or two. Those punches would have sent a horse to the ground. But the fighter from Leipzig merely shakes himself like a wet dog, and grins wickedly. His left shoots out, as his opponent follows up. It lands square on the Russian's nose with a sickening crack. They dance round one another, spitting and breathing hard through their noses. A punch lands on the German's face, splitting his

284

eyebrow open. Blood stripes his cheek. His lips swell. His face seems partially paralysed.

'Holy Mary,' whispers Gregor, his eyes bulging. 'It's like hitting bulls with your bare fists!'

'Bulls couldn't take that,' considers Porta, biting thoughtfully into a sausage he has taken from the hand of a Bavarian, who is staring, glassy-eyed, at the scene of violence in the ring.

The Caucasian begins to go for the face, but this does not seem to worry the German. He ducks neatly, allowing the punches to pass closely above his head, and replies with a wicked left. It looks as if he is attempting to open the Russian's guard with his left, and several hooks land heavily. To the crowd's amazement the Caucasian only gives a grunt, and dances round in the ring.

'Murder 'im! Smear the sub-human bastard out!' howl the true-blue Germans, clashing their mess-tins and steel helmets together. 'Stamp 'im back into the ground where he come from!'

The 6th Westphalian Cavalry goes at the 5th Prussian Panzers with a roar. 'Bastards! Sausage-eaters! Swine!' they scream.

The battle between the two regiments sways back and forth in the great artillery storehouse. The noise can be heard miles away.

Bavarians from the 8th Panzer, and the 116th Infantry choose sides and fling themselves happily into the fight. Watchdogs, with drawn batons, pour in through every entrance, and hammer at the heads of the excited crowd, indiscriminately.

'Death to Germany!' roars Tiny, fanatically, from an up-ended empty beer barrel.

'Hey there! You there! Cannibal!' shouts a Bavarian, throwing a case of empties at Albert which knock him off the table he is sitting on.

'Drop dead!' howls Tiny, lifting a Watchdog up above his head.

'You're under arrest,' screams the MP, desperately, kicking his boots about in the air. One of them comes off and hits a QMS, who looks as if he has been rolling in mustard and ketchup, on the head. 'In the name of the Führer, I order you to let go of me!'

'Order heard and obeyed,' yells Tiny. He throws the watch-dog at two Bavarians. They go over backwards and slip down underneath the stands. Their wildly kicking feet are all that remains visible of them.

At last the MP's manage to quieten the crowd sufficiently for the fight to continue. They retire and hold themselves in readiness behind the church, where they pray to God they will never have to go inside the stores building again.

'That kind of sporting event should not be allowed,' says their leader, an elderly major. All his men nod their heads violently, in agreement.

The fight is on again, and it seems as if both heavyweights have gone amok. They show a complete disregard for the rules of the game. The German rushes at the Caucasian and kicks him in the stomach. In reply the German gets a bite on the cheek. Blood spurts over both fighter's faces.

'Jesus'n Mary,' yells Tiny, excitedly, knocking over a beer barrel. 'Now they're *eatin*' each other!'

The referee, a tiny rat-like Jugoslavian, tries to separate the two boxers. Suddenly, he finds himself jammed between two murderous mountains of muscle. It seems as if he will be crushed. He wrenches himself free and staggers to the ropes where he hangs, arms dangling, until two medical orderlies take him away to the M.O. for treatment.

A new referee takes his place. He talks seriously to the two boxers, shaking his finger in their faces. They look as if they feel like throwing him out of the ring into the roaring crowd of spectators.

In the third round the Caucasian plants a punch below the German's ear, which causes him to stagger and go into a clinch. The referee moves forward, but before he can shout 'break!' the German has broken the clinch, and goes at the Caucasian with an attack the like of which has not been seen since the Carnera-Sharkey bout in 1933.

The crowd is dead silent for a few seconds. Then an infernal roar breaks loose. Everybody is slapping the back of the man

286

next to him, and shouting his approval. If the man next to him does not agree with him, then everybody is ready to knock the next man's block off!

'Hurra!' shouts the sporting fools in the ringside seats.

The Caucasian drops his head like a water buffalo about to charge, and drives a steel-hard fist, with terrific force, into the German's kidney region. The sport-lovers scream in furious protest, naturally. The German's killing left hand goes to work again. As it lands he emits a short scream. The hand has gone. The noise of its breaking can be heard at the ringside. A thrill of perverse horror runs through the knowledgeable.

There is no doubt now that the boxers have forgotten all about any prior agreement which may have been reached. They go at one another like wild beasts. Murderous intent is expressed in every bone of their bodies. Chief Mechanic Wolf gets nervous. Tiny and Porta have to hold him back physically from rushing up into the ring with an Mpi, and reminding them of their agreement.

The roar of the crowd threatens to lift the roof of the ordnance stores. It must be audible over on the other side of the front, 50 miles away.

The boxers are no longer civilised human beings. They have gone completely ape! Their screams would have made Tarzan green with envy.

'We'd ought to've given that Caucasian sod a coupla 'orseshoes in 'is gloves,' mumbles Tiny, worriedly. 'Then 'e'd 'ave been certain to 'ave smashed that German bastard's bleedin' face in!'

'Hell! Hell!' curses Porta, viciously. 'We're ruined if that bloody German goes and knocks the Caucasian twit for a burton!'

'He *promised*,' moans Gregor unhappily. 'He *promised* to *lose*. Rotten German lies, as usual. Propaganda!'

'Jesus,' cries the Old Man, terrified, as the German lands a terrific punch which lifts the Caucasian from the floor and drapes him on the ropes.

'I'll cut your soddin' mother's tits off! I'll piss on your grave! Oh you fuckin' German *shit*, you!' roars Tiny, shaking his fist threateningly at the German.

'Lets cut his crazy head off,' suggests Albert, ashen-faced, 'an' send it in a parcel to his wife!'

Gregor puts his hands together and sends up a silent prayer as the German buries his fist in the Caucasian's solar plexus. The blow is followed by a terrific uppercut which seems as if it must rip the man's head from his shoulders.

'Man born of woman, an' created in God's image,' stammers Albert, hiding his face in his hands. 'I can't stand to *look* at it, man!'

'Shit, we're *ruined*! Poor as when we started!' babbles Barcelona.

'We can't allow this,' roars Wolf, excitedly, chewing his cigar to bits. 'Poor, Goddamit! Poor! When you're poor they piss on you! An' you're *dumb*! Dumb as snot!'

Seating breaks under stamping feet. The crowd roars with excitement. Men embrace one another, all differences forgotten, when the German smashes home a left hook, and follows it up like lightning with a right hook with the whole weight of his body behind it. It lands on the Russian's shoulder.

'Its all over,' declares Gregor in despair. 'Now we're goin'to have to live off Adolf's tiny, little wage packet!'

But now the fortunes of the fight seem to change. To the advantage of the Caucasian. The German's left hand has gone. It cannot stand up to much more. It is already swollen to twice its normal size. He is using his right as much as possible, and protecting the damaged hand. The Caucasian has changed his tactics. Now he is going for the German's throat.

'*Cojonudo*,' screams Barcelona, happily. 'He's gonna *get* that German shit!'

Porta opens his mouth to say something, but closes it again, engrossed in the scene in the ring. The Caucasian attacks the German, who has more than enough to do to avoid the whirl-wind of punches smashing at him from every angle. He is up against the ropes. A punch crunches into his temple, and he goes down on one knee. Blood streams from his nose. He is bathed in blood. As he rises, a brutal kick stretches him to the canvas.

'Smash 'im! Tramp 'is guts out!' roars Tiny's huge, beery bass.

The new referee rushes forward, arms flailing, only to find himself on the receiving end of a kick which sends him flying over the ropes. The medical orderlies carry him off to their first aid post behind the dustbins, where his colleague is still lying, trying to regain his breath. It is not a boxing match anymore. It has turned into a murderous fight, in which every dirty trick, any hard-boiled American movie has ever shown, is being used. Growling they go into a clinch and fall to the floor. They roll round the ring in a knot of twisted, intertwined muscle.

The Caucasian lets out a scream of anguish, as the German's teeth bury themselves in his testicles.

'Not goin' to fuck for a bit, that boy,' roars Porta. He kicks at an empty beer barrel, which rolls into the standing room area, knocking over spectators like ninepins.

With an upward kick, and a punch which lands on the German's neck, the Caucasian gets free and up on to his feet. The German is no slow-coach, either. He starts off like Jesse Owens, moving at a pace which would leave a world champion sprinter standing. He sinks a right, deep into the Caucasian's middle region. The Russian responds with a straight right, which seems to make the German sag, followed by a sizzling left, which, would have sent him straight to the heavenly hunting grounds if it had connected.

With the exception of the boxing fanatics, who do not like it, the crowd roars ferociously. Seats are torn up. Boots thud on the floor.

'Tear 'is ears off!' comes from the cheap seats.

'Jesus'n Mary, this is the best fight I ever did see in all my life,' shouts Tiny, happily. A size 15 boot crashes into the German's knee. He screams and goes down, both hands clasped round the smashed kneecap.

'I'll *flatten* you,' he hisses, getting back on his feet with a face twisted with pain. 'Say your prayers, you Russian bastard. You're for the boneyard!' In his rage he has apparently completely forgotten that he is supposed to lose in the final round.

289

'Kill him,' roars Porta, excitedly, as the two boxers, clasped in one another's arms, sway round the ring employing, as certain circles say, 'every dirty trick in the book'!

The boxing enthusiasts rage in protest. They do not want, they say, to see a good boxing match turned into a street brawl. But all the others who, like Tiny and Porta, think they have never seen such a lovely boxing exhibition, hit them on the heads with whatever is to hand.

The fight goes on. The noise resembles that of an air raid on a large-sized industrial city. Suddenly it stops. It is as if we were at the quiet vortex of a typhoon. There is a dead silence. The German lifts the Caucasian, holds him for a moment above his head, and throws him to the canvas. He lies there, unmoving.

The 8th Panzer Regiment rises to its feet in a body, and begins to sing, solemnly, '*Wacht am Rhein*'.

'These bloody patriots,' says Porta. 'They don't know where they are half the time. They shouldn't be singin' "*Wacht am Rhein*". "*Wacht an der Volga's*" the thing!'

The Russian is on his feet again, and the match moves into its final phase. The German patriots are at fever pitch, as their man draws back his left for the decisive punch. But the Caucasian goes at him again like a weasel at a sleeping hen.

He kicks him on the wrist, then brings down both fists on top of his head. His entire skeleton gives off cracking sounds. The German's mouth opens in a scream of agony, and he bends forward. The blow that follows, from the Caucasian's right hand, throws him into the air. He almost somersaults, and in some unexplainable way lands on his feet. He smashes his right into the Caucasian's face. In his rage he forgets his broken left and sinks it with all his force into his opponent's solar plexus.

'Oh, no!' moans Wolf, seeing his winnings begin to fly away from him.

Porta begins to make panicky plans to desert to the Russians. If the Caucasian loses, which now seems probable, there is no earthly possibility of them being able to pay out the winners.

But the Russian is not finished yet. He literally jumps at the German, who whirls like lightning in an 80° turn, and aims a wicked kick at the Caucasian's crotch, but misses his mark. The

Caucasian evades the kick, and attempts a risky manoeuvre aimed at breaking his opponent's neck. The German has seen it and jumps high and to the right. From there he rushes forward and hammers a right into the Russian's shoulder. The Russian gives out a roar as he sees the opening to the German's throat. The German's head rocks back twice. It is as if it had been torn loose from the spine. With a scream he falls to his knees, spits, and grunts, and goes purple in the face. Quite slowly he falls over on his side, and brings up what is in his stomach. With great difficulty he gets to his knees, spitting a great deal of blood. With the aid of the ropes he brings himself to his feet.

'Now that German shit's *gotta* be finished,' roars Tiny, delightedly. 'The neighbour's boy's only got to give 'im one more, an' 'e's out!'

But Tiny is wrong. The German is *not* finished. After his seconds have emptied a couple of buckets of water over him, he is back again hammering away at the Caucasian like a mad elk which has been chased away from the cows. The Caucasian lands a blow on his throat, directly on the larynx. He is thrown back over the ropes, smashing his stool and flattening a water bucket in the process.

The Caucasian goes roaring round the ring with his hands above his head. Every now and then he takes a kick at the German, who is lying stretched out in the ring like a man who has been crucified.

The crowd goes wild. A Bavarian Unteroffizier rushes down to the ringside seats, swinging a bag above his head. When he catches sight of Chief Mechanic Wolf, in his tailor-made uniform, he throws the bag straight in his face. It breaks open, and smashed tomatoes, corn cobs, pieces of roast duck, and many other things fly through the air.

A fat Feldwebel from the Air Supply Service comes yelling down from the cheap seats with one boot dragging on the end of a boot-lace behind him. He demands his money back. The match was a swindle, he claims.

Porta makes a V-sign with the forefinger and middle-finger of his right hand.

'*Faites vos jeux!*' he yells, and drives his fingers into the eyes of the onrushing Feldwebel.

'Long live Greater Germany,' screams an Obergefreiter from 8, Panzer Regt., fanatically. He presses a large black bucket down over the head of a Feldpolizeiispektor. The stinking contents spray up over his own face.

'Good God Almighty,' shouts Porta, jumping to one side. 'What's in that'd kill a man off quicker'n a whole chemist's shop!'

Soon after, the Bavarians begin using the noodles and black puddings, which they have brought with them for lunch, as missiles. In only a few minutes of time the whole storehouse begins to look like a blown up field-kitchen. A huge soft cheese sandwich, with onions, comes flying through the air and smashes, like a grenade, against the wall, close to the Old Man.

A piece of tripe comes arcing towards us. Porta ducks and it hits Tiny in the face with a loud slap. Porta turns round to see where the tripe has gone and gets a large *meefischli* in the neck. The head of the fish flies off and sticks in Gregor's open mouth, almost choking him.

Porta goes after a little artilleryman, attempts to kick him but misses and goes down on his back. The artilleryman picks up a soft salami and smears it round in Porta's face. Porta gets back on his feet, trips the man with an *osotagari* swing of his foot and sends him stumbling away.

Tiny saves Albert from being strangled by two Rheinlanders, at the very last moment.

'The panther,' screams Porta, 'let that black bastard loose, somebody. *He'll* show 'em where Moses used to buy his beer!'

With a great deal of shouting and jungle roars Tiny gets the black panther up the stairs and into the ordnance stores. The panther can smell food. Its tail begins to whip from side to side. It shows its long fangs.

'Jesus Christ,' shouts Tiny, expectantly. 'The sod's started! Go on Ulrich, you can 'ave 'em all!'

'Old men are often better off dead,' shouts Porta, swinging a plank at an elderly Stabsfeldwebel from Divisional Workshops.

The panther gives out a rolling roar, and prepares to spring.

'No-o-o!' howls an artillery Wachtmeister, in terror, swinging a broken bottle above his head. He looks into the panther's open jaws, and his legs give way under him. It hunches its back, measuring the distance to the long counter, which is swimming with burst salami sausage, fish, tripe and sauerkraut.

Two alert-looking Watchdogs, the half-moon badge winking on their chests, stop in horror, as the panther shoots through the air like a black arrow, lands on the counter with a heavy thud, and slides in the slippery mess of food. It begins to eat, as if it were preparing for ten lean years.

One of the Watchdog's tears off his helmet, and throws it to one side. He sinks to the floor onto a heap of tripe.

The other Watchdog, whose nickname is 'Bollock-breaker', because of his preferred method of interrogation, stares, with rolling eyes, at the panther's open mouth, and feels the heat of its breath. Shaking with fear he rolls down behind the counter, and forces himself in under a shelf where there is not normally space for more than a ten-year old child, and certainly not room for a 200 pound Watchdog.

Ulrich looks down curiously. He is probably wondering if he can get himself in under that low shelf.

'Mein Führer, save me!' screams 'Bollock-breaker,' helplessly.

The panther's yellow eyes glitter in the half-light. With a pleased grunt it puts out a large paw, and pats 'Bollock-breaker' playfully.

He had had enough.

'He's goin' to *eat* me,' he screams. With a long-drawn whine he rolls out from under the shelf, and crawls rapidly across the floor, sliding in the thick layer of food-scraps which covers it.

Ulrich believes he wants to play.

Happily, he springs through the air, and lands with a hollow roar on the back of the terrified Watchdog. He gives him a little friendly slap with his paw.

The Watchdog emits a long howl of terror, and rolls over onto his back, arms and legs thrashing.

Ulrich is having a wonderful time.

He bites the Watchdog's foot, playfully, then slaps his shoulder. His uniform jacket is slashed open. He looks into

Ulrich's open mouth with its huge fangs. It is the last thing he sees in this world.

'Shock,' says the doctor, who examines the body.

'Two large vodkas, and a bottle of red wine to wash 'em down,' says Porta, provocatively, when we arrive, noisily, at 'Natascha's'.

'No credit here,' shouts 'Anna the Bait', keeping a tight hold on the bottles.

'Credit?' grins Porta, pulling a large bundle of notes from his pocket. 'I can *buy* the place, if I want to!'

Anna's eyes open wide, and she suddenly becomes very friendly.

'Would you like to see my pussy-cat?' she asks Tiny, liberally filling his glass.

'Not interested,' says Tiny, turning his nose up. 'Probably all wrinkled up an' old-lookin', anyway!'

'No trouble-makin' here,' warns 'The Drummer', who is in reality a Feldwebel of Security ordered to the brothel to keep the peace. He is called 'The Drummer' because he *was* a drummer before the war. In the nightclub 'The Yellow Wolf' in Leipzig.

'You can just shut your face,' says the Old Man, hiccoughing into his vodka glass.

The Drummer goes red in the face and gives out a cackle of protest.

'I said you can shut your face,' hiccoughs the Old Man, stubbornly. 'I'm an Oberfeldwebel, an' I've got a star more'n *you*!'

'It's got fuck-all to do with *stars*,' screams Drummer in a womanish voice. 'You all behave yourselves the way I say.'

'Wonder if he ever had sexual intercourse with his mother?' grins Porta noisily.

'They sent 'im to war 'cos 'is sister was frightened of 'im,' roars Tiny. He doubles up with laughter at his own wit.

'Now you all be nice to one another,' admonishes Anna. 'We'd all be sorry if we had to throw you out!'

'Why don't you try that? Now, for example!' whinnies Barcelona. He bangs a chair down on the floor, challengingly, in front of Drummer.

'How'd you get so black?' asks 'Danube Dolly', a girl who has been extradited from Rumania. She pushes Albert ingratiatingly.

' 'E's black 'cos 'e's a Prussian nigger,' explains Tiny, with almost closed lips, in the Humphrey Bogart manner. He is a fanatical admirer of Humphrey, and does his best to imitate him. They once showed a film at the front in which Bogart pushes two old ladies in wheelchairs down a steep flight of steps, and then cuts their throats. Tiny was so enthusiastic about this film that he stayed and saw it three times. The following day he stood three hours in the queue to make sure he was the first to get a ticket at opening time.

'You *are* a lovely bit o' stuff an' no mistake,' fawns Tiny, posturing idiotically in front of a tall, slender girl who is sitting on a barstool showing every bit of leg worth showing. He bends over her and says, in the middling loud lion's roar which he thinks is a whisper, 'I'd like a lot to get a feel of you. An' you could play a bit with me, too!'

'Tryin' to be funny?' she asks in a deep, husky voice, putting half a yard of cigarette holder to her crimson lips.

Tiny whimpers with pleasure, and runs a none too clean finger up and down an area of bare leg.

'Not too far, now, big boy,' she husks, sensuously, smacking his hand. 'I ain't a fan of Frankenstein's, *nor* his descendants. Just remember that, soldier!'

'Obergefreiter, please,' Tiny corrects her, 'the backbone of the Army. Take 'eed of that, lady!'

'The bottom end of it?' she smiles, sweet as sugar.

' 'Ow should *I* know?' roars Tiny, missing the point. He sniggers, happily, pinches her in the breast and gives her a noisy smack on the behind. She lets out a scream of pain. Porta has taught him that when ladies defend themselves they mean just the opposite. 'You'n me lady, we're goin' to play the zoo outin' game!' He explains himself by giving the international sign for a round of sexual intercourse.

'I never go into the monkey-house,' she replies in rebuff, pushing at his broad chest with both hands.

'Whatcha mean, monkeys?' grins Tiny. 'Once you've intertwined your legs with mine, you won't have any use for monkeys!' He drags her firmly out onto the dance-floor, where the trio has started up with a rousing hot number.

'My *toes*!' she groans.

'Stand up on my feet,' he suggests. 'It's the easiest way to learn 'ow to dance. I tell you, I learnt 'ow to in "Lausen" on the Reeperbahn at 'Amburg.'

'I bet the ambulances were doubled-parked outside,' she says, sarcastically.

'No, there ain't no fightin' allowed at "Lausen",' explains Tiny, belligerently. 'You're thinkin' of "The Red Lantern" on Davidstrasse. A set o' teeth goes out there every night.'

She gives a shrill scream when Tiny executes a step which he believes to be part of the tango, and kicks her above the knee with his steel-tipped size 14 boots.

'Where's that horse that just kicked me?' she asks, rubbing her aching leg.

'Shall us two go upstairs?' asks Tiny with a wolfish grin.

'For *what*?' she asks, tearing herself from his grip.

'Don't keep it goin' *too* long,' he warns her threateningly, whirling her round and going into the kind of spin he has seen professionals do on the pictures.

She groans loudly as her head contacts a chair with a crash.

'Goin' up for a rapid round of all-in without shorts?' asks Albert, dancing past with a girl whose head comes no higher than his navel.

'Won't be long now,' roars Tiny, spinning his partner again. This time she hits her head on the floor.

She forgets to call him out. Porta passes, dancing at such a rate that they are pulled after him by the suction of the slip-wind.

'What in the world was that?' she asks, staring after Porta. He thunders on over the dance-floor with a matronly lady known as 'Petunia the Pig', because she is so enormously fat, and because her mouth resembles a pig's snout.

'I don't feel like dancing any more,' says the tall girl, going over to the bar. She sits down, deliberately on the other side of the bar from Tiny, and asks for three aspirins.

'Where you come from?' roars Tiny across the bar.

'Moscow,' she answers, sourly.

'Many 'ores there?' asks Tiny.

'Swine,' she snarls at him.

'You two feel like nippin' upstairs with us an' puttin' our

things together?' asks Porta frankly as he and the sweat-dripping matron reach the bar.

'You two are, perhaps, the harbingers of German culture?' asks the tall lady with a sneer.

'You've 'it the nail on the 'ead,' answers Tiny, proudly, sticking out his chest so far the stitches of his uniform begin to stretch threateningly. 'When we've been here a bit you lot won't be wipin' your arses with gravel any more. You'll be usin' paper, just like us westerners. Can all that bleedin' eargas, now, an' let's get up them stairs so's we can show you 'ow a cultured people does its mountin'!'

'You goin' to buy a drinky-winky for your little girl?' Petunia asks Porta, sending him a false smile.

'Crimean rum and orange,' he orders, rapping in a lordly manner on the bar.

It soon gets round that we have money. A lot of money. Suddenly we are surrounded by willing ladies. Two girls, who have been dancing together, make inviting, money-laden eyes at Wolf. He is half sitting, half lying, on one of the special bar-stools with a moveable back rest.

'You look as if you'd like to do more than drink,' fawns one of the girls, rubbing her body in catlike fashion, up and down his left side. 'I don't think I'm wrong in thinking you want to fuck?'

'That is maybe what they call a hint in the Soviet Union?' grins Wolf, slipping a finger up between her thighs. 'Hell, you gone bald?' he asks, in surprise, lifting up her dress.

'Shaved, dearie,' she giggles, 'a special effect. Usually costs 10% more, but you're so handsome I won't charge *you* extra. 500 for the night. What d'you say? French, German, Swedish, the lot! Two hundred extra for the Japanese touch.'

'That the selling price?' asks Wolf, letting his hand investigate her more closely.

They agree on four hundred, and disappear through the door marked PRIVATE.

A few minutes later Wolf puts his head back through the door and whistles up his wolf-dogs.

Barking happily they bound after him.

'They gonna fuck 'er too?' asks Tiny, gaping.

297

'Very like,' says Porta. 'Wolf's terribly kind to animals.'

A slim hand, with green painted nails, begins gently to rub the inside of Gregor's thigh. The hand works its way inside his trousers, in a manner which shows that it has made this kind of entry before.

'I could sharpen your sabre for you. You'd think you were floating into heaven,' she says, seductively. 'I fuck *good*!'

Gregor giggles with delight.

'Come on then. Let's get up there an' frame 'im!'

'We dance first and get real warm,' she twitters, pulling him out on the dance-floor.

Shortly afterwards they too disappear through the door marked PRIVATE.

Albert, who is always a little shy, cackles like a drunken parrot when a girl with slanted, black, business-like eyes takes his hand, and presses it gently between her legs.

'You are lovely, my black darling,' she breathes, twisting her hips, and sighing. She rubs herself against his hand. 'Come, little soldier,' she invites him. 'Let us go in and fuck, so that you will not have to go out and be shot at by those wicked Red Army men without having had a good screw first. You are my first cannibal,' she confides to him, as they cross the floor towards the door marked PRIVATE, 'I will give it to you for half-price. But you must not bite me! I am not food!'

We are hardly back in the bar when a series of animal roars put a sudden stop to the music and the chatter of voices.

'Ulrich,' cries Porta, fearfully, letting go of Petunia, who falls to the floor with a crash.

'Oh, hell!' groans Barcelona, emptying a glass of *Krazisom* in one gulp. *Krazisom* is a drink one can get down if one has never developed a taste for nobler liquids, and one's sense of smell has been reduced to a minimum.

Albert, who is shovelling away at his favourite dish, sour-sweet fish, quite forgets to eat, as he stares at the long black bunch of muscle and sinews hunching by the door, making ready to spring.

The Mongolian boot-black, who is busily polishing Wolf's handsewn riding boots from Rosseli's in Rome, keels over after two deep breaths when he looks straight into the eyes of the panther, and it wickedly grinds its teeth.

Piercing screams of terror come from behind the door marked PRIVATE. Everybody looks up, forgetting even the panther for a moment.

'Murder, murder,' howls the tall, slender lady. She comes rushing in with Tiny roaring after her. He is stark naked, and swinging a chair over his head.

'Stand still, you dirty arse'ole reamer. I'll tear your rotten prick off,' he yells, in a furious rage.

'Poor unlucky boy!' The little Legionnaire laughs heartily. 'He has bought himself a transvestite!'

'Take *that*,' roars Tiny, throwing the chair after the terror stricken transvestite. 'Five 'undred chips 'e says, an' only for snatchin' *'is* broken-down, rotten ring!'

The transvestite is so frightened he does not even notice the panther crouched, snarling, by the door. He goes past it with a rush, and slams the door behind him. The panther's tail is in the way. It gives out a long scream of anguish, which clears the dance-floor in seconds. It whirls and hisses wickedly at the door. With fur standing up all along its back it stretches its muscles in readiness for action. In an elegant spring it is up on the bar. Its hot breath plays across 'Danube Dolly's' neck. She goes down, emitting a strange grunt, with her thickly-painted face in a bowl of warm sweet-sour fish. People standing at the bar drop everything they have in their hands. A roast sucking-pig goes down inside the panther in one long, slobbering gulp. Ulrich marches along the bar-top, and reaches out a great black paw towards a dish of macaroni and kidney. In passing, he gives 'Shells Carlo' from the ammunition unit a slap on the shoulder which makes his Army issue dentures fly out of his mouth. He collapses like a house of cards exposed to a high wind.

SS-Oberscharführer Gerner, from the T-Division, who is known for his brutality, pushes his plate of sucking pig away from him, as the panther comes sliding towards him with splayed paws. He only manages to give out a small scream, before the panther crashes onto him. He faints completely away. The panther sniffs interestedly at the still body, then turns to the remains of the sucking pig and begins to consume it, making a crackling sound which everybody thinks is the Oberscharführer being eaten.

'There'll be trouble,' says the Old Man, foreboding in his voice.

'We'd best get him out of here,' considers Barcelona. He throws a freshly-killed rabbit to Ulrich, who is lying on a broad divan, after having cleared the whole brothel.

'He's going *nowhere*,' states Porta, angrily, 'he stays here!'

'Hell, man, he's going to cause us incalculable problems,' cries the Old Man fiercely.

'The problems are *yours*,' comes from Chief Mechanic Wolf. '*I* never met a panther in all my life. In fact I never even *heard* of one. Write it down if you like!'

'You rotten shit,' sneers Porta contemptuously. 'I don't think I know anybody who's as treacherous and false as you are. Even the Chinese wouldn't accept fireworks from you, if you had any.'

'I won't have my section turned into a sodding Zoo,' shouts the Old Man, banging his fist on the table.

' "Panther-Ulrich" stays in No. 2,' decides Porta brusquely. He points a dirty finger at the Old Man, 'If *not*, both him and me gets us a posting, and *that* you would surely regret!'

'I'll put in a report,' shouts the Old Man furiously.

'Don't make me die laughing,' grins Porta. 'That's just what you *won't* do. You know what'll happen if they find out who's responsible for all this panther business. They'll throw the book at him, for everythin' from illegal exposure to murder an' high treason, or whatever it's called. He'll get life fifteen times over, plus a couple of death penalties for good measure. Him and the panther'll get strung up side by side, with the wind ruffling their hair, playful-like!'

The very next day the telephone of Staff HQ begins to ring violently.

'A what? A panther, you say?' asks the Chief Clerk, Stabsfeldwebel Weingut, blankly.

'A *black panther*, dammit,' shouts the Divisional Clerk, excitedly.

300

'You're crazy,' says Weingut, with a short laugh. 'All *our* Panthers are yellow or grey, and they've got a Maibach engine in their arsepart!'

'Just you wait. You'll get that grin wiped off your face,' threatens the Divisional Clerk, darkly. 'General von Hühnersdorf's hoppin' mad! Went straight up out of his boots! Our telephone exchange is jammed with calls complaining about panthers. 'Fore we know where we are the Generalfeldmarschall'll be here in person to see first what's goin' on!'

'I can't see what your complaints have got to do with us,' answers Weingut, pleasantly. '*Our* Panthers are where they're supposed to be. The only people who can complain about *them* are over on the neighbour's side, and I don't reckon complaints signed by Ivan carry much weight!'

'*You've* got a black panther, and it's running round giving people heart-failure, and brain lesions. The General demands an investigation. A *thorough* investigation. Mark *that*, my dear stupid pig of a friend!'

'Why don't you just nip down to the M.O. and get yourself a powder?' suggests Weingut, in a fatherly voice. 'There's nobody here at 27. Panzer Regiment who's weak-minded enough to go pissing around with anything as nutty as a black panther. They *bite* people, you know!'

Half an hour later the Divisional Adjutant is on the telephone.

'What's all this about your having a black panther with you?' he asks the Regimental Adjutant, an inexperienced young Leutnant, newly arrived from the depot. 'There are all sorts of wild rumours down here at Division.'

'What colour Panther?' asks the Regimental Adjutant, blankly. 'We haven't got any *black* Panthers!'

'Hell, man, it's not tanks I'm talking about,' snarls the Divisional Adjutant, wheezing like an overheated steam engine. 'It's a big *cat*, a real jungle cat, that eats Watchdogs by companies. Do you realise that the Watchdog battalion's C.O. is lying in a strait-jacket out at the looney-bin after a meeting with *your* bloody, black panther?'

'But, sir, I can assure you we *have* no black panther,' whines the Regimental Adjutant, in a servile voice. 'The only animals we have are two wolf-hounds, belonging to Chief Mechanic Wolf, and these are properly taken on strength, by permission of the C.O.'

'Animal crackers,' sighs the Divisional Adjutant, resignedly. 'You can look forward to one hell of a row about this. Rumblings are coming down already from Corps, and complaints are *pouring* in from the civilian population of the area!'

'Sir, I don't understand a word of it,' replies the Regimental Adjutant, helplessly. 'I know *nothing* about a black panther at 27. Panzer. It must all be a regrettable mistake. Why not ask the Veterinary Corps?'

'You'll be advised,' grins the Divisional Adjutant, maliciously, banging down the receiver.

Oberst Hinka is shaving when the telephone on his direct line begins its excited, impatient ringing.

'Hinka,' he says, brusquely.

'Hühnersdorf! What the devil's going on at your regiment?' the General of the Division commences, without any kind of polite preliminary.

'What is *happening*?' asks Hinka, with a certain trepidation.

'You're the C.O., aren't you? If *you* don't know what's happening then who the devil *should*? But *I* can inform you that your people are playing around with some kind of a carnivorous animal, and frightening everybody in the area into fits! Half my Watchdogs are already in the nuthouse because of it. If you tell me you know nothing about this, Oberst Hinka, then I must tell you that you are the only person in the whole of 4. Panzer Army, who *doesn't*! The Generalfeldmarschall himself *demands* a clear report on the matter, *within the hour*!'

'It all sounds like some kind of crazy joke, General,' answers Hinka, truthfully enough. 'What kind of carnivorous animal is it?'

'Didn't I *tell* you?' roars the General, raging. 'It's a panther, in the name of all the hells! A *black* panther called *Ulrich*!'

Hinka closes his eyes and curses silently. He is no longer in doubt of where to find the black panther, Ulrich, and his human accomplices.

He takes a couple of deep breaths, and wipes the lather furiously from his face.

302

'A report will be forthcoming within the hour, sir,' he promises.

'I hope so for *your* sake,' hisses the General. 'This case is more serious than you think. The Generalfeldmarschall has demanded the panther shot, and the guilty men in front of a courtmartial. Damnation, Oberst, this is *rough*. I want your report inside sixty minutes!'

'Oberleutnant Soost,' roars Hinka, in a voice which rings throughout Regimental HQ. 'Oberleutnant Soost,' he repeats impatiently, throwing his towel violently into a corner.

'Oberst, sir!' stammers his adjutant in terror, clicking his heels together.

'Find that villain Porta and drag him here,' curses Hinka, viciously.

'Porta?' asks the adjutant, who has never heard of anybody called Porta.

'Dammit, man,' roars Oberst Hinka, 'don't you understand *anything*? Obergefreiter Porta, in hell's name! No. 5. Company, 2. Section. The scoundrel is to report to me now, immediately, and to bring a black panther called Ulrich with him!'

The adjutant staggers out into a Kübel, firmly convinced that he has been posted to a regiment which is completely made up of maniacs.

'Where to, Oberleutnant, sir?' asks the driver with a wide grin, dancing his foot up and down on the accelerator.

'To arrest an Obergefreiter Ulrich, and a panther named Porta,' stammers the adjutant confusedly, lighting a cigarette with shaking hand.

'5. Company, *that'll* be, then, sir,' grins Obergefreiter Helmer, taking off like a rocket.

'Drive properly,' the Oberleutnant scolds, straightening his uniform tunic nervously.

'That's just what I'm doin', sir,' grins Obergefreiter Helmer, beginning, unregimentally, to open a large sandwich packet as they pull up in front of 5. Company Office.

Staff and Hauptfeldwebel Hoffmann sit, broad-shouldered and self-confident, behind the large desk he has inherited from a former Political Commissar. This early in the day he is still wearing his Russian morning slippers. He snaps off a salute, and positions himself so that the adjutant cannot see his red embroidered footwear.

'By order of the Commanding Officer I am to arrest a panther,' yells the adjutant, attempting to look severe. 'It's name is Ulrich,' he adds, after a long, painful silence.

'Very good, sir,' mumbles Hoffmann, already seeing problems of unbelievable dimensions towering up. 'Gefreiter Müller,' he roars to the company runner. The soldier is standing by the filing cabinet, close to him so that his roar is quite unnecessary. He could have whispered. 'Off with you, you sad sack. No. 2. Tell Obergefreiter Porta and the panther Ulrich to report to me on the double. Has it got through? Come back without 'em and I'll see you further! Further on over to the neighbours, where a hero's death is waiting for wetnecks like you!'

Most of an hour has gone by before Porta turns up. He thunders into the Company Office, where he clicks his heels three times, twice for the adjutant and once for Hoffmann. He gives a Nazi salute and a ringing 'Heil' in front of the large picture of Hitler, which has taken the place of one of Stalin.

'That's enough of that,' warns Hoffmann, sending a glance at him which is so hard it should have knocked his teeth half way down his throat.

'Am I *not* allowed to salute the Führer?' asks Porta, with assumed astonishment.

'Idiot,' roars Hoffmann, 'not when he's hanging there!'

'Where *should* he be hanging then?' smiles Porta.

'You're under arrest,' roars the adjutant, in a cracked voice. 'You're under arrest,' he repeats, pointing accusingly at Porta.

'Arrest?' asks Porta, blankly. 'Me? What for, sir?'

'For running around with a panther, and frightening the life out of people,' screams the adjutant, who is beginning to lose control of himself.

'Ain't we allowed to keep pets in the German Army any more?' asks Porta, naively, clicking his heels together again, three times. He is about to give Hitler's picture another salute, when he catches Hauptfeldwebel Hoffmann's vicious look, and stops himself.

'A panther is not a pet,' decides the adjutant, shortly.

304

'Beg to state, Herr Oberleutnant, sir,' babbles Porta, in his usual village idiot manner, 'there's all kinds of pets all over, sir. The Emperor of Abyssinia keeps lions for pets, sir, an' in India they keep elephants. So why can't I have a sweet little panther for a pet?'

'*You* are under arrest,' declares the adjutant, red in the face. 'You can explain about your pet to a courtmartial. You *and* your panther'll go in front of a firing squad. You've ruined the morale of half the *Wehrmacht!*'

'Very good, sir,' answers Porta, turning his eyes up towards the ceiling, resignedly. 'Beg to say, sir, that as a German soldier I have the right, in accordance with Army Regulations, paragraph 209, sub-paragraph 5, subject: arrest and detention of military personnel, to resist any arrest not in accordance with the Greater German Wehrmacht military penal code. Beg the adjutant to be allowed to report, sir, that Obergefreiter Porta. Joseph, resists arrest on the grounds that the charge is without foundation.'

'Are you completely and entirely out of your mind, man?' froths the adjutant, losing control of himself completely. 'Don't you try to tell *me*, an *officer!* Do you understand what you are saying, Obergefreiter?'

'Beg to report, sir! The Obergefreiter understands perfectly, sir!'

'Shut your mouth!' cackles the adjutant, hysterically. His fingers play nervously around his yellow pistol holster, as if he were thinking of shooting Porta.

'Back to regiment,' he orders Obergefreiter Helmer, as they come out to the Kübel. Helmer, who is consuming a leg of turkey and a jam sandwich, pretends not to hear the order. He looks quietly at the turkey leg before taking a bite at it.

'Are you deaf, man? Didn't you hear my order?' screams the adjutant, at white-heat.

'What order?' asks Helmer, his mouth full of turkey.

The adjutant loses his self-control completely. He throws out a mixture of undecipherable orders and threats, to the unconcealed enjoyment of Porta and Helmer. Behind the smeary window of the Company Office, Hoffmann's fat, piggy face can just be seen.

'Beg to report, sir,' trumpets Porta, 'am I a *free* German Obergefreiter, sir, or an *arrested* German Obergefreiter, sir?'

'You're under arrest,' howls the adjutant, madly, without taking time to think about why the question has been asked.

Helmer salutes, dismounts from the Kübel, and removes the keys.

'Where the devil are you going, man?' roars the adjutant.

Helmer salutes again, and smashes his heels together so hard that mud splashes up all round him.

'Beg to report, sir, accordin' to Army Regulations, sir, prisoners under arrest may only be conducted by authorised personnel. Only personnel who have taken a special oath, can be ordered to service of that nature, sir!'

'Then *march* back to HQ,' decides the adjutant, shortly. 'Give me the starting-keys and the vehicle documents.'

'Beg to report, sir. I may not allow this vehicle out of my charge without written orders from Regimental HQ, sir,' roars Helmer, saluting again. 'But, sir, if the adjutant, sir, will throw Obergefreiter Porta out of the vehicle, sir, or declare him to have been released, sir, *then* I can drive the adjutant back to HQ, sir.'

After thinking the matter over for a while the adjutant declares Porta temporarily released. He is just about to settle down in his seat in the Kübel again, when something long and black flashes past him and lands with a thump on the back seat. It is Ulrich who has found Porta again, and now sits proudly beside him on the back seat.

The adjutant sways, and sinks down, with a gurgle, into the mud alongside the Kübel.

'Is he dead?' asks Helmer uncaringly, stretching his neck. 'My God, man, you'll soon have a job just keeping count of all the heart attacks your cat's been the cause of!'

'Let's pick him up,' decides Porta, 'and push off home to HQ. The C.O. wants to talk to Ulrich and me.'

There is great alarm and confusion in HQ office when Porta and Ulrich march through it. Three clerks have a nervous breakdown, when the panther shows them its long fangs.

'What in the devil's name makes you tick, Porta?' asks Oberst

Hinka, in a quiet, threatening, voice, when Porta clicks his heels in front of the chart-table. 'Do you know what the book of animals tells us about that beast you have acquired? It is a killer. It kills every living thing it comes in the neighbourhood of! And it kills, because it *likes* to kill!'

'Beg to state, sir, the book's full of lies from beginning to end. Ulrich's gentle as a lamb, sir. Just *playful*!'

'I don't want to have any more trouble with you, Porta. The panther must *go*! And if it doesn't go quickly, *you'll* go — in front of a courtmartial. How I'm going to be able to save your hide *this* time I can't for the life of me think, but, mark my words, this is the very last time I'm going to help you. My patience is finally at an end. Get out of here, and be good enough to take that black monster with you!'

Porta crashes his heels together, salutes, and steps backwards out of the door, together with Ulrich.

'By the way, where's Ulrich got to?' asks Helmer, when we run across him one day, at the Charkow goods station where we are picking up new Tiger tanks.

'Emigrated to Sweden,' says Porta sadly. 'He'd had enough of the German dictatorship.'

'To *Sweden*?' asks Helmer, his mouth falling open. 'A panther can't go off to Sweden just like that!'

'If you know the ropes he can,' answers Porta. 'He took a hospital train from here to Libau. There he went on board a Swedish boat. He is, most likely, strutting round Stockholm now enjoying the lights in the shop windows. He may even have got himself a new fur coat, with spots on, instead of the black one he had. If the Gestapo's still after him a bit of camouflage wouldn't come amiss.'

If it is necessary to save time, and it almost always is, then we drop a thousand, or three thousand, bombs on a city which is delaying us, and leave only a heap of rubble behind. We cannot afford to pity the civilian population. Our task is to press forward and destroy the enemy as quickly as possible. War is war, and it is unmerciful.

General Bradley

A gaggle of geese waddles talkatively across the dusty square. They stretch their necks, and flap their wings. Peace and quiet pervades the whole place.

'This hole's deserted,' says the section leader.

'Hang on a minute,' says the tank-man. 'You never know with Ivan.'

The section's four tanks have been waiting, prepared to attack, for an hour. There is something about the village they do not like, but the only sign of life, in the course of that hour, has been the cackling geese.

'We got to go in,' says the section leader. He makes a signal to the other three tanks. 'But we'll go in from the river. The bridge could be mined, and who want's to go to heaven on the top of a blast wave?'

They roar across the river, rock up the opposite bank, knocking down a couple of mud huts, and stop in the middle of the village square.

The geese cackle. An aggressive gander rushes at the tanks, hissing and flapping its wings. Everything is quiet. Not a treacherous sound.

'Driver and turret gunner stay in the car,' orders the section leader. 'The rest out! We could use some of these geese!'

Turret flaps fly open. With roars of laughter, the tank crews jump down and run at top speed after the cackling geese. One of them has just caught a goose, when a machine-gun opens up, spraying the square with bullets. In a moment, it resembles a slaughterhouse yard. Tankmen are thrown about amongst the frightened geese. Two badly wounded men try to crawl back towards their vehicles.

Russian soldiers stream from the huts. Grenades explode, turret

308

hatches bang shut. Guns roar, and machine-guns snarl.

Explosive charges are thrown between the tracks of the tanks, rendering them unmanoeuvrable. Mines are thrown up under the turrets. In the space of a few minutes the four tanks are the centre of an exploding, hellish sea of flame.

Shortly afterwards the wrecked tanks are found by an advancing Panzer Regiment. A brief intermezzo in a summer's day of war.

309

8
The Tigers

'You lot'll soon be where the shit's flyin',' shouts Chief Mechanic Wolf, who is risking his precious skin for once, close behind the front. 'When I hear you've got yourself grilled, in a few days time, my good Porta, I'm goin' to get stewed as a newt on the very best French champagne.'

'You've got mud between your ears, you great shit,' hisses Porta, from down inside the Tiger tank's engine.

'Mind that sewing-machine of yours doesn't hit you on the head,' Wolf warns him with an anticipatory grin as the heavy Tiger engine is swung up and out of the tank.

As he says the words the wire snaps, and the motor falls, pinning sour-faced Werkmeister Brandt's arm beneath it. It takes some time to raise it and get the white-faced man's arm free. His hand has been crushed.

We bandage him up crudely and lay him in the shade of some fir trees. He begs for a doctor, but there is no doctor available, nor even a medical orderly. He will have to wait until a supplies waggon can take him back to the depot.

One of the mechanics asks Wolf to take the hurt man back with him.

'You must have nuts'n bolts where your brains ought to be,' Wolf roars with laughter. 'Think I'm goin' to have my waggon mucked up by a bloody mechanic?'

When a lorry finally arrives the Werkmeister is already dead from loss of blood.

Over on our right Barcelona's Tiger roars forward. The little Legionnaire rattles off on our left, his tank's long 88 mm gun-muzzle angling towards the sky.

'2. Section, battle stations,' orders the Old Man over the radio. 'Guns loaded and safe!'

Tiny opens the ammunition lockers, ready to load quickly when the Old Man commences giving fire orders. On his right he has yellow-tipped H.E., on his left black-tipped armour-piercing. Behind him hang blue-nosed S-shells. It is important that the right ammunition be chosen — and used. It can be a catastrophe for both vehicle and crew if the loader makes a blunder.

'*Panzer, Marsch, Marsch,*' orders the Company commander, Oberleutnant Löwe.

In wide, arrow-head formation the Tigers roar forward, crushing everything in their path.

A spear of flame shouts from the ruins of a house. A shell hits the turret, glances off, and ricochets vertically into the air.

'Dead ahead. Enemy anti-tank position. Turret one o'clock,' orders the Old Man. 'Panzer halt. Load H.E.!'

'Breach released,' echoes Tiny, and pushes a yellow-tipped shell into the firing chamber.

A deafening roar splits the awakening morning and the anti-tank gun is thrown up into the air, together with the bloody remnants of its crew.

'Close turrets, *Panzer Marsch,*' orders the Old Man.

The Tiger's 700 horses roar, and with ringing tracks we rattle down through the village. Hens flutter, fearfully, up into the air.

A party of Russian soldiers rushes madly towards cover in the undergrowth. A stream of tracer, from the turret-M.G., hastens after them, catches them and smashes them down into the dust of the road. They scream, and glare in terror at the oncoming tanks. Broad tracks crush them into the substance of the roadway.

We roar across a wide open place, where laundry is hanging to dry. Underclothing, sheets and towels festoon our vehicles' turrets and guns, like flags waving on May Day.

'It'll be in PRAVDA tomorrow. German Panzer troops loot Russian washing,' grins Porta, pressing his foot down on the accelerator. 'Damn their eyes,' he shouts, 'I can't see a thing. There's a pair of blue drawers hanging down in front of my viewing-slit.' With a loud clang the tank goes down into a anti-tank trench.

311

'What the hell are you up to?' scolds the Old Man.

'I *said* I couldn't see anything,' Porta defends himself. 'There's a pair of Commie drawers blocking me view! What a diversity of weapons these Russians do use! Why have we no plan of action ready for when the neighbours bombard us with women's drawers? A circular from Sally's paper factory is what we need!'

The radio buzzes nastily. The Old Man answers it.

'What the devil are you doing, Beier,' roars the Company commander impatiently. 'Come up out of that hole, dammit, or you'll get yourself a court-martial! You must *not* stop!'

'Got nothing but shit in their heads, every single one of 'em,' shouts Porta, irritably. He rocks and twists the tank round on its tracks in an attempt to get the Tiger out of the tank-trap. It takes the aid of another tank to get the 68 tons of metal up out of the hole.

In the twenty minutes we have been stuck, the whole battle-scene has changed. Russian tanks swarm forward, also in arrowhead formation.

We stop, fire, send shells into countless anti-tank positions, roll over infantry units, grind foxholes closed, and crush the men hiding in them.

The enemy tanks are still almost 2,000 yards away. They are not dangerous to us until the range closes to 800 yards, while we can hit them at 1800 yards. Our long-barrelled 88 mm tank guns, with their fantastically high muzzle velocity and flat angle of fire, can wreck any enemy tank.

Both Tiger companies form up in one great arrowhead and literally shower shells onto the advancing Russian armour.

In a moment the steppe has become one great tank graveyard. The clear, pleasant summer's day is darkened by oily, black clouds of smoke rising from countless burning tanks. It seems, though, as if we have taught the Russians something. At breakneck speed they race fearlessly forward, attempting to get inside their 800 yard range limit and use their 76 mm guns.

'Keep them at a distance,' orders the Company commander over the radio. 'Spread out! Out to the flanks!'

The heat inside the tank becomes insupportable. Sweat runs

from us in rivers, and we are all as black in the face as Albert. Only our eye-balls and our teeth gleam white.

A T-34 flies up over a mound, and lands, with an ear-splitting crash in a quarry. It is as if it were trying to force its way down into the earth. The next second an armour-piercing shell bores its way through the tank's 60 mm thick front armour. The turret flips over and its gun-muzzle goes down between two large rocks.

A company of heavy, 57 ton, KW-2's advances in a line and halts on the edge of the forest. Gouts of flame come from the muzzles of their 150 mm guns.

Barcelona's Tiger, which is standing slightly behind us, seems to bulge out, like a balloon blown up too hard, and explodes in a giant ball of fire. Three of its four-man crew roll desperately around on the ground in an attempt to extinguish the flames which dance gaily on their uniforms.

The Legionnaire's Tiger swings round to go to their assistance.

Before the Old Man can stop him Tiny is out of the turret and dashing towards the burning tank. He swings Barcelona up onto his shoulder, like an empty sack, and sprints back with him. Albert comes limping after them, his face ashen with fright.

Quickly we help them in through the hatches. Tiny waves, and runs back to get the turret gunner, who has had his left arm torn off.

Some Russian infantry come down at a run from the heights. Bullets whistle and buzz around Tiny, who is galloping along with the wounded tankman over his shoulder.

I pull myself up from the turret, swing the air target M.G. round and open fire on the Russians.

Sweating and cursing Tiny crawls up on the tank, and forces himself through the side-hatch. A shell splinter gouges a long channel in one side of his face. Blood spurts over the gun and drips down on Heide.

'Fuckin' Commie 'oresons,' curses Tiny, smashing the hatch-way shut.

My eyes are glued to the periscope sight. Three hundred

yards away a KW-2 is taking aim at us. I stare, literally, straight into the barrel of its enormous gun.

'Tank attack,' I scream, in terror. And, at the very second Tiny shouts: 'Gun clear.' I bring my foot down on the firing pedal. With a sharp crack the shell leaves the gun and penetrates the front armour of the KW-2. The high turret is torn from its mounting ring, and falls alongside the tank, which is already on fire. A long lance of flame shoots up from it. Two burning tank soldiers seem to balance on the tip of the flame.

One of our Tiger's goes up in a volcano of fire. None of the crew manage to escape. If one has never seen it, it is impossible to imagine the sight, when 102 H.E. and armour-piercing shells, 6,000 machine-gun bullets and 800 litres of fuel all go off together.

Afterwards it seems as if a storm of flame has burned off the terrain for many yards around the fire centre. Vegetation, houses, everything above the surface of the ground has disappeared, leaving no trace. Pieces of the tank are spread out over a huge area, and not a shred is left of the five-man crew.

Continually we stop and fire. Shell after shell pierces enemy tanks and destroys them. Six hours of fanatical battle has given the regiment 116 hits. Our company has 29 of these. That evening 27. Panzer Regiment is named in Army Orders. All the officers and Julius Heide, strut around lapping up the praise. The rest of us would have preferred a bowl of mashed potatoes with diced pork. But Julius Heide's disappointment is endless when he finds that there is no Iron Cross, First Class for him. The regiment gets only two, and these are hung on two Leutnants who are short of them.

Porta is so large-minded he offers to give Heide his own Iron Cross.

'What use would it be, without the paper that goes with it?' Heide whines, miserably.

'If it's that bit of paper you're worrying about,' laughs Tiny, 'I can soon get you that! Sally's sittin' there in the War Ministry, like some kind of minister, and 'as got all sorts of pieces of paper. Piece of paper'n a rubber stamp's nothin' to 'im!'

'You filthy psychopath,' spits Heide, contemptuously. 'D'you think I'd dream of wearing a medal I wasn't entitled to?'

'Dry those big, blue eyes, now, Julius,' Porta comforts him. 'This world war's not over yet, and one fine day it'll be your turn. Just keep on being a good, brave German soldier, and Uncle Adolf'll give even *you* a cunt-magnet to hang on your best suit.'

'*Panzer Ma-a-a-a-rsch,*' rasps over the radio.

'2. Section, mount,' orders the Old Man, and edges his way through the turret hatch.

We inspect weapons, ease springs, and place our pistols in our uniform breast pockets. They are easier to get at there when you are in a hurry. Usually your pistol has hardly cleared a regulation holster before you are dead.

The Old Man swings his arm in a circle, the signal to start engines. With a thunderous roar, the twelve-cylindered, 700 H.P. Maibachs come to life.

A whole pack of T-34's comes from the maize fields. They move forward at a great pace, shooting as they go.

'Stupid waste of ammunition,' snarls Heide, condemnatorily. He cannot bear such undisciplined waste. 'They must, in hell's name, have learnt to stop before they fire! Ought to be court-martialled, the half-trained idiots!'

'I wouldn't stop for a bloody second, if I was sitting in one of those "Tea rooms",' declares Porta. 'They need another 200 yards before they can even scratch our paint, while we can blow *them* off the face of the earth easy as scratchin' our arses! They're banging away to try and frighten us, and maybe some *will* be frightened!'

'It's what's called psychological warfare, that is,' says Tiny, importantly. 'They used to talk a lot about that when I was at the ammo' place at Bamberg. We used to sod around with little yellow tins what made a bang as'd stop a bloke both shittin' an yawnin'. Psychology they said it was called. You drop the tin, it goes off "Bang!", an' there stands the enemy gapin' at you an' you've got plenty of time to pull your shooter'n knock 'im off!'

'2. Section, swing right, broad arrowhead,' shrills Oberleutnant Löwe's voice on the communicator.

As if on a string 2. Section's four Tigers swing right and go into formation. There is deafening report, and a tongue of flame several yards long spits from the thick growth of young trees at the edge of the forest.

'150 mm Anti-tank gun, straight ahead, 300 yards,' screams the Old Man in horror, ducking involuntarily below the commander's dome.

I find it immediately in the periscope sight, and spin the fine-sighting hand wheel. It is a low, broad colossus of a gun, its muzzle aimed straight at us.

'Left,' roars the Old Man, excitedly. 'Portal Left, goddammit! He'll *smash* us!'

'Like hell he will,' grins Porta, carelessly. 'Hang on to your piles, Old Un!'

Instead of turning left Porta stamps the accelerator down all the way, and goes straight for the heavy self-propelled gun at breakneck speed.

'Have you gone mad?' protests the Old Man, terrified. 'Stop man, in hell's name! You'll kill us all!'

I dive below the sights and wait for total destruction. The sharp muzzle report stabs at my ears.

The enemy shell passes closely above the turret, but almost before we realise we are still alive, we are thrown across one another in a confusion of arms, legs and bodies.

I hammer my head against the elevation control, and my back against the fine-sighting wheel. A stream of warm blood runs down over my face, blinding me.

Armour plating screams, groans and buckles as Porta attempts to pull the Tiger away from the enemy S.P., which we have rammed head-on at top speed.

Three men spring from the hatchway in the side of the gun and run towards us with explosive charges in their hands.

A long, rattling burst from Heide's front MG flings them to the ground. Flaming petrol streams from the capsized gun, and ignites the clothes of the three figures on the ground. A hare springs high in the air and bounds away out into a stream, where it appears to believe it will be safe from the madness of human beings.

'What the devil, can 'ares swim?' cries Tiny, in wonder.

'Seems to *think* he can, at any rate,' grins Porta.

'Turret 3 o'clock, T-34, 1200 yards. Panzer halt! Fire!' says the Old Man into the radio.

As Porta stops the tank I tread on the firing pedal. Quite clearly, I see the shell enter the T-34's turret. The turret becomes a glowing ball of fire, then breaks up with a terrible crash into millions of steel fragments.

'*Hit!*' howls Heide, triumphantly, and enters it on his list.

'Did you get the number?' he asks Porta.

'You *must* be cracked,' hisses Porta, irritably, 'I'm a tank driver, not a bloody book-keeper. My job's driving you there where you can blow the shit off the crust of the earth and nothing else.'

A tinny scream for help comes over the radio. The Legionnaire's Tiger has been hit. Deep-red flames leap from the engine and the turret.

Tiny and I climb up and lift the Legionnaire out. His face has been badly knocked about. We hand him up to the Old Man. His turret gunner is beyond aid. The man's whole stomach has been torn open, entrails dangling down in red and blue loops. The driver, Obergefreiter Hans, is hanging half out of the turret, his body burning and blistering. The blisters crack sharply as they burst.

'Let's get out of here,' shouts the Old Man. 'If it goes up now, we'll go with it!'

We are barely 200 yards away, when the Tiger's ammunition explodes, splintering the vehicle completely. One set of tracks comes flying through the air and crashes into the side of our tank. For a moment we think we have been struck by an enemy shell.

'Come death, come. . . .' hums the Legionnaire, softly, blinking his eyes in the bloody face.

'Shut that piss,' scolds the Old Man. 'No need to *ask* for death. It'll be there soon enough!'

A T-34/85 comes up over a hill-top in a flying leap and lands with a crash a couple of hundred yards in front of our Tiger.

'The devil,' cries the Old Man, in amazement, 'where the hell'd he come from?'

'God of all the Russias dropped him from heaven,' grins Porta, turning to avoid a smashed P-4. The crew's charred bodies hang from its hatches.

'Fire, you fool,' shouts the Old Man, kicking me in the back. The T-34's 85 mm gun is beginning to swing round towards us.

'Take it easy,' laughs Porta, unworried. 'Those chaps won't be able to either hear or think after that trip. Landing like that must've sent both their balls an' their arseholes up into their throats!'

I swing the turret on the hydraulics, but before I have managed to get the gun fine-sighted, a jet of flame comes from the T-34's long gun-muzzle, and the Tiger is thrown back. A blinding yellow flash lights up the inside of our tank.

'Jesus'n Mary,' screams Tiny, in terror, dropping an armour-piercing shell to the floor. 'The bleeder's shot us!'

By a miracle the steel-capped shell ricochets, and howls harshly off to one side.

As if working in a fog I take aim at the T-34 and press the firing pedal down. The sounds of the shot and the strike come almost simultaneously. The shell penetrates to the engine, and a yellowy-red spurt of flame goes up.

'They're evacuating her,' roars Heide in jubilation. He sprays the crew with bullets, and they fall from the burning wreck.

Tiny is sweating like a galley slave, as he works with the heavy ammunition. The job of loader in a heavy tank can only be compared with that of stoker in the old steam-driven ships.

A T-34/76 crashes through the leafy forest at breakneck speed. Its broad tracks flatten bushes and trees and throw them far behind it.

Even though there are 25 Russian tanks to every one of ours, their superiority in numbers does not make up for their primitive sighting mechanisms and poor-quality radios. These last make communication difficult for them, and communication is an important factor in a tank battle where the situation changes from second to second. But their biggest handicap is their poorly trained crews. This often leads to catastrophically large losses, which even their fanatical courage cannot make up for. Another thing which is surprising is the slowness of Russian reactions in battle situations.

The Tiger's turret hums round, and the gun is sighted carefully. A fiery tongue many yards long licks from the muzzle and with a muzzle velocity of over 3,600 feet per second the shell howls towards its target. The T-34's turret is hit. It flies backwards, rolling like a child's ball, and smashes the tracks of a T-34 behind it. The lower half of a man's body dangles from the command seat. His dark blue trousers and new yellow boots are covered with blood.

'I'd like a pair of boots like that,' says Porta, craning his neck. 'You could march all over Russia, in boots like that, without getting blisters.'

'Boots,' coughs Tiny, bringing black slime up from his soot-filled lungs, 'let's go out an' get a breath o' fresh air then, and bring 'em back with us!'

'Looting of bodies carries the death penalty,' Heide says, warningly.

' "Organising" a pair of boots from a body ain't looting,' protests Porta. 'People don't march into paradise wearin' boots. *I* never heard of an angel in boots, anyway?'

'Turret, 4 o'clock,' the Old Man breaks into our boot discussion. 'T-34, 1,700 yards.'

I swing the turret quickly into the required position, and bring the sights to bear on the T-34 which is breaking through a stone wall. I cannot possibly avoid hitting it. I press the firing pedal confidently, but only a click sounds from the gun. No shot!

Everybody turns and looks at Tiny, who is sitting unconcernedly on the floor throwing dice.

'What in the name of all the devils in hell, are you up to?' roars the Old Man, beside himself with rage. 'Why the hell haven't you loaded the sodding gun, you giant fool?'

'No more ammo',' replies Tiny, casually, throwing a six, to his great pleasure.

319

'That's all I need,' shouts the Old Man, furiously. 'Why the devil haven't you reported it, the way you're supposed to?'

'You told us to shut up,' answers Tiny. 'You said you'd say anythin' there was to say!'

'Heavenly Father,' moans the Old Man. 'What have I done to be burdened with a section like this? Let's get out of here! Full speed, back!'

Porta makes the Maibach give everything it has in it, and the Tiger crashes into a deep quarry where we can get a little more cover from the murderous Russian tank. Half an hour later we roar into Tortschin, on the outskirts of which the ammunition and petrol unit awaits us.

We are surprised to find Chief Mechanic Wolf there. He is sitting, relaxed, in his general officer's Kübel, wearing his tailor-made uniform and the highly-polished riding boots made by Roselli in Rome.

'You look as if you're nearly dead already,' he laughs, catching sight of Porta. 'I hope the neighbours clawed your backside about a bit for you!'

'Piss up your own arse,' suggests Porta to him, sourly. 'You sound like a bloke with termites chewing on his balls! You talk more crap'n a whole college of priests!'

'Easy now, lad,' says Wolf, fawningly. 'I've got a plan. I've found out where some of the Kremlin fellers've stashed away a load of Commie gold. No more'n three thousand kilometres from here. I'll organise it. All you do is go out an' pick it up!'

'*Is* there money in it?' asks Porta, immediately showing interest.

'More'n you've ever dreamed of,' grins Wolf. 'Get this stupid tank-battle over sharpish, an' come back without too many scratches so's we can get it fixed up quick an' take everybody's arses for 'em!'

Barcelona gets a whole new tank. Albert is already in the driver's seat, with a heavy bandage swathing his black head.

'This man's army ain't goin' to be satisfied 'fore we're all blown to bits'n pieces,' he complains, racing the tank's engine with unnecessary violence.

The petrol men rush to fill us up with the 700 litres we can take. Two 500 litre drums are fastened firmly over the engine housing as a reserve.

'Wish the bloody stuff'd catch on fire,' says Porta, audibly, 'then we might have a chance of some kip and a bite of something good to eat!'

'*What* did you say, you there, Obergefreiter?' shouts Werkmeister Müller, red in the face. He is known all through the division as 'Nazi Müller'.

'What *I* said?' asks Porta, pointing stupidly at himself. 'What I *said*?'

'Nazi Müller' goes dark blue in the face, and begins to emit the screams which NCO's always give out when they can find nothing better to do.

'Do you know who I *am*?'

'Beg to say, Sir! You, Sir, are Werkmeister Müller, Sir, the Werkmeister responsible for the petrol supply unit,' cackles Porta, clicking his heels together. 'Beg to report, Sir, Werkmeister Müller, Sir, there was once a railway crossing keeper named Heinz Schröder. He watched over the German National Railway's railway crossing, between Paderborn and Bielefeld. A cruel fate caused him to fall out of a goods waggon one day. It was, unfortunately, just prior to his being appointed Chief Railway Crossing Keeper with the right to wear a red lanyard at his shoulder. This promotion was not effected, since, when he woke up after the fall, he could not remember who he was. He kept running around asking everybody:

'Do you know me? Do you know who I am?'

Porta breaks off his stream of words, and examines Werkmeister Müller's purpling face, which is swelling up as if about to explode at any moment.

'Beg to enquire, Sir, has the Werkmeister, himself, ever fallen off a goods waggon?'

'I've had enough,' fizzes 'Nazi Müller', stamping his foot angrily on the panzer's deck. 'I warn you! Don't try to make game of me!'

'Beg to report, Sir, no intention of making game of any kind with the Werkmeister, Sir, but it reminds me, Sir, of Herr Weinhuber, who was employed as a lifesaver by the German

National Corps of Life-savers, Sir. Herr Weinhuber also believed that everybody he met was trying to make game of him. It was when they promoted him to Chief Lifesaver at Zell-am-See that things began to go really wrong. The final breakdown came one Sunday morning in July when he was on his way to Zell-am-See, as usual, on the bicycle provided for him by the Life-saving Corps, Sir. It was raining terribly hard that Sunday. Nobody even thought of bathing outdoors, so that National Chief Lifesaver Weinhuber, Sir, he could just as well have stayed at home. Even the stupidest of men ought to be able to understand that a lifesaver won't have anything to do on the beach when nobody is out bathing.'

'Nazi Müller' lifts his hands towards the heavens in the attitude of a man praying. He opens and closes his mouth as if trying to give out a scream of protest, but only a few strange gurgling sounds, like water running out of a bath, become audible.

'The trouble was really in the service regulations for lifesavers,' Porta continues, smiling up at 'Nazi Müller', who is standing, swaying, up on the tank. 'These regulations lay down that the service is to be commenced at 08,00 hours., and there is no mention of weather conditions, such as rain or snow, causing this to be altered so that lifesavers can stay home. In any other country in the world our lifesaver would not have gone out that day. Not in Germany, however, Sir. Beg to say, Sir, I recall, now, an interesting matter in which a set of German Service Regulations led to an unusual happening. Down in the cellars, Sir, at the War Ministry, Sir, they print regulations on a printing press supplied by the company. Graphik A.G., of Heidelberg. There was a compositor there, Sir, named Ludwig Kaltblut. This Herr Kaltblut got a completely crazy idea, one day. . . .'

'I refuse to listen to any more of this,' howls 'Nazi Müller', desperately. He falls backwards off the vehicle, and hits the ground with a thump.

'*Always* seems to happen,' sighs Porta, shaking his head, despairingly, 'as soon as I start giving them a detailed explanation about anything, so that they can understand it properly, something *always* seems to go wrong with them. . . .'

Porta is interrupted by the ammunition squad, which comes to our aid as usual. We stack the long-bodied shells in the ammunition lockers.

I get the worst job. Opening the boxes, removing the protective rubber and taking off the anti-rust caps. It is hard work. Each box holds three shells, and they are heavy. The rest of the crew shouts at me continually to get a move on. We want to get finished before the Russian Jabos come diving out of the clouds laying phosphorous eggs on our heads.

We finish up by cleaning the gun. A dirty gun can cause accidents, and a premature is no fun at all.

Porta comes back to us, puffing, with a case of sausage and a large round cheese, which he has purloined from the supplies people.

'5. Company,' the CO's voice comes over the radio. 'Right wheel. Arrowhead formation. Over the bridge. Shoot at anything which moves. The regiment has to cross that bridge before they blow it!'

At top speed No. 5. Company, consisting of sixteen Tiger tanks, goes rattling down towards the river. The hellish clangour of the tracks drowns out the noise of the infantry.

Russian soldiers spring from foxholes, and go running through and over ruins, in flight from the onrushing giants. Many of them do not succeed in escaping, and are crushed under the tracks.

Three 5. Company Tigers are hit and set on fire. In an amazingly short space of time the several kilometre deep battle area is covered with the burning wreckage of German armour. Krupp Sports, Panzer-3's and the legendary Panzer-4, as well as Panther and Tiger tanks. But by far the majority of the wreckage is Russian. BT-7's, KW-2's, T-34's, together with countless American Christie's and British Matilda's.

To avoid a KW-2, Porta turns his vehicle and crashes straight through a house, showering the turret with domestic fittings and furniture. We jolt to a stop in the middle of the house, and peer, cautiously, through the observation slits.

A white grand piano stands in one corner of the large room. A Russian officer hangs, lifelessly, across the keys. Two others sprawl across chairs, their faces covered with blood.

'Let's get out of here,' mutters the Old Man, whispering as if he were afraid someone might be listening.

'This German bloody motor's given up,' curses Porta. 'Russian bloody dust flyin' all over the place's probably blocked the filter. A couple of you'd better get on the handle. The self-starter can't manage it.'

'Up you, mate,' shouts Tiny. 'I'm not gettin' out an' swingin' no startin' 'andle!'

'You and Sven,' orders the Old Man, 'and no more arseing about. That's an order!'

Violently protesting we creep out through the hatchways. Our hands are soon torn and bleeding as we work at the retaining clips which keep the starting handle in place. At first we can hardly force it to turn. Then Tiny is gripped by a seizure of mad rage. He jumps into the air and comes down on the handle with all his weight. I just manage to throw myself into cover behind one of the tracks when a long burst from a machine-pistol goes off just above our heads. I whirl and catch sight of a Russian, fumbling with the magazine of a Kalash-nikov. Like lightning I pull a personnel grenade from my pocket and throw it at him. It explodes with a sharp crack, tearing his entire chest open.

'What the bleedin' 'ell are you *about*?' shouts Tiny, white with rage, and kicking out at me. 'You can't go throwin' explosives about like that in other folks 'ouses! You coulda bleedin' well killed me, you war-mad sod, you!'

The engine fires. A flame a yard long shoots from the exhaust-pipes, and the engine starts up with a thunderous roar. Plaster from the ceiling rains down on us.

The starting handle spins round, sending Tiny arcing through the air. With a crash he falls on the piano, smashing it to pieces with a jangling as loud as a whole orchestra at full blast.

'I've 'ad enough!' he roars, rising up from the wreckage of the piano, festooned with strings. 'You're *tryin*' to kill me,' he yells. He is up on the Tiger in one giant leap, P-38 in his hand ready to kill Porta in return for the air-trip on to the piano.

'Drop it,' snarls the Old Man, pressing his Mpi against the big man's forehead.

Tiny's eyes follow the barrel of the Mpi slowly. It is pressed against the bridge of his nose. His eyes cross in idiotic fashion.

With a rueful grin he replaces his pistol in its holster, and crawls complainingly inside the vehicle. A hand-grenade hits him in the back and rolls down inside the waggon.

'Bleedin' arse'oles!' he roars, fearfully, picking up the grenade. He gazes at it in confusion and discovers that the safety-pin is still in place. 'Jesus,' he yells, tears out the pin and hurls the grenade back where it came from.

A thunderous explosion rings through the house, and two bodies are thrown up towards the ceiling.

'Bleedin' 'ell,' mumbles Tiny, white in the face with terror. 'The devil nearly 'ad us that time, all right. Think if that Commie shit 'ad pulled the pin!'

'Well, then the inside of this tank'd have looked like a mediaeval painting of hell. Blood and bodies all over the place!' sighs Porta, taking a deep breath.

The 700 hp motor gives out a roar, as Porta turns the Tiger in a circle. The long dining table and the silk-upholstered chairs are smashed to firewood. A sofa hits the ceiling, followed by a bookcase. Books rain down on the turret.

Both machine-guns rattle viciously. The Tiger goes straight through a wall and smashes a kitchen as large as a ballroom to pieces. Dividing walls go down in a cloud of mortar and plaster dust. With a tinkling crash we go down into a garden, smashing a glassed-in terrace in the process. We tear up a lilac hedge by the roots, and the Tiger is covered in a cloak of blue and white lilac, as if it were a bridal coach on the way to the church with a bride.

We go through an outhouse, which is crushed flat. Twenty yards in front of us we catch sight of a 55 ton Stalin tank. The crew are changing the tracks. They stare at us, paralysed with fear. Two seconds later and there are only scorched earth marks where the heavy tank and its crew had been standing. The house beside it has disappeared with it. The steel-cased high explosive shell must have made a direct hit on the reserve ammunition, and the eighty-five shells gone up together in one disintegrating explosion. The blast throws the Tiger several yards backwards, back into the flower garden from which we had emerged.

In a split tree a Russian captain is hanging, spitted like a piece of meat on a grill.

Countless batteries of Stalin Organs lay down a wall of fire and steel, aimed at destroying our tank support infantry. They stay close behind the tanks but in short order whole battalions are reduced to a shamble of meat, blood and bone.

Two T-34/85's come racing towards us like greyhounds. They fire, stupidly, while on the move, their shells going over us harmlessly without doing any damage.

'Turret ten o'clock,' orders the Old Man, calmly, 'Panzer halt. Range 800. Armour-piercing. Fire!'

The first shell glances off without damaging the T-34, but the second tears open the front armour, like a can-opener cutting into a can of peaches. The driver's headless body hangs out over the ripped-up plating. The telegraphist has lost the bottom half of his body.

Two shells crash against our forward armour, without penetrating the four inches of armour plating. They ricochet, howling, straight up into the air.

'God'd better get his arse moving before *they* get there,' Porta screams with laughter.

My next shell tears a track off the closest T-34. It swings round and crashes into one alongside it.

'Hit it in the face,' shouts the Old Man. 'S-shell. Fast!'

'Take a deep breath, mate,' protests Tiny. 'I've got an armour-piercer in this pea-shooter already, an' I ain't bleedin' takin' it out again. There's a limit to the amount o' work as can be expected of a feller for the money the Army pays!' He dries his black face with an even blacker piece of waste, and takes a long swallow of water. 'Bleedin' slavery, that's what this is,' he grumbles, sourly. 'The German Army treats us worse'n any slavedealer in America ever treated Albert's forefathers when they pinched 'em from Africa.'

'Shut up,' shouts the Old Man angrily. 'Fire!'

'You said "S",' I protest, folding my arms. 'There's

armour-piercing in the chamber. What do I do?'

'Fire, was my order!' yells the Old Man, furiously, stamping on the steel deck. 'Some day I'll bloody *strangle* you!'

A ringing crash almost splits our eardrums. We are completely deaf for several minutes. The radio falls from its shelf into Heide's lap, and loose cables fly around our heads. A burst oil pipe spurts oil onto Porta, making him look like some kind of monster in an American horror film.

'Hit,' howls Heide, and is halfway out of the hatch when Porta pulls him back inside again.

'Just a moment, Unteroffizier Heide. We're not finished yet. Our wonderful, valuable, teetotal, sex-despising Führer wouldn't like to see his model soldier running from the subhuman enemy! He couldn't *bear* it. He might even be disappointed enough to go back home to Austria and let the Germans go their own way.'

Our next shell is a strike. Straight into the ammunition lockers. The Russian tank explodes like a ripe melon dropped from a skyscraper. The other tank rolls over and over like a kicked tin-can and ends in the river. It explodes under water like a submarine volcano.

No. 2. Section's four Tigers crash through the forest, breaking off thick-boled trees like matchsticks. A forester's house is reduced to a pile of rubble in seconds. A small boy stumbles and is mashed under the wide tracks.

To the time of the engines we press forward through a thick hedge. Branches of thorn, as thick as an arm, catch at the whipping tracks. As if trying to hold the tanks back. In front of us appears a seemingly endless column of green lorries, horsedrawn waggons, tanks, and bus after bus packed with women soldiers. The column is stationary, caught hopelessly in a mile-long traffic jam, which grows longer by the minute.

OGPU soldiers rush round like excited sheepdogs, trying to get the column on the move. Heavily loaded lorries, blocking the road, are pushed ruthlessly over the edge, and go rumbling down the incline alongside it. The shouts and screams can be heard for miles. Every now and then a burst of Mpi fire comes from the OGPU-men's ready Mpi's. There is no grousing allowed here. The OGPU soldiers, with the blue caps, do all the talking that is necessary.

'God save us,' mumbles the Old Man. 'They've been handed to us on a plate. Just sitting there waiting to get shot all to hell. 2. Section! Hear me! Aim at the fuel transporters, and the fuel transporters *only*. Load with incendiary. The rest'll look after itself!'

'What about picking up that bus-load of carbolic soap perfumed lovelies before we set fire to the shithouse?' suggests Porta, pointing to a white bus filled with nurses.

'Close hatches,' orders the Old Man. 'Fire at will!'

The Russian soldiers catch sight of us. A murmuring quiet falls over the long, jammed-up column. Then a concerted scream of terror goes up.

Crews and passengers pour from their vehicles and run off across the plain. They all know what is going to happen.

Women soldiers fight desperately to escape from one of the long, grey buses.

The tank guns open fire. Incendiaries smash into the tankers' inflammable loads. Giant tongues of flame roar up towards the heavens, flaming petrol sprays out over ammunition-packed lorries. In the winking of an eye the column has become one great roaring bonfire. Hundreds of humans perish immediately in the glowing inferno.

A small group of Russian soldiers come rushing towards us, when we stick in a deep hole.

I tear the MG from its mounting, and crash open the flap. Quick action is needed if we are to prevent them from destroying us, with the close-combat bombs which are every tankman's secret fear.

I am only half way through the hatch when I look up to find myself staring straight into a twisted face. A tangle of long red hair and beard.

'*Schort*,' he roars, drawing back a hand holding a grenade. I pull the trigger and loose off a whole magazine.

The hail of bullets throws him backwards, splintering his face. Gouting blood he slides down from the tank and lies half in

328

between the rollers. The grenade goes off, with a hard crack, alongside him.

'Hell and tommy,' curses the Old Man. 'Did that take a roller out?'

I bang the hatch shut. I have had enough fresh air.

The Old Man calls Barcelona on the radio and orders him to come and pull us out of the hole. Towing is, in fact, strictly forbidden, since the effort strains the Maibach's power resources. We did it, nevertheless, in serious emergency, although it almost always meant serious damage to the tank doing the hauling. It was an order for all types of tank, but the decision was usually a difficult one. It cost a crew their heads to abandon a useable tank. It was the glasshouse for ruining a motor by aiding another tank in distress.

'Whose turn for a walk?' asks the Old Man, with a crooked smile.

'The Führer's super-soldier and Sven,' grins Porta, maliciously.

'Out you get. Ready the wire!' orders the Old Man, brusquely.

'It was us *last* time,' protests Heide, affrontedly.

'What you cryin' for?' asks Tiny, with a pleased grin. 'This is goin' to give you a chance at the 'ighly-praised 'ero's death, mate! Out you go, an' pull Ivan's pud for 'im!'

'We're here,' comes Barcelona's voice over the radio. 'Get your arses movin' an' make that wire fast. The competitors are on the way with machine-popguns!'

'Give baggy-arsed Ivan our love,' grins Porta, as Heide opens the flap, and edges out.

I throw myself into cover between the rollers as a machine-gun burst whips up dust all along the side of the Tiger.

'Get those fingers out, you devils,' shouts Barcelona, impatiently, from up in the turret. 'We'll have a charge down our throats 'fore we know where we are!'

'Shut up, you silly man,' snarls Heide, raging. 'You'd do better to come down here and give us a hand. This wire's as stiff as a board!'

Cursing and sweating, our hands pouring with blood, we

finally get the wire up over the heavy towing-hooks.

'*Pull*,' screams Heide, furiously.

I let out a terrified shout, as a hand-grenade lands beside me. From pure reflex I kick at it. The kick sends it flying back. It lands by a corporal and explodes, sending him up into the air.

'What the hell are you doing, fucking about down there?' jeers Barcelona, his head just visible above the edge of the turret.

'You can see they're shooting at us, can't you?' I shout, angrily.

'What did you expect, then?' he laughs. 'Ain't you found out yet, you're taking part in a world war?'

The engine roars. Flames shoot from the exhausts, and the tracks throw large clods of earth up over us.

'Get out of there, in the name of hell,' roars Barcelona, warningly, bending down from the turret. 'Want to get your bollocks rolled flat, you lame turtles, you?'

I roll over, and lose my Mpi under the tracks.

'You're going to have to pay for that,' yells Heide, in his insulted unteroffizier tone. 'Every penny of it'll be held back from your pay!'

'Squarehead!' I shout at him, rolling under cover from an MG burst.

'Let's get that wire off, now,' orders Barcelona, super-ciliously, when our Tiger is out of the hole.

'How was the weather out there?' asks Porta, as we edge through the hatches. 'Neighbours' boys got any new stories?'

We don't bother to answer him.

Later that afternoon the regiment is lying in ambush at the edge of a wood. The long gun-barrels are pointing at the Charkov-Kiev road, which goes via Orel straight to Moscow. Many of us doubt we will ever get that far. In our section only Heide believes it, but his belief is strong enough to carry all of us along with him.

Down from the river fog comes rolling, sweeping across the maize and sunflower fields. A battery of heavy Stalin Organs send rockets over at the German positions. It is fascinating to watch a rocket come rushing through the fog and explode above ground level. It reminds one of those old-fashioned gaslamps which always looked as if they were about to go out, and then suddenly brightened up again, to shine with a wavering white light.

Up on a hill-top flames dance up from a burning house. It must be the residence of a highly-placed official. The whole hill is covered with an artistically planted carpet of flowers. A fantastically beautiful sight in the flickering light of the fires.

A whole village burns in the distance. It seems as if the flames from it are licking the clouds.

Clouds of velvet-textured black smoke swell up from Russian T-34's and German P-4's, on fire down by the river bank.

The order has been given for radio silence, and there is a strange, threatening feeling in the air. All round us stripped trees loom like huge, naked sentinels. Down by the railway station, or rather the ruins of what once was a railway station, stand shell-damaged locomotives and burnt-out goods waggons. A personnel train must have suddenly driven in under the rain of steel and fire. Bodies of soldiers lie scattered everywhere.

An old woman scuttles around, in the ruins of what was once her village. She sniffs cautiously about her, like a cat moving through a dark forest. A single rifle shot sounds, wickedly. She goes down, crawls a little way, then goes rolling, faster and faster, down over the ruins like a fluttering bundle of rags.

'Why'd they have to do that?' sighs Porta, sadly. 'Enjoy life while you can, boys. You can soon lose it!'

'Wonder what a bloke thinks about when 'e gets shot dead?' says Tiny, interestedly. 'Wonder if there's time to be sorry for all the time you've wasted?'

'It goes that quick, you don't even know it before it's all over!' says the Old Man.

'Some of 'em scream for a long time,' protests Tiny, thoughtfully.

'Yes, you're right, I suppose,' the Old Man gives in, tiredly.

Red-hot shells stream across the sky from the far side of the river. They hammer into the ruins, knocking down walls pitted with empty, gaping window openings. German rocket batteries reply from behind the woods. A blanket of fire sweeps across the

331

heavens. The air is filled with howls, whines and the roar of explosions, as if a thousand mad demons were on their way towards the earth. The huge OGPU building in Styrty goes down in a great sheet of flame. A whole salvo of rockets crashes through the roof. Tiles are thrown over onto the opposite bank of the river. Yard-thick walls go down, sending giant clouds of brick and mortar dust billowing out across Proletariat Place.

A long row of tiny prison cells is revealed behind the collapsed wall.

'Jesus'n Mary,' shouts Tiny, mouth agape. 'There goes the bleedin' jug!'

'It's what a long-term jailbird dreams about all his miserable life,' says Porta, taking one of the Legionnaire's cigarettes. 'Hell, it must be annoying for the place to be empty when some mad shit or other in uniform finally gets to draw a bead on it.'

'Seen the sky?' asks the Old Man, quietly. He folds his hands behind his head. 'There's so many stars up there you wouldn't believe it.'

We stretch out on the dew-wet grass and enjoy the mid-summer's night. The river glistens, and throws out flashes of light, like a necklace set with diamonds.

A long way away, on the far side of the river, the Russian heavy artillery rumbles. The shells pass far above our heads, with a sound like a long goods train moving across a steel bridge. Suddenly, the stars are wiped from the sky by the brilliant white light from a rain of magnesium, parachute flares. The bright glare reveals everything. Ruins, corpses, smashed trains, shattered tanks, twisted guns, a desolate, broken landscape frozen in the cruel harshness of burning magnesium. The deathly light illumines every nook and cranny, warning of sudden, violent death. The flares seem to hang in the sky for an eternity of time, light dripping from them like white blood, ruins, and the banks of the river, glittering like glass in their monstrous white brilliance. A long time after the last flare has gone out, and the stars twinkle above us again, we rise carefully to our feet and stare, nervous and tense, out into the night, where death lurks behind each tree and each rock.

The guns roll again, sending a long, thousand times repeated echo along the river. Flames and flashes blink, in every imaginable colour. The stinking smoke from the burning tanks takes on a reddish violet tinge. An automatic rifle coughs, and a long line of tracer snakes across the river. A rattling scream cuts through the night. Flares go up! Soldiers press their bodies to the ground, and hide their faces in the wet grass.

The maize fields are burning. Crackling and popping, as if thousands of rattles were being swung out in the shrouding dark. The grass is soaked with night-dew, but we take no heed of it. We stretch out tiredly under our tanks, with only one thought in our minds. To sleep for a hundred years.

The thirty-six Tiger tanks waiting inside the edge of the forest, are the remnants of three heavy companies, which have escaped the hell of fire and steel. Every one of them is black with soot, and their yellow-green paintwork is blistered and peeling. Track shields are gone from most of the vehicles, and there are dents and holes in their armour from shells which have not succeeded in penetrating it. Their yard-wide battle tracks tell the tale of the mire of flesh and blood through which they have ploughed. Parts of humans and animals hang from every link. The crews have grown used to it. The smell is the worst part. It hangs in our uniforms and on our skin. The Old Man says it will stay with us for as long as we live.

Partridges take wing immediately in front of us, with a great clatter. Porta and Albert are off the mark like hunting dogs, and go after the fleeing birds. Albert is first to give up, but Porta is optimistic enough to follow them right down to the river, before he has to admit defeat. He glares after them disappointedly and champs his jaws dreamily.

'Think, those devils have been squatting there in front of us all the time, just waiting to jump into the pan. And I didn't see them,' he says, almost crying with disappointment.

'Do you know, by the way, the Peruvian dish called "Partridge in hiding",' he asks, licking his lips. 'First go out and catch four partridges. Then their necks must be wrung, they must be cleaned carefully, plucked, and cut in two, lengthways, with a sharp knife. Five onions must then be sliced in thin rings. Two of those Commie-coloured peppers, sliced into nice even strips. White celery, two, chopped fine. Three cloves of garlic are an *absolute* necessity, and one single bay-leaf, which must be torn across. Then do not forget, for the sake of the Holy Virgin, salt and parsley. Half of this must now be spread out on a small roasting pan, and the partridge laid on top of it, with the fatty parts upwards. Cover them nicely with the remainder of the greenery, and make up a mix, which finer cooks call a marinade. Thereafter, take three tablespoonsful of olive oil. *Not*, repeat *not*, butter or rifle oil. *That* would frighten our partridges so much that they would pull themselves together and fly away.'

He follows, with his eyes, the howling path of a shell, before going on:

'*Now*, we take a drop of tarragon vinegar, a splash of white wine, a knife-tip of white pepper, a teaspoonful of Chili pepper, and, in honour of the devil, we press one lemon to the very last drop of its juice. The whole mixture is then poured over the partridges as they lie on the pan. Over the fire with them, and there they stay until they are tender. After, this, place them on one side to cool. The essence of the thing, you see, that one must enjoy them cold.'

'Oh shut up, for Christ's sake,' groans the Old Man, fishing a piece of dry bread from his pocket. 'Makes a man more hungry than ever listening to you!'

'It occurs to me, seeing you sitting there chewing on that ancient crust of yours,' Porta smiles, broadly. 'It comes back to me, that there is a Moroccan dish they call coconut bread. First steal two pieces of white bread from a baker while he is chatting up a girl or something, dip them in cream, pull them through a pan of coconut flour, which you can also steal from the same cunt-crazy baker, and toast them lightly over a small coal fire. They should be served piping hot, with, for example, ice-cold cherries or stewed apricots. *I* prefer cherries. A cultivated Moroccan eats three or four slices, before taking off his baggy trousers, and moving on to the pleasures of the harem.'

'One word more'n it'll be your last!' screams Barcelona, drawing his pistol, 'I'll blast your brains out, so help me!'

'You, Albert, whose forebears come from wilder parts, will perhaps know the Indian dish known as "Sweet Noodles"?'

Porta continues, disregarding Barcelona's threats. 'I got the recipe from a tame savage, who kept a cannibal kitchen in Berlin.'

'See all them mushrooms we drove past this mornin'?' remarks Tiny, from the darkness.

'*No!*' shouts the Old Man, putting his hands over his ears, 'and we don't want to *know* about 'em!'

'Mushrooms,' sighs Porta, smacking his lips. 'If you can find that place again, we can fix up that Chinese dish, "Singing Mushrooms". The recipe for that one I got from a Chinese major, who visited the Army Ammunition Depot at Bamberg. I had to explain to him how the new explosive cans worked, but there must have been some kind of misunderstanding, language or something I suppose, because he blew himself straight down into the Chinese hell, or up maybe, with two of 'em. Anyway, I was lucky enough to get the recipe for "Singing Mushrooms" from him before he went off. Its a *pièce de résistance*, both with a meat or a fish course. It is also a source of comfort to the stomach with boiled rice or. . . .'

'Knock his bloody wig down round his ankles,' roars Gregor. 'That madman's driving us all *nuts!*'

Shortly before dawn the regiment moves off. Two hundred and sixty tanks with the heavyweight Tigers in the lead. A broad earth road lies, straight as a string in front of us. We crash right past Russian units, who stare after us in amazement, without making a move. With a roar and a rattle of tracks we rush through a village, a gigantic cloud of dust rolling up behind us. We send short, wicked, bursts of MG fire at Russian soldiers we see in full flight.

'What the hell's this?' shouts Porta, braking the heavy Tiger close to a bridge. The road in front of us is packed with animals. Sheep, thousands upon thousands of sheep. They press around us, pushing and shoving so that the framework of the bridge creaks.

The radio quacks impatiently.

'Company Commander to 2. Section. What in the world are you stopping for, Beier? Forward! Move! Move! Movement, blast your eyes! Under no circumstances must you stop! How often do I have to tell you?'

335

'But, sir!' the Old Man attempts to protest.

'I won't hear a word,' screams Löwe, hysterically. 'Forward! Roll over anything that stands in your way. Want me to cut it out in cardboard for you? You stop again, and you're on a courtmartial! Message ended!'

'2. Section! March! March!' orders the Old Man, sharply.

'Oh no,' groans Porta, in despair. 'All that lovely *food* ! I've got a wonderful recipe for lamb chops with cognac and fennel seeds. So stimulating for people with strong stomachs. I've been told it gives a man a special increase of sexual potency. Just the thing, before visiting a knocking-shop!'

'Shut up and drive,' snarls the Old Man irritably, sliding down from the turret.

'It's such a shame,' protest Porta, 'but have it your way!'

Until now none of us knew that goats and sheep could scream. Now we find out. Their screams are like the screams of terrified children.

The bridge and the road are turned into a shambles of steaming blood, meat and bone. Clouds of torn-off fleece are blown into the air, as we press through the crowding herds of animals. We are hardly free of them, when, a couple of miles further on, we overtake a column of civilian refugees, who press forward, shouting and screaming, choking the whole road from side to side.

'Come death, come,' hums the Legionnaire softly over the radio.

'I'll strangle that little sod someday,' snarls the Old Man, furiously.

'What now?' asks Porta. 'I can't go round them. Not a chance. It's pure swamp. Go out there and we won't stop going down till we're balancin' on the tip of Old Nick's prick!'

As if answering his question, the radio blares. 'Forward! Go over them! The crew that stops, goes on courtmartial!'

'Panzer Marsch! 2. Section follow me!' orders the Old Man. He bangs both fists down on the edge of the turret in helpless despair.

The civilians flee. Out into the swamp. A boy throws his

bicycle in front of the tanks. A crazy, desperate thing to do to stop a Tiger. Perambulators, carts with small children in them, invalids. All are left to their own resources.

Those who escape the clattering steel tracks of the tanks, are drawn down into the clutches of the swamp. The last we see of them, are their helplessly clutching hands, appealing uselessly to heaven, before they disappear with a gurgling, sucking sound into the green ooze.

'It's sheer murder,' groans the Old Man, in horror.

Russian motorcycle escorts come, with horns tooting, from a side road, leading a line of tractors pulling factory-new howitzers.

OGPU soldiers, with Mpi's held across their chests, signal us down with stop signs. They discover, too late, that we are Tiger tanks from the competition and that we do not let stop signs get in our way.

A commissar gets to his feet in the leading sidecar, waves his arms about feverishly and goes down riddled with tracer.

'Enemy target straight ahead,' orders the Old Man, shortly. 'Range 350 yards. H.E. load! Halt! Fire!'

The heavy artillery tractors are blown to pieces. Howitzers go over on their sides. The motorcycle escorts are blasted into the forest, their machines draped around the heavy-boled trees.

An OGPU NCO is thrown up over the turret, hangs for a moment on the motor cover, then slides down, sizzling, onto the red-hot exhaust pipes. The fat in his body ignites and burns with small, wavering flames. The stench finds its way inside the tank, making us feel sick.

The sun has risen. The countryside lies in front of us bathed in a lovely, golden light. We open the hatches, take deep gulps of the invigorating air, and forget the war for a second or two. A flock of pheasants flies noisily low across the road.

'Holy Mary,' shouts Porta, staring after them with the eyes of a starved fox. 'If we'd got hold of a couple of those chaps there, I'd have given you "Pheasant à la Hannibal". All we'd have needed, besides the birds, was a few bits of cinnamon, a handful of dried apricots, plums, cherries, a little saffron, cloves and some chopped mushrooms. Finally a glass of white wine and a teaspoonful of sugar. A marrow-bone from a calf would not hurt since these lovely birds are plump at this time of the year.'

'Haven't you finished *yet*, you wicked swine?' roars the Old Man, throwing an empty shell-case down at him.

A large infantry personnel carrier turns out of a field road at full speed, spins round like a top and turns over on its side. The soldiers in it are thrown, headlong, out into the road.

Barcelona's Tiger roars down a hill and tries to brake, but the 68 ton tank continues to slide on, with tracks blocked. It crashes through the soldiers lying in the road, turning the tipped-up lorry to a heap of scrap, and continues on until stopped by the wreck of a personnel carrier.

'What the hell,' shouts Porta in terror, peering through an observation slit, 'the road's on fire!'

'They've put out flamethrowers,' groans the Old Man. 'We've *had* it!'

Barcelona's Tiger is already in the middle of a hell of fire, with the Legionnaire's tank only a few yards behind. Hundreds of flamethrowers jet fire out over the road, turning it into a seething oven of flame. Paintwork bubbles up in great blisters. The air is so hot that our breath burns in our throats and lungs.

'I can't see a rotten *thing*!' coughs Porta, pouring water over his head.

'Get *on*!' screams the Company Commander on the radio. 'If you stop we're lost!'

Half-way through the sea of flame the engine begins to cough. The flame-throwers are taking all the air.

'Gear down,' shouts the Old Man, 'bottom gear needs less air!'

'Don't teach your grandmother to suck eggs,' snarls Porta, irritably. 'Look after the shooting end of it and leave the machinery to me! *I'm* Chief Engineer on this ship!'

Suddenly we are out of the fire belt. Careless of what may be outside, we throw open all the hatches, only one thought in our minds — air!

'Well, at least we know now what it's like being roasted,' moans Porta hoarsely, dabbing his swollen face with damp cloths.

'Forward! Full speed ahead!' rages the Company Commander, impatiently, over the radio. 'Don't *stop*!'

No. 5. Company storms through a village, ignoring infantry fire from the houses, and rolls on through endless fields of sunflowers. Exhausts flaming, we rattle into a large market town where Russian soldiers, in summer uniform saunter carelessly about as if they were on garrison duty in peacetime.

Outside a house which resembles a castle a couple of squads are drilling. They are practising saluting on the march. They goose-step past the NCO, bring their hands up to their caps and turn at the hips in typically clumsy recruit fashion.

With a rattling crash the company comes to a stop, turrets swinging round to cover us against attack from any direction.

The Russians stare at us as if we had dropped from the skies. One soldier continues to march at the salute, because the NCO has not given the order to halt. If he had not walked into a wall he could have marched straight across Russia, through China, out into the Pacific Ocean, and drowned. An officer with broad shoulder straps throws open a window and shouts something unintelligible.

We are almost as surprised as the Russians. Nobody fires a shot. Nobody runs away. Even the skinny hens stand still, staring with necks stretched.

A party of officers comes out of the castle. All kinds of hand-weapons are thrown together in a great heap in the middle of the town square, at the foot of a memorial from the First World War, which points up at the heavens like a stone finger.

A Russian Lieutenant-general, Commander of a Reserve Tank Corps, is taken prisoner by No. 2., together with his whole staff, without a shot being fired.

'What the devil are we to do with them?' asks Porta, worriedly. 'If they start thinking things out, our backsides'll be black as Albert's before we know where we are!'

'Let's shoot at 'em a bit,' suggests Tiny, 'then they might run away'n we're rid on 'em. A general like 'im with all that staff can give us a lot o' problems!'

Before the Old Man has reached a decision, Oberleutnant Löwe swings into the square at the head of No. 5. Company.

'What the hell're you stopping for, Beier?' he screams, white with rage, from the open turret. 'Didn't I order you not to stop? D'you *want* to spend the rest of your life at Germersheim?'

'Beg to report, sir, No. 2. Section has taken a general, corps commander, and his staff, prisoner!'

'*What* have you done?' gapes Löwe, looking around him for the first time.

Hatches clatter open, and Löwe springs from the turret, tugs his oil-stained uniform straight and adjusts his grey field-cap regimentally. He salutes the Russian general formally, and his salute is returned in a reserved manner. Hands are shaken, and civilised politenesses observed.

'There you are, you see,' snaps Porta, throwing out his hand in the direction of the officers clustering on the broad terrace, 'just one dirty big *clan*! That's what those shiny-buttoned sods are. Us coolies they've completely forgotten. Löwe'll get something nice to hang round his neck and we'll get a kick up the arse for havin' stopped!'

A little later HQ Company rattles into the square. Oberst Hinka salutes the general and his staff and, soon after, 5. Company is on its way again at breakneck speed.

'Where the devil's the neighbours got to?' asks Porta, wonderingly, when we have driven for several hours without seeing a sign of a Russian.

'Ivan's gone 'ome! 'Ad enough of this bleedin' World War, I reckon,' thinks Tiny, optimistically.

The forest spreads around us like an endless green ocean when we stop for a moment on a hill to check the oil level. This is one of the Tiger tank's weaknesses. If there is too little oil the engine over-heats and may catch fire.

The careless chatter over the radio becomes less as we go deeper into the endless forest. Even Porta is silent. We fill up at a deserted Russian petrol depot before continuing.

I press my eyes against the rubber-padded periscope eyepiece, staring tensely at every single climb of trees where an anti-tank gun could be in ambush. I long to hear the sound of a rifle shot. It would ease the nervous pressure of this ominous silence.

Porta is pressing the Maibach engine to the uttermost of its power, snaking his way past shell-holes and burnt-out vehicle wrecks. Bodies of soldiers and civilians are strewn across the road. Bloated corpses, covered with millions of fat, blue flies. They buzz up in clouds, disturbed by the roaring passage of the heavy Tigers.

The Legionnaire is in the lead when he sights, luckily for the section, a heavily fortified tank barrier, covered by the new Russian A.A. guns which can be turned into highly effective anti-tank weapons by a simple adjustment. At 300 yards they are deadly to Tiger tanks. At that range the shells go through our four inches of front armour like a knife through butter.

The Old Man gives the order to halt, and examines the dangerous obstacle carefully through his binoculars.

'Further advance completely impossible,' he reports over the radio.

'Go round, down to the river arm, and cross there,' the order comes back.

We crash through the forest, stopped for a moment by a forest lake, large enough, almost, to be called a sea. 'Seal hatches,' orders the Old Man. 'Up schnorkel!'

In line abreast we continue out into the lake. Tigers can go down to about twelve feet below water level, but we are always feverishly nervous when we go down in places we do not know. Tanks have been known to stick in the bottom ooze, and sink down into it in short order. When, and if, the tank is hauled up again, the crews are long dead from suffocation.

'Hell, but that lake looks *wet*,' curses Porta, lifting his shoulders and shivering.

'Look 'ere then. See this. There's 'erring swimmin' all round us,' shouts Tiny, in amazement, pressing his eyes eagerly to the periscope eyepiece.

'If we were to stop for a minute,' suggests Porta, 'we could nip outside and shovel up a bushel of mussels, maybe. Then I could do my "Mussels *à la Normande*" for you. We can easily find some charlotte onions, chop 'em together with parsley an' chervil. . . .'

The Old Man draws his pistol and presses the muzzle into Porta's neck.

341

'One word more about grub, and that bloody Berlin brain of yours'll get splattered up on the ceiling!'

'*You'll* never be a gourmet, I'm afraid,' sighs Porta, contemptuously. 'You remind me strongly of Herr Kamphalter, who used to live in the rose gardens outside Paderborn. . . .'

'Shut *up*,' roars the Old Man, wildly. He is cut off by a crash which makes our ears ring. We are thrown forward onto the instruments and up against the steel armour.

'What the hell was that?' asks the Old Man, shocked, wiping blood from his forehead, which has been in collision with the turret edge.

'A great big atheist Commie rock got in our way,' answers Porta, taking a long pull at his water-bottle.

'Can you get round it?' asks the Old Man nervously. 'The bottom here's soft as fresh cow shit you know!'

'Stop shitting in Adolf's pants, will you,' Porta says confidently, swinging the tank round and stirring up so much mud that we are totally unable to see anything. We drive along the side of the cliff Porta has run into for what seems an eternity before he manages to find an opening big enough for the Tiger. Finally we feel firm ground under our tracks, and come up on land again with the dangerous anti-tank position behind us.

A company of T-34's is lined up a little behind the spot where four roads meet the main highway to Charkow. We open fire on them from 15 yards range. They burst into flames and we roll straight on over the wreckage.

A couple of squadrons of Russian dive-bombers howl down on us, but their bombs explode out on the steppe and in the woods with a wet, muddy "plop", doing us no damage. Without meeting serious resistance we are through, and see the silver glitter of the river in front of us. Capsized boats whirl on its surface. Bloated bodies sail along between green banks, where flocks of wading birds stand, staring in wonder.

Shells fall behind us, throwing earth and snapped-off tree trunks up into the air.

'2. Section at river,' reports the Old Man, over the radio.

'Cross,' comes the brusque order.

'2. Section follow me,' orders the Old Man, signalling with his hand in the direction of the bridge.

A pair of Russian Jabos appear, flying just above the treetops. They strafe the road with machine-cannon. Soviet troops in large numbers come from the *dachas* along the river, and from behind the burning buildings of a *kolchos*. A herd of pigs, maddened with fear, run screaming in front of them, turn around and run straight back again into the sea of flames. Both soldiers and civilians spread out their arms to show that they are not carrying weapons. Apathetically they wade out through mud up to their knees, stream down the hills and walk like a solid wall of humanity, directly towards us. Those in front fearfully slacken their pace but are pushed forward by the press of humanity behind them.

They sit down around our tanks, and look up at the viewing-slits, waiting tensely for what is to happen to them.

'What in heaven's name are we to do with them?' asks the Old Man, looking at the mob surrounding us with a defeated air.

'They are unarmed,' decides Heide, playing nervously with the forward MG.

'How are we to be sure of that?' mumbles Porta, doubtfully.

'What the hell am I to do with this lot?' asks Barcelona nervously over the radio. 'There's that many of 'em they could pick the blasted tanks up and run off with 'em, if they wanted to!'

'Keep cool, now,' orders the Old Man. 'Above all keep 'em off the vehicles! One magnetic and they'll have pulled the chain on us!'

'Rotten shits! Nothings!' growls Heide, angrily. He feels his soldier's honour touched. 'It's high treason in the Soviet Union to surrender!'

'Yes, those chaps don't seem to have accepted the soldier's highly thought of oath of faith: To die for the Fatherland is sweet and honourable,' grins Porta, jeeringly.

'*Dulce et decorum est pro patria mori,*' quotes Heide, importantly.

One of the ancient 'coffee-grinders' swings low above the soldiers who have surrendered. It is near enough for us to be able to see the pilot threatening them with a clenched fist. It rises and is soon no larger than a moth in the sky.

343

A few minutes later a howling becomes audible, and a salvo of shells explodes in the middle of the crowd, blowing many of them out into the river.

A pack of KW-2's and T-34's waddles through the sun-flower fields in broad-arrow formation. Their machine-guns send bullets in long bursts into the mass of humanity in front of them. Guns roar. Flames shoot up from the ground. It literally rains with torn-off parts of human bodies.

'Let's smash those lousy bastards,' roars Porta, in a fury, 'the dirty, rotten sons of bitches.'

'No. 2. Section. All vehicles. Fire at will!' commands the Old Man, harshly.

'S-shell,' I order, and the breach closes. The shell ploughs its way into the nearest KW-2 and blows off the turret.

'Come death, come. . . .' hums the Legionnaire over the radio.

A Panzer-3 is splintered to atoms. Two Panzer-4's suffer the same fate. The tank commanders of the T-34's are wise enough to concentrate their fire on the lighter tanks, where it is effective at a greater range.

Our tank fills with thick, poisonous, cordite fumes. Our teeth and eyes shine whitely in soot-blackened faces.

More and more tanks crash into and through the panic-stricken mass of humanity. War is celebrating a triumphant orgy, and humanity has become a farce. Ammunition explodes in burning waggons, turrets weighing tons are thrown into the air, and fall to earth with shattering force.

Armoured planes roar out of the sun, and send rockets hissing at the tanks which are dancing their murderous saraband of death on the ground below.

On the heels of the armoured planes come the fighters, ME 110's and YAK's bulleting through the sky. The dive bombers and armoured planes flee in panic. Many do not succeed in escaping and go whirling down to explode amongst the tanks.

In a short space of time all the men who sat and lay around the Tiger tanks have been reduced to an unrecognisable, bloody mass, pulped by steel tracks and shells.

'Turret, 3 o'clock. T-34,' orders the Old Man, quietly.

I rotate the turret like lightning, and get the T-34 in my sights. I see the shell go into the side of it, quite clearly, but to our amazement the green monster goes on as if nothing has happened.

'Gun. Load. Ready,' says Tiny, mechanically, ready with the next black-nosed armour-piercing shell in his hands. Steel clangs on steel. There is a rattling and crashing. Smoke billows around us, making the inside of the tank pure hell.

Again the shell goes into the T-34. A long tongue of flame shoots from the turret. Three of the four-man crew jump from the tank and take cover behind it. The uniform of one of them is in flames.

Heide sends a long burst of tracer at them, but the bullets fall short. Bullets spray earth up behind them as they run.

'Stop pissing about,' scolds the Old Man viciously. 'We don't need to be worse murderers than we *have* to be!'

Red flames lick up from the T-34's hatches, and oily, black smoke goes up towards the clear, blue sky. To our horror it starts to move again, and comes rattling at ever increasing speed towards us.

I swing the turret on manual control, and send three fragmentation shells at the approaching tank without achieving a hit.

'Is that mad son of a bitch tired of life?' shouts Porta, pressing the engine's 700 horses to give him every ounce of power available, so that the Tiger seems almost to rear up and rock on its tracks. With a roar, Porta sends it straight at the T-34 on collision course.

'Stop!' screams the Old Man. 'Have *you* gone mad too?'

'Hang on to your false teeth,' growls Porta, like a baited wolf. 'This is a matter between a German and a Russian tank driver. Get out an' walk if you're scared. I'm going to show that weak-minded neighbour twit where Moses bought his beer!'

I have never in all my life completed a fine sighting so quickly. The shell leaves the barrel of the gun at 3,500 feet per second, and smashes into the edge of the T-34's turret. Sparks and shreds of steel buzz through the air like angry wasps, but the 88 mm armour-piercing shell ricochets and goes screaming off towards the clouds. The glowing ball of fire which is the T-34 rolls on towards us unchecked.

'He *must* be mad,' screams Heide, crouching down in fear under the radio, 'or else he's the very devil himself!'

With a clang and a crash the burning T-34 runs into us. In the course of seconds we are surrounded by a wall of flames and pitch-black, oily smoke.

'Get back! Get back!' roars Oberleutnant Löwe over the communicator. 'Are you crazy?'

For a moment it seems as if the great tank battle has stopped to watch the mad, single-combat struggle, between the fanatical Russian tank-driver in his burning T-34, and ourselves. The whole battle area seems to hold its breath. Any second the T-34's ammunition can go up, and cause a chain reaction of dimensions seldom, if ever, seen before.

Porta tries to back out of the death grasp of the T-34, but it seems as if the enemy tank is held to us with grappling irons. It follows us.

'Let's get out of here before his ammunition and petrol goes up,' screams Heide, in terror, tearing open the hatch.

'Fasten hatches,' orders the Old Man, harshly. 'Nobody goes outboard without my order.'

'What the hell's happening?' asks Tiny, blankly, pressing his eyes to the viewing eyepiece. 'Are we gettin' brown-'oled by a T-34?'

'Hold on to your cock,' grins Porta. 'We're getting ready to take the air trip of all time with one of the neighbour's mad sods!'

The interior of the tank is filled with black, stinking smoke, and we double up in violent fits of coughing. The heat is unbearable. Through the observation slits, flames throw a ghostly flickering light in to us.

Porta curses and swears sulphurously, trying every way he can think of to twist the Tiger round. But we are caught helplessly fast. Twisting metal screams and cracks.

'Give 'em a pill, then, in hell's name,' shouts Porta, furiously. 'Shoot that Commie sod off the face of the earth!'

'I can't,' I babble, desperately. 'This shit of a gun is pointing above 'em!'

'Try anyway,' shouts Porta. 'The shock an' the blast might make the bastard lose his breath.'

'S-shell,' orders the Old Man. 'Muzzle flame ought to burn the clothes of that crazy fool!'

The shell leaves the muzzle with a deafening clap of sound, but seems to make no impression on the suicidal driver of the T-34. He has managed to force the burning tank up on to our front plating. Flames lick over the Tiger.

'Must have his brains in his arse,' cries Porta, as he sees the belly of the T-34 tower up in front of his observation slits. 'He can't come with us.'

'Hell, he's smashing my gun,' I shout, fearfully, as the muzzle of the gun is torn from its mounting with a scream of tortured metal.

'Goodbye gun,' says Porta, pumping the accelerator pedal as the engine begins to cough for air. With a thunderous roar the Tiger seems to spring forward with such force that the T-34 topples backwards. We crash our way onwards and over it. It seems as if the very earth explodes. A blanket of flame covers us, and blast sucks all the air from our lungs. Cables, radio, all the instruments, ammunition, fly around our ears. Oil and petrol spurt from countless broken leads. The interior of the tank looks as if ten wild devils have passed through it.

I am stuck fast between the clinometer stand and the gun sled. Tiny breaks me loose with a lifting bar. I lie on the deck, shaking with terror, while my heart does its best to pound its way out of my chest. The Old Man throws a fire extinguisher down to me. All five of us begin to pour foam on the dancing flames, which waltz like lightning round the firing room.

'Back,' orders the Old Man.

'Then it's out an' push, Old Man,' answers Porta, laconically. 'The engine's in a thousand bits.'

'How's the radio?' asks the Old Man.

'Scrap,' croaks Heide, pitifully.

'Dammit,' curses the Old Man. 'Can you fix the engine so we can hobble back?'

'Maybe I could,' answers Porta, nose in the air, 'but I'm not allowed to according to the Collected Appendices to Army

Regulations: Major repairs to Tiger tanks must only be carried out by Army technical staff.'

'We can't stay *here*,' the Old Man explodes.

'No? It's pretty peaceful round 'ere now all them war-mad bleeders've gone rushin' off elsewhere to bite one another's bleedin' throats out,' grins Tiny, looking round him with an air of satisfaction.

'Listen here, Porta,' the Old Man says, with an attempt at being diplomatic. 'You *can* repair that engine, if you *want* to. It's not that badly damaged. We'll help you, an' hand you down what you need to get that shit back together.'

'I'm sticking to Army Regulations,' says Porta, stubbornly, making sure that he gets his share of a passing sausage. 'All I'm allowed to do is change plugs an' oil, but *this* is the *lot*. The cylinder head! Obergefreiter by the grace of God, Joseph Porta, won't *touch* that! That's what all the clever sods've said he mustn't!'

'It's also forbidden to leave the Tiger here,' shouts the Old Man, desperately.

'Blow it up then,' suggests Porta. 'That's what they put explosive charges in the turret for.'

'You know damn well,' rages the Old Man, turkey-red in the face, 'that that vehicle mustn't be demolished without it's completely wrecked, and can't be towed back.'

Porta stretches himself out at full length, and lights a cigarette thoughtfully, disregarding the fire risk from the petrol which is streaming out all over the place.

'Wake me when a tow turns up that can give us a lift.'

'Shut that piss,' shouts the Old Man, infuriated. 'Let's get lookin' at that engine! Outside everybody!'

Porta saunters carelessly once round the waggon, singing softly:

Es geht alles vorüber
es geht alles vorbei. . . .

A little later he sits down in the grass alongside the Old Man.

'Half one track'll have got to Moscow by now. Two of the four rollers are blown all to hell, and the gun's dangling like a limp, ministerial prick.'

'Damn,' the Old Man swears, viciously. 'They'll throw us to a courtmartial, if we demolish her. One of you'll have to go back and requisition a rescue vehicle.'

'I've got an idea,' cackles Tiny, putting up his hand. 'Even a bleedin' psycho sod couldn't 'ave thought of anythin' better!'

'Holy Mother of God,' groans Porta. 'I *know* you and your ideas! They always end up with us getting knocked on the head!'

'Spit it out,' demands the Old Man, willing to accept any plan, however mad, to get us out of the spot we're in.

'Over there back of that line of big oaks,' explains Tiny, 'there's a lame T-34/85. The four mateys sittin' fartin' inside it, keep peerin' out of the viewin' slits like Indian chiefs on the warpath. What about nippin' over to 'em, an' suggestin' they knock our bleeder for six. *Then* there won't be nobody as can say we've abandoned it needless like!'

'I don't want to know it,' protests Heide, shocked. 'The worst kind of sabotage is what that is. It will cost you your head. You must be quite crazy!'

'You are dumb as a pile o' cowshit, Julius,' jeers Tiny. 'If your Führer's got as little up there as you 'ave, we're 'eadin straight for the world's biggest defeat.'

'*Not* so crazy,' says the Old Man, thoughtfully, looking at the T-34, from which a leather-clad head peeps up cautiously over the edge of the turret.

'We just 'ave to wave a white flag,' says Tiny, optimistically, 'so they can get it into their nuts we only want to 'ave a little chat with 'em.'

'On the surface this sounds completely mad,' says the Old Man, 'but it's a chance. Those four over there get a pretty medal for smashing up a Tiger, and *we* get out of a courtmartial. But why the hell haven't they shot at us already?'

'Clear as mud,' grins Porta, broadly. 'Their tracks've gone, just like ours have. They can't move. They also can't see our guns buggered up from where they are. If they miss with the first shell, they think we'll blow 'em to bits and pieces before they've had time to scratch their backsides.'

'To hell with everything,' the Old Man gives in. 'Let's give it a try!'

Tiny waves the white signal flag enthusiastically. A little later a white flag comes slowly into view from the turret hatch of the T-34.

'Well I'll be damned,' cries the Old Man, in amazement. 'They're playing along with us!'

'I feel as ashamed as a Jew-boy's dog that's had his nose up an Arab's backside,' protests Julius Heide, furiously. 'You don't talk to *untermensch*. You destroy them. The Führer himself has said it.'

'Go an' 'ave a good cry, be'ind a tree somewhere,' advises Tiny contemptuously, waving his signal flag even more enthusiastically.

'Let me have the rest of the cognac and sausage,' demands Porta, practically. 'I'll go over and place the case before 'em. Keep waving that white flag. And no shit tricks from *you*, Julius. I'm *not* interested in getting my balls shot off.' With the cognac and sausage under his arm, he begins to walk towards the green T-34, which is half hidden behind the oaks.

A tall, thin sergeant, with a large, wildly-flowing red beard jumps down from the T-34, and approaches Porta cautiously. The sun sparkles on a pair of binoculars which are aimed at us, and sends flashes back from our own glasses, which are aimed at the T-34. Porta and red-beard meet around the half-way mark. With healthy, but restrained, suspicion they hesitantly offer one another their hands. Porta offers the cognac bottle and cuts off a piece of sausage. The sergeant pulls a bottle of vodka from his pocket. They exchange bottles. After several hearty swigs they have reached the stage of embracing and cheek-kissing. They take a couple more pulls at the bottles and come, laughing loudly, over towards us.

'Peace is now a fact,' grins Tiny, triumphantly. 'Up my arse with the rest o' this bleedin' world war.'

'Sergeant Gregorij Poleshajew, 43rd. Guards Armoured Brigade,' Porta introduces him with a wide-sweep of his arm, almost falling over in the process.

Cautiously, we greet the sergeant, who looks like the very devil himself with his bushy whiskers and black eyes.

Porta explains the workings of the Tiger, hiding nothing.

350

Everything is examined. The wild-looking Russian shows unconcealed admiration for the equipment, and says he is only sorry Germans are not Russians.

'With a machine like this we would have reached both Paris *and* London by now,' he declares.

A little later the three other members of the crew of the T-34 come across to us. We sit down in the burnt-off stubble of maize, share what we have, and discuss peacetime and women. Porta explains to them how caviare omelettes and oysters in champagne should be prepared.

We leave them at dawn, after watching, in cover of the T-34, the Tiger being shot to pieces. They have to put five shells into it before it begins to burn. After that we help them to repair the T-34's broken tracks.

'*Dassvidánja,*' they shout, as we disappear between the trees.

When we are some way into the forest we hear the Otto engine begin to roar. The noise of it disappears gradually in the distance.

'Let's hope they don't run into some mad German sod an' get their arseholes shot off for 'em,' says Porta.

We sit down on a fallen tree trunk, and stare dreamily out across a lake. Heide is surly, and refuses to talk to the rest of us.

THE END